The Elephant Girl

Henriette Gyland

First published 2013 by Choc Lit Limited
Penrose House, Crawley Drive, Camberley, Surrey GU15 2AB, UK
www.choclitpublishing.com

A CIP catalogue record for this book is available
from the British Library

ISBN 978-1-78189-020-2

Printed and bound by CPI Group (UK) Ltd, Croydon, CR0 4YY

Dedicated to the memory of my friend
Terhi Hannele Campbell
1968–2008

Acknowledgements

First of all, a huge thank you to the Choc Lit team for helping me knock this story into shape, and for the gorgeous art work. You're a real pleasure to work with.

A very special thank you to my critique partner and friend Pia Fenton, and my beta-readers Jenny Haddon and Kate Thomson. Also, to my sister Pernille, my parents Elsebeth and Bjørn, and my friend Jane Coulthard for their unwavering support.

A lot of ingredients go into writing a book, and not just coming up with a story, but also the technical or subject-specific references. Many people have been kind enough to help me with those, suffering lengthy phone calls and late night e-mails. Thank you to Lesley McCall for information on childhood epilepsy, and to Zofia Millar for her personal experience of living with epilepsy. She also has a mightily brutal red pen! To Jussi Kaur and Manjit Rooprah for help with Indian customs and for sharing their personal memories of Goa, Darshana Thakrar who proofread the phrases in Hindi, and Kelvin Woolmer for references to police procedures.

Also thanks to Liz Harris, Myra Kersner, Janet Gover, Jean Fullerton and all my other friends and colleagues in the Romantic Novelists' Association. I'm proud to be a member of such a supportive organisation. (The parties are good too.)

And, as always, to Tim, Oliver and Ruby, who accept that I can be an absolute bear to live with at times.

Prologue

The car has pulled up alongside the park. Helen knows it because this is where she went to the circus with Mummy in the summer. Ealing Common. Mummy has told her that in the olden days people used to keep donkeys there. There aren't any donkeys now, only muddy grass and heaps of yellow leaves blowing under the trees that go all around the common.

She knows it must be early, because it isn't light yet. The street lamps are glowing orangey-red, and it's very quiet. Other cars are parked near them, but the people who own them must still be asleep, because there's no one around.

Someone brushes past the car. Helen flinches away from the window because he looks like a spaceman, but it's only a cyclist all bundled up in black clothes, gloves and glasses that look like mirrors. He leans the bike against a tree and lights a cigarette, tapping the lighter against the palm of his hand.

Turning her head, she spots another man walking his dog. He's huddled in a coat and hood and seems to be looking right at Helen although she can't see his face. The dog is big with curly brown fur and a silly face, and it bounces around its master as they walk. She follows them with her eyes, glancing beyond them to the edge of the park where she can see more cars and a red double-decker bus driving past on the big, dangerous road. The bus is nearly empty, and the cars still have their lights on.

Helen yawns. She's feeling sleepy, but it's not the real sort of sleepy like when it's bedtime. It's the kind of sleepy that Mummy says she has to be a good girl and take her medicine for. The doctor calls it a medical condition, and

Helen knows the name for it. It's a long word which rolls off her tongue when she says it.

Epilepsy.

Plepsy, plopsy, flopsy, she chants silently. Flopsy is the name of her pet rabbit, who lives in a cage in the garden, and who eats carrots and apples and his own poo. She smiles. He sleeps a lot too, even when you hold him, and that's why she called him Flopsy.

The dog is back. Fighting back the drowsiness, Helen watches it running playfully from tree to tree. She wishes that she didn't feel so tired, then perhaps she could've played in the leaves too instead of sitting in the car, which is boring, boring, boring, but she can't because they have to meet someone. Who, she asked, but Mummy wouldn't say.

A little light flashes inside her head, and she blinks and rubs her eyes. This is what happens if she doesn't take her medicine, she sees lights and colours that aren't really there, and she worries because she doesn't think Mummy gave it to her this morning. Mummy was in a strange mood, dressing her roughly without a word, no breakfast and no teeth-brushing. Helen didn't dare remind her of the medicine.

Mummy's big shopping bag is lying on the back seat next to Helen's car seat. It's a cream cloth bag edged with red ribbon and red carry handles, and it has a picture on the front of an Indian prince riding an elephant. Mummy has a lot of handbags – and lots of nice clothes too – but Helen loves this bag best because it's embroidered with gold beads and red sequins.

She lifts the top of the bag and peers inside. Perhaps Mummy put the medicine in there. Secretly she hopes not because she doesn't like taking it. She only really likes Calpol. The epilepsy medicine is a red liquid which tastes horrible, and she has to wash it down with something. Water is best; orange juice just makes it taste even more yucky. But the medicine isn't in there, and instead the bag is stuffed full of boring-looking papers and computer discs. She sighs and looks out of the window again.

Her gaze falls on a car on the other side of the road. She can't remember if it was there when she and Mummy got here, but she's sure she's seen it before. She looks at it more closely. It's a small blue car with a dent in the door. She cranes her neck, straining against the seat belt which is attached to a clip on the side of her car seat, but she's firmly stuck.

A lady is sitting in the blue car, and even though she's wearing a large coat and a thick scarf around her neck, Helen recognises her. This lady used to be Mummy's friend, but not any more. Now she sometimes stands outside the house where they live, and when Helen points her out, Mummy runs out into the street and shouts go away, leave us alone. Helen feels sorry for the lady who looks like she's lost something precious, but she doesn't like to say anything. Sometimes Mummy can be a bit scary, a bit like Auntie Letitia, actually. Helen likes Auntie Ruth better, even if she cries a lot when she thinks no one is watching.

Helen lifts her hand and waves, but the lady tugs up the collar of her coat then slides down in her seat as if she wants to sleep, and Helen can only see the top of her head. She considers telling Mummy about it, but Mummy is busy talking on the car phone. She's keeping her voice down, and Helen can't make out what she's saying. She knows she's not allowed to interrupt, and she doesn't really want Mummy to go chasing after the lady anyway, leaving her alone in the car, so she keeps quiet.

Blue streaks of light blink in her head, and everything around her turns a hazy sort of purple, like smoke. Helen knows what's happening to her. It's called fitting, and it means that her head goes funny. She doesn't like the fitting;

before it starts, it makes her tremble all over, and it's always horrible afterwards. But there's nothing she can do. Helpless in her car seat she gets that sick blue feeling of being all alone which she knows so well. Terrified, she tries to call out to Mummy, but the words don't seem to come out of her mouth ...

Helen returns to the world around her. Her eyelids flutter but feel like they've been glued together, and she's too tired to try and open her eyes yet. Her arms and legs are heavy, and she's thirsty. She rubs her eyes and opens them slowly. She doesn't remember why she fell asleep. Was it night time? So why isn't she in her bed like she always is when she wakes up in the morning? Then she remembers that she's in the car with Mummy, and that Mummy was on the car phone when Helen started fitting.

Except Mummy isn't on the phone any more. She's still sitting on the front seat, but her head is dangling in a funny way, and her arm is lying on the other seat as if it just fell there. The lady from the blue car is leaning over Mummy and has both her hands on Mummy's chest.

'Oh, God!' she cries. 'Oh, dear God!' She lifts Mummy's chin up and puts her mouth over Mummy's as if she wants to kiss her, but it's a weird kiss where she blows air into Mummy's mouth.

Helen twists in her seat and presses the button on the seat belt clip. The seat belt snaps out. She isn't supposed to do that when they're driving because Mummy says they might have an accident, but they're not driving right now so she thinks it's probably okay.

'What's the matter with my mummy?' asks Helen, and leans forward. She doesn't like what the lady is doing, and she can't understand why Mummy doesn't push her away. There's a knife with red stuff on it on the other seat next to Mummy's hand, and Helen recognises it as the one Mummy uses for opening letters. She doesn't understand why Mummy would bring it in the car.

The lady ignores her and keeps blowing air into Mummy's mouth. Helen is just about to push the lady away because she doesn't think Mummy really likes what she's doing to her, but then she sees that Mummy's white shirt has gone completely red at the front as if someone has spilt paint all over her. Her eyes are open and looking at Helen, but she doesn't seem to see her, and some red stuff is coming out of her mouth where the lady is blowing. It's all over her neck too.

Helen hits the lady on the shoulder with her fist. 'Leave my mummy alone!' she shouts angrily. 'Stop biting her!'

The lady pulls away from Mummy. She has tears in her eyes, and her lips have gone red from the stuff from Mummy's mouth. 'I never meant …' she whispers hoarsely. 'I'm so sorry.'

Helen freaks out. Shrieking, she jumps back and cowers in the corner of the back seat looking for somewhere to hide, something to hide behind, but there's nothing there, not even the elephant bag with the papers.

'I'm so sorry,' the lady says again. 'Oh, you poor, poor baby!' She stretches out her hand towards Helen. It's covered in the same bright red stuff. When Helen finally realises what it is, she screams in horror, a loud piercing sound like a seagull. As she flails her arms, kicking her feet spasmodically against the seat in front of her, her brain scrambles and short-circuits, and everything goes black …

Chapter One

This is the first day of the rest of your life.

The thought struck Helen as she watched the sun setting over Arambol Beach, the Goan resort area where she'd lived and worked for the past two years. It hung like a fiery orb from a breathtaking rosy sky, the sea below an expanse of weathered gold, broken only by lazy white-tipped waves.

Sunsets sometimes did that. They made you take stock of your life, think about all the times you'd been at a crossroads and chosen one way over another, even if that way turned out to be a mistake.

She'd lost count of how many times she'd had that exact thought. She never welcomed the realisation that the rest of her life lay in front of her. It meant making plans, and she'd grown used to thinking only of one day at a time. The only responsibilities she had were her shift at The Sundowner bar and paying her rent. Sometimes she went to the market in Anjuna but not much else.

And every second of every day she pretended she wasn't unhappy.

Sighing, she rose from the palm leaf she'd been sitting on and put out her cigarette in the wet sand. For a moment the sweet cloying scent of cannabis lingered, then it dissipated in the crisp evening air. Goa was a liberal place compared to the rest of India but not like it had been at the height of the hippie era, and she didn't want to provoke anyone.

On her way back along the beach to the bar she met some local boys playing cricket. When the ball rolled along the sand, she picked it up and bowled with them a few times, to their delight. The boys, about eight or nine, timed their batting well, and when one of them hit a particularly fast ball she ruffled his black hair in encouragement.

Then she left them to their game and waved to Mamaji Madhu and her daughter-in-law, who were standing in the sea in their saris. Together they ran a convenience store on the high street, which sold food, toys, shoes and more, all in one big jumble, and everyone knew they loathed each other. There was no sign of that now, as they splashed and giggled and cooled themselves down after yet another humid day.

'*Namastē*,' called Mamaji as Helen passed them.

Smiling, Helen returned the greeting. 'Hello.'

Outside the beach bar she glanced over her shoulder at the fading light. A haze was quickly settling over the sea with threatening clouds blowing in from the south, and it wouldn't be long before it started raining again. Late May and the start of the monsoon was characterised by sudden downpours and thunderstorms, but between the rainfalls you got the true flavour of Goa as a lush and fertile land. Helen loved the monsoon. With fewer tourists to cater for she had time to read and meditate, to steer her thoughts in the direction she wanted them to go.

Although not to where they'd taken her earlier.

A sudden gust of wind lifted and tossed her hair across her face and made the loose cotton shirt she wore billow around her like a tent. Shivering, she hugged herself and ducked inside the shack.

The Sundowner was a typical palm thatch and bamboo shack with solid wood floor and a raised verandah facing the sea. Three of the walls were fashioned from bamboo wattle whereas the fourth wall was made from an old advertising hoarding, proclaiming the delights of Kingfisher beer. In stark contrast to the clapped-together exterior, the interior was cooled by ceiling fans and lit by colourful electric lanterns. A row of downlighters reflected against the gleaming hardwood bar.

Behind it Joe, the owner, was drying glasses. 'Been out for a tea break?' His lilting Australian accent made her wonder if he was being sarcastic, although she knew it often just sounded like that.

She searched his face for signs she'd annoyed him. 'I haven't been too long, have I?'

Joe simply tossed her an apron. 'Here, give us a hand.' He knew it wasn't a tea break, but by tacit agreement neither of them ever talked about Helen's epilepsy and her use of cannabis to prevent seizures. She wound the strings of the oversized cook's apron twice around her slim waist and tied them at the front.

They worked in silence broken only by the gentle tinkling of the wind chime. Through the front of the shack where the doors had been pushed open to the verandah, Helen saw a flash of lightning followed by a low roll of thunder, but the storm was still far away over the sea.

The bar was deserted apart from a small group of local fishermen discussing the day's meagre catch over *chai*, a sweet tea stewed with milk and sugar. A young Indian couple entered, hand in hand, and chose a table in the corner. Helen put the tea towel down, picked up a pad and went to take their order.

Approaching the holidaymakers, she mentally pigeon-holed them as she did with all the customers at the shack. Newly-weds, with eyes only for each other. When the weather cleared, they'd probably write their names in the wet sand and enclose them in a heart, and maybe later they would take that obligatory post-nuptial trip to the sacred Darbar Sahib in Amritsar.

She envied them their obvious happiness but flicked on the charm in the hope they might leave her a decent tip.

Their order taken, she lit the tea light on their table and returned to the bar.

Joe lit a cigarette and stared out across the sea. 'Rain's coming.'

As if on cue the wind chime jerked violently, and the heavens opened. Soon water poured from the edges of the roof, and although partly covered, the raised verandah was instantly awash with torrents of water, making the boards slippery and treacherous. The beach had emptied as quickly as it had filled earlier during the lull in the weather. No one in their right mind would be outside in a downpour like this.

And yet …

A lonely figure was making his way across the sand pockmarked by heavy raindrops. As the rain increased, he made a run for it, thumping clumsily up the steps and under the palm-leaf roof. He was a short, rotund man with a shock of white hair and a white beard, and his polo shirt and chinos were soaked. Shaking off the worst of the rain, he stumbled into the shack and chose a high chair by the bar.

'Horrible weather we're having,' he said.

Joe wiped the counter with his tea towel. 'What can I get you, sir?'

The stranger's eyes met Helen's, and she had a curious feeling that she ought to know who he was, but she couldn't place him.

'I'd like to try some of your fire water.' The stranger grinned at Joe, but his eyes slid back to Helen. She turned away and loaded a tray.

'One *feni* coming up,' said Joe.

He took down a shot glass from a shelf behind the bar and poured a generous measure from a colourful terracotta bottle, then placed the glass in front of the customer with an utterly neutral expression on his face. Despite herself, Helen stopped what she was doing and watched surreptitiously as the man downed the drink in one.

Predictably he gasped for breath. *Feni* was double-distilled and fearfully potent, and the uninitiated were well-advised to try it with cola first. The fishermen jeered and roared with laughter, and even Joe had trouble concealing a smirk. Yet all the time the stranger's eyes had been on Helen, giving her the impression this was nothing but a show, entirely for her benefit.

What did he want from her?

She thought of herself as a good judge of character. In the two years she'd been here, she had learned to spot the different types of holidaymakers. She recognised the middle-class, middle-aged English divorcees seeking spiritual healing through meditation and Ayurvedic treatments after their husbands had done the clichéd bunk with a younger woman. Then there were the honeymooners, like the couple in the corner, and the old hippies drifting north from Anjuna, one time a hippie haven but now a ravers' paradise, seeking the quieter beaches where they could chill out for a while. Sometimes there were families who wanted to experience a holiday away from the exclusive resorts further south, but mostly it was people like herself, whose faces spoke of a recent pain and a need to find themselves. Helen avoided that type more than any other.

The man at the bar didn't seem to fit into any of these categories. He appeared normal enough, although more conservatively dressed than most beach tourists, but behind the Father Christmas beard and the apple cheeks, redder now after the *feni*, lay a certain hawk-like awareness that made her feel uncomfortable. Involuntarily, she clasped the silver elephant pendant she'd inherited from her mother, which hung from a chain around her neck.

The movement didn't pass him by, and a small smile

creased his lips. Pulling a photograph out of his pocket, he turned his attention to Joe. 'I was wondering if you could help me,' he said. 'I'm looking for one Yelena Dmitriyeva Stephanov. I was given to believe she'd be here.'

'We don't have a Yelena – what was it? – Stefanov,' Joe replied without looking at the picture.

Helen felt her stomach muscles tighten at his next words. 'She probably goes under the name of Helen Stephens. Honey-coloured hair, hazel eyes, five foot seven. No?'

Joe crossed his arms and said nothing. He'd never give her away, but this stranger already knew who she was. Why keep up the pretence?

'Who's asking?' She clenched her fist around the pendant to stop herself from grabbing him by the collar and yelling at him to just leave her the hell alone.

Grinning widely, he stuck out his hand. 'Ronald Sweetman, solicitor. I represent your grandmother, Agnes Ransome.'

She shook his hand but only because it would be rude not to, and wasn't surprised by the strength of his grip. As she'd suspected, the whole teddy bear demeanour was a front. 'I don't have a grandmother.'

'You seem to have a grandmother when you withdraw your allowance every month.' He sent her a sharp look from under bushy brows. 'I should know, I deal with the paperwork.'

Helen glared at him. 'For your information, Aggie has threatened to cut that off many times. I don't know why she doesn't just do it. I couldn't care less.'

It was pure bravado. The money was useful. Besides, she knew Aggie would never stop sending it, because Aggie had abandoned Helen to the 'care' of social services and a children's home at the age of five and was still atoning for it. As she would for the rest of her life if Helen had anything to do with it.

Probably Mr Sweetman was aware of this too, for his

expression softened a little. 'Step-grandmother, then,' he said mildly. 'She wants you to come home.'

'She does, huh? Fat chance.' Joe touched her briefly on the shoulder. Mr Sweetman noticed and probably made his own assumptions about their relationship. *Let him*. He'd be wrong. 'This is … where I've chosen to live. There's nothing for me in England. Nothing.'

'Mrs Ransome needs you.'

'Needs me?' Helen scoffed. 'Aggie's never needed anyone in her entire life, and she certainly doesn't need *me*. That's just bullshit.' Her voice rose, and the few customers in the shack turned to look at her. She sometimes wondered what drove her to keep fuelling this inextinguishable rage she carried around inside her, but it had become as natural to her as breathing. She could never stop feeling that way. Couldn't and wouldn't. *Ever*.

Mr Sweetman eyed her for a moment the same way a lazy, fat cat might look at a mouse, deciding whether it was worth the bother, then he shrugged and got down from the bar stool. 'Well, if that's your final word …'

The rest, if there was more, was drowned out by a flash of lightning and a tremendous boom. A vicious gust of wind sent needle-sharp drops of rain up under the awning and in through the open door where they bounced off the wooden floor. The few lighted tea candles extinguished, and the electricity fizzed and cut out, then returned unsteadily.

In the flickering light the solicitor's eyes were bright and hard like polished granite. Shivering, Helen felt her nerve failing. 'It is,' she said in a tired voice. 'Please just tell her I'm not coming back.'

'I see,' he said and returned the photograph to his pocket. 'It looks like I've had a wasted journey, then. Sorry to have troubled you.' He left a few coins on the bar for Joe, nodded to Helen, and turned towards the door.

His comment was probably designed to make her feel guilty, and it might have worked if it wasn't for an overwhelming sense of relief. This was another person she'd never see again, and all the painful memories could go back in the box where they belonged. Memories of her mother and of Aggie's betrayal.

One day when she had the strength, she might take them out again.

As Mr Sweetman paused in the doorway for the rain to ease up, it suddenly seemed odd to Helen that Aggie had chosen to send her minion all this way when she must have known what Helen would say. A pointless wasted journey indeed. Aggie could be accused of many things, but doing something on a whim wasn't one of them.

The solicitor turned around as if he sensed her thoughts.

'There was one other thing Mrs Ransome asked me to tell you,' he said. 'Fay is out of prison.'

Chapter Two

Looking around his father's London office, Jason Moody stretched his long legs out in front of him and regretted wearing a T-shirt and jeans. This was the kind of place where deals were made, and who you were and how you presented yourself counted for everything. Appearing too casual made him feel inferior when he'd prefer to be the one in charge of the situation.

The converted warehouse was a very familiar environment to him, with its sanded oak floor, raw bricks painted white, and a large floor-to-ceiling window giving him an expensive view of Tower Bridge. The furniture complemented the décor: a sleek Scandinavian oak desk, minimalist floating shelves, and two brown leather sofas forming an *L* around a coffee table made from smoke-coloured glass. In the far corner stood a life-sized bronze statue of a naked Adonis with, incongruously, an owl in the place where the head should have been.

Jason's lips twitched. It would be so tempting to dress that statue in a canary-yellow Borat-style mankini, but somehow he didn't think his father would see the funny side. Derek collected ornaments and curiosities, antique as well as modern, and was very proud of his collection. Like a magpie he'd never been able to resist anything shiny, no matter how tacky, although Jason had to admit that the statue in the office was one of his better pieces, if a little unnerving.

He'd grown up in this environment and should be used to it, yet his father's world was completely alien to him. Derek Moody did his best to appear a respectable businessman, but Jason knew he had a sideline or two. His father was, for want of a better word, a gangster.

'Remind me again, what are you using the house for?'

The question brought him back to why he was here. His father spoke with a pleasant baritone, but with a flinty undercurrent if you listened hard enough. As Jason turned to face the suit-clad figure across from him, he was all ears.

'A halfway house. I've already told you that a hundred times.' Impatience crept into his voice, and he hated the way it made him sound like a spoilt brat, never mind that he was almost thirty. 'For people who come out of prison and have nowhere to stay.'

'Just checking.'

Infuriatingly calm, Derek Moody started opening the small pile of letters on his desk, slicing through the top with a paper knife. Jason gritted his teeth. How like his father to do his admin during a conversation with his only child.

'I think you're wasting your time,' Derek said. 'Housing murderers, rapists and paedophiles. Just scum.'

'I'm not offering a home to either paedophiles or rapists.' Jason felt his hackles rise. 'As for the "scum" you're referring to, I want to help the little people, the small fry who always pay the price while the big fish get away scot-free.'

'The big fish, eh? Anyone particular in mind?' Derek's eyebrows rose.

Jason felt his cheeks grow hot. 'You know what I mean. The pot dealer who's sent down while the organised crime boss gets rich. The hired gun who takes the fall so the posh git can inherit his wife's money. The ones who work for those who always pay their way out of trouble.'

'You're an idealist, son. How sweet.' Derek put down the paper knife and rested his chin on his folded hands. 'Why don't you come and work for me instead? Business is booming, and I'm sure I could find something useful for you to do.'

'What? Cooking the books? Acting the goon, like Jones?'

His father's mouth curved in semblance of a smile. 'You have a strange perception of what I do. I'm a run-of-the-mill property developer …' Jason scoffed, but his father ignored him. 'True, I sometimes circumvent a law here and there, and, yes, I didn't get to where I am without making a few enemies – that's why I need "goons" as you call them – but there are worse characters than me out there. Where would you draw the line? What sort of crime would qualify for a room in your house?' Derek smirked. 'Murder? Fraud? Rolling over little old ladies? Do you keep a score? Allocate points based on evilness?'

His father was mocking him. Not only that, he was demonstrating that he had the means of unearthing every little detail about his son's life if he chose to. Derek Moody knew exactly what sort of people were already living in the house Jason had been renting from him for the past six months. It was frankly galling.

'Do I get the house or not?' he snapped.

He met his father's ice-blue stare across the desk and cursed the fact that it was like looking at a mirror image of himself. Why couldn't he be more like his mother, all blonde and peaches-and-cream? He'd be happy looking florid and jowly like his uncle if it meant not having to share the angular jawline, the thick dark hair, and the well-defined cheekbones with the man in front of him. Hell, he'd even settle for resembling one of his mother's Pekingese dogs. Anything not to be like his father.

Derek said nothing, just opened another letter with a *ritsch*. The sound set Jason's teeth on edge.

'The lease is coming to an end, Dad. I need an answer.'

Still his father said nothing, but instead scanned the letter he'd just opened.

'I have a lot of plans for the place,' he continued with a sigh. 'You know, new plumbing, rewiring, refurbishing the kitchen.'

Finally, a response. 'Where are you going to get the money for that? If you think—'

'I've got my stall. I work six days a week there, so it's doing all right. I was going to do most of it myself and just pay for materials, and besides, I don't expect to be able to do it all in one go.'

'My son, the plumber,' Derek mused and tossed the letter aside. 'No, is the answer.'

'No?'

White-hot rage suddenly welled up in Jason, taking him by surprise. Gripping the arm rests hard to restrain himself, he wondered how it would feel to leap across the desk and throttle his father. Or push him through that big window behind him just to see if he would bounce on the ground four storeys below. He could imagine the sense of release after years of pent-up anger, the rush of adrenaline, the freedom …

He controlled himself. They'd be evenly matched, and his father had a bodyguard waiting outside ready to turn Jason inside out if need be. Maybe a dose of Derek's own medicine would work.

'How's Mum?'

His father sent him a sharp look as if wondering where this was going. 'Your mother's fine. She's just bought another dog.'

'Lucky you.'

'How is that "lucky me"? I hate the stupid mutts.'

This was the first time his father had shown any sign of passion, and Jason savoured it. *Fifteen-love to me.*

'She'll be too busy to notice your new bit on the side, then, won't she?'

Thirty-love. Derek turned a fraction paler, visible to Jason but probably not to anyone else. His father was a devout Catholic and believed strongly in commitment within a marriage, but as Jason had discovered in his late teens, Derek did have a slight problem with the fidelity issue. Or maybe it was about control, Jason could never figure out which.

'I don't know what you're talking about.'

'Brunette. Former *X Factor* contestant. Nice legs, lives on Finchley Road.'

'How do you know?'

'I have my own spies.' He didn't, but had followed his father himself a couple of weeks ago in a fit of pique.

Derek regarded him for a long moment, a small muscle twitching over one eye, but Jason held his father's gaze with steely resolve. Finally Derek said, 'All right, I'll consider it.'

'You're forgetting, I need an answer now. Next week might be too late.' Jason waited to see how far he could push the old man.

'You expect me to just give you the place?'

'Well, it's not as if it's worth much. And you've got plenty of houses like it.'

Derek hesitated a fraction of a second longer, then capitulated. 'Fine, drop back in a few days and I'll have the papers ready for you.'

Forty-love. Game over.

Jason felt like shouting it out loud but decided his father would probably change his mind if he realised Jason was comparing their squabble to a tennis match. Derek hated losing. He also had a tendency to become suspicious when something was important to his son. Better to remain neutral.

'Thanks. I appreciate it.'

'You realise there's no way back. This is the life you've chosen. I can't be seen to be involved. I can't jump in and protect you. My business associates would be rolling on the floor with laughter.'

'I don't need you to.'

'That,' Derek paused for effect, 'remains to be seen.'

'You seem awfully pleased with yourself today.'

His father's secretary eyed him over her spectacles as he left the office. Ms Barclay – he had no idea if she was a Miss or a Mrs – was a formidable woman of indeterminate age, dressed in a timeless uniform of grey skirt, unadorned white blouse and black pumps. Her only concession to fashion and femininity was a pair of red-rimmed reading glasses and blood-red lipstick which she applied generously several times a day.

She was the sort who could tell even the Krays to wait in reception and expect them to obey, and she guarded the door to the inner sanctuary like a dragon. Jason liked the old battleaxe.

'He's just signed over the house in Acton to me,' he explained.

'Well, good for you. Now if you don't mind, he has *important* matters to attend to.'

Jason grinned at her and left. This was as close to praise as she'd ever come, and he was happy with that.

The week after Sweetman's visit passed in a blur for Helen. As he'd intended, the solicitor's words had hit home. No way could Helen carry on hiding out in India, or anywhere else, with Fay out of prison.

Fay who'd killed her mother.

Giving up her rooms, she bunked in Joe's apartment for a few days. She said her farewells to the boys on the beach, to some of the long-term visitors, whom she'd got to know, and to Mamaji.

The old woman kissed her on both cheeks. The gesture brought a lump to Helen's throat. She didn't think she'd ever see her again, but she'd been like a thing possessed since Sweetman delivered his bombshell.

'No tears, *bhachē*.' *Child*. 'Life moves on and so must you.'

She snapped something in Hindi at her daughter-in-law, who stood behind the counter of the shop. The daughter-in-law gave a petulant shrug and Mamaji gestured wildly, sending a torrent of words in her direction, some of them clearly expletives. Helen caught the word *āalsī*, *lazy*.

The younger woman rolled her eyes demonstratively and disappeared into the back of the shop. She returned with a small parcel wrapped in a strip of saffron-coloured cloth, the Hindu holy colour. She handed it to Helen and put her hands together in the traditional Indian greeting.

'You didn't have to …'

'You open.'

Inside was a silver amulet, shaped like a coin, with the Hindu elephant god Ganesh seated on a lotus, in relief on one side and flat on the other, and with an inscription in Hindi. She held it up by the leather cord, and it glinted in the sunlight that fell in through the open door. Mamaji must have noticed the pendant Helen always wore and decided to match it. Her heart constricted at this unexpected kindness; they were so poor and so generous at the same time. She didn't deserve it.

'I can't possibly accept this.'

Mamaji's face split into an almost toothless smile, and she closed Helen's hand over the parcel with more force than you'd expect from her bony hand. 'Ganesh will remove all obstacles for you. He is the god of learning, and of peace. He will give you strength.'

Joe helped her pack. Clothes, mainly jeans, T-shirts and a few floaty skirts. A vintage leather bomber jacket she'd picked up in Hong Kong on impulse. A pair of Doc Martens boots. Jewellery made from Thai silver filigree, ornaments. Five years of travelling and her belongings took up precious little room in her rucksack, but they both pretended it amounted to the contents of a proper life.

On the morning of her coach journey back to Mumbai, Joe cooked breakfast in his cramped kitchen. Helen sent him a questioning glance when he placed an enormous plate of crispy streaky bacon and fluffy scrambled eggs in front of her and sat down, his own plate untouched.

'You don't have to do this,' he said.

She avoided his gaze. Outside, below the flat, on Arambol High Street, the clamours and smells of early morning rose. People shouting, street dogs barking, cooking tins rattling, and above it all the sound of impatient *auto-wallahs* honking the horns on their three-wheeled auto rickshaws. The din was impossible, and she was going to miss it.

'You can turn your back on the past,' he said. 'I don't know what's eating you, but you *can*. I did.'

Helen weighed her words carefully before answering that. She'd told Joe about how her father had died before she was born, that when her mother died when she was five, it left her with no living relatives to speak of, but she'd never elaborated on what actually happened. With only hours to go before her coach left, this was hardly the right time to begin. But she owed him something.

'A long time ago someone, a woman, did something terrible to my family, and she went to prison for it. Now she's out, and I have to—'

'Have to what? Kill her?'

'Of course not!' How come Joe could read her so well? That was exactly what she had been thinking. 'But she has to pay.'

'And a couple of decades weaving baskets isn't payment enough?'

'Not for me.' Fay had ruined her life. How could any punishment ever be enough?

'Then God help you,' he said and began picking at his food.

Helen pushed her own half-eaten food away, all thoughts of breakfast gone. 'I don't expect help from anyone, not even God. I gave up on that a long time ago.'

'And what's back home? Is there no one you care about, or have kept in touch with?'

Helen thought of her family who had rejected her, the countless foster homes where her epilepsy had been a source of either mirth or disgust. A bitter taste welled up in her, and she clenched her jaw to bite back the tears. 'No. Although I suppose I ought to see my grandmother.'

'I thought you said you didn't have one.'

'Step-grandmother. It's complicated.' She shrugged. 'And I'll need to see my neurologist. He's all right.'

Joe nodded and went back to being taciturn. She was grateful for that.

She'd known him for two years. With Joe what you saw was what you got. He never pretended to be a friend and then groped her when her guard was down, like some blokes. He never cross-examined her either. She could lean on Joe. And now she was saying goodbye and going back to ...

What exactly? Even her mind hadn't played the scenario that far.

At the coach stop she hugged him and briefly leaned into his strength. 'There will always be a place for you, here,' he said. 'You know that, don't you?'

Helen nodded, unable to speak.

The driver stopped at midday at a *chai* place along the route. The heat hit Helen as soon as she left the air-conditioned coach, and she pulled at her T-shirt to fan herself. She bought a Coke and a couple of onion *bhajis* from a stall. Pressing the ice-cold can to her cheeks, she found a rickety bench under a graceful ashok tree, its downward-sweeping branches and shining green foliage providing perfect shade. The bench was deliberately placed so it overlooked a sludge-coloured river.

When she'd finished eating, she leaned back and watched a group of boys of different ages washing an elephant in the murky water. The boys, wearing only shorts, were lithe and tanned with bright white teeth and reminded her of the cricket boys on the beach.

The elephant was a young female if the way it only reached up to the shoulder of one of the older boys was anything to go by. Helen could still see remnants of decorative paint on the front of its head and trunk, an intricate design of swirls, circles and stars in turquoise, red and white. Unfazed by the chattering boys around her, the elephant dipped her trunk in the water, raised it over her head and emptied it over her back, splashing herself and the boys as they scrubbed her sides and legs vigorously with palm-sized stones.

It wasn't an uncommon sight in India, but it was a peaceful scenario. Sighing contentedly in the pleasant shade from the tree, she closed her eyes and dozed off.

A high-pitched trumpeting pulled her out of her slumber, and she sat up, disorientated. Then she remembered where she was: the coach stop by the river. She lifted her hand to rub her eyes and knocked over the rest of her Coke which she'd left on the bench beside her. The liquid hissed and bubbled before soaking into the ground.

The boys had rinsed the decorations off the elephant and were joined by another young handler shepherding a baby elephant forward with a twig. Trumpeting again, the calf made his way into the river on long clumsy legs and headed straight for his mother, where he drank from her teat.

There were sighs of '*oohs*' and '*aahs*' and 'isn't he just adorable?' from other travellers nearby as they watched.

The spectacle held Helen's attention. Somewhere, inside her, a dull ache throbbed.

When the calf had had his fill, the handlers gently guided him forward and began to wash him in full view of the spectators, while another boy walked among the tourists collecting coins in an old condensed milk tin.

'Please, for baby?' he said, over and over again, with pleading large eyes. A gross manipulation, as the animals looked well-fed, but no one seemed to mind.

The mother elephant had curled her trunk around that of her calf, almost as if they were holding hands, and the small, black eyes of the formidable beast held an expression of utmost gentleness.

Stirred by a sudden, vague memory, Helen hardly noticed the smiling young boy in front of her rattling his tin, but dropped a few rupees in it like the others had done. He quickly moved to his next victim while Helen kept her eyes on the elephants.

'You like elephants?'

She turned to find the coach driver leaning against the tree behind her. He was a squat man with a sheen of sweat on his forehead and red-black teeth from chewing *paan*, made from betel nut, lime paste, spices and sometimes a dash of opium. Grinning widely at Helen, he now displayed his teeth in all their discoloured glory. It looked like blood.

'They are supposed to be very clever, aren't they?' she said.

'They have good memory.' He nodded enthusiastically and pointed to the young men who were now preparing to round up the two elephants. 'They are *reghawan*. What you say? Good handlers. They use love. A *balwan* is cruel, and elephants remember.'

He continued talking about elephants, a subject he seemed to know a lot about. Helen wasn't really listening. The young men had ushered the animals out of the water and were heading back to where they'd come from. She watched the baby follow on his mother's heels, faithfully and trustingly, on unsteady legs, occasionally chivvied forward by the boy with the stick if it fell too far behind.

The pain caught her off guard.

Mother and child.

Tears welled up in her eyes as the elephants and their handlers disappeared behind a group of silver trees, a cloud of dust the only evidence they'd been there in the first place.

'Are you okay, lady?' The coach driver patted her arm.

'What?'

'You're crying.'

Helen brought her hands to her face. She hadn't realised she'd cried for real, and she quickly brushed the tears away and wiped her hands on her jeans. 'I'm fine. Everything's fine.'

Eighteen hours later she stumbled into Mumbai airport still wondering why Aggie needed her to come back to England so urgently that she would use the dirtiest, most rotten trick there was.

It was obvious that sending Sweetman to Goa with the message that Fay had been released from prison was pure manipulation. Aggie knew nothing else would get Helen to come back, not even the threat of being cut off without a penny. And it worked.

But it wasn't Aggie's motives which kept her awake for the entire coach journey. That bitch Fay was free, and when Helen found her, she was going to show her what hell on earth was like.

Chapter Three

Jason's good mood lasted until he reached the front door and the bodyguard who held it open for him. Then something curdled inside him like sour milk, because the goons always reminded him of what his father was.

'Have a nice day, Master Moody.'

I bet you practised that one, thought Jason tetchily.

It sounded like mockery. Jason remembered the teachers calling out names for the register every morning when he was at school. *Moody, Jason.* That always raised a few titters, and it wasn't far from the truth. Throughout his time at boarding school he'd been Moody Jason.

Suddenly he felt the need to take it out on someone that he'd had to come crawling to his father yet again. Even if he had won this time.

'Get stuffed, moron.'

'Whatever you say, sir.' The goon kept an almost straight face, and he was tempted to plant a fist in the man's already crooked nose.

Then he was shamed by his own hypocrisy. This guy doing the dirty work for people like his father was the kind of person he was trying to help. It was just that there was something about his father and his whole operation which had made Jason see red for as long he could remember.

It wasn't difficult to see that the problem stemmed from never having fitted in. His father had set out to give him everything he himself never had as a child. That part was easy to grasp; what parent wouldn't want the best for his kid? So, he'd had the best bike, the coolest clothes, the most exclusive education, the exotic holidays, the swankiest twenty-first birthday bash.

There was a time when he'd enjoyed the attention. Until the tender age of thirteen when he'd begun to realise his father didn't give him these things out of the goodness of his heart or even for Jason's benefit. It was entirely for his own sake. Jason had become a showcase for Derek's wealth. Everything was bigger and better than what his friends had, which started out as being fun, but in the end set him apart.

Sure, he had the school tie and the songbook, but he'd never be part of the old boy's network because of his background. For his father to think that you could move from nouveau riche to posh in one generation was both cringe-making and pathetic, and Jason had wanted nothing to do with these attempts at social climbing.

'I want to go to a normal school,' he'd tried to tell his dad, but was met with blank incredulity.

'Are you out of your mind, son? You don't know how good you've got it. I'd have killed for an education like yours. Now get on with it, I don't want to hear about you slacking. The money I'm paying, you'd bloody well better get straight As, you hear?'

On top of that, despite the trappings of wealth and the appearance of respectability, there was no way of hiding what his father was, what the goon at the front door epitomised. His friends knew it, their parents too. The childish outburst 'I'll get *my* dad to beat up *your* dad' took on a unique significance. People were afraid of him. It wasn't empowering; just plain embarrassing.

The final straw came when, at twenty-three, he'd got a girl pregnant. Sexy Cathy, whose hips moved as if on ball bearings, was from Australia and worked in an Aussie pub in London. Brash, golden-haired and with respect for nothing, she was the exact opposite of the girls his father paraded in front of him and a whole lot of fun. They partied, cooked and slept together. Every day. Sex with Cathy was like an exuberant dance between the sheets.

But sex occasionally resulted in babies, and while he was still reeling from the impact of her shocking news and psyching himself up for marriage and fatherhood, Cathy disappeared off the face of the earth.

Six months later he received a letter postmarked in Perth with no return address, in which she told him she'd had an abortion, thanked him for the money, and called him every name under the sun. He knew then he had to get out from under his father's influence.

'Stay the fuck out of my life, Dad. I mean it! I don't interfere in yours, so just leave me the hell alone.'

His father tried to play the innocent. 'What? All I did was offer the girl some money – and for the record, I didn't have to offer it twice. You're a fool, Jason. I've saved you the trouble of having to support the kid. Hell, who knows, maybe it wasn't even yours?'

'Did you threaten her?'

Derek's eyebrows rose, and he looked almost affronted.

'Well, did you?'

'I didn't have to.'

Of course his father didn't have to. One look at him and the muscle-men flanking him would have been enough to intimidate even Cathy.

'Oh, really? And did you know she had an abortion? Hmm?' Jason knew that would rankle. His father didn't approve of terminations. The barb hit home and Derek's mouth tightened.

'She said nothing about that. You told me she was Catholic.'

Jason had never discussed Cathy with him and hadn't been the one to tell him she was pregnant, but what was the point in arguing about it? What was done, was done.

Instead he said, in a voice marred by both pity and disgust, 'I've always suspected what sort of man you are, but now I know. Owning other people is the only kind of love you understand, and you'll do anything to keep us all under your thumb. Even if it leads to the slaughter of an innocent child.' And he'd stormed out of the room but not before he'd seen his father turn pale.

Since then he'd had only casual girlfriends and very few friends in general, careful not to leave himself exposed to the same kind of manipulation again.

It was working with young offenders at a music recording studio which showed him a way forward. He became passionate about helping people who were less fortunate than himself, and, if he had to be completely honest about it, it was also a way of getting up his father's nose. When annoying his father slowly became less important, Jason knew he'd finally found something to do with his life which truly mattered. Somewhere he could make a difference.

Derek had only given in about the house because he'd played him at his own game, but it seemed to be the only language he understood. Jason sensed a grudging respect, but the victory felt hollow because he didn't want to be respected for the part of himself which he loathed the most.

The part that was like his father.

After the sweet air in Goa the smells of London were like an assault on the senses. Helen checked into a hotel in a cheap but bustling part of town and slept off her jet lag.

Aggie's Kensington home was a Victorian semi-detached house covered in white-painted stucco. The roof of a summer house could just be seen over the top of the walled garden, and yellow climbing roses spilled over the iron railings that bordered the small paved area outside the entrance. The front of the house was almost entirely covered in a trailing wisteria, its flowers resembling succulent grapes. The air was heady with their perfume, and if she turned her back on the traffic and shut out the noise, Helen could almost imagine herself back in Goa.

Almost.

She'd called beforehand because with Aggie you didn't just 'drop in', and the voice on the phone, a secretary perhaps, had told her to come at eleven. It galled her that her step-grandmother had lured her back from India and then expected her to schedule a meeting like some office junior, but sometimes you had to play by the rules to get what you wanted.

And Helen wanted something very specific – answers.

On the front step she stopped with a feeling of déjà vu. Same time of the year with the wisteria in bloom, clutching her mother's hand and staring up at the house which she'd thought belonged to a witch. She wore a rose-pink velvet dress made by someone called Laura. Her mother had been particularly fond of that dress and told Helen it made her look like a little princess, so it became her favourite too. They referred to it as 'Laura's dress', and for years she'd believed this Laura was a friend of her mother's until she'd walked past the Laura Ashley store on Oxford Street, and the penny dropped.

The woman who opened the door now was unfamiliar, but Helen wasn't surprised. When she last saw Aggie's housekeeper Mrs Ingram, seven years ago, the old lady had looked ready to drop.

'Yes?' She looked Helen up and down, took in the scuffed Doc Martens boots, the ripped jeans and the long tie-dye top, and wrinkled her nose. 'We don't buy or sell at the door.'

'I'm here to see Mrs Ransome.'

'I doubt it.' The woman made to shut the door.

Helen stopped it closing with her boot. 'Excuse me, but I have an *appointment* to see my *step-grandmother*. Unless she's popped her clogs or moved out, I suggest you let me in.'

The woman opened the door reluctantly as if she still suspected it to be a con. 'Why didn't you say so in the first place?'

'You didn't ask. Anyway, who are you?'

'Your grandmother's nurse. You can call me Mrs Sanders.'

Hard as nails, this one. 'Nurse, you said. Is my grandmother ill?'

'When did you last see Mrs Ransome?'

'About seven years ago. Why?'

Mrs Sanders sent her a sly look. 'Well, then I'd say you're in for a surprise.' She motioned for Helen to follow her across the chequerboard hall floor to the lounge facing the garden. Helen clomped after her with some misgivings. Aggie normally received visitors in the front parlour. Things had obviously changed since she was last here.

Mrs Sanders pushed the door open, and Helen was hit by the strong smell of Dettol and old age, which made her recoil.

Despite the smell it was a lovely room really, sunny and bright, decorated in shades of primrose and buttercup, and connected with the large garden through a set of French doors. Old-fashioned spindly furniture, covered in exquisite damask with matching loose cushions, dotted the room and gave it an air of opulence, reinforced by the priceless artwork on the walls. A splendid marble fireplace dominated one wall, its mantelpiece covered in Meissen figurines.

Aggie reclined in a high-tech adjustable chair, out of place among the antiques, at the back of the room. Her hawk-like features, which Helen remembered, had filled out, and her face seemed to float on a sea of sallow flesh. Her belly rose like a mound under a cellular blanket, and her arms appeared short and ineffectual like the clipped wings of a bird. She was quite simply gargantuan, and Helen swallowed back a feeling of revulsion.

How the mighty have fallen, she thought, though without the rancour she'd expected to feel.

When Aggie didn't respond to the door opening, Helen crossed the room and put her hand on her step-grandmother's shoulder. The old lady started and opened her eyes. For a moment she looked puzzled as if she'd forgotten where she was, then she squinted at Helen and then at a digital clock on a small table next to her chair.

'You're here,' she said briskly, 'and on time. Evidently some things do change.'

'You certainly have.'

'Mm, yes, indeed. Here, let me have a look at you, girl.' She put a fleshy hand on Helen's arm and pulled her closer. 'You're too thin.'

'And *you* are bloody enormous.'

For a moment Aggie stared at her in outrage, then she laughed. Against her will Helen felt a pull at the corners of her mouth.

'*Touché*. I'd forgotten what a foul-mouth you can be, but I suppose you've put me in my place. What a terribly granny-like thing to say. I never thought I had it in me.'

'That's probably because you're not my granny.'

'I'm the only grandmother you've got.' A haunted look appeared in her eyes and disappeared almost as quickly as it had come. 'Why don't you pull up a chair?' she said, indicating a Chippendale.

Helen dragged it across the floor, scraping the legs against the varnished floors boards, while Aggie rang a small silver bell.

The door opened and Mrs Sanders reappeared. 'Yes, Mrs Ransome?'

'Oh, Sanders, now that my granddaughter has arrived

would you be so kind and serve elevenses. We'll have tea and some of that Victoria sponge cake with Fortnum's strawberry preserve.'

'But, Mrs Ransome, that's far too rich for you.'

'Nonsense, woman. When did a little cake hurt anyone? And I don't see my granddaughter every day. The child has been to *India*. Heaven knows what they get to eat there.'

'Egg and chips,' Helen remarked.

Mrs Sanders left them again, muttering to herself.

'Why aren't you allowed cake?' Helen asked though she knew the answer.

'I'm diabetic and under strict orders not to eat anything nice.' Aggie's small eyes twinkled behind their folds of flesh. 'And Mrs Sanders takes her job very seriously. Letitia engaged her.'

'Didn't you have any say in it?'

Aggie harrumphed. 'If I had, I wouldn't have let that old sourpuss darken my doorstep. Anyway, Letitia means well. She does her best with me, and I don't suppose I'm an easy patient. I do wish she'd stop fussing so.'

'Auntie Letitia fussing?' Helen snorted. That wasn't how she remembered her step-aunt.

'People change.'

Helen leaned back in her chair and looked at Aggie. 'Why did you send for me?'

'*Send* for you? My dear, I merely thought it was time for you to come back. Five years is a long time to travel.'

'Not long enough.'

'Running away never served any purpose. As you young people say, "it's time to face the music". You have responsibilities.'

'Responsibilities?' Helen choked on the word. 'What, looking after you in your old age? Just like you looked after me when I was a child?'

Aggie flinched. 'Not at all. You're twenty-five years old, and your mother's shares in the company, which were put in trust for you, are now yours. You're entitled to sit on the board.'

'Shares?' Helen blinked. 'The *board*?'

'Surely you knew? Ransome & Daughters is a public limited company, has been for twenty years now. When William and I married, we both had grown children of our own. I had Ruth and Letitia, and William had your mother, Mimi. When we merged our respective families and auction houses, it was always the intention to build up the company to float on the Stock Exchange. Your place is there too. Sadly William never saw any of this happen …' she paused and looked away.

Helen couldn't believe her own eyes. Hard-hearted Aggie had softened, in every sense of the word.

There was a knock on the door, and at Aggie's curt 'enter' the nurse came in with a tray of tea things. Aggie went uncharacteristically quiet, which puzzled Helen because her grandmother had never moderated her behaviour in the presence of servants. It was almost as if she expected Mrs Sanders to eavesdrop.

'Would you pour, please?' Aggie asked when the nurse had left.

'Sure.'

Helen filled the delicate bone china cups with fragrant Earl Grey tea and cut two slices of the cake. While Aggie continued talking about the history of the company and singing the praises of a grandfather she had never met, Helen wolfed down her cake and helped herself to another slice without asking permission, a gesture Aggie chose to ignore.

'Before William passed away,' Aggie droned on, 'we agreed that when the company eventually floated, sixty-three per cent of the shares would remain with the family and each of our children would have a stake in it, as well as myself. Your mother died, so her shares went to you, and you now effectively control fifteen per cent of the company.'

'*I* do?'

'Yes, dear. As of your twenty-fifth birthday you've become quite a wealthy young lady. The company is performing well, and the annual dividends to the shareholders are ... well, let's say very generous.'

'How generous?'

'Our annual turnover is about fifteen million.' Aggie sipped her tea. 'Out of that the company's net profit is five to ten per cent, depending on performance, so a good year would yield, say, one and a half million. Fifteen per cent of that is ... well, you work it out. You'll need to see Sweetman about all that.' She waved her hand dismissively as if it was unimportant.

Helen's brain kicked into gear. *Two hundred and twenty-five thousand pounds.* Stunned, she sat back in her chair. She'd never imagined she would come into money, *and* without lifting a finger too. For years the loss of her mother had eaten away at her so sometimes it was the only thing she could think of. She'd known Aggie was wealthy, but had seen the monthly allowance as Aggie's way of paying for her bad conscience. Compared to what she would have at her disposal now, the allowance had literally been a pittance.

Still, she was convinced Aggie hadn't lured her back to England to talk about her inheritance. She could have written a letter, saving Sweetman the trouble and herself the unpleasantness of facing Helen's anger. Because it was still there.

'Is that really why you sent for me?'

'Certainly not. I wanted you back here so you could take your place on the board of Ransome & Daughters. I'm getting a little old for that sort of thing.'

'But I'm not interested in sitting on the board. I don't know anything about the running of a business. What if I make a mistake?'

Aggie made a dismissive gesture. 'Oh, you won't. You're a bright girl, and Letitia is there to advise you. She's practically been in charge single-handedly for the past five years now. I'm only there for important meetings, and Ruth's more or less dropped out. Letitia is good at what she does. She'll fix you up with something.'

'Fix me up?' Helen grimaced.

'With a job, so you can learn the trade. That's what your mother did.'

Aggie rarely mentioned her mother. and the snarky remark died in Helen's throat.

A smile creased the corners of Aggie's piggy eyes. 'Mimi was quite a woman. She persevered and worked her way up. If she wanted something, she found a way to get it, through her own application. She had integrity,' Aggie added when she noticed Helen bristling. 'You may not believe this, my dear, but I truly admired her. She was a fighter.'

Like me, thought Helen. *Or am I?*

She only had hazy memories of worshipping her mother as a child, and although she hardly remembered her now, Aggie's unexpected praise warmed her. Some of the tightness in her chest lifted, and for the first time her grandmother seemed almost human, fallible even. Maybe she was a fighter too, even though she hadn't fought for Helen when it really mattered.

'Ruth and Letitia won't have anything good to say about my mother,' she commented, not quite won over. 'They couldn't stand each other.'

Aggie grunted. 'Certainly there were ructions between the girls. Letitia adored her late father and didn't want me to marry William, so she resented the set-up. It didn't help that your mother was so pretty. As are you, if you would only make the best of yourself.' Her gaze fell on Helen's scruffy clothes.

'I don't like drawing attention to myself.'

'That's understandable, given what you witnessed as a child, but maybe it's time to say goodbye to the ugly duckling and turn into the swan you were always meant to be. To come into your own, as it were.'

Ignoring Helen's glare, Aggie nibbled a piece of sponge cake, like an automaton as if she didn't really taste it. 'I admit that William and I didn't do as much as we could've done to make the girls get on. We were too preoccupied with the merger. The company was our passion. When we did notice that all was not well between our daughters, William fell ill, and I divided my time between nursing him and running the company. Letitia was a great help, as was your mother, though she was barely out of school.'

'What about Ruth?'

Aggie scoffed. 'Ruth was in love. She always was in those days. Nothing else seemed to matter to her. One after the other, and they were all disasters.'

'But then she married Jeremy.'

'Eventually. He was a disaster too.'

It suddenly dawned on Helen what Aggie was driving at. 'And now you want me to do what Ruth can't, or won't. You want me on your side against Letitia. That's why you wanted me to come back.' She hadn't imagined she could be useful to Aggie, and now she saw the role she was expected to play, it wasn't quite what she'd hoped for.

Aggie's mouth tightened. 'Letitia will do as I say. I still own eighteen per cent of the shares. That's enough to throw a spanner in the works, with a few of the other shareholders on my side. You, my dear, read too many trashy novels.'

'I haven't read a book in years. Reality is strange enough.'

'You're right about that.' Aggie put her fork down, suddenly looking very tired. 'I'm sorry, but would you mind awfully if we continued this conversation tomorrow? These confounded medicines sap my strength so.' She pulled at a lever on her chair which pushed her halfway up, but still she had difficulties getting out of her seat.

Overcome by a sudden pity, Helen got up to help her, but her grandmother waved her away.

'I'll manage. Be a good girl and ring for Mrs Sanders so she can tidy up.'

Mrs Sanders appeared almost immediately as if she'd been waiting right outside. With expert hands she helped the old lady into an electric bed at the other end of the room, took off her too-tight pumps, and pulled a blanket up to cover her hips. This done, she cleared away the tea things and left the room without a word.

'Do you want me to go?' Helen asked.

Aggie patted a chair next to the adjustable bed. 'Stay a while, Helen.'

This was the first time she'd used Helen's name since she got here, as opposed to 'child' or 'girl'. Helen experienced a rush of something. Affection? 'You never really liked my name, did you?'

'Helen is a perfectly sensible name.'

'I meant my real name. Yelena. Ridiculous, I think you said.'

'Hm. I may have said something like that. It seemed a little too … exotic for a girl like you.'

'No one in your social circle had daughters who married foreigners. My mother brought shame on the family, is that what you thought?'

'It seemed unnecessary, when there were so many suitable English men vying for her attention. But I wasn't ashamed of her.' Aggie leaned back against her many pillows and closed her eyes. She sat like this for a while, and Helen thought she'd fallen asleep when she said, 'They're trying to put me in a home, you know.'

'Who?'

'My daughters, who else? Letitia doesn't think I'm able to look after myself. Getting me a *nanny* was just one step in that direction. Ultimately I think she'll have me declared mentally incompetent in order to control my shares. I don't blame her,' she added in response to Helen's look of disbelief. 'That's how I brought her up, to have a head for business. I just don't think I can hold out against the pressure much longer.'

They sat in silence for a while longer, then Helen blurted out the question which had been on the tip of her tongue throughout. 'Tell me about Fay.'

Aggie eyed her through half-closed lids. 'You took your time.'

'I didn't exactly get a word in edgeways, with you going on and on about the company, did I?'

That brought a flicker of a smile to Aggie's pale lips. 'Go on.'

'Where is she? How long has she been out of prison?'

'A few months. You're not going to do anything silly, are you? Anyway, what makes you so sure I know where she is?'

'Why else would you send your trained monkey to tell me she'd been released?'

'It was the only way to get you to come home.'

Helen jutted out her chin.

'All right, all right.' Aggie sighed. 'Sweetman has all the details. I'll get Mrs Sanders to call him this afternoon. I take it you're staying here.'

'Well, you're wrong. I'm not. I'm in a hotel for the time being. My home was never with you. You made that quite clear a long time ago.'

Aggie had the decency to look shamefaced but soon

recovered. 'Fine. If you let me have a phone number for where you're staying, I'll make sure the information reaches you. Also, I do think you need to see our doctor in Harley Street about your, er … well, condition.'

'My epilepsy. It's okay, you can say the word. I've had plenty of time to come to terms with it.'

'Yes, your epilepsy. I'd feel more at ease if I knew you'd seen Dr Urquhart.'

'As it happens, I called from India and wangled an appointment with my old consultant. The NHS is good enough for some of us.'

Her grandmother gave a sort of disgusted grunt, but the conversation had depleted the last of her energy, and she closed her eyes with a sigh.

Helen rose to leave. It was gone noon, and an intrepid shaft of sunlight had broken through the morning's cloud cover. It fell on a swarm of hover flies by the open window, hanging motionless in the air like the unspoken words between herself and Aggie.

Turning the door handle quietly, she threw one last glance at the only grandmother she'd ever had, in a way. Aggie had her eyes open, and a weary smile appeared briefly.

'It's good to see you again, my dear.'

Mrs Sanders showed Helen out with a sullen air, almost slamming the door behind her. Outside she bumped into another woman who stared at her with an equally sour expression. Plump and middle-aged with short, coarse, iron-grey hair and thin lips, she was dressed in a tweed skirt and a drab olive-green Barbour gilet over a beige shirt, and she clutched a brown handbag to her chest as if she thought Helen was a bag-snatcher.

Helen did a double-take. 'Auntie Ruth! I almost didn't recognise you. It's Helen.'

'Yes, I know. What are you doing here?'

She hadn't seen Ruth in years, nor Letitia, not since she'd graciously been invited back into the fold. She'd almost completely blocked out her old life when, on the morning of her eighteenth birthday, a chauffeur-driven car had collected her from her last foster home and brought her here. In Aggie's dining room they'd made it clear that she'd been kept apart from her family for 'practical reasons' but they now considered her mature enough to understand the complexities of the family set-up. In other words, know her place. They were blood relations, and she was not. That even though it would appear they considered her family after all, she was still an outsider. The gesture had felt like a cruel joke.

They'd met her screaming rage and frustration with stony-faced silence. She'd adored Ruth as a child – strangely the memories of her aunt were stronger than the memories of her mother – and once she'd thought the affection was mutual, but of the three of them Ruth was the one who hadn't looked her in the eye.

It was therefore a shock that her aunt looked straight at her now, and with undisguised hostility.

'I came to see Aggie,' she explained.

'Why? So you can break her heart again?'

As a way of showing she didn't care about any of them either, Helen had spent the following two years saving money to go travelling, then took off. She'd seen Aggie a few times during those two years, always at Aggie's instigation, and had mellowed a little since that traumatic family meeting, but the sense of rejection was still there, inside her. Ruth's accusation was too much. 'I'm not the one who breaks hearts,' she said, and tasted the acid of her own words.

For at moment it looked as if Ruth would burst into tears, but then she controlled herself. 'Well, you could've fooled me.'

41

She pushed past Helen on the narrow garden path in a miasma of the lemon verbena scent she always wore and which never quite managed to disguise the smell of gin. Then she threw Helen a bitter look over her shoulder.

'Whatever your reasons, we don't want your sort of trouble here. Just leave her alone.'

Chapter Four

Helen hadn't seen Dr Boyd in nearly six years, but he hadn't changed.

'Hello, stranger,' he said with a smile.

'Thanks for fitting me in at such short notice.'

'I had a cancellation. How are you? I take it you managed to get replacement medication while you were abroad.'

'I paid to see a doctor in Hong Kong and showed him my old prescription,' she explained. 'It cost me an arm and a leg, so after that I ... experimented a bit. For the last two years I've been smoking cannabis. While I was in India I met someone who recommended it.'

'Another epilepsy sufferer?'

'Er, no, but he had a friend with epilepsy.'

'So let me get this straight: on the say-so of someone who knows someone you decide to play around with your medication?'

'Pretty much.'

'Lordy!' He threw up his hands. 'Have you been seizure free?'

'Not completely, but I never was, not even with the tablets.'

'Hm.' For a moment Dr Boyd regarded her with a curious expression, then he shook his head. 'Well, you're clearly in one piece. However, as your consultant it's my duty to tell you that experimenting like this, without any kind of medical supervision, is dangerous. You do know that, don't you?'

Helen nodded, swallowing hard. She'd said to Aggie that she'd come to terms with her condition, but it was only a half-truth. Most of the time she managed to hide it, controlling minor seizures as well as she could, but the thought of having a major seizure terrified her. It had happened a few times in her life, and she'd either frightened the people around her or become the subject of their ridicule. And each time the shame of it had made her distance herself that little bit further from the world around her.

'I haven't had any major seizures.'

'Hm,' he said again. 'I practise conventional medicine, but that doesn't mean I completely pooh-pooh alternative remedies. *Epilepsy Action* has written about the connection between cannabis and seizure control. Since controlling these episodes is the goal, I'm happy to support you, although I think you should use it with your normal medication. I just can't prescribe it on the NHS.'

'Of course not,' said Helen. 'Anyway, I'd like to go back on the Carbamazepine, because, well, I don't really feel comfortable buying weed.'

'Fine, fine, we can get you back on the medication. I want you to keep a diary of seizures to see if there's a pattern and if it changes, your general well-being, what you eat and drink. You know the drill.'

'Sure,' said Helen, knowing she wouldn't. She'd tried before, starting each time with a certain amount of enthusiasm, then stopped, because keeping a diary was a constant reminder that she wasn't like everybody else.

'Include your interpersonal relationships this time,' he continued. 'That'll give me an idea of your mental state.'

Helen thought of Aggie and Fay, and Ruth who hated her, and clenched her jaw. 'My mental state is fine. I'm just not very good at forming relationships.'

'Right,' he said and typed something on the computer. 'A word of warning: as always when you mess with your medication, there'll be a period of readjustment. You may experience a higher number of seizures, and possibly even have grand mal seizures.'

'Any new tips for how to avoid them?'

At that Dr Boyd gave a little laugh. 'Same advice as always, I'm afraid.'

'Okay.' She knew the score. No alcohol. Pace yourself. Eat properly. Avoid getting excited because adrenaline can lead to seizures. Yada, yada.

She wondered if wreaking vengeance counted as getting too excited.

If so, she was doomed.

Back at the hotel, Aggie's solicitor had left a message with Fay's address. A map told Helen it was in Shepherd's Bush, only a stone's throw from her first foster home.

Trundling along what had once been familiar territory with a curious feeling of detachment, she felt as if that early part of her life had all been a dream, and India was the only place she'd ever really existed.

Fay's home was a four-storey Edwardian town house which must once have been an elegant middle-class residence, but was now in a sorry state. Peeling plaster, rotten woodwork, crumbling concrete steps leading to the basement area at the front. Venturing downstairs looked like suicide. Incongruously, the brass knocker on the front door gleamed in the sunlight as if in defiance against the rest of the decay. Higher up, a set of curtains billowed from an open window, flapping in the gentle breeze. That, combined with the gleaming knocker, was the only sign that someone actually lived in this pile of old bricks.

Helen dug her hands into her jacket pockets. Who lived in this house with Fay? There was only one doorbell so it couldn't be bedsits. Did she live with friends? Did she have a social life? A boyfriend maybe? Kids? Or did she, like Helen, go out of her way to avoid sharing too much of herself with others?

Her sudden interest in Fay irritated her. She wasn't meant to feel like that.

As she debated with herself whether to knock or not, the door creaked open. Instinctively she turned away and pretended to be walking past. A couple of doors down, she ducked behind the thick round pillar to the portico of another house in need of renovation.

A middle-aged woman shuffled down the steps bumping a tartan shopping bag on wheels behind her. She stopped at the foot of the stairs to catch her breath, then unfolded the telescopic handle of the trolley.

From her hiding place Helen watched her. Was it Fay or one of her house mates? Her question was answered when the woman pulled up her jacket collar. The gesture was both furtive and familiar, and a tingling ran down her spine when she remembered how the woman in the blue car had done the same.

She was standing only a few feet away from her mother's murderer. Her stomach churned suddenly, and her hands went sweaty inside her pockets. Now that she was here, nothing seemed quite as simple as it had when she left India.

Fay headed towards the main road and Helen hung back for a minute or so then followed her at a safe distance.

Walking behind her, she made a mental note of every detail, the quirks and physical features, the clothes. Prison had taken its toll. Fay was dressed in a shapeless raincoat and sensible, flat shoes, and her hair, once a frizzy, brown mop, was sparse and nicotine-grey, limp and unstyled. She hadn't quite shed her prison pallor and walked with a slight stoop as if she carried the burdens of many people, or maybe the sin of what she'd done.

I hope you burn in Hell, Helen thought.

When Fay reached the main road, Helen found it was easier to follow her without being spotted. Here she could hide behind other shoppers and various racks and rails spilling out of the local shops onto the pavement. She didn't want to confront Fay yet, just needed to find out what sort of entity she was before …

Before what?

Before she killed her?

Joe had said something like that, but she'd swatted the thought away. Obviously Fay had to pay for what she'd done, but even after years of thinking about this moment, Helen didn't have a plan. And now, watching her had made her curious. Fay had known her mother. In fact, she'd have been the same age if she'd lived. They were friends.

So what *happened* for Fay to stab Mimi in the throat?

Helen fingered a Swiss Army knife she always carried in her jacket pocket. No one else was about; it would be so easy to just unfold the blade, plunge it into Fay's back, and then melt away. There would be a certain ironic justice in that.

'*An eye for an eye*' and all that.

No, there had to be another way. Fay would pay for what she had done, but not like that.

Shepherd's Bush Market was an open-air market, running parallel to the railway line. Helen passed under a painted metal arch and into the middle of the throng. A stall holder selling CDs and vinyl records was playing dub reggae on a portable stereo, and everywhere in this happy, bustling chaos the Afro-Caribbean influence ran high. The atmosphere took her right back to some of the places she'd visited while travelling.

Fay was still ahead of her, at a greengrocer's. Helen kept her distance and pretended to be interested in tea towels. A sudden awareness made her turn around and meet the gaze of the guy manning the record stall.

Young, maybe a little older than her, he was dressed in jeans and a tight white T-shirt, which showed he was no stranger to working out. He had thick brown hair, which curled at the nape of his neck, and a small strip of beard shaped in a thin line from the middle to the curve of his chin. Clear, blue eyes. Helen supposed a guy like that would be considered attractive, if you liked that sort of thing. Sexy even.

He winked at her and smiled, but she ignored him in case he waylaid her and pressed her to buy something, another thing she'd learned while abroad. You were trapped if you met the eyes of a market trader.

A smell of fried onions and doughy bread drew her towards a refreshment stall. Next to it, two smartly dressed young mums were chatting, their plump babies slumbering contentedly in designer pushchairs. Suddenly conscious of her own dishevelled state, Helen ran her fingers through her unkempt hair as a spurt of angry jealousy surged through her. Life was so easy for people like that. How did they know what true survival meant? They'd never woken up in the dark, afraid and lonely, with no one to comfort them, never felt ostracised because they were different. And nor would their cute little babies when they woke up.

She clenched her fists to get her feelings under control. These women weren't to blame for her bad luck.

One of them had left her keys and wallet on the counter behind her back and wasn't paying attention to her belongings. It would be as easy as pie for a pickpocket to run a hand over the wallet and scoop it up unnoticed. Helen had seen this trick often enough and wondered if she ought to warn her, when again she felt as if she was being watched and turned around.

The stall-holder shook his head imperceptibly. At first she didn't know what he meant, then her cheeks flamed. He thought she was a thief.

Trembling with anger and embarrassment, Helen tried to regain her focus on Fay. The stall-holder didn't give up. He changed the dub reggae to 'Pretty Woman'. His taste was nothing if not eclectic, but Helen saw it for the ploy it was and stalked off. Screw that guy and his Roy Orbison album. His stupid little goatee looked like a gravy stain anyway.

Jason saw the girl long before she became aware of him. She was moving from stall to stall aimlessly, as if drifting was second nature to her.

She was pretty, in a slightly unusual way. Slim and athletic with a deep tan and hair the colour of honey. Her eyes he couldn't see, but he imagined they were either green or hazel. She had a nice shape too, with just the right amount of curves.

He thought about calling out to attract her attention, but something about the way she moved held him back. Like a puma waiting to pounce on some unsuspecting prey.

Then he saw where she was looking – an unattended wallet on a table.

Don't do it, Jason wanted to say to her. *It's not worth it.*

Suddenly she stiffened as if she'd heard him. When she turned, slowly, and met his gaze, a virtual truck slammed into him. Her eyes *were* hazel, and they were blazing with fury.

Bad call, Jase, he thought, and shook his head at himself.

Actually, no, it wasn't. He'd prevented a theft by letting the girl know he was keeping an eye on her, and had saved the young mum from the pain of losing her wallet.

More importantly, he'd stopped this pretty girl from getting herself into trouble.

'Antipodean, I reckon,' said Neil, the stall-holder selling net curtains next to him.

'Who?' Jason heard his own voice coming from far away.

'The girl you can't take your eyes off. Not that I blame you.'

Another Australian. Bitter-sweet memories welled up in Jason, taking him by surprise, although it had happened a lot lately.

'Yeah, maybe she is. Although it's hard to tell these days.'

'All I'm saying,' the man went on, 'is you don't get that kind of tan in this country.'

'True.' Jason looked towards the girl again, but she'd turned away. For some reason he felt he owed her an apology, but was stumped for ideas on how to communicate with her. Then it came to him, and he put on a different record.

His choice of track had the opposite effect. The girl flounced off in a huff, and disappointment washed over him.

It would have been nice to see her smile.

Helen tried to forget about the annoying stall-holder. Ahead of her, Fay was chatting to the fishmonger. Although she wasn't close enough to hear what they were saying, it was obvious from the way the vendor gesticulated that they were talking about preparing fish.

The anger she hadn't quite managed to quell rose again. It wasn't right that Fay could stand there and talk about something so trivial when the crime she'd committed was anything other than mundane.

'Are you buying or just fingering my goods?' said a lilting Caribbean voice behind her.

In her attempt to stop Fay from noticing her, she'd used a strip of fabric from a nearby stall as a makeshift curtain to hide behind.

The owner, a Rastafarian with greying dreadlocks and a cap in the colours of the Jamaican flag, was frowning. 'It's silk, you know.'

Viscose more like, she thought and smoothed down the fabric to get rid of any creases. 'Sorry, I was just—'

'Following old Fay, yes, I saw. What might you be doing that for?'

'I'm not following anyone. Why do you think that?'

He tapped his nose. 'You don't fool me, girl. I seen you ducking and diving like you up to no good. You'll make a lousy spy.'

'I'm gutted.'

He laughed and revealed a stunning set of even teeth. 'What you want with her?'

Helen gave up pretending. There was obviously no getting around this guy, and she didn't want Fay alerted. 'Information,' she said.

'Don't we all, my love, don't we all? If you want information, Winston's the person to see.'

'Who's Winston?'

'That'll be me.'

'Thanks, I'll bear it in mind.' She turned around, but Fay was gone. Without being too obvious, she glanced down both sides of the narrow market. Fay had either finished her shopping or realised she was being followed and given Helen the slip. She muttered a curse. She knew where Fay lived but people were safer in their own houses. She wanted Fay exposed and vulnerable, as her mother had been, when she confronted her.

The Jamaican trader was watching her with wry amusement. Helen drove her fists deep in her pockets before frustration got the better of her.

'You sure I can't help you with something today?'

'No thanks.' Swallowing her frustration, Helen headed in the direction of the main road. She figured Fay would have to go home at some point.

When she reached the market gate, she nearly collided with her prey and had to duck aside again to avoid being seen. Fay didn't seem to notice, and Helen managed to stay behind her, stopping when Fay stopped to look at a shop window. Away from the buzz of the market Fay had somehow returned to what she'd been like before, just another hunched over, poor London pensioner. Helen almost felt sorry for her.

Almost, but not quite.

Turning into her own road, Fay was stopped by a beggar. Over the din of the traffic Helen could just about make out their exchange.

'I don't have much,' said Fay, 'but you can have a bag of apples.'

She handed him a brown paper bag from her shopping trolley and he smiled deliriously, like a small child who'd just been given a huge treat.

Fay left and Helen followed her again but was also stopped by the beggar. He was surprisingly young, perhaps about her own age, although life hadn't been kind to him. His head bobbed up and down continuously and so did his right arm, which he was holding up like a dog begging at the table. Under the other he clutched the bag of apples, and he reeked of old dirt and urine. Helen drew back in disgust.

'Spare some change, please?'

India had desensitised her to beggars because there were so many of them, and she'd developed an ability to see right through them as if they weren't there, weren't talking to her, weren't suffering, but she wasn't prepared for this guy.

How was it possible that someone could live like that in an affluent society? There was no dignity in begging wherever you were in the world. In a moment of kinship she realised that she too had swallowed her pride many times and accepted what others could offer. It didn't matter whether it was food, shelter, or simply words of encouragement.

'Sure,' she said and found a pound coin in her purse. 'Here, go get yourself a cup of tea.'

She watched him wobble along the pavement. Did giving him money make her a good person? And if it did, did it mean that Fay, who'd given him a bag of apples, was a good person too? Her mind couldn't allow that. It simply wasn't right.

Absent-mindedly she played with the knife in her pocket, unable to accept that Fay might be nice. That Fay might have been pushed into doing what she did by some desperate circumstance, just like this beggar had thrown himself at the feet of a stranger, shoving all integrity and self-respect aside, because *he* was desperate.

Her mind was conspiring against her with all these doubts.

Fay seemed to enjoy being outside on this mild spring morning. She stopped to stroke a cat sunning itself on a garden wall, picked up a stray crisp packet and put it in a plastic bag which hung from the handle of her shopping trolley.

She's picking up litter now. Helen bit back an angry outburst. She couldn't believe her eyes. Fay was doing it on purpose. To wind Helen up.

Suddenly, eyes narrowed, Fay swung around and manoeuvred the shopping trolley to create a shield between them. 'What do you want?'

Adrenaline surged through Helen, and she took a step back. Fay might be old, but she was a killer. Dangerous.

'You look familiar. Do I know you?'

Helen shook her head.

'Then why are you following me?'

The way Fay was standing took Helen right back to the old nightmare. Crazy-haired and wild-eyed this woman had stuck a knife into her mother's throat. Blood – sweet, dark, and life-giving – had ebbed away, splashing the inside of the car. Helen's life plunged into darkness.

The terror of the memory almost paralysed her, but her rage was as fresh as ever, and her hand closed over the knife.

Bitch.

Murderer.

Something shifted in Fay's eyes, and the demon who'd killed Helen's mother was gone, replaced by an unremarkable middle-aged woman who just looked sad.

Helen eased her hand out of her pocket. Reality hit her with a thump. Even in a moment of rage, did she have what it took to kill another person? Did Fay, who gave apples to beggars?

What *really* happened that day?

For years she'd been so certain of what she'd seen, but she'd been five years old at the time and had suffered an epileptic fit. It occurred to her now this didn't exactly make her a reliable witness.

'Well?' said Fay. 'I'm waiting. Are you going to tell me what you want or do I call the police?' She produced a mobile phone from her coat and held it like a weapon while directing her challenge at Helen.

Helen supposed that prison made you expect the worst of others, but she had no pity for the time Fay had spent inside. Her mind blank, she was struck dumb. All the things she'd wanted to say for such a long time floated around her, unformed like mist. After all, what *did* you say to the woman who murdered your mother?

Hello?

Long time no see?

No way.

She needed an excuse for being in the area, and heard herself say, in a chirpy, happy voice she didn't recognise as her own, 'I've heard that there's a room to let in this road.'

'Who told you?' Eyes narrowed again.

Think, Helen, think. 'Winston.'

Fay relaxed. 'Oh, yeah, Winston knows everything that goes on around here. Don't tell him anything you don't want other people to know.'

'I followed you down the road because I thought you might know where it is,' said Helen, encouraged.

'You did, huh?'

The challenge was still there, and Helen backed down. There was time for revenge another day. She'd find a way to make Fay's life miserable, and *then* she'd make sure Fay knew why.

Suddenly Fay smiled, losing ten years in an instant. 'Trust Winston to only give you half the picture. You're standing right in front of it. For what it's worth.'

Chapter Five

Taken aback, Helen blinked. Was Fay having her on? Was it possible for a fabricated excuse to turn to gold like this?

Fay didn't seem to notice her surprise. 'Come in,' she said. 'See if you like the room. Jason will be back soon. He deals with the official stuff. He'll fill you in.'

She began to hoist the shopping bag up the steps to the front door, pausing on every step, with the strain showing in her face after each heave.

Without rationalising it, Helen put her hand on the trolley handle. 'Here, let me help.'

'No!'

Helen withdrew as if she'd been slapped.

'Sorry,' said Fay. 'It's not you. It's a matter of principle. As long as I can haul this thing up the steps every day, I can persuade myself I'm not getting old. Silly, isn't it?'

'No, not really,' Helen murmured, surprised she was chatting with this murderess.

Fay unlocked the door and beckoned Helen inside a spacious hallway. Despite the cracked floor tiles and yellowed and stained wallpaper, you could see the house had once been a grand family home, but two world wars and economic decline had reduced it to a humble state.

Running her hand over the wall, Helen didn't see the neglect. Instead she saw the house as a gentle giant, patiently waiting until someone lavished tender loving care on it.

'I like it,' she said.

'Wait until you see the kitchen. It's ancient. This way.'

The back of the house opened up into a large kitchen which doubled as a communal living room. Mismatched kitchen units on the walls provided a frame for a large scuffed dining table in the centre with a collection of odd chairs around it. A pepper grinder stood between two old wine bottles which served as candle holders. Years of use had created a multicoloured-wax drip pattern, red, green, white, blue and even black. A stack of unwashed dishes stood on the kitchen counter next to a chipped ceramic sink with some antiquated plumbing which might possibly be original. At the end of the room a set of double doors led into an untended garden with a dilapidated shed leaning against the fence at the back.

From a battered sofa a young woman was watching TV with a black cat on her chest and a ginger one by her feet, but she put the cats down when she saw them come in, switched off the TV, and began to help Fay with the shopping.

She had blonde dreadlocks, tattoos on her arms and silver rings through her nose, eyebrow and bottom lip, and she stared unashamedly at Helen.

'Another one of your strays, Fay?'

'No, this is ...' Fay frowned at Helen. 'Sorry, I didn't catch your name.'

'I didn't give it.'

The girl with the dreadlocks snorted with laughter.

'It's Helen. Helen ... Stephens.' She'd almost lied about her name before remembering that Fay would never have heard it before. Yelena Stephanov had died with her mother. Helen Stephens had been born at age five, when Aggie put her in foster care.

Opening the fridge, Fay sent her a sideways glance. 'Are you sure I don't know you?'

'I don't think so.'

'There's something very familiar about you. You weren't at New Hall, by any chance?'

'No.'

'Holloway?'

Helen shook her head, puzzled by this line of questioning. 'I get that a lot. Apparently I look like Sheryl Crow.'

'Perhaps. Anyway, this is Charlie. Helen's interested in the room,' she added for Charlie's benefit.

'Lucky you,' said Charlie. 'So where *did* they bang you up, then?'

She was saved from answering as the door opened and a man came in. Her eyes wandered from his trainers and jeans to his brown hair and blue eyes, and instantly she felt her cheeks go hot.

It was the annoying stall-holder with the fancy goatee.

'Jason,' said Fay, 'this is Helen. Potential new house mate.'

Jason managed to hide his surprise thanks to years of keeping his thoughts to himself. It was the pretty girl from the market, and this time she was smiling. Or rather she had been until she recognised him. He knew what she'd been up to, or rather what he'd stopped her doing, and she obviously knew that he knew.

He decided to make light of it. 'Hi, there. Finished your shopping, then?'

It was entirely the wrong thing to say, and he could have kicked himself for his big, stupid mouth. She flinched visibly as if he'd slapped her.

Jason, you complete shit.

Without realising it, Charlie came to his rescue. 'Have you met before?'

'I saw her at the market. Looking at Winston's fabrics, I think?' Jason sought her eyes, read the gratitude in them. He'd seen that same look in other people before: friendless, exposed, remorseful, yet defiant at the same time. In recent probationers. He wondered if she'd recently been to prison and what had made her come here. Then he wondered what her crime was, and thought from the haunted look in her eyes it was probably something more than theft. Something momentous and life-changing.

Whatever it was, she clearly didn't want to be reminded of the one she'd almost committed half an hour ago.

'I was just browsing,' she explained, falteringly, then her confidence seemed to return. 'I haven't been to Shepherd's Bush in ages, so it was a bit full-on. You run a stall there, don't you?'

'Yes, I sell vinyl and CDs. Collectors' items. Recordings which are difficult to get hold of, that sort of thing. You should come and have a look some time.'

'Maybe I will.'

She met his stare, and Jason thought perhaps her earlier blip wasn't a relapse at all and he was losing his ability to read other people. He hoped not.

'Well, you'd better come and see the room,' he said. 'It isn't much but it's clean and we've given it a fresh coat of paint.'

He spoke in the clipped tones he inadvertently returned to whenever he was on thin ice, and which he knew flagged up visions of boarding school and top universities in his listeners, but he couldn't help it. He wondered what she made of it, if she found it hard to equate with a person who manned a market stall and ran a shared house for apparent losers. It annoyed him that he should care about her opinion but he did.

As soon as the kitchen door had swung shut behind them, she touched him lightly on the arm. Jason felt as if someone had tasered him and was grateful for the dim lighting in the hallway.

'Listen, about earlier, I wasn't planning to, well, you know, take that woman's wallet,' she said.

'That's okay, you don't have to explain yourself.'

'You seemed to think I was.'

He shook his head. 'My mistake. I just didn't want you to get in trouble, that's all. You looked like you'd lost your way a little, if that makes any sense.'

'Like I said, I hadn't been to the Market in a while.'

'That's not what I meant.'

He led her up the wide stairs to the first floor, running his hand along the dado rail as he often did. The paint on it was chipped and uneven where it had been painted over countless times, but beneath it the wood was reassuringly solid. The stairs also had a dependable feel to them despite the threadbare carpet, and the water stains on the wallpaper, which appeared here and there, were bone dry because the problem with dampness had been superficial. It was one of the things he loved about this house, that it was solid. Whatever else might happen in life, this old relic would still stand.

Glancing over his shoulder, he was amused to see the new girl do the same, tracing her fingers where his had been.

On the first floor he opened the door to the vacant room which had a view of the street and the houses opposite. He had recently redecorated it in neutral colours, and although it was sparsely furnished with only a bed, a narrow wardrobe, a desk and a chair, he'd tried to make it as bright and welcoming as possible. Catching her expression, it looked as if he'd succeeded. Her lips were slightly parted and her eyes had lit up with appreciation.

The window was open, and the pale curtains were billowing in the breeze. Tentatively, she crossed the room to the cast-iron fireplace and, resting her hand on the mantel piece, turned to face him.

'Very nice,' she said

'Interested?'

'Yes, but er—'

'But what?'

She bit her lip. 'Aren't you going to ask me for some

kind of identification? Or references perhaps? I mean, I just walked in from the street. I could be anybody.'

Taken aback, he replied, 'At some point, I suppose. Why? Do I need to check you out, is that what you're saying?'

She shook her head. 'I was just wondering.'

'I'm not worried about you,' he said, 'so long as you understand that the people who live here, apart from myself, have all had trouble with the law and have been to prison. This is a halfway house.'

'Yes, I got that impression. I should fit right in, then.'

Jason ran his hand through his hair. 'I'm glad to hear it. Usually we get sent people from the Probation Service, but you've beat them to it.' He closed the door. 'If you don't mind me asking, how did you know about the room?'

'Winston.'

'Ah, that figures. Anyway, let me show you the rest of the house. There's just the four of us at the moment. Fay's across the landing from you, and the bathroom is up here as well.'

He opened another door to show her the shared bathroom. This room he wasn't quite so confident about. It was in dire need of replacement, but he'd been putting it off until he knew where he stood regarding the lease. The toilet had an old-fashioned porcelain cistern with a pull-cord, the claw-footed tub was stained grey-green from lime scale, and one of the brass taps in the basin dripped continuously. He stepped past her and tightened the tap.

'It needs a firm hand,' he explained.

'So I see.'

He heard the laughter in her voice and wished he could explain the situation to her, but decided it could wait until another time. Chances were, she hadn't heard of his father anyway.

Closing the bathroom door, he said, 'Charlie has the big

room on the ground floor, next to our shower room, I'm in the basement, and Lee, whom you haven't met yet, is on the top floor. We also have a small spare room for emergencies up there.'

'Emergencies?'

Her amusement was gone, and she was wary now.

'People don't usually stay here for very long. A couple of months on average. Sometimes after they've moved out and gone back to their friends and family, things don't always work out. I let them stay here for a few days until they can sort something else out. I've never closed the door on someone who's come back, not unless he's given me grief. It can be a shit world out there.'

'Yes, it can,' she said. 'So if I move in, Fay and I'll be the only two people on this floor together?'

'Does that bother you? I mean, do you feel uncomfortable sharing a floor, because I could probably persuade Lee to move down. His room isn't as big as this one, though.'

'No, no,' she said quickly.

Too quickly. Alarm bells rang in his head, but she seemed so sweet and so lost that he decided to give her the benefit of the doubt.

'It really doesn't bother me,' she added as if she'd read his mind. 'Would it be okay to take a look at her room?'

He shook his head. 'House rules, I'm afraid. We don't enter other people's private space without being invited. Anyone who does will be out by the end of the week. I hope it won't be a problem for you?'

He could tell from the sudden pink spots in her cheeks that she'd caught his warning. It was the same expression she'd worn at the market, when she'd been furious with him. Jason experienced a toe-curling and gut-churning sensation of having kicked someone who was already down.

'I was just curious,' she said. 'I wasn't going to invade her privacy. I'd hate it if someone invaded mine.'

He assessed her for a moment. 'Obviously you've got principles. Why do I have this feeling you haven't been in prison?'

'Why would I want to live in a halfway house if I hadn't?' she retorted.

'You tell me. Usually principles are some of the first things people put on hold when they're locked up. They can be difficult to find again.'

'There's nothing wrong with my principles.'

'Okay, fine, no need to get on your high horse. There's just one other thing. If you don't mind me asking, what was your crime?'

'*My* crime?'

Her eyes flew to his and suddenly there was such a fiendish rage in them, a deeper and older rage different from the one before, that he almost stepped back in alarm. Then her shoulders slumped.

'Let's just say someone died who shouldn't have,' she said softly.

'Who?'

For a moment she stared at a point somewhere over his shoulder. He feared this was her way of saying she wasn't going to answer his question, and if she didn't, he couldn't allow her to have the room, simple as that.

Which would be a crying shame.

Finally she said, 'A child.'

'A child?' he repeated and sent her a startled look.

It was the first thing which had sprung to mind because there was a certain, odd truth to it – a part of her *had* died that day and her childhood with it – but she could see now that perhaps it hadn't been the smartest thing to say.

Everyone hated child killers, and rightly so. However, it was too late to take it back. No matter what she said, he wouldn't believe her now.

She found herself torn. She rarely went out of her way to make people like her, would often push them away because it was easier that way, and she'd prefer Jason's condemnation to him knowing the real reason she was here. At the same time the thought of being condemned by someone who seemed so tolerant of others was almost unbearable. Dammit, she wanted him to like her.

When he said nothing, just continued to stare at her, she turned away and headed down the stairs. Talk about messing up. Story of my life, she thought.

He caught her arm, the lightest of touches. 'Was it an accident?'

'Yes,' she replied, surprised he even bothered with her.

Something must have made him think she wasn't the devil incarnate. He smiled suddenly, and she basked in the glory of that smile like a sun-starved tourist. It transformed his face, lit up the intensely blue eyes, and the little goatee she'd scoffed at so rudely no longer looked like a gravy stain, but instead soft and beguiling, inviting her to trace it with her finger. She stopped before she made another mistake.

'Okay,' he said. 'There'll be time enough to talk about that another day. Now for the boring bit. The rent money covers bills and council tax. I don't charge much because most of my tenants are on benefits of some kind. I'm not making a profit, but that's not why I do it anyway.'

They had reached the bottom of the stairs and Jason pushed open the door to the kitchen.

'Why *do* you do it?' she asked.

The television was blaring and Fay was grinding coffee beans. Helen didn't quite hear his answer but it sounded like 'indulgence', which puzzled her because he didn't seem like the self-indulgent type.

'So what do you think?'

Coffee ready, Jason put mugs on the table with a carton of milk and a sugar bowl. Helen counted five cups, so they obviously expected her to stay for coffee whether she moved in or not. As she wondered about the last mug, she caught the eyes of the woman who'd made her life a misery. Fay was smiling.

One day you won't be smiling like that.

'I like it,' she replied to Jason's question.

'Fantastic,' said Charlie. 'We could do with another woman in the house.' She reached for the coffee pot, sloshed coffee into four mugs, then passed them around. There seemed to be a special unity between the three of them, the way they would follow up on each other's actions. It was like a strange, modern dance, beautifully choreographed, and Helen wondered if she'd ever find that.

The last mug was still standing empty in the centre of the table. As if on cue, the kitchen door banged open and a young man came in. He was lanky with mocha skin and almond-shaped brown eyes framed by thick dark lashes, and his black hair was arranged in thin plaits running across his scalp in a sideways pattern. He wore a tight-fitting T-shirt, low slung hipster jeans, and a chunky silver chain around his neck, and looked like a cover model for a hip hop fashion magazine.

She wasn't the only one affected by his presence. Charlie had gone rigid, but it was hard to say whether this was due to attraction or dislike.

'This is Lee,' said Jason. 'He lives on the top floor. Lee, Helen's going to move in across from Fay.'

Lee filled the last mug, stirring in milk and sugar. 'C-cool,' he stuttered and left the room.

'He doesn't say much,' Jason explained.

Charlie scowled. 'That's because he has nothing to say for himself.'

Definitely dislike.

'Charlie,' Jason warned.

Charlie ignored him. 'He's nasty. He mugged some old lady and kicked her in the stomach when she was too terrified to let go off her handbag. I just think Helen ought to know before she moves in that Lee's done time for violence.'

Helen's eyes cut to Fay, but Fay was staring at her mug. She then sent Jason a questioning look, wondering if she'd been mad to agree to stay. The thought of a mugger in the house didn't bother her as much as the idea of having walked in on someone else's argument.

Jason seemed to pick up on her concern. 'Don't worry, Lee's harmless. You know what I'm trying to do here, Charlie. I don't judge based on the past, but on what people do now and what they contribute.'

'He doesn't contribute anything. The old dear died of fright. You talk to her family about c-c-contribution,' she mocked.

Jason held his ground. 'It's a tough one to swallow, but he's got to live somewhere. I'd rather it was me making sure he sees his social worker than no one doing it. Besides,' he added, 'I think everyone deserves a second chance.'

Chapter Six

'Do you have a lot of stuff to bring?' Jason asked when Helen was about to leave. 'I have a small van if you need transport.'

'One of those little three-wheeler thingies?'

'Almost. It has four wheels, though. It's even got advertising on the sides.'

'Yeah?' She cocked her head to one side, gently mocking. 'What does it say?'

'Vinyl Destination.'

'Really?' She laughed and shook her head. 'No, it's all right. I've moved around a lot recently, so I don't have much.'

Part truth, and partly an excuse, Jason thought. Maybe she had been asked to leave from her previous address, and he could guess the reason. Maybe she didn't want him to run into her old flatmates in case they bad-mouthed her. Keeping him at arm's length made sense.

This child's death would weigh heavily on her conscience. It would for anyone, unless they were made of stone, so he hadn't pressed her when she confided in him on the landing. Instead he'd suggested going back to the kitchen for a cup of coffee to give her some space. His was a policy of one step at a time. When she was ready to talk, he'd listen, but he wouldn't force any details out of her.

Her caginess and the way she'd looked away, then met his gaze full on as if challenging him told him something else too. A part of her story was a lie, or at least an interpretation of the truth. At this stage it hardly mattered. He'd find out the truth eventually.

He remembered what Neil had pointed out. *You don't*

get that kind of tan in this country. One thing he was pretty certain of: you didn't get it in prison either.

This was the piece he had the most trouble fitting into the puzzle, because who would say they had been inside if they hadn't? It was an odd thing to do. Most ex-offenders would put it off for as long as possible because of prejudice and mistrust in the generally-law-abiding public. And if she'd lied about prison, was the bit about the child also a lie?

It takes one to know one, he thought. Most people would back away when they were up against someone who clearly couldn't be trusted, but he wasn't about to because he understood it. Hadn't he always been vague and skirted around the issue of who his father was and how he made his money?

He saw her to the door and held it open for her. As she passed him, he got a whiff of her perfume, something fresh and floral and strangely at odds with the heavy sadness surrounding her. He liked her scent, and when she brushed against him by accident, a thrill ran through him. He caught her eyes for a nano-second, felt the attraction connecting them by an invisible string. She was the first to look away, but he spotted the faint smile and wondered if the nearness had affected her the same way.

Watching from the top step as she headed back to the main road, he thought of a silly game he used to play with his school mates.

If she turns around, she's interested.

Her stiff shoulders and self-conscious way of walking told him she knew he was watching her. When she never looked back, he couldn't say for sure whether this was sheer bloody-mindedness on her part, or whether she truly wasn't interested in him.

Which was probably just as well if they were to live under the same roof.

Closing the worm-eaten front door, he smiled grimly. She was a total mystery, and he was the idiot walking right into the snare, eyes wide shut. It couldn't be helped. He had to get to the bottom of it, to satisfy his own curiosity and because she looked like she could do with having someone on her side. After all, he had to practice what he'd preached to Charlie, that everyone deserved a second chance.

Then why did he have this peculiar feeling that a second chance, in the strictest sense of the word, wasn't what she was seeking?

He returned to the kitchen where Charlie was washing up the mugs. Grabbing a tea towel, he began to dry the crockery.

Charlie handed him a mug dripping with suds. 'Do you like her?'

'She seems all right,' he replied non-committally.

'She didn't say where they locked her up.'

'I'm not sure she was. Does it matter?'

Charlie shrugged and rinsed the last mug. 'I can't put my finger on it – and you can say what you like – but I smell trouble.'

Jason laughed. 'Please don't let that overactive imagination of yours run away with you. I think she'll be quite nice to have around.'

'You're not getting it.' Charlie wrung out the sponge and dried her hands. 'I don't mean us, or the house. It's just that you have such a big heart, Jase. I meant trouble for *you*.'

Helen felt his gaze scorching the back of her neck. She nearly turned around but the thought of what she might see stopped her. He'd sensed that zing between them as much as she had, a feeling that had been there at the market too and which was a complication she could do without.

Why did he have to be so damn nice?

Everything screamed at her that moving in was a bad idea, but Jason's house was cheap and convenient for her purposes, and she was only staying long enough to complete her task.

A quick trip back to her hotel in Earl's Court to collect her bags, and she was installed in the magnolia-painted room in time to eat a Caribbean takeaway by herself.

Then she tried to make herself at home. She covered the bed with a blanket from India, hung a couple of posters and put her knick-knacks on the mantelpiece. Her statue of the Hindu god Shiva she placed on the desk, then she hung her clothes in the wardrobe. They barely took up half the space.

One day, she promised herself, when she'd got over the hurdle Fay represented, her life would be normal, and she'd have all those lovely useless things which cluttered up the lives of average people.

Slipping across the landing to the bathroom with her toothbrush, she noticed the light from underneath Fay's door and tiptoed closer to put her ear to the door. She could hear music, faintly, but wasn't sure whether Fay was in there or not. Tempted by the proximity to her mother's murderer, and by curiosity, she put her hand on the door handle, but pulled back when she caught a flicker of movement out of the corner of her eye.

Lee the Mugger, as she now thought of him, had come up the stairs without a sound and was standing right behind her, eyeing her curiously.

'Hi,' she said, heart thudding wildly.

'Hnh.'

He continued to the top floor without a backwards glance. She stared after him, thinking that there must be someone up there, among the gods, watching her and rolling on the floor with laughter. Even she had trouble explaining how she'd ended up sandwiched between a murderer, a stuttering street thug, and an infuriating do-gooder. Plus whatever it was Charlie had done.

You couldn't make it up.

It surprised her how quickly she settled in. Charlie turned out to be easy to get along with, and Jason worked at his music stall and then did jobs around the house. Helen offered to help, and he set her the task of clearing out some of the kitchen cabinets which he was planning to replace with new ones.

'Where do you want the stuff?' she asked.

'Just put it all in those boxes over there. We'll sort it out later when the new cupboards are up.' He indicated a stack of cardboard boxes by the back door and sent her another of those smiles which did peculiar things to her insides.

This could get complicated. Really complicated.

As for the others in the house, Lee would, to Charlie's immense irritation, turn up only at dinner time to scoop some food on his plate and take it to his room.

Fay was okay, if a bit reserved. Helen wondered if whatever had caused her to kill a friend wasn't still lurking beneath the surface, but there was no sign of it. Still, no one ever completely knew what went on inside other people, so she kept an eye on her.

When she wasn't helping Jason, she hung out with Charlie, mainly watching TV, and when Charlie wasn't around either, she'd stand outside Fay's door listening for sounds from behind it. Joe had been right, the pull of revenge was just too strong to resist. She just didn't know how to go about it.

At the same time she wanted to hear Fay's version of events first. Except Fay kept herself to herself. Everything was definitely more complex than she'd expected. It didn't help that she was beginning to like her.

She had to do something to take her mind off things.

Recalling what Aggie had said about getting a job at the auction house, Helen rang the offices of Ransome & Daughters expecting short shrift, but was instead given an appointment with her aunt Letitia two days later.

She dressed carefully for the interview. Letitia was always so elegant, but the best Helen could come up with was a white blouse of Indian cotton and a layered skirt in the most sombre shade she could find. As for shoes, it had turned cold again lately, and she had to rely on her trusted Doc Martens.

Charlie whistled when Helen entered the kitchen.

'Going anywhere nice?'

'Job interview. Of sorts. At an auction house.'

'Of sorts?'

'Well, you know. I'm hoping they won't mind me not having any experience of the trade.' The lie slipped off her tongue easily enough. Too easily, but she doubted the personal connection and her part-ownership of the company would go down well with Charlie.

'Lucky you. I haven't had much luck finding a job. Everywhere I go, they take one look at my record and all my piercings, and then they suddenly don't need me any more.' Charlie pushed a brown teapot across the table. 'Here, I just made it.'

Helen poured a cup. 'Shouldn't I be paying something towards food and drink? Or does it come out of the rent money?'

'Don't worry about it. Fay comes around with the kitty tin once a fortnight. It used to be my job, but Jason gave it to Fay when she moved in.'

'Why?'

Charlie sent Helen a direct look. 'I'm a thief. I'd steal from my own granny, or so they said at the juvie. Trouble is, I don't have a granny. Or anyone else.'

'I'm sure that's not why he asked Fay to take over.'

'It doesn't bother you?'

'I don't have anything worth taking, except these.' Helen showed Charlie her mother's elephant pendant and the silver amulet Mamaji had given her, then tucked them back inside her blouse. She ignored the voice in her head which reminded her about the two hundred and twenty-five thousand pounds a year she was supposed to get. It was just too unreal, and she hadn't really taken it in yet. Besides, she wanted to make her own way in life before accepting handouts from her family.

'I don't steal from friends.'

'I wouldn't have shown them to you if I thought otherwise.' Helen sipped her tea. It was scalding hot and bitter, just the way she liked it. 'So, you don't have any relatives at all?'

'Me going to prison wasn't part of my parents' plan, so they'd rather pretend I don't exist. The people that matter live in this house. Even that bastard Lee.' Charlie looked at her fingernails which were bitten to the quick.

'Why don't you like him?' Helen didn't like him much either, especially not the way he crept about silently and popped up when you least expected him to.

Charlie scowled. 'Because he could do so much more with his life. Unlike me. Because of what I did.'

'Why unlike you?' What had Charlie done?

'I ran with a bad group, right. A gang of girls. We'd hang around on street corners after school, you know, just being a general nuisance. There was this one girl we liked to pick on. She had some sort of facial deformity, and we just didn't give her a break. Then … one day she killed herself. That's when I flipped because I realised what I'd done. Ruined the life of another person. And why? Because I was bored, didn't care about other people's feelings. Didn't have any prospects.'

Helen digested this in shocked silence. The dead girl could have been her. Almost was her, except she knew she was stronger. And Charlie was taking all the blame on her shoulders, which was unfair because there was a whole group of them.

'It wasn't just you,' she said.

'I had a choice, I could've said no.' Charlie shrugged, as if she wasn't sure about that herself. 'So, I decided I was going to make good some of the harm that I'd done. I took a college course in computing and got a job working for HM Revenue & Customs. Then I made sure her family got a big tax rebate.'

Another person who thought money could make up for everything. 'How?'

'Oh, it was a piece of cake, but of course it all got found out because these people really were too good to be true and they queried it, the silly bastards. Then I got sent down for hacking the system, and I knew there was no justice in life. It should've been manslaughter.'

'You didn't kill her.'

'I almost did.' Charlie looked at her fingernails, then back at Helen with a grin. 'I hope you still like me.'

The joke was skin deep. Helen felt it, and Charlie knew it. 'Of course I do. I'm glad you told me.' It was still a shock, though.

'Yeah,' mumbled Charlie with a far-away look in her eyes.

'And what about Fay?' said Helen.

'Fay's a good person. Believe me, if she could wave a magic wand and turn back the clock, she would. She suffers daily. She just doesn't show it. Anyway, what do you know about what Fay's done? She hardly ever talks about it.'

'Nothing, really.'

'I care about the people here,' said Charlie, chewing her thumbnail. 'That goes for Lee as well, but he's just too bloody stupid for his own good. He never learns. He's been in and out of prison like a yo-yo. The time he's lived here is the longest he's been straight, but I don't expect it to last. With a face and a body like his there's so much more he could do with his life, and this is as far as his imagination stretches? That really gets to me!'

'Yes, I can see that.'

Charlie stopped gnawing on her finger and laughed. 'I'm glad you moved in. I haven't had a real friend in years.'

A warm feeling fanned out inside Helen's chest. Me neither, she thought. Smiling back, she was about to say something when the kitchen door opened. She tensed, and so did Charlie, but Charlie relaxed when she saw it was Fay. Helen didn't.

'There's tea in the pot,' said Charlie.

'Ta.' Fay was wearing a threadbare towelling dressing gown, and her grey hair lay flat against her skull. Her hand shook as she poured.

'Bad night?' asked Charlie.

Fay nodded.

'Helen's got a job interview.'

Fay's face lit up with a genuine smile. 'Already? That's great! Good luck and all that.'

She put her hand on Helen's shoulder and gave it a little squeeze. Helen stiffened, and Fay immediately withdrew her hand as if she'd been stung.

Helen got up, pretending this hadn't happened. 'I'd better go.'

Ransome & Daughters was situated near Berkeley Square, in a four-storey town house with arched windows and the company's name in gold lettering. Facing the green-painted façade, Helen knew immediately that she must have been here before, yet couldn't quite remember it.

But there was nothing for it.

In the foyer she approached the receptionist who sat behind an imposing walnut desk. The woman ran a lacquered fingernail down a clipboard list and tapped it audibly. 'Oh, yes, here we are. Meeting with Ms Walcott at ten. Please take a seat. I'll send for someone to take you upstairs.'

Helen sat down on an imitation Regency style sofa – or was it the real thing? – and looked around her. The foyer was large, with marble flooring, mahogany-clad columns, a red-carpeted staircase and a corridor at the far end leading to a darkened room. In front of an imposing fireplace stood a polished table with an arrangement of white lilies, their cloying scent filling the air.

Helen closed her eyes briefly. There had been white flowers on her mother's coffin.

'Miss Stephens?'

She looked up to find a craggy-faced, bald man in a brown workman's smock smiling down at her.

'Yes?'

'If you'd follow me, please?'

They climbed the stairs to the first floor, their feet moving soundlessly on the thick carpet. Everywhere Helen turned she saw opulence, or a good impression of it. The banister gleamed golden-red, up-lighters enhanced the lichen-green wallpaper with its velvet *fleur-de-lis* pattern, and English Romantic paintings were hung to maximum effect in strategic places.

The company was making serious money, a stark contrast to what Helen was used to, but she hadn't imagined this to be reflected in the surroundings, and she nearly gasped. Her annual dividends began to seem like a paltry sum.

'Are you here about the job?' her companion wheezed as he opened the door to an outer office with two doors leading off it. A large desk stood in front of the doors as if it had been placed there in order to form a bastion against invaders. Behind it a secretary was tapping away at a computer.

'I'm here about *a* job.'

'You look familiar,' he said.

'Really?' It was possible he'd known her mother if he'd worked here long enough, but she knew from the only photograph she had of her parents, and which she carried in her wallet, that she didn't look like her. He couldn't have recognised her.

She didn't know whether Letitia had announced she was expecting her niece, but she suspected her aunt wanted to keep the association between them private. She'd never showed herself to be an auntie in the true sense of the word, so why start now?

He scratched his chin, rasping his fingers against his grey stubble. 'Not sure, but I expect it'll come to me.' To the secretary he said, 'Helen Stephens for Ms Walcott.'

Still *Ms* Walcott, Helen noted. So, perhaps she hadn't married. It didn't surprise her. Letitia had always lived for her work.

The secretary ran her eyes over Helen's outfit and curled her lips in barely disguised contempt. Sticking her chin out, Helen was tempted to reveal her family connection, if only to wipe that look off the face of the snooty bitch, but decided not to. Perhaps the secretary already knew.

Oh, who cares, she thought impatiently. 'I have an appointment at ten,' she said instead.

'You're a little early.'

'Isn't that better than being late?'

'I suppose so.' The secretary sniffed and rose, then knocked on one of the doors.

The workman winked at Helen and left them.

'I'll just see if Ms Walcott is free,' said the secretary.

'I hope so because I've arranged to see her today.'

'Maybe, but we have to leave room for emergencies. Ms Walcott is very busy.'

'I bet,' Helen muttered. Busy oiling the wheels of the family company and scheming behind her own mother's back, if Aggie was to be believed. But that wasn't Helen's problem.

The secretary stepped into Letitia's office and Helen followed, refusing to wait. Immediately she took in the sumptuously furnished room: gleaming oak desk, tall windows hung with designer curtains, Art Deco lamps, works of art in heavy gilded frames.

Letitia was on the phone, and Helen shuddered at the sound of her husky laugh. There was something about her laughter which had always made Helen feel she was the butt of the joke, but Letitia's smile was genuine when she hung up and asked the secretary to leave them.

'But, Ms Walcott …' the secretary protested, holding out her notepad.

Letitia waved her hand. 'There'll be no need for note-taking. You may go.'

The secretary retreated reluctantly, and Letitia came forward to meet Helen, putting her strong, almost masculine hands on Helen's shoulders and kissing her on both cheeks.

'Helen, my dear niece. You have been away for far too long.'

In stark contrast to her sister, Letitia was slim, almost bony, with rich chestnut hair in an expensive cut, a hooked nose and an angular face, which wasn't exactly handsome, but striking nonetheless, its lack of prettiness part of the charm. Her posture was effortless but at the same time commanding. She wore a peacock-blue Thai silk dress under a cream jacket with gold buttons, and matching blue heels.

The 'dear niece' bit flummoxed her because they had never had that sort of relationship. 'Hi, Letitia.'

Her aunt stepped back so she could take a proper look at her. 'You look very … mm, tanned. The epitome of good health, I'd say.'

But I'm not, Helen wanted to say. *I have epilepsy and take drugs.*

'Thank you.'

'Come, let's talk.' Letitia indicated an armchair in front of her desk, then sat down in her own executive desk chair. 'So, are you back for good now? Mother said you wanted to work with us. I'm happy to find something for you to do if you're prepared to muck in.'

Helen grimaced. So like Aggie to jump the gun. 'I don't mind hard work, but just so you know, I didn't come home expecting special favours.'

'I understand,' said Letitia briskly. 'We haven't exactly been the most loving of families, have we? I expect you've felt rather abandoned over the years.'

This was the closest thing to an apology Helen had ever had for her family's deception. Although she welcomed the acknowledgement from her formidable step-aunt, it didn't have the impact she'd hoped for. All these years of bearing a grudge – when someone finally said sorry, it was almost as if they got let off too lightly.

'I suppose.'

Letitia smiled. 'I'm not completely heartless.'

'I never said that.'

'We didn't do the right thing by you. I'll be the first to admit that. But Mother thought it would be best for you if you grew up away from us. Didn't think it was the right environment for you. She may have had a point.'

'It still bloody stung,' said Helen. 'Learning to forget about you all, and then suddenly you expected me to come back and be part of a family.'

Letitia nodded. 'I appreciate that. But let's move on, shall we?'

Helen shrugged.

'So, er, how have you been? Any significant other?'

'I don't have a boyfriend, no.'

'Mm, understandable with your condition, I should think, but still …'

What do you know of my condition? Helen thought sourly. 'No one wants the responsibility,' she said.

'A shame. Anyway, where were we? Oh, yes, a job for Helen. Let me see.' Letitia riffled through a stack of papers on her desk, then rose and opened a drawer in the filing cabinet behind the desk, while she continued to talk.

'As you may know, in the last eight or nine years the company has really taken off. This is reflected in our share prices and in the dividends to the shareholders. I'm sure Mother must have filled you in on that.'

A rhetorical question. Helen merely nodded.

'Of course, you could easily live on the dividends alone,' Letitia continued, 'but we'd prefer your involvement. One of the strengths of Ransome & Daughters is that we're a *family* company. When you have a personal stake – not just financial, but a desire to see the results of your hard work – then it really matters. I believe only family can achieve that. We're the only ones who share that passion. Do you follow me?'

'I think so.'

'Would you agree?'

Helen thought of the tempestuous relationship between Mamaji and her daughter-in-law, and how they managed to run the shop together despite their obvious dislike for each other.

'Yes, I'd agree with that.'

'Good. We're on the same wavelength, then.'

Letitia found the file she was looking for and slipped on a fashionable pair of reading glasses.

'You'll be getting our starter wage, but naturally you'll have your dividends as well.' She sent Helen a schoolmarmish look over the top of her spectacles. 'I'd advise you not to mention to the other staff that you receive dividends, nor your relationship to me. We have a couple of malcontents around here, and I don't want to be accused of favouritism.'

'I know how to fit in.'

Letitia snapped the file shut again. 'Good. I'll see you on Monday bright and early. And by that I mean eight o'clock sharp. Wear jeans and a jumper or something; there'll be some lifting involved.' Her eyes slid over Helen's boots and hippy skirt. 'Later you'll be required to dress more conservatively. My secretary will provide you with a list of where to find the kind of clothes I have in mind.'

Resentment prickled between Helen's shoulder blades, but she pushed the thought aside, aware that her wardrobe needed some attention. Who better to make suggestions than her elegant aunt? She got up to leave.

At the time of Mimi's death Letitia had been focusing on her career and hadn't wanted to be saddled with the responsibility of a child. Now, in hindsight, Helen could see that Letitia just wasn't the maternal sort and living with her might not have been so great after all. Ruth would have been okay, she supposed, but Ruth didn't want her. Both Aggie and Letitia had said so. Sure, they'd packaged it nicely, but that was the bottom line.

For a moment the old bitterness welled up in her, then she let it go. Practical to the core, Letitia was right, it was all in the past. The issues surrounding Fay were different, but the aunts were probably a bit screwed up in each their own way. Perhaps it was time to move on from that.

She paused in the doorway and looked back at Letitia. 'I never thought I would hear myself say this, but I'm actually glad to be back,' she said.

Letitia smiled. 'That's good to hear. By the way, on Monday make sure you go round the back.'

'Well, that's me put in my place,' Helen muttered and caught the look of surprise on the secretary's face that she'd actually been hired.

Chapter Seven

Helen Stephens, Jason mused as he bagged a vinyl record for another customer, a rare gatefold Pink Floyd album.

It was a perfectly ordinary name, shared by lots of people in Britain alone. He should know, he'd spent hours googling for information on her. A waste of time.

She'd lived in the house for over a week now, and with every minute he spent in her company he became more and more intrigued by her, and convinced that she was lying through her teeth.

Which only made him even more interested. And concerned.

It didn't help that she was so attractive either. Yesterday morning he'd watched, fascinated, as she flicked back her honey-gold hair while looking through the job adverts in the local rag with Charlie. Charlie was always job-hunting, so newspapers were usually strewn about the place.

Suddenly she'd looked up, and Jason had been treated to a smouldering look from those hazel eyes. Back off, it said, and it was like a full frontal assault on his senses. It had hit him right in the gut, or more specifically, the groin.

It disturbed him, this heat coming from her. He suspected she must know, at some level, about the affect it had on him. Her vulnerability just added to her attraction, made him want to shelter her, although he doubted she'd welcome it.

Scarily independent, that one, he'd thought, and broken eye contact.

He couldn't stop himself from thinking about her, though, and swore under his breath. How could he help her, if he didn't know who or what she was hiding from? And if there was one thing he hated, it was not having the answers. He needed to know.

As her landlord he had the right to press her for certain details, like her prison information, and ask for references, but what if she got spooked and simply took off …?

Turning to Neil, who was threading display curtains on a pole in his own stall, he asked, 'Do you think you could look after the vinyls for me for a couple of hours?' The stall-holders had a thriving community and would help each other out when needed.

'Should be able to. Not very busy today, by the looks of it.' Neil glanced up at the sky. 'Probably because it's going to rain.'

Jason thanked him and set off in search of answers.

As Neil had predicted, the heavens opened as soon as he arrived at his aunt Lucy's home in Fulham. A streak of lightning flashed across the sky in the distance, and for a moment he felt his father's shadow on him. He had to pull himself together not to turn around and check if he was being followed.

He wasn't, of course. Derek Moody had better things to do with his time, and anyway what could be more innocent than visiting his aunt?

Lucy was the youngest of his father's three sisters and only about fifteen years older than him, so it was more like a friendship than an auntie/nephew relationship.

That didn't stop her fussing over him like he was the golden child, but he put up with it because he knew she enjoyed doing it.

'Jason!' she squeaked. 'Where have you *been*? I haven't seen you in *months*.' She planted a couple of loud *mwahs* on his cheeks, and Jason grinned.

Lucy was a slim brunette with a figure that spoke of hours at the gym. She wore skin-tight white jeans, a skimpy emerald-green blouse, which showed off her impressive cleavage to its advantage, and caramel-coloured peep-toe ankle boots giving her at least five extra inches. Gold rings on eight of her ten fingers glinted as she waved him inside, and a heavy gold pendant with Queen Nefertiti dangled to below her bosom, drawing the eye to where she no doubt wanted it.

Jason gulped. Lucy was, as always, just a little overwhelming.

Attracted by the commotion, Lucy's Rottweiler came up behind her, growling. His aunt was another dog lover, and although Rottweilers weren't Jason's favourite breed, he preferred them to his mother's dogs. You got more dog for your money.

'Don't growl at Jason, you silly girl!' Lucy dragged the enormous dog away by the collar so she could close the door.

'It's okay.' Jason dropped to his haunches. 'Come, Jessie. Come, girl.'

Tentatively, the dog stopped growling and stepped forward to sniff Jason's hand which he held out palm facing upwards to show he wasn't a threat. After a moment or two, Jessie began licking his hand then rolled onto the floor to have her tummy rubbed.

Crossing her arms, Lucy shook her head. 'I don't know who's the craziest of the two of you. She's supposed to be a guard dog and you've got more balls than sense sitting down in front of a Rottweiler like that. She could rip your throat out.'

'But you're not going to do that, Jessie, are you? No, no, we're not going to do that at all.' He continued talking baby-talk to the dog while it groaned with pleasure, then he rose with a grin.

'Dogs like me,' he smirked. 'Besides, you know how I like to live dangerously.'

'Lunatic,' she said. 'I was just getting the roast out of the oven. Come and have some dinner. Trevor is carving once the footie's finished.'

'I didn't stop by for you to feed me.'

'*That* is a barefaced lie, but I'm prepared to let it go. Anyway, who says I can't invite my favourite nephew for dinner now and again?'

'Your only nephew.'

'Who's counting? You're still my favourite.'

Jason followed her to the back of the house and commented on her tan.

'We're just back from Dubai.'

Lucy went on to talk about their holiday to a destination which had never held much fascination for Jason, then handed him a G & T and told him to get out from under her feet. He joined Lucy's husband, Trevor, who was slurping gin and shouting at their massive flat-screen TV in the den just off the kitchen.

Trevor turned away from the screen. 'Well, if it isn't Master Moody! What brings you here?'

'Very funny. Like I haven't heard that one before.' Jason perched on the armrest. 'Thought I might watch the game with you. How's it going by the way?'

'They're a couple of clowns short of a full circus, that's what. And you, young sir, are a terrible liar. What can I do for you?'

'It's complicated.'

'I'm good at complicated.'

'Okay, then, what would you do if you knew someone was lying to you?' Jason sat down on the sofa properly.

Trevor raised his eyebrows. 'I dunno. Try to get the truth out of them?'

'What if you knew they'd either disappear or feed you another line?' A sudden roar from Trevor caused him to nearly spill his drink.

'Oh, you complete fucker! You're depriving a village of an idiot somewhere!' Trevor continued hurling abuse at the

TV, then turned to Jason with a sheepish grin. 'Sorry. Tell you what I'd do. I'd drop them like a hot potato. Life's too fucking short.' He swirled the ice cubes in his drink with a pained expression. 'You know, you're not making a lot of sense.'

'What if you couldn't bring yourself to do that?'

'A girl, is it? Does your loving father know?'

Jason hesitated. Trevor had once worked for his father as a chauffeur and general fixer, and had strengthened the bond by later marrying Lucy. He wanted to keep this matter out of his father's reach for as long as possible, but he needed Trevor's help because of his various contacts. Which meant trusting him.

'Not yet, and I'd like to keep it that way.'

'This "no parental involvement" thing you have going, will it lead to conflict of interest for me?' Trevor asked.

They both knew what he was referring to. Trevor was the one who'd let slip, inadvertently, that Jason's involvement with Cathy had developed into something more than a fling. Derek had put the screws on, then, got the whole story. Jason had tried not to blame Trevor when the whole sordid affair went belly-up, but it had cost him.

'It shouldn't do,' he said. 'It's just an enquiry.'

Trevor downed the last of his drink. 'Okay, so let me get this straight: you've met this girl, you like her, she's lying to you about something, and you want to know what and why.'

Jason nodded.

'Christ, you don't ask much,' Trevor grumbled. 'Why don't I discover a cure for cancer while I'm at it? Who is she?'

'Her name is Helen Stephens, and she's just moved into my house. Claims she's been to prison, but I think she's lying about that.'

'Why on earth would anyone do that? I mean, the other way around, yes, but ...'

'Beats me,' Jason shrugged. 'She said a child died, in an accident. I think she might be telling the truth about that bit, but there's more to it than that. Perhaps she used to be a nanny or something and is hiding because she's worried about the family coming after her. I'd like to help her if I can. Except I can't find any information about her. Do you know how many people are called Helen Stephens in this country? I tried everything, Google, combinations with *murder*, *child*, *manslaughter*, *drink-driving*, *Münchausen Syndrome by Proxy*, you name it, but nothing came up.'

'Maybe she's the sort who just falls under the radar,' Trevor suggested.

'No one falls under the radar, you know that. Not completely. Something would show a connection.'

'Mhm.' Trevor's eyes had slid back to the TV screen. 'Oh, you twat!'

'Could you look into this for me?'

'You're not giving me much to go on.'

'That's all I have, I'm afraid.' Jason handed him a slip of paper with a description of Helen and a guesstimated age of somewhere in her mid-twenties. 'And while you're at it, could you check that she isn't one of Dad's spies?'

Trevor put it in his shirt pocket. 'I'd need to take a look at this bird myself, though.'

'Won't be difficult. She hangs around the house at the moment, going in and out.'

They were interrupted by Lucy dressed in an apron with a bikini-clad torso on the front. 'Could one of you be a real darling and lay the table while I get the roast out of the oven?'

Leaving Trevor to his game, Jason followed his aunt back into the kitchen. The Rottweiler was lying prostrate in the middle of the floor, and as he stepped over the huge lump of a dog to get to the dinner plates, he realised how much he felt at ease here, amidst the noise from the TV, the homely smells and the gentle chaos. He couldn't recall his own home-life ever having been anything like this, and it gave him a sense that he'd been deprived of something which was both normal and rare.

'Have you found a job yet?' Lucy asked, stirring an Oxo cube into the pan of meat juices.

'I'm still at the Market, and that's going well. Dad's finally signed his Acton house over to me, and it needs a lot of work.'

Lucy looked at him sharply, her carefully plucked eyebrows coming together in a frown. 'He did? That's a first. Did you hear that, Trevor?'

'I heard. Good for you.' Trevor paused. 'What a load of rubbish!' he shouted, to the TV.

'You do know he'll want to have a finger in the pie,' Lucy added in a low voice.

'Actually, he says he doesn't want to know.'

'He might say that, but trust me, I know my brother extremely well.'

Jason decided to play it down. 'Then I'll just have to make sure I don't draw attention to myself, won't I?'

'Yeah? How?'

'By staying out of his line of sight.'

Lucy snorted.

'Naïve, I know,' said Jason, 'but I thought once the house was in my name, and since I don't ask him for money or anything, that I really would be beneath his notice.'

'Go home, Earth is full!' Trevor bellowed.

'You'll never be beneath his notice. He loves you.'

'He has a funny way of showing it.' All of a sudden blue-eyed Cathy and his own fantasy image of the child that never was popped up in his mind. Some loving father. He tried to suppress the memories once and for all. It was in the past, he had to let it go.

'I wouldn't know what the right way is,' said Lucy. 'I never had children.'

A shadow crossed her unlined face – Botox, and why not? – and he was cross with himself for touching on the one subject which could make his tough, loud-mouthed aunt go quiet.

'Don't worry about it, Jason,' she said, guessing his thoughts. 'We're happy as we are, aren't we, Trevor?'

Having switched the TV off, her husband joined them in the kitchen and was rummaging in a drawer for a carving knife.

'Happy as Larry,' came the reply. 'Or I would be if it weren't for bleedin' referees.'

Lucy shrugged. 'I was quite sad about it a while back, but I got over it. Some people don't. They become totally obsessed with what they can't have, and it eats away at them until there's nothing else that matters. It can make a person very bitter and twisted. We're not like that, me and Trevor, are we?'

Brandishing a lethal-looking knife in one hand, Trevor smiled and caressed her cheek lightly with the other. 'No, we're not, dolly.'

Feeling like an intruder all of a sudden, he admired their quiet resignation. His own sense of loss was nothing compared to theirs, yet he thought he understood. And just like them, he had to learn to accept what he couldn't change.

Helen left Letitia's office and stopped outside on the pavement to think about what had just happened. Then she laughed. The look on the secretary's face had been priceless; the woman clearly didn't think Helen fit in. Nothing strange about that either, because, in truth, she didn't.

For her it had never been about money and status. That was Letitia's world. And Aggie's. What drove Ruth heaven only knew, but Helen had a feeling she was different.

What little she remembered of Ruth from her early childhood had been drowned out by resentment when the doors to the family had been shut in her face. Back in the office Letitia had hinted it was all Aggie's decision, and she believed it, but it still angered her that Ruth hadn't stepped in. Ruth had been her favourite, her husband Jeremy too, even if Aggie thought of him as a 'disaster'.

They could have been a proper family, the one she never had even when her mother was alive. It could have been perfect. Ruth never had children of her own and desperately wanted some. So why had she rejected Helen?

A series of images flashed through her head. Ruth, angry and wistful, staring at Helen as if she wanted to scoop her up and never let go, yet hating her at the same time. Those images had stayed with her all these years, as clear as day, but no matter how hard she tried she couldn't conjure up any real memories of her own mother. In the past she'd had the odd recall, but as soon as she tried to pin it down, it was gone.

Lost in thought, she crossed Berkeley Square and headed for the Tube. It had rained recently, but the sun was shining now. A young woman played catch with a little boy in the dappled sunlight under the large trees. A lady in a Burberry raincoat walked two frisky poodles who kept getting entangled in their extendible leads. On a bench a man in a black suit lit a cigarette and then stared at nothing in particular through mirrored sun glasses.

Helen frowned. The ordinary scene struck her as very familiar, but her mind refused to cooperate.

She reached Piccadilly and stopped for a moment, squeezing her eyes shut. If she squeezed hard enough, perhaps she could force her memories to come back. Nothing happened except for a dull ache in her chest and a feeling of exhaustion. Sighing, she opened her eyes again.

A grey mist rose from the pavement, obscuring her vision.

Her arms twitched involuntarily, her fingers tingled. She picked at her clothes, only partly aware she was doing it, and swallowed back a metallic taste in her mouth.

'Not now,' she whispered.

Brief, excessive electrical discharges fired in her neurons, a simple partial seizure. Her mind told her this rationally, but powerless to stop it, she was suddenly gripped by terror and a feeling that this was the end of the world. Putting her shaking hands on the wall beside her, she anchored herself so even when her brain switched off, her body wouldn't continue walking and send her right out into the traffic without knowing it.

The raw stone scraped reassuringly against her knuckles as the seizure took hold of her ...

'Bit early in the day, wouldn't you say?'

Someone was shaking her gently, an old guy with dark, bushy eyebrows. Helen registered the look of concern, the hand on her shoulder. For a moment she had no idea where she was or what she was doing, but slowly the pieces fell into place again.

He was a newspaper salesman, from a nearby stand. She'd been to Letitia's office, had thought of Ruth, had become distressed because she couldn't remember her mother. Then the seizure had imploded inside her.

Her arms down by her sides, she leaned against the wall. The traffic was roaring past, clogging the air with car fumes. The pavement teemed with office workers, tourists and shoppers too busy to notice a person whose brain had just glitched.

Except this guy.

'S-sorry, I didn't catch that.' Helen's tongue felt enormous in her mouth. Somewhere hidden above her pigeons cooed, a reassuring sound, a sign of normality returning.

'I said,' he repeated, slowly as if he were talking to an idiot, 'it's a bit early in the day to be knocking them back, innit?'

Another piece fell into place. He thought she was drunk. 'I'm not …' she protested but he'd already turned his attention to a customer wanting to buy a paper.

The temptation was there to blurt it all out, to seek comfort, to shock and horrify, anything so she didn't have to be alone with this secret. She didn't, of course, never had, never would.

A lot of people thought epileptics were freaks, that the condition was some kind of mental instability which could affect them if they got too close. The same way some people thought you could catch cancer. A stigma was attached to Helen's condition as if this loss of brain control was voluntary, and that epileptics could stop the seizures happening if they just pulled themselves together.

Some shied away in horror, others wanted to show how tolerant and efficient they were by restraining the epileptic during the seizure or even put something in his mouth, the idea being to stop him biting his own tongue off. Too many myths and half-truths, too little general understanding of the illness drove sufferers underground.

Helen lived in that half-world, like so many others.

'What business is it of yours?' she snapped.

The man looked over his shoulder at Helen. 'Steady on, love. Steady on. I was only concerned. If you can't hold your drink, you shouldn't be out and about like this. You should be at home sleeping it off.'

'Who are you to tell me what to do?'

She didn't wait for an answer but turned her back on him and headed for Green Park tube station.

'I've got a daughter just like you,' he called after her.

No, you don't, she thought as her unsteady legs found the escalator. *No, you bloody don't.*

The kitchen rang with Charlie's laughter when she got home. Ignoring the pull in her stomach at the delicious smells of cooking wafting up the stairs, she headed straight for her room, kicked off her boots and collapsed on top of the bed.

It was dark when a gentle knocking woke her. She ached all over as if she'd been in a boxing match. Before answering the door, she scooped up her packet of tablets which lay on the desk and shoved it in a drawer.

It was Fay holding a tray with a covered plate, a glass of juice and a knife and fork.

Knife. *Blood.*

The memory was suddenly so vivid Helen swayed.

'Did I wake you?'

Helen shook her head.

'I did, didn't I? Sorry, I just thought you might like something to eat. Charlie heard you come in earlier but we missed you at dinner. May I come in? This tray's a bit heavy.'

Helen nodded, her tongue still tied in a thousand knots.

Fay put the tray on her desk. The food smelt inviting, and Helen realised she hadn't eaten anything since ... well, nothing all day.

'You've made the room look nice,' said Fay. 'I like all the little statues.'

Helen's eyes were on the tray. She was ravenous, but reluctant to eat in front of Fay in case the food tasted like it often did after a seizure. Fay had gone to the trouble to bring her a plate, and maybe even cooked the food herself. Spitting it out again would be rude, even if she was a murderess.

Fay's shoulders slumped. 'Well, I'll leave you to it, then. Enjoy. It's veggie curry. I hope you like it.'

'Stay a while.'

Fay must have interpreted Helen's silence as a brush-off, but that hadn't been her intention. Besides, she had to get to know Fay so she could find her weak points. That had been her plan all along, so why did it suddenly seem like the most underhand thing in the world?

'I got the job,' she said.

'That's wonderful! When do you start?'

'Monday.'

'And what will you be doing?'

'Oh, this and that. Starting from the bottom, but I don't mind.'

'Everyone has to start somewhere. Who knows, it may be the first step to something bigger.'

Smiling her wary smile, Fay picked up a statue from the mantelpiece, uninvited. 'What sort of company is it?'

'It's an auction house.' Helen removed the top plate which was keeping the food warm and wolfed down a forkful of curry.

Fay's smile disappeared as she weighed the little statue in her hand. It was Helen's favourite. Carved from soapstone and about the size of a man's fist, it was an Indian elephant with a smaller elephant inside it, and as a test of the artisan's skill, with an even smaller elephant inside the second one. Like the traditional ship in a bottle scenario it was impossible to imagine how it was made, but you couldn't dispute the evidence.

'An auction house? How odd.' Fay replaced the statue on the mantelpiece. 'I had a friend who worked for an auction house. She liked elephants too. She used to say that elephants have long memories and would remember every little hurt and kindness that ever happened to them. She said that's why she liked them so much. Because it made them very human.

'I gave her a bag with an elephant on it once. A big blingie shopper type bag.' Fay smiled. 'She was just like that, a real magpie. Anything that glittered, and she'd be all over it.'

Helen felt a sliver of ice run down her back. A memory

sliced through her aching head, ripping open an underbelly of memories and spilling the contents into her brain.

The car, the elephant bag on the back seat, Mimi telling her sternly not to touch anything because it had important stuff in it. Herself disobeying and looking in the bag for the medicine, then the agony that Mummy died because Helen didn't do what she was told, it was all Helen's fault, and she was a naughty girl.

She remembered not understanding what had happened, remembered the immense loss. Emotion pressed at the back of her throat, but she quelled it before Fay noticed. She wondered what had happened to that bag and the rest of her mother's things. It had never seemed important, not until now. She saw herself as a blank sheet with virtually no history, but Fay had reminded her that she had a history, even if she had no memories of it.

Maybe Sweetman knew where her mother's things were. But she'd deal with that soon enough. Right now she wanted to get some answers out of Fay without revealing herself.

'Where's your friend now?' she asked.

'She died a long time ago. She was murdered.'

'God, how awful,' she said on autopilot. *Awful* didn't begin to cover it, but hearing those words from Fay shocked her.

Her hands tightened around the cutlery. What would happen if she stabbed Fay right now? You could do a lot of damage if you stuck a fork in someone's eye. And then what? Back to not knowing what really happened? It wasn't worth it.

'They say I did it. That's why they locked me up.' Fay's eyes took on a glazed look.

'And did you? *Did* you kill her?'

Fay took a long time before answering. 'Yes, I believe I did.'

Chapter Eight

'You *believe* you did? How can you not know for sure? If you'd killed someone, you'd know about it, wouldn't you? I know I would.'

'It's complicated.' Fay wrung her hands. 'Would you mind if I sit down?'

It was at the tip of Helen's tongue to say, yes, I would mind, but politeness forced her to swallow that retort, and she pointed to the bed, which was the only other place in the room you could sit.

Did she really need to hear this? Life was a lot simpler when she was convinced of Fay's guilt. Now she wasn't sure of anything. Fay's kindness had punctured her old certainties, and the air was slowly going out of her metaphorical hate-filled balloon.

'We fell out,' Fay explained. 'Over a man, would you believe it.'

'A man?'

Fay sighed. 'My husband. They had an affair. I felt betrayed, as you would. Began stalking her. I saw her as more guilty than him because she was supposed to be my friend. It's hard to explain, really, when it was just as much his fault.'

Helen nodded because she sensed agreement was required, even if she didn't agree. Her mother, stealing someone else's husband? She hadn't considered that Fay might have had her reasons, however wrong they were, and she'd never thought of her mother as anything other than a mother either. Then again, maybe it was all a lie.

'The police got involved,' said Fay. 'My husband found out what I was doing and wanted a divorce. I was too immersed

96

in the whole thing to get legal representation, so he more or less walked off with everything. I continued to follow her, hung around outside her house despite a restraining order. Made obscene phone calls, wrote letters … I was mad, quite literally. She'd ruined my life, and I was going to ruin hers.'

Helen's hand tightened around the fork, and she put her hands in her lap to stop them from shaking. She'd been waiting for years for this moment, for Fay to confess, except it didn't feel like a proper confession. It wasn't satisfying enough.

'I was doing drugs, booze and God knows what. High as a kite half the time. The next thing I know she's dead, murdered in her car, and they say I did it, except I don't remember anything at all.'

Her appetite gone, replaced by a sudden queasiness, Helen put the fork on the tray and swallowed back the bile rising in her throat. She'd heard enough.

But Fay hadn't finished.

'My friend's daughter, who was on the back seat at the time, pointed the finger at me. There was other evidence as well, but if the child had seen it, I must've done it. I just don't …' She sighed.

'Did you ever find out what happened to the child?'

'No.'

'Did you even try?' Helen's voice rose a notch, and Fay sent her a curious look. 'I mean, if you weren't sure what happened, perhaps the child was the key.'

'I tried, but obviously I wasn't allowed anywhere near that little girl, and her family made sure I had no contact whatsoever. I don't blame them. I'd have done the same, to protect my child.'

Family. Protection.

The words rang false, because the reality of the situation was so different.

'That's quite a story.' Her voice cooled, certain that it was just that, a story for her benefit, and Fay was looking for sympathy.

Well, you picked the wrong person if you're looking for pity, she thought.

Had Fay guessed who her new flatmate was? Helen didn't look like her blonde, petite mother. She was just as slim, but with a taller and stronger build, and she tanned well like her father, Dmitri. But if Fay and Mimi had been friends, she may have seen a photo of him.

The thought unsettled her. She needed to be more careful, at least until she'd decided what she was going to do about Fay. Because someone had to pay.

Fay rose from the bed. 'I didn't mean to bore you.'

'I wasn't bored.' Far from it. 'Thanks for the curry. I'm not really hungry. I appreciate it, though. You must let me give you some money.'

'Oh, yes, I forgot.' Fay produced a tattered notebook, held together with an elastic band and a pencil tucked in between the pages. 'Household stuff. Charlie said you wanted to give something towards food and things. There's no fixed sum, just give me what you can afford.'

Helen set her mouth in a thin line. 'I'll pay what everyone else pays.'

'All right. In that case, it's forty quid a fortnight. Sounds like a lot, but it covers food, basic toiletries, and cleaning materials.'

Helen reached for her wallet in her rucksack and counted out forty pounds. Fay ticked her name in the notebook, pocketed the money and took the tray from Helen's desk.

'Why don't you let me carry that downstairs?' said Helen.

'I'm fine.'

Fay shut the door behind her, and Helen listened to her soft footfall on the landing. She'd missed a golden opportunity to confront Fay.

She wasn't ready.

Later as she went to bed, she sat for a moment in total darkness, hugging her knees to her chest. Although Fay said she couldn't remember anything, that didn't mean she wasn't guilty, but it did make Helen question how much she actually remembered herself. She had a vague memory of some time afterwards – when, exactly, was still hazy – that Aggie drove her to Ealing police station …

… 'Is Mummy going to be there?' she asks eagerly.

'No, darling, your mummy won't be there.'

Disappointed, Helen sits back in her seat. She frowns. Aggie has never called her 'darling' before, and somehow this frightens her though she doesn't know why.

At the police station Helen and Aggie are taken down a long corridor, past many closed doors with letters on them. People's offices, Aggie explains. Finally they're led into a room with a large window looking into another room, which is empty. A man and a woman are waiting for them. The man has light-coloured hair and wears a blue suit, and the lady is dressed in a baggy green jumper and red trousers. Fascinated, Helen stares at the lady's trousers. They're not the sort of clothes Mummy would wear, and from the horrified look on Aggie's face when she sees the lady, she's sure Aggie is thinking the same.

'I didn't know the handover was today,' Aggie says and puts her hand on Helen's shoulder, where she leaves it. Helen shifts uncomfortably; Aggie's never done that before either.

The lady nods. 'Your daughter Letitia called me. I told her this isn't how we normally do things, but she insisted. Said you'd prefer it to be dealt with quickly. It's not a problem, I hope. We don't really want a scene in front of—' She stops and bites her lip when she sees Helen staring at her.

The man looks at Helen too, then at Aggie, and his expression isn't kind.

Aggie's voice is small when she says, 'The child is ill. Neither of my daughters are willing to take the responsibility, and I ... well, I'm too old.' She turns away, fiddling with the clasp of her handbag as if she can't open it.

Helen has a feeling Aggie is upset about something, but she has no time to think about it because the man kneels down in front of her, smiling. Involuntarily she takes a step back. When grown-ups kneel down like that and smile in a certain way, it's because they've got something to say that you don't want to hear.

'Hi,' he says. 'My name's Barry. I'm a detective. Do you know what a detective is?'

Helen shakes her head. *Why isn't Mummy here?*

'A detective is a policeman who doesn't have a uniform on, and who has to ask people questions when something bad has happened. He has to ask people if they saw anything, or anybody. Do you understand what I mean?'

Helen stares at him, unblinkingly. Her tummy feels hard, like there is a big lump inside it.

'Did you see anyone that day you were with your mum in the car?'

'I saw a lady.'

'If you saw her again, would you be able to point at her and say "that's her"?'

Helen nods. 'She's a vampire,' she says and waits for the grown-ups to laugh and say there are no vampires, they don't exist, but no one does.

'I see.' The man looks at her closely for a while then takes a tube of Smarties out of his jacket pocket and hands it to her. 'Tell you what,' he says, 'why don't you have some Smarties while you think about this vampire, because in a minute that door in there'—he points to a door which is inside the room behind the window — 'will open, and some people will come in, and maybe you can tell me if that vampire lady is one of them. Yeah?'

Helen hesitates. She loves Smarties, they're her favourite, but Mummy says she can only have sweets on Saturdays, and she's not sure it's Saturday. Plus she's not allowed to accept sweets from strangers. But she doesn't want to disappoint him, so she nods and smiles in the way she knows is expected of her. Where *is* Mummy?

'Good girl.' He gets up and asks over her head, 'Does she know?'

'No,' says Aggie quietly. He doesn't look pleased, and neither does the lady with the red trousers. 'There were fears it would bring on another seizure.'

Helen knows they're talking about her, but she ignores them and concentrates on her Smarties. She pours them out into her hand and picks the blue ones first. She likes them the best, even though they're full of nasty colouring, and she hurries up and eats them, just in case someone tries to get them off her.

When she's finished, the man takes her over to the window.

'Are you ready?'

Helen nods.

'Remember to tell me if you see anyone you know.'

He presses a button, and the door opens at the back of the room. Some women walk in, each carrying a piece of paper with a number on it. Helen knows them, because she can count to twenty, but she's more interested in the women's faces, and even before they're standing still and looking at the window, she sees one she recognises.

'That lady there,' she says and points. 'With the funny, wild hair. The one who looks like a witch.'

'Are you sure?'

'She did something to my mummy.'

'Yes, she did,' says the man.

'Where is she?'

None of the grown-ups answer her question. They just stare at each other as if they all have a secret that Helen isn't supposed to know about.

'There's something else I'd like you to do for me,' he says instead.

Aggie puts her hand on Helen's shoulder, and this time she doesn't move away from it. 'Don't you think the child has been through enough?'

'Just one more thing, I promise. It's important', he says to Helen. 'Is there anything else you remember that you haven't told anyone already? Anything at all?'

'There was a knife. It was my mummy's.'

'We didn't find any knife. Are you sure?'

Helen nods.

'O-kay,' he says. 'In that case, do you think you can tell me what the knife looks like?'

'No, but I can make you a picture. I'm good at drawing.'

'That would be very helpful.' He smiles and takes a small notepad out of his jacket pocket, and hands it to her with a pen.

She would rather have crayons, but she takes the pen and draws a picture in the notebook. 'This is gold'—she points—'and where you hold it, it's made of swirly blue rocks. They're called leopards,' she adds, proud of her own knowledge. 'A man had it in the olden days. He was a king, but then the commas came and killed him and his family in a forest. It was very sad.'

The policeman just stares at her, and she thinks he must be a little bit stupid.

'If I may,' says Aggie, 'I think I know what the child is referring to. My step-daughter had a pair of paper knives, period pieces with lapis lazuli inlay. Fabergé, I think.'

'Would you be able to get me their complete specifications?'

'I should think so. It's a well-known set, and collectors are often on record.'

Helen can see from the man's face that what Aggie has said must be important, but she's getting tired now and wants to go home. 'Can we go now, Aggie? I want to see Mummy.'

The lady in the red trousers, whom Helen has forgotten all about, is the only one who answers. 'You need to come with me, darling. I see your granny has brought your bag with you. Have you got all your nice things in there?'

Helen stares at her. What does she mean, go? *Go where?*

The lady holds out her hand. 'Come, sweetheart, we're going to a nice place where there's lots of other children you can play with.'

Helen shakes her head. 'I don't want to play. I want to see Mummy!'

The lady just smiles sadly. 'I'm sorry, darling, but you can't see your mummy.'

'Now!' Helen stamps her foot. She's close to tears. Why are they keeping secrets from her? It's not fair.

Without another word the lady lifts her up and carries her towards the door. Suddenly it hits her, from the look on Aggie's face, that the bad thing which the policeman talked about happened to Mummy, and that she isn't coming back.

Mummy is dead.

Furiously she kicks and beats her fists against the lady's chest, but the lady is strong and doesn't drop her. Whispering soothing words, she carries her out of the room and down the long corridor, but Helen can only hear herself screaming at the top of her lungs.

'I want my mummy! I want my mummy!'

Helen woke, disorientated and cold, her body leaden. She'd

fallen asleep on top of the covers and realised she'd been crying. With no tissues handy she wiped her face on the bedspread and tried to make sense of her thoughts.

She knew this was a real memory, but she also knew her mind had always had a tendency to fill in the blanks when she tried to focus on it, leaving vital impressions tantalisingly out of reach.

Except this time it had been different. This time she'd pictured herself firmly in that room, tasted the Smarties, felt Aggie's shaking hand on her shoulder. She *had* been there, and the sequence of events was probably pretty much as she'd just pictured them. But how could she begin to make sense of it?

Rising early, she met Jason in the kitchen.

'Rough night?' he asked when he saw her blotchy face, which no amount of ice cold water had managed to soothe.

'You could say that.'

He handed her a cup of tea, and gratefully Helen wrapped her hands around it, allowing the warmth from the mug to quieten her nerves.

'You know, I'm here if you want to talk,' he said.

'That's okay. I can't imagine you'd be interested in what goes on in my head.'

'But I am.'

She looked up and read not only curiosity in his eyes but openness and sincerity as well. Was he really just a nice guy, or did he have an agenda? It was on the tip of her tongue to tell him all about her mother's murder, about Fay, and about her epilepsy and fragmented memories, but she had no doubt what the outcome would be. He'd reject her, like everyone else had done, because people always did. For that reason she'd learned to rely only on herself. It might lead to loneliness, but it kept her safe from hurt.

So why did she find the thought of confessing so appealing? Was it simply his kind blue eyes? The carefully shaved goatee which showed someone who took good care of himself without worrying that it made him less of a man? Or maybe the way he wore a pair of old jeans, low-slung and hugging his backside like a second skin, inviting you to reach out and run your hand over the soft, worn fabric. She couldn't decide whether it was the sex appeal which attracted her, or Jason the person.

So it was probably best to leave well alone.

'Another time,' she said and felt like a meanie when the eager light in his eyes went out.

Armed with the business card Aggie's solicitor, Ronald Sweetman, had given her in Goa, Helen tracked down his office in a less salubrious part of town with a strong Asian influence, above a shop selling fabrics. Access was through an alley, at the backstreet level via an entry phone.

Someone buzzed the door open. Inside, narrow steps led upstairs. Water damage had caused the plaster to crumble in the corners, and the hall itself smelt very faintly of cat piss.

A woman, presumably the one who'd buzzed her inside, met her at the top of the stairs. Dressed in a black trouser suit, she was tall and angular with flat straw-coloured hair and horsey smoker's teeth. Clutching a stack of files, she had a harassed air about her.

'Third door on the right,' she replied when Helen asked for Sweetman. 'Tell him I'll bring some coffee in a tick. And don't worry if he snaps at you, he's as tame as a pussy cat.'

Puzzled that she hadn't been challenged about an appointment or asked who she was, Helen knocked on the door at the end of the corridor.

'Come in!' bellowed a voice.

Ronald Sweetman was sitting behind his desk with his

feet on the windowsill, staring out through the grimy glass while twirling a pen in his hand. He was wearing a polo shirt like last time they met, which stretched tight across his belly, grey trousers, worn leather belt and scuffed black shoes, and looked more like a down-at-heel private detective than a solicitor. Turning in his chair, his eyebrows rose when he saw Helen, and he quickly righted himself, extending his hand.

'Miss Stephens. I was hoping I'd see you again, but I didn't expect you so soon. Obviously I was mistaken.' A teasing look accompanied his outstretched hand.

Helen shook it politely then withdrew quickly. There was something about his demeanour which didn't sit right with his cuddly exterior. She'd sensed it in Goa, and did so even more now. Pussy cat, my arse.

'Just Helen,' she said.

'I see, Just Helen.' He ran his tongue over his lips as if tasting her name. Maybe he had synaesthesia, she thought, the ability to taste and smell sounds. She wondered what hers tasted like, fancying the idea of sticky toffee pudding, but maybe it was more like earwax. The thought made her smile.

Ronald Sweetman caught her grin. 'That's quite a different expression from the one you greeted me with in India. Never has one man travelled so far to be so cruelly dismissed.'

His paraphrasing of Winston Churchill's famous blood, sweat and tears speech broadened her grin despite the serious business she wanted to discuss. 'I was horrid, wasn't I? Sorry about that.'

'But you're better now, Just Helen?'

'Much better. By the way,' she jerked her head towards the door, 'your secretary said she'd bring you coffee in a minute.'

'My wife, yes. Let's hope she remembers to bring two. Shall we sit down?'

Sweetman's office was small, and apart from the desk and the chairs, there was only a yucca plant in the corner and a row of steel-grey filing cabinets against the back wall. Everything looked as if it had been collected haphazardly from second-hand furniture shops, apart from the filing cabinets which appeared strong enough to withstand a terrorist attack. The shabbiness gave Helen a sense of being on an equal footing with him.

'So to what do I owe this unexpected pleasure?' he asked and rested his steepled fingers on his desk.

'I've been to see my st—, er, grandmother. She's explained to me that I own a share of Ransome & Daughters, but said you have the paperwork. I'd just like to know where I stand. My legal position, if you like.'

There was a knock on the door and Sweetman's voice boomed in response. The secretary, his wife, came in with a tray. The conversation stopped while she poured coffee and milk, adding two sugars and stirring Sweetman's mug for him. The mugs were proper fine bone china, Helen noticed, and the coffee the real thing, strong and aromatic. A smile teased in the solicitor's eyes as he gauged her reaction, and he accepted the mug from his wife without looking up, his eyes still fixed on Helen's face, like a fighter weighing up his opponent. Mrs Sweetman left as unassumingly as she'd entered.

Leaning back in his chair, Sweetman balanced the mug on his large stomach. 'It's simple. You own a percentage of the company, which gives you the right to vote on the board. We keep the share certificates in the safe here, but if you'd rather store them yourself, I can arrange to have them biked to you when I've located them.'

Helen thought of the long-fingered Charlie, and decided not to put temptation in her way. 'It's fine, you can keep them here.'

Sweetman continued. 'We also store your grandmother's share certificates plus her will, but I've never had dealings with either of your aunts. Can't say I'm losing any sleep over that.'

He sipped his coffee, and Helen hid a smile. She didn't think Letitia would lose sleep over it either. No doubt she had a team of very expensive City lawyers at her fingertips, which befitted her social standing. Ruth too.

It made her wonder why Aggie had chosen this humble practice. It didn't fit with a person whose doctor was in Harley Street. Her grandmother could afford to hire a service costing four times as much, probably more. Was she trying to become invisible? That never happened to the super-rich. A beggar in the street, yes, but not a person like Aggie.

'Did you have dealings with my mother?' she asked.

Sweetman hesitated before answering. 'Not as such. She was with the same firm of solicitors as your aunt Ruth. I do, however, have a copy of her will.'

'My mother's will? But how come you have that if you didn't represent her?'

'Your grandmother requested a copy and lodged it with me. She wanted to safeguard your interests, as legal guardian. Anyway, wills are public property once probate has been obtained. As for your share certificates, well, the company didn't float on the Stock Exchange until after your mother's death, and Mrs Ransome ensured they were placed with us.'

'And have my interests been safeguarded, as you put it?'

'Perfectly.'

'What about the monthly allowance?'

'Came out of your inheritance from your mother. The rest was put in trust for you until your twenty-fifth year, which is now.'

'If the allowance came out of my inheritance, why did

Aggie go on pretending the money came from her? It doesn't make any sense.'

Sweetman put his mug on the desk. 'There are a lot of things in life which don't make sense,' he said, and his previous supercilious manner seemed to have been replaced by kindness of sorts. 'If I know anything about human nature, I'd say your grandmother did it because she wanted you to feel you had a link with the family. You may have resented it as patronising handouts, but at least it signalled that there was someone who cared, if only from a distance.'

'But I'm not her relative.'

He shrugged his shoulders. 'If you want to split hairs, in the eyes of the law you're not, but people aren't governed entirely by legalities, are they? We see that time and time again.'

'Since you're such an expert on human nature, what governs Aggie, then?'

'If you really don't know that, then you're more stupid than I thought!' he replied hotly.

Helen glared at him, but his words had found their mark. She fought hard to hang on to her old anger, that familiar feeling, but it was too tiring. Her shoulders slumped.

I'm not ready for this, she thought. She didn't want to believe Aggie had real feelings for her, only to find out it wasn't true.

Could she trust Sweetman? He was Aggie's representative and probably didn't move a muscle without consulting her. Aggie had broken Helen's trust before. There was no one she could rely on, apart from herself.

'How much did my mother leave me?'

Sweetman smiled, the twinkle in his eye telling her he understood she wasn't in this for the money.

'Well, there was the sale of her house and contents when she ... when she died. I have a list by the way. She had a substantial inheritance from her father, Mr Ransome, and she was hard-working. Without the papers in front of me, I'd guesstimate it somewhere in the region of the half million mark, give or take a few grand.'

Half a million.

In ready cash, on top of her dividends.

Helen's mouth fell open. All that money, and she never knew.

Anger rose in her. 'Why was I never told? I grew up in a children's home and then foster homes. It was bloody miserable! Oh, yes, there was enough to eat and a roof over my head, but if I'd had that money, I could've had a nicer life. I could've … I don't know, paid someone to look after me maybe, or Aggie could have paid someone with my money. I could've had a proper home!'

'You can't buy love no matter how much money you have,' said Sweetman, and there was genuine pity in his voice.

'Well, screw you!' Helen clenched her fists in her lap to stop herself from hitting him.

'Sorry, no can do. I'm a married man.'

'Screw you anyway,' she muttered.

'If it's any consolation, I suspect your grandmother had her reasons for placing you in a children's home.'

'Yeah, like what?'

'*That* is as much a mystery to me as it is to you.'

Her anger abated, and she kept her eyes on him while finishing her coffee. His gaze never wavered, but stayed fixed on her until she was the one who had to look away.

'My mother,' she said.

'Yes?'

'Do you know anything at all? Anything about the murder, or the court case?'

He shook his head. 'It was before my time as your

grandmother's legal representative. You'll have to speak to the police.' He rose and rummaged in one of the filing cabinets, then returned to the desk and handed Helen a large brown envelope as well as a manila folder.

'In the envelope you'll find a countersigned copy of your mother's will and that list of contents I mentioned. The file, well, you'd better see for yourself.'

Helen opened the file as if it was a bomb about to explode in her face. Inside were several pages of newspaper clippings relating to Mimi's murder. It was like a step back in time, a window into a past she hardly remembered. Perhaps this was a chance for her to put together the pieces of who she was.

She sent Sweetman a questioning glance.

'Before you ask, no, I didn't compile it,' he said. 'Your grandmother did. She placed it in my care a few months ago, at the same time she asked me to find you. She thought you might like it.'

'Why couldn't she give it to me herself?'

'She's quite unwell, you know. Maybe she didn't think she'd get an opportunity. Who knows? I personally haven't the faintest idea. Your grandmother is an enigma, but I expect you've worked that out for yourself.'

'May I keep it?'

'Of course. It's yours. To do with what you want. Burn it, treasure it, colour it in, whatever takes your fancy.'

'Reopen the case?'

Sweetman chuckled. 'On the basis of newspaper clippings? I doubt it, but who am I to tell? I'm not a criminal lawyer.' Heaving a sigh, he looked at her with his chubby chin resting on his hands. 'To use the sort of psychobabble my wife is overly fond of, Mrs Ransome has long suspected you of needing closure. Maybe this will help.'

'What if it doesn't?'

'Then I hope you'll think before you act,' he said.

Chapter Nine

When she left Sweetman's office, she spent a little time taking in the ambience of the area, browsing the garish pavement displays and breathing in the spicy aromas from various food vans. A man on a street corner handed her a flyer for cheap foreign phone calls, Indian pop music droned from an open doorway somewhere nearby.

She stopped to stare at a jeweller's display which sparkled with an unearthly light. Indian jewellery had always both fascinated and repelled her. It was too sophisticated to be called bling, but just as ostentatious, and the prices in the window made her almost queasy.

I can afford things like that now, she thought, but knew she'd never dream of buying it. Cold stones and metal like that belonged in Aggie's and Letitia's world, not hers. There had to be a better way for her to spend her new-found wealth.

On the bus she hung onto her bag tight, resisting the pull of the folder because she wanted to be somewhere without distractions and the risk of anyone looking over her shoulder.

Until last night all she'd remembered was Fay bending over her mother, covered in blood, and that she'd had a seizure. But then Fay had reminded her of the sequinned bag. Who knew what sort of memories the contents of this folder would trigger?

The house was quiet when she got back. Charlie was signing on at the local Job Centre today, and Fay must have gone to the market. The door to Jason's basement room stood open, but a quick glance told Helen he wasn't in either. She heard Lee's door closing on the top floor when she went to change into more casual clothes, and she decided to read the file in the kitchen.

The kitchen was baking hot. She threw open the doors, enjoying the way the gentle breeze played with her hair and the sound of the bees droning lazily in the jasmine bush which was in full flower. The grass, which hadn't been mowed in a while, was springy and soft when Helen crossed to the bush and broke off a stalk of jasmine. The flower's heady scent reminded her of India.

One of Fay's stray cats was sunning itself on the shed roof. When a dog barked somewhere in a neighbouring garden, it didn't move a whisker, although Helen dropped the flower with a start. Picking it up again, a flash of memory swept through her.

A dog had been there that morning, a big brown one, the breed she didn't know. It had played in the leaves, and she remembered how she'd longed to play too, to kick and toss the leaves high in the air, but couldn't because she was stuck in the car.

If a dog had been there, the dog owner had been there too. He or she must have seen something. Had they come forward, helped convict Fay?

Sighing, she went back inside, dropped the flower in a jam jar with some water, and put the kettle on.

Tea in hand, she sat down on the sofa and opened the folder, which had been arranged like a scrap book with newspaper articles stuck in it. The first article, with a photo of her mother, was from a tabloid newspaper.

Mother Murdered with 5-Year-Old Daughter in Car
A 34-year-old woman was found stabbed to death in the front seat of her car in the early hours of October the 12th. The victim, identified as Mimi Stephanov, was discovered at 6.35 a.m. on Ealing Common.

Police were alerted to the scene by a 999 call made by the postal worker who found the body. Mrs Stephanov's 5-year-old daughter, who had been asleep on the back seat, was in shock but appeared otherwise unharmed.

Investigators say Mrs Stephanov was bleeding from a stab wound in her throat. Emergency services responded and pronounced her dead at the scene.

'I'm totally shaken,' said Darren Morris, a Royal Mail employee. 'I cross the Common every day to do my rounds, and you don't get a quieter neighbourhood than this.'

Authorities are holding a 37-year-old woman for questioning. Neighbours talk of recent disturbances near the victim's home, and that the woman held in custody had been harassing Mrs Stephanov.

There were several articles from different newspapers reporting the story in the same factual terms, others dealing with the court case, one long article detailing the history of the family company, plus a snippet from a trade magazine which commented on the company's recent quotation on the stock exchange.

On the 15th of December the family-run auction house Ransome & Daughters, with offices in London's Mayfair district, began trading on the London Stock Exchange small business section for the first time in the company's short, but hitherto extremely successful, history.

The article went on to talk about share prices and expected turnover, and Helen skipped to the end.

This comes only two months after the tragic demise of founder William Ransome's only child, Mimi Stephanov, who was killed by a one-time friend.

A spokesperson for the company, Bill Collins, gave the following statement: 'It's been a difficult time for all of us. Naturally we're delighted that the company is doing so well, but the loss of a member of the Ransome family and one of our most dedicated co-workers has been a terrible blow.'

She read the newspaper clippings through once, then dropped the file in her lap and stared out into the garden. The dog was still barking next door, the timbre of his voice suggesting it was a large dog.

Her mother's life, and her own too, compressed to a series of stills reported as bare facts. There was no mention of the incredible upheaval in Helen's young life or what sort of person her mother was. Or at least the person Helen assumed she was from her fragmented memories.

She wished she hadn't read the articles. The factual clippings and just the one photo of Mimi meant that her mother now only existed in a vacuum, beginning and ending her life in a tragic murder.

She wanted to weep, but her brain had other ideas. Her eyelids flickered, and her hands twitched. Outside, falling jasmine petals hung suspended in the air, and sounds rang out from the far end of a very long, dark tunnel. Another seizure was slowly squeezing her.

I don't care any more, she thought. Despite the familiar terror which sent her heart racing, she felt herself slipping away.

Just let me die this time …

Jason came in the kitchen in time to see Helen knocking over a cup of tea. 'Mind out,' he said.

She lolled her head sideways, roughly in his direction but he got the feeling that she didn't really see him. Her expression was vacant and twisted as if she was suffering discomfort or even pain. Instinctively he put his hand on her shoulder.

'Are you all right?'

She didn't answer. Instead she blinked rapidly several times, or rather her eyelids quivered, involuntarily. Slowly life returned to her eyes, her focus realigned itself, and she squirmed under his hand. He removed it but remained standing in front of her. Something wasn't right. In fact, something was way off the chart.

'You okay?' he asked again.

'Mm?'

'You just knocked over your tea,' he said.

Only then did she seem to notice the overturned mug and a mud-coloured puddle by her feet. Picking it up, slowly almost painfully, she said, 'Sorry, I must've dropped off.'

'That boring, is it?' Jason grinned and pointed to the open folder on her lap.

Helen reached for the folder, sluggishly, then closed it and clutched it to her chest as if she was afraid he'd snatch it off her.

'Abysmal,' she said and stood up to put the empty mug on the draining board.

'Are you sure you're okay? Because you've gone all pale and twitchy.' His eyes searched hers, seeking the truth. But seeking the truth with Helen Stephens was like catching a slippery bar of soap in the bath.

What had he just seen? She hadn't dozed off. Dozing off looked different. He'd had a school friend once who had absences like that, but Simon was an epileptic. Did Helen have the same telltale signs of a seizure? Jason hadn't seen Simon in years, and anyway the signs could be difficult to spot unless you knew what you were looking for.

'Yeah. I'm fine … fine.'

'Sure?' He didn't know why he kept asking that, but it seemed important to keep her talking.

'No, really I'm okay, just tired,' she said. She looked at

the tea on the floor. 'I'd better clean this up. Have we got a mop and a bucket anywhere?'

'In the cupboard. Why don't you let me do this? You look like you need to sit down.'

She sent him a testy look. 'I'm fine. I can do it.'

'Go on,' he said. 'Do me a favour and sit down. I don't mind, honest.'

'No.'

'God, you're stubborn! Sit down, for Christ's sake.'

Almost manhandling her back down on the sofa, he could tell that her instinct was to fight him, but he wasn't having any of it. Sometimes it was nice to be a man and be stronger than the girl. And this girl looked like she needed someone strong to lean on now and again, preferably without losing face. He could understand that.

He felt it through the palm of his hand as she allowed her body to relax, and when he lifted her booted feet off the floor onto the sofa, she even laughed.

'Oh, stop it!'

Armed with mop and bucket, Jason began to clean the floor. Helen watched him whisk the mop from side to side with the efficiency of a seasoned cleaning lady. His calm fascinated her. He was so un-self-conscious, just himself, and not at all bothered by her stare.

His muscles rippled, and when he stepped outside to pour the dirty water down the drain, her eyes wandered to his backside. He was wearing jeans, as always, and his bum was pert, there was no other word for it.

She looked away. Relationships had never been easy. Sex she could do, because it didn't require giving anything of herself, and this had led to a number of one night stands. For a time she'd even kept a scorecard before throwing it away in a fit of self-loathing. Meeting Joe taught her that it was possible to be just friends with a man, without strings attached.

Jason treated her the same way Joe did, with kindness and respect, but with an undeniable heat in his eyes now and then. For the umpteenth time in his company she slammed a lid on her lust. If anything ever happened between them – a big *if* – she wanted to get it right this time.

He returned to the kitchen and made them both a fresh mug of tea, which they took outside on the grass. Opening a packet of Hobnobs, he offered her a biscuit, then wolfed down two without drawing breath.

Impressive, she thought, amused, and watched him out of the corner of her eye.

Jason lounged on the grass supported by an elbow, his legs stretched out before him, and, completely untroubled by the world, continued munching biscuits. Helen realised she knew nothing about him. She'd been so focused on Fay that she hadn't given him much thought, except in the sexually attractive sense. Then there was Charlie who was pretty unavoidable, and creepy Lee who was the exact opposite.

It was a confining environment, living in a shared house, yet it was a much bigger world than Helen had ever been part of. All she had to do was to come out from her shell, and there'd be someone to talk to.

'Tell me about yourself,' she said.

He smiled. 'There's not much to tell.'

'There must be something.'

'Well, if you want the whole boring life story …'

'I do.'

'Okay,' he drawled, finished the biscuit he'd been eating, and brushed the crumbs from his hands.

Jason had only caught a glimpse of the contents in the folder which had lain open on Helen's lap, the one she seemed so keen for him to forget about. A headline about a murdered woman and her child, a picture with the name Mimi Stephanov underneath it. A company logo of an *R* and a *D* cleverly intertwined like a royal insignia. No dates, but the newspaper clippings were yellowed with age so it couldn't be that recent. Was Helen related to this woman? The child who was mentioned? Her reaction had told him it was private, not work-related.

Her face was animated now that the focus had shifted away from herself, and he supposed he ought to let her have this little triumph. Another time he might try to delve deeper with her, but for now let it be the other way around.

Of course, it was possible she was interested in him, which was flattering, and he wasn't going to discourage it. He was certainly interested in her, one way or another, the mystery or the woman. Or even both.

She was smiling expectantly. Jason took in the full lips and that cute little dip above her mouth he hadn't really noticed before, and wondered how it would feel to kiss those lips. Probably very nice.

Then he stopped himself. One thing at a time. Right now she wanted to know more about *him*, the rest could come later, perhaps.

The question was how much to tell her.

'I'm an only child,' he said. 'My father is a, well, I suppose you'd call him a self-made business man. He worked himself up from humble beginnings, and then tried to give me everything he never had as a child, you know expensive toys, the right clothes, boarding school. It all meant that I was a spoilt little brat until I discovered how the other half lives.'

'I can't imagine you being spoilt.'

'Why is that so difficult to imagine?' he said, with more feeling than he intended. He snapped off a blade of grass and tossed it aside irritably. 'You'd be surprised. I was intolerable. Of course, the perverse thing about parent-child relationships is that parents try to show their love in one particular way, *their* way, but the children only see that they're not loved in the way they think they ought to be loved. It can get into a right old muddle sometimes.'

Helen watched him quietly with those arresting eyes of hers. Could she tell there was more going on between him and his father than met the eye? At the best of times he found it hard to hide his irritation with his father, and it must have sounded like the sore point it was.

'And what about your mother?' she asked.

'My mother keeps dogs.'

'What?'

'Dogs, yes. Day in, day out, dogs, dogs, dogs. That's what she does.'

'What kind of dogs? Does she own a kennel?'

'Pekes. Pekingese,' he explained in response to her confused look. 'And she doesn't run a kennel, more's the pity. She has them at home. Five of them. Drives my father around the twist. Can't say I blame him. Annoying little yappers if you ask me, but she adores them.'

Helen laughed, and the sound of her carefree laughter did something funny to his stomach.

'What?' he said, both peeved and delighted.

'You. Your mum and her dogs. Your poor dad.' She laughed again. 'I can just see them. It's wonderful.'

'Wonderful? It's bloody awful. My family are messed up and get on each other's nerves, and you think it's funny, do you?' He made his voice sound extra stern but for some reason she'd managed to take the sting out of his bust-up with his father. When he thought of it now, it was almost irrelevant.

'At least you have a family,' she said.

'And you don't?'

120

She shrugged. 'Not really. Just aunties and stuff.'

'Yeah, I have a few of those, on my father's side. They're a bit younger than him, so he doesn't see much of them.'

'And what are they like?'

He picked up another biscuit and sent her a look of mock despair. 'WAGs. Think *Footballers' Wives*, and that should give you a pretty good idea. Opinionated, expensive hair, lots of bling. But they're very nice.'

She smiled. 'I like the sound of your family. A strange mix of posh and middle-class, if you don't mind me saying so. Not that there's anything wrong with that,' she added. 'It's just a bit off-beat.'

'That's a pretty good description,' he muttered darkly. 'Posh 'n Trash, that's us.'

'Does it bother you?'

She was sharp, he had to give her that. Once, when he'd tried to conform to his father's ambitions for him, it *had* bothered him a lot. Back then he'd been ashamed of his background. Then he grew up.

'It's not what people *are* that matters,' he said, 'but how they behave, what they do. I think I've proved that here, in this house. Anyway, let's not talk about me. Let's talk about you.'

He sat up, crossed his legs and smiled at her in a way which he hoped was roguish. It had the desired effect. Her eyes widened, filling with humour and promise.

'Oh, no, let's not,' she said. 'I'm really boring.'

'That's not the word I'd use to describe you.'

Leaning back on the palms of her hands, she stuck her chest out, deliberately he reckoned. She wore no bra under her sleeveless top, and his eyes followed the curves of her breasts and settled on her nipples, which showed through the fabric like a cherry on a cake. His lips parted slightly, then his eyes cut back to hers.

'What, then?' she taunted.

Man, she was something else.

'Intelligent, self-reliant, interesting.' He paused. 'Secretive.'

'Secretive?' Her eyes went wide with surprise. 'What makes you say that?'

'It was the business with that folder. The way you closed it. There's something in it you don't want me to see.'

'Anything else you want to say about me?'

The look she sent him was nothing short of sassy. 'You're sexy,' he said.

Her mouth curved at that.

He couldn't help it. She was like a siren, an urban Lorelei reeling him in like a fish on a hook. He leaned in, and before he knew it his hand cradled her neck in a firm hold, and his mouth was on hers.

Her reaction was a series of spasms which electrified him, turned him on like he'd never felt turned on before. He crushed her to him, and felt another shudder run through her which almost took his breath away. Sliding her hand up, she curled her fingers into his hair and, for one long, sweet moment, returned the kiss.

Then she pushed him away.

'Don't,' she said in a thick voice and got up, pressing the folder to her chest like a shield.

Jason was still trying to control his baser instincts when he heard the kitchen door bang shut behind her.

Shit.

Chapter Ten

Heart racing, Helen ran upstairs and threw the folder on her bed. She could still feel Jason's mouth on hers, still taste the intoxicating mix of sugary biscuits and something Just Him on her lips. She'd tried so hard not to, but what she'd both wanted and feared at the same time had actually happened. If she hadn't stopped the kiss, how far would it have gone? To sex? Was that what he wanted? *She* didn't just want that, she wanted …

Oh, hell, I don't know, she thought. To be part of something special, maybe. Love. All the things she'd never had.

A tumble between the sheets wasn't going to give her that, not long-term anyway. Guys like Jason might look at her, but when they discovered what a freak she was, she wouldn't see them for dust.

She pushed the thought aside and focused on something else, something she'd just figured out. Jason had been as loath to be upfront with her as she was with him. It made her wonder what *he* had to hide.

Had he seen inside the folder? He'd certainly had the opportunity because she had no idea how long she'd been out. A couple of minutes maybe? Enough time for him to get the gist of the content and know more than he'd let on. Perhaps he'd only seen the top page.

For legal reasons her name wasn't mentioned in the first few articles. She'd only been referred to as 'Mimi Stephanov's five-year-old daughter'. Fay wasn't mentioned either, not to begin with. Jason had told her Fay had been to prison for murder, but he'd made it clear that Fay never offered him the specifics, and it wasn't his place to ask.

The question was, how much had he seen and had he put two and two together about Helen?

She spent the evening poring over the newspaper clippings and taking notes, again finding it completely unreal to read about her mother's murder strictly in reported terms, but being sentimental about it would get her nowhere.

The only useful information from the articles was that the investigation had been headed by a detective named Barry Wilcox, of Ealing Police, so he had to be her next move. Her head buzzed from overload as she half-stumbled to the bathroom to brush her teeth.

Opening the door, she came face to face with Lee, and the shock made her drop her wash bag. He picked it up and handed it back to her, his eyes darting from side to side as if looking for an escape route.

'Thank you.'

'No prob-b-blem.'

He was in slouchy trousers and bare feet, showing off his flawless golden chest. Charlie was right, what a waste for him to spend half his time behind bars. She decided to give him the benefit of the doubt, like Jason had.

'Listen,' she said, 'I appreciate you keeping to yourself and all that, but could you please make a bit of noise when you're around? I get sort of freaked out when you're suddenly behind me, and I haven't heard you.'

Lee grinned.

'You like freaking people out?'

He shook his head.

'So do you think you could let me know you're there next time?'

He nodded.

'You don't say much, do you?'

'My big m-m-mouth. Always gets me into trouble. I

k-keep my head down now.' He sent her a dazzling smile and disappeared into the bathroom.

In a way, what he said made sense to her. Just like Lee retreated behind his stutter, she'd been hiding away behind her epilepsy, allowing it to define her. To come out she needed to have faith in other people that they would treat her like a normal person.

But where did you find such faith? It didn't grow on trees.

Heading back to her room, she saw a flickering light from under Fay's door and stopped.

Candles.

In Goa she'd lit candles every night before going to bed. One for her mother, one for her father, and one for herself. Plus a handful of others for practical reasons as the electricity supply was sometimes unpredictable. By candlelight her demons diminished so they were no bigger or threatening than the shadows she could make on the wall with her hands. It was in daylight people might spot the aberration behind the façade.

Did Fay light candles for the same reason? She was tempted to just ask.

She lifted her hand to knock, then hesitated. Aggie's scrapbook had been screaming Fay's name at her all afternoon, but the more the newspapers were convinced of Fay's guilt, the less Helen was, now that she'd met her. Still, she was hardly a friend.

Dropping her hand, she returned to her room.

Her sleep was plagued by confusion, and she woke, exhausted and full of doubts as to whether she was doing the right thing. Her mother died twenty years ago – even if she contacted the detective named in the newspaper clippings, he probably couldn't be much help.

When she entered Ealing police station, her heart beat

a little faster. Last time she was here she'd screamed the building down when she realised her mother was dead, and she tried hard not to look at the door she'd come through then. Instead she headed straight for a clerk behind a glass partition who informed her that Wilcox had long since left and was now a Chief Superintendent working at Scotland Yard's Homicide Unit.

'I can call him if you like,' he offered.

'That'd be great, thanks.'

The clerk disappeared to a room behind the reception, was gone for ages and left her wondering whether his absence meant good news or bad news, but when he returned, he was smiling.

'He says he remembers you and would be happy to see you this afternoon if you're not busy.'

Not busy? Helen could hardly believe her luck. Could it really be that easy?

At Scotland Yard she made her way to Back Hall as instructed, where she was asked to empty her pockets and step through a metal detector. Then she waited. Eventually a uniformed officer showed her upstairs.

Chief Superintendent Barry Wilcox rose as she entered his office. Looking every bit the career detective, he wore a grey suit, a smoky-blue shirt and tie. His hair was blondish-grey, his eyes sharp, and Helen took him to be in his mid-fifties now.

When he held out his hand, she almost expected him to give her another tube of Smarties.

'Little Yelena Stephanov. This *is* a surprise.'

She shook his hand. 'I'm not so little any more. I grew up very fast.'

'I bet you did.' His eyes searched her face. 'Please sit down.'

'And I haven't gone under that name in years.'

'You're married?' he asked.

'No, just Anglicised.'

That produced a laugh. 'Fair enough. It was quite a mouthful.'

'It was my grandmother's idea,' she said. 'In the children's home they had me down as Helen Stephens. Apparently she was afraid I'd be teased. New identity, new life, and all that.'

Not that it did her much good. Some things you couldn't run from.

Wilcox nodded sagely.

'No Smarties today, Detective?'

If her comment wrong-footed him, he didn't show it. Instead he grinned. 'No, but I can offer you a cup of tea. And please call me Barry. That's how you knew me back then.'

'I'm fine, thanks. How well do you remember the case?' It felt odd saying 'the case' but it helped her to get straight to the point.

'Well enough. Some cases you forget quickly, others stay with you. This was one of them. And when I knew you were coming, I read up on it.'

'The thing is,' she began, 'lately I've ... well, I've started to remember some things from that morning. Stuff that doesn't quite make sense.'

Wilcox raised his eyebrows but didn't interrupt her.

'I want to talk about my mother's bag.'

'Her handbag? Nothing was taken as far as we could tell.'

'Not her handbag. The other bag. It was a cloth bag or shopping bag, something like that, on the back seat. It had an elephant on it.'

He shook his head. 'I don't think there was another bag at the crime scene. The SOCOs, sorry, that's Scene of Crime Officers, will have photographed everything they found. That'll still be on record. I can dig it out for you, but you do understand that I can't show you the file.'

'I understand. I just need to know what happened.'

He nodded. 'I'll tell you everything I remember.'

He explained how he was called to the scene. 'Uniform was already there, acting on a 999 call. Ambulances too, although by then your mother was beyond help. They found Fay Cooper in hysterics and covered in blood. You were slumped on the back seat. The postman who'd called 999 thought you were dead, but one of the paramedics recognised the aftermath of an epileptic seizure.'

Helen swallowed, and for a moment Wilcox's room tilted on its axis.

'Mrs Cooper was taken into custody,' Wilcox continued. 'We never found the knife, but you were able to describe it for us. A fancy inlaid paper knife. Actually, you drew it for me. Do you remember that?'

'Vaguely.' So she hadn't imagined that bit.

'To cut a long story short, your grandmother was able to supply us with details of your mother's knife set. When we showed a picture to Mrs Cooper, she broke down and confessed that the knife was hers, something her husband was able to confirm. Ironically, your mother had given it to her. We were able to make a replica – and I'm sorry for the grisliness – but the blade matched the defensive wounds on your mother's arms and hands. The only problem was we couldn't find the damn thing. Mrs Cooper had no recollection of what she'd done with it. We also couldn't find your mother's remaining knife amongst her possessions, but in the end it was irrelevant. Mrs Cooper's presence at the scene, her own knife unaccounted for, and the fact that she'd been stalking your mother for months ... well, it was pretty cut and dried as far as we were concerned. Premeditated murder. Your mother even had a restraining order against her. I think it was just luck that she was so hysterical over what she'd done that she didn't attack you as well.'

Helen shuddered. It made a morbid sort of sense, except it didn't tally with the picture she was beginning to form in her own head. Only this morning Fay had given her some shampoo because she'd run out. A small thing perhaps, but done as if kindness came natural to her. Fay killing her mother, yes, that she could picture, but a five-year-old child?

Then there was the missing bag.

'No jury would've failed to convict on that kind of evidence,' said Wilcox.

Helen nodded. 'Yeah, I get that. Problem is, the more I think about it, the more I see a bag with an elephant on it, yet you don't remember it.'

'Not off-hand, no.' A defensive undertone crept into his voice. 'Like I said, I'd have to check the files.'

'But don't you see, if Mrs Cooper took it from the car then you'd have found it with her at the park. I can understand the knife going missing, it was much smaller, but this was a big bag. So if she didn't take it, then who did? The same person who took the knife maybe?'

Wilcox regarded Helen with undisguised pity and something else, which was better hidden. Irritation perhaps. 'Do you still suffer from epilepsy?'

She flashed him a look. 'It's not like a cold which goes away. It's how my brain works. Anyway, what's that got to do with it?' she said, ignoring the fact that she'd asked herself the same question. She hated the idea that the condition made her into a less than reliable witness.

'Nothing, I suppose. I don't mean to patronise you, but this was a long time ago, and you were five years old. Couldn't you have got things muddled up in your mind? We all do it sometimes. Written records are important, because they help us to remember.'

His irritation and defensiveness she could deal with, but his pity got up her nose. 'And because I was a sick child and have no written records, you can't take me seriously? I'm telling you, the bag was there.'

'No, it wasn't.'

'There was a dog. Did you speak to the owner?'

'You were the only witness, Helen …'

'There *was* a dog,' she insisted.

He sighed. 'What sort of dog?'

'Oh, I don't know, a big brown one!'

'Be reasonable.' His voice was kind. 'What do you expect me to do?'

'Maybe we can find the dog owner and ask if he saw anything.' Helen set her mouth in an obstinate line.

He shook his head. 'We appealed for further witnesses. No one came forward.'

'They wouldn't if they'd stolen the bag, would they?'

'The car was checked for fingerprints. We only found yours, your mother's, Mrs Cooper's, and a colleague's, but he had an alibi and no motive. We checked with your mother's local garage. She'd recently had the car valeted.' He gave an exasperated shrug. 'I'm a police officer. It's my job to build a case, and the courts pass judgement. Fay Cooper killed your mother in a fit of jealous rage. It's small and sordid, I know, but it's life. You have to let it go.'

'Where is the bag, then?' Helen's eyes stung, and she blinked.

'Among your mother's things, I imagine.'

'Everything's been sold. It's like she never existed.' She brought her hand to her mouth. *I'm not going to cry. Not here, not now.*

Wilcox put his hand on her arm. She wrenched it away from this unwanted pity.

Get a grip.

'What's so special about that bag anyway?'

Unformed images flitted around in her head like bats on a summer night. Why was the bag so important? She'd only thought of it recently when Fay inadvertently jogged her memory. Nothing sentimental had been in it as far as she knew, just stuff, but it had belonged to Mimi, and that made all the difference.

'It was pretty,' she whispered, 'and it's about the only thing I can remember of my mother.'

Trevor called Jason two days after his visit. Balancing a spirit level on top of a kitchen cabinet, Jason stretched to pick up his mobile which was within reach, but only just.

'Yeah?'

As usual Trevor didn't beat about the bush, a trait Jason both admired and found a little un-English at the same time.

'I've had a nosey 'round,' he said, without elaborating where this nosing-around had taken place, 'and there's no connection between someone named Helen Stephens and a dead kid, at least not something she'd have gone inside for. It could be a cot death, but that's gonna be a helluva job digging up. It'd show on the kid's medical records, but as I haven't got a name, that's a non-starter. You're gonna have to give me a bit more info than that, mate.'

'I under'and,' Jason replied with a pencil between his teeth. He tugged the phone under his chin and began to mark the required drill holes with his pencil, when the cupboard slipped out of his grasp and landed on the work surface below, smashing a teapot he hadn't had the foresight to move. Dropping his phone, he cursed loudly.

'Everything okay?' Trevor asked when he picked it up again.

'I'm just trying to do two things at once.'

'Multi-tasking is the key.'

'Some things are not meant to be multi-tasked, unless you're an octopus.'

Trevor laughed. 'Exactly *what* are you doing?'

'Putting up a kitchen cupboard. A heavy bastard from Wickes.'

'Best there is if you're on a budget. Solid, not made of cardboard, like some crap I can think of.'

'You sound like an advert. Wickes paying you?'

Trevor snorted.

Enough man-talk, thought Jason. 'Listen, I appreciate what you've done. Could you check something else out for me?' He could almost hear Trevor roll his eyes. 'Does the name Mimi Stephanov mean anything to you? I've googled it, but nothing came up. I'm guessing she was around before Internet news was a big thing. What I need you to check for me is if there's any link between Helen Stephens and this Mimi.'

'I can't say that it does.' Jason detected a cautionary note in Trevor's voice. ''What I can say is it's an unusual surname, sounds Russian, and I'm not altogether comfortable with this Stephens woman having a Russian connection. That always smells of bad news to me.'

'Not all Russians are Mafia. Anyway, it was only something she was reading but I got the feeling it was important to her.' Jason quickly gave Trevor the low-down of what he'd seen in Helen's folder. 'A five-year-old daughter was mentioned in the headline. It was in what used to be called the *Evening Standard*.'

'*Now* you're giving me something proper to go on. Shouldn't be too difficult to work that one. I'll give you a buzz when I've finished.'

Trevor rang off, and Jason picked up the sorry remains of the teapot and tossed them in the bin. It was a particularly nice teapot too, a traditional glazed Brown Betty, which his aunt Lucy had given him years ago when he left home, claiming that it made the best cuppa.

'She'd better be worth it, whatever her story is,' he muttered. Recalling their kiss and the way she'd responded, he thought she might be.

And then some.

Chapter Eleven

Helen woke early Monday morning, annoyed that she'd have to spend the day working instead of sleuthing.

Reluctantly she had to agree with Detective Wilcox. Her mother was murdered a long time ago, and Helen had brooded, fantasised and searched for clues in her own head. Perhaps her mind *was* playing tricks on her by planting images which had no basis in reality. She had to let it go, but just couldn't. Not yet.

She dressed in jeans and a sweatshirt as Letitia had told her to do, dreading the prospect of having to eventually shop for smarter clothes. She hated clothes shopping, saw it as an unnecessary expense and a waste of time too, but she wanted to fit in and would have to bite the bullet at some point.

Charlie was in the kitchen.

'How come you're up so early?' Helen asked, then regretted it immediately.

'You mean because I don't have a job to go to?'

'I didn't mean it like that.'

Charlie shrugged. 'I guess I'm hoping that someone will call me about a job, and then I'll be ready to go.'

Helen finished her coffee and left her mug on the draining board. She should've eaten breakfast, but the coffee had been like sand in her mouth, and she knew from experience that food wouldn't taste any better. It never did in the mornings.

She turned in the doorway. 'If you like, I can ask at work if they need someone.'

'Yeah, I'd like that.' Charlie smiled, but didn't sound hopeful.

Arriving at the auction house, Helen walked through a large wrought-iron gate at the back. An eclectic mix of vehicles were parked in the enclosed yard, including a couple of dark green vans with the company logo, an old Ford estate, a nimble hatchback, a scooter and a bright yellow Lotus Elan, which was probably Letitia's.

So Letitia hadn't been putting her in her place after all – *everyone* came in around the back.

A gangly youth in a thin, light brown overcoat was smoking a cigarette by the loading bay. Pale and spotty, he wore a surly expression as if he'd got out on the wrong side of the bed, or perhaps even the wrong bed.

'You need Personnel,' he mumbled, pointing over his shoulder to a door at the back of the loading bay. 'Oh, hell,' he added, 'I'm supposed to take you there.'

He stubbed out the cigarette and led the way up a narrow staircase to one side of the loading bay, then unlocked a door with his security pass which hung from a lanyard around his neck. The door opened into a long corridor lit by flickering strip lighting where the youth pushed open another door without knocking. 'The new girl's here, Mrs Deakin.'

A middle-aged woman frowned at Helen over the rim of her reading glasses, clearly resenting the rude interruption. 'Thank you, Jim. Why don't you come in?' she said to Helen with a sudden smile which made her seem much more approachable. 'We need to get a few formalities out of the way before you can start. Hope you don't mind filling in forms?'

'Not at all.'

'Good, good.'

Mrs Deakin handed Helen some forms and carried on with her work. When Helen had finished, Mrs Deakin explained the job, confidentiality and security issues. Finally she handed her a coat like the one Jim was wearing and a padlock.

'When you come out into the corridor and turn left,' she said, 'you'll find a staff room. Take any locker which isn't occupied and use the padlock. It's unisex I'm afraid, but if you need to change your clothes, you can do it in the loo. Everyone else does.' Removing her reading glasses, she let them dangle from her neck on a chain. 'It's good to see you again, Helen. You won't remember me, of course, but I used to work with your mother.'

Surprised, Helen turned before reaching the door. 'I didn't think it was common knowledge that I'm sort of related to Letitia.'

'Oh, it isn't, no. Ms Walcott was quite specific about that, but she must've known I'd recognise you, so that's why she told me. You have your mother's chin.'

Sticking out said chin, Helen approached Mrs Deakin's desk again. 'Did you know my mother well?'

'We were friendly, the kind of friends you make when you work long hours together. I was absolutely horrified at what happened to her. Everyone was. It was so awful. I can't begin to imagine what it was like for you. You must've been traumatised.'

Clutching the coat to her chest, Helen felt her throat constrict. How could she answer this question without getting too caught up in the emotions which rose in her?

'It was a pretty tough time.'

Perhaps sensing Helen's reluctance to talk about it, Mrs Deakin put her reading glasses back on and busied herself with some papers. 'At least you seem to have pulled through. I'm sure having your family around was a great comfort.'

Was this woman for real? She clearly didn't know that Helen had more or less been shunted out of the family before her mother was even cold in her grave. She ought to put her right on that score, but perhaps it was better to wait until she knew where Mrs Deakin stood in relation to Letitia. If the woman was loyal, there'd be no point maligning her. Instead she smiled politely and left the office.

She found the staff room easily enough. A long narrow room, it had lockers along one wall, a low bench along the other, and a window at the end with frosted glass and security bars. In front of the window stood a Formica table and a set of orange plastic chairs in a haphazard arrangement as if everyone had got up in a hurry. Helen hung up her jacket and backpack in an empty locker and put on her brown coat. As she was locking it, Jim skulked in followed by an older man, the one who'd met her in reception the week before.

'This is Bill,' said Jim listlessly, showing that at least he had some manners.

'Hi,' said Helen.

Bald as an egg, with weathered and craggy skin as if he'd spent a lifetime outdoors squinting against the sun, Bill's brown coat hung from a set of scraggy shoulders like a shirt on a wire coat hanger, but his hand was strong when he shook Helen's. His face crinkled into a spider's web of wrinkles. She recalled a 'Bill' from one of the newspaper clippings. If this was the same chap, he'd known her mother too.

'I remember you from last week,' he said in a deep and melodious voice. 'Welcome on board. I said to Jim – didn't I, Jim? – I said, "she's all right, that one, I hope she gets the job".'

'Yeah, you did, didn't ya?'

'I hope you like it here. We're a friendly bunch, except for old misery guts over there.'

'I can be friendly.' Jim sent him a dirty look and left the room, muttering something about 'going for a smoke'.

Bill took Helen on a tour of the premises. They started with the behind-the-scenes bit, as Bill called it. He showed her the storage rooms and introduced her to the Shipping Manager, who nodded briefly while shouting instructions down the telephone.

'Mrs Deakin's office you've seen,' said Bill as they entered what was known as the packaging hall.

'Hall' was a rather grand word for what was really a large, square room lit by a skylight and a few strip lights. It was a bright working space, yet stuffy at the same time, and smelt of dust and pine resin from the wooden packing crates.

Three men, dressed in coats identical to her own and white cotton gloves, were packing a large painting depicting a man on a horse with his sabre raised, set in a heavy gold frame. They gave her a cursory nod, but concentrated on their delicate task.

'The Duke of Wellington,' said Bill, 'from the studio of Sir Thomas Lawrence. Or so the story goes. We're sending him home to his new owner today.'

He led Helen down another wide corridor to the auction room. Several steel trolleys, some designed to move large items, others for smaller artwork, stood against one wall. He pushed aside a pair of thick, olive-green velvet curtains, and it was as if Helen had gone through a magic portal to a different world.

In contrast to the shabbiness of the back rooms, the auction hall glittered. Gold-painted chairs with red velvet seats were arranged in neat rows on either side of an aisle, a plush red wall-to-wall carpet covered the floor, and the room was lit by four large crystal chandeliers and a row of candle lamps on the walls. The back wall was hung with the same olive-green curtain as the one which hid the entrance to the back rooms, and in front of it stood a raised dais with a mahogany lectern and a state-of-the-art microphone. The auction hall had an air of unashamed opulence and unimagined wealth.

Helen's jaw fell open. She'd seen Letitia's office, but it was nothing compared to this.

Bill chuckled. 'Impressive, isn't it? Can't blame you for being a bit overwhelmed, but just remember the old saying, "all that glitters is not gold".'

Helen wasn't really listening. The place was empty at the moment, apart from a large suit-clad bloke sitting on a chair in the far corner, and whom Bill whisperingly referred to as 'Ms Walcott's chauffeur', but it didn't take a lot of imagination to see it full of eager collectors, to hear the auctioneer's rapid chant as he sold item after item to the highest bidders. To fantasise about the astronomical sums changing hands here.

In India the contrasts between rich and poor had been staggering, but for the first time since she'd returned to England she realised that they existed here too. She tried to picture Charlie's reaction, but found it difficult, perhaps because she couldn't imagine this kind of wealth herself.

And yet she was associated with it. That was the hardest part. One of the clan, she had her feet firmly under the table now. So why did it feel so wrong?

'Wow,' she said, for want of something more appropriate.

'Come on, love, let's go back and see if Jim's finished his coffin nail.'

Bill was quiet when he took her back to the staff room, and after they'd collected Jim from his illicit cigarette break, she returned with Bill to the packaging hall. She spent the rest of the day helping the men unpack crates shipped from a private collection and marking the items with sale tags.

One oil painting caught her attention. Christ on the crucifix, it was done in brown, burnt umber, gold and sienna, with a touch of royal blue in the dress of the Virgin Mary kneeling with her hands folded in prayer. Helen guessed the age to be Renaissance, but the most remarkable feature of the painting was the light that seemed to flow from a source inside Christ himself, bathing the faces of those who beheld him. Set in a gilded frame, there was no signature, but she thought she knew who the artist was.

'Rembrandt?' she asked, a little breathlessly, as Bill placed the painting on a trolley in preparation for an auction that afternoon.

'School of, I should think.' He turned the painting over carefully with his cotton gloves to inspect the small white label at the back. 'Yep, just like I thought.'

Jim laughed. 'Yeah, there's a lot going on in this place what doesn't meet the eye.'

'Easy, son,' said Bill. 'Remember, the walls have ears.'

Jim rolled his eyes and continued to work in silence.

Helen was still wondering what he'd meant by that when she left at five that evening. Everyone else had already gone, but there was a lot to learn so she'd spent the last hour reading up on various things. Mrs Deakin had said something about her mother working long hours; if she could do it, so could Helen.

Using her own, shiny new security pass, she released the lock on the loading bay door and let herself out. A sharp gust of wind tossed a bundle of wood shavings used for packing across the yard and behind a car. Helen caught up with it, but when she bent down to pick it up, she found herself staring at a pair of shiny black shoes.

A squeak of alarm escaped her, and she drew back to look up at the owner. He was a big guy with short cropped hair and biceps straining against his black suit jacket. Arms crossed, he stared back at her with virtually no expression on his face.

Helen felt the rush of blood in her ears. It was still light, but the office buildings surrounding the auction house were deserted, and she was alone with a gargantuan thug and only a handful of wood shavings for a weapon. Fighting back was out of the question.

Before she could ask what he was doing here, he beat her to it.

'I am here for business purposes,' he said in heavily accented English. Eastern European or Russian, Helen wasn't sure.

'What kind of business? The office is closed now.' Surprised at herself for being so cocky when her heart was practically jumping against her ribcage, she tossed the wood shavings in a rubbish crate.

'With boss.'

'And where's your boss?' Even bolder now.

'He is there,' he replied and looked over Helen's shoulder.

Helen turned. Across the yard Letitia was coming out through the loading bay with someone, a man. He whispered something in her ear, and Letitia's husky laugh echoed in the thin evening air.

Any further words died in Helen's throat. It wasn't the fact that Letitia had a lover – if it was a lover – which made her stare, it was the man himself.

In her wallet Helen carried a faded Polaroid photo of her parents, the only picture she had of them together. Her father, who died before she was born, had thick dark hair, arresting eyes and a rather prominent nose.

The man descending the steps with his eyes boring into hers was a walking ghost.

Dmitri Stephanov had returned from the dead.

With several conspiracy theories racing through her mind, Helen stared at him numbly. Had her father faked his death? He couldn't have. You could fake an accident but not dying from leukaemia …

If Letitia was annoyed at being caught out with her boyfriend, she didn't show it. Instead she did something which took Helen completely by surprise. Putting a well-manicured hand on his, she motioned for Helen to come closer.

'Helen, I'd like you to meet a business associate of mine. Arseni,' she said, with an elegant movement of her wrist, 'this is your niece.'

Suddenly – nastily – the pieces fell into place. Helen's father had a brother, but she'd never met him, and when her mother was killed and he hadn't come forward to claim her, she'd thought ... well, what? That he'd died? That he didn't know his brother was dead and his niece an orphan?

No.

She'd thought he'd rejected her.

Like everyone else had. Because she was a bad child who had epilepsy. Who'd want that?

'Hello, Uncle. Nice to meet you. At last,' she added, barely holding back a sneer.

Her uncle's face had gone white, and he'd stopped in mid-movement as if frozen. After a few long seconds he turned to Letitia.

'What? You wanted to meet your niece. Well, here she is.'

Arseni ran his fingers through his dark brown hair, so like her father as he was on that faded Polaroid and so like herself except for the hair colour. Then, as if remembering a role he was supposed to be playing, he spread his arms wide and grinned broadly.

'Yelena.' He came towards her and kissed her on both cheeks. Then, frowning, he held her at arm's length with his hands firmly on her shoulders. 'A young lady now. Not beautiful like you mother, but like Dmitri. You are my poor, dead brother – what you say? – come back to life, *nyet*?'

Unhappy with this level of closeness, Helen tried to move away, but his grip remained firm.

'Well, girl, have you no kiss for your poor old uncle Arseni?' The Russian inflection got heavier with each word.

He wasn't old, and he didn't look poor. Nevertheless she planted a kiss on his cheek, expecting to feel something, affection, happiness, revulsion even, but she was like a dead thing. She didn't even have the energy to slap him for not being there when she could have done with a real flesh and blood relative, not just a step-this or step-that. She experienced no connection at all.

Then the anger came, shocking in its intensity, poison in her veins. Sensing this, Arseni let her go.

'Why you do this to me?' he said to Letitia. 'Is not fair.'

'Seni, don't be dramatic. I didn't know she was here. Most of my staff have normally left by this hour.'

'I wanted to meet her when I was properly prepared,' Arseni went on. 'When I could give her gifts and show her my love. She is family, she deserve only the best proper Russian welcome, not like you English, so stiff and upper lip. God in heaven!'

Letitia shrugged. 'How touching. A proper family reunion. Seni, you've had twenty years to get to know your niece. You could've looked her up sooner. I expect she's thinking the same. Give her some space.'

Helen's eyebrows rose at this unexpected insight from Letitia.

'You are hard woman, Letitia,' said Arseni. 'And cruel too. Russia is very busy country now. Life got in the way. I would have found her sooner and clasped her to bosom of family.'

'Oh, no doubt,' said Letitia dryly. 'Helen, if you'll excuse us, Arseni and I have business to discuss. Come by my office on Friday afternoon and we'll talk about your first week.' She turned away, fully expecting her Russian lapdog to follow.

Arseni winked at Helen. 'Always business with your aunt. All work and no play. It makes me very dull boy.' He laughed at his own joke. 'But you must come to my home, and I'll make up for you all my neglect, *da*?'

As she watched them get into a black Mercedes parked behind Letitia's sports car and drive out through the gate, two things struck her in rapid succession: her uncle was as phoney as the accent he cultivated, and everything had just got ten times more complicated.

Why couldn't he have stayed in bloody Russia?

When Jim came back from his early deliveries the next day, he handed Helen an envelope. Inside was an invitation to a black-tie dinner, at the Knightsbridge home of Mr Arseni Stephanov, on Saturday. Below the printed invitation was a scribbled note to Helen promising that they would get to know each other, followed by an *A* and a smiley.

Irritated, she crumpled it up and threw it in the staff room bin. She had no interest in false friends like her uncle. Almost immediately she fished it out again, wiping off a tea stain, and smoothed out the paper. Arseni had known her mother, and might be able to fill in some of the blanks.

For the rest of the week she shadowed Bill in the packaging hall and helped Mrs Deakin with a backlog of paperwork, and saw nothing of Letitia until Friday when they had their talk about Helen's first week at work. Afterwards Letitia's secretary provided her with the promised list of shops where Helen could buy the sort of clothes Letitia deemed suitable for representing the corporate image of Ransome's, and her scathing look revealed all too well what she thought of Helen's fashion sense.

Ignoring the put-down, Helen scanned the list and was tempted to chicken out of the dinner party altogether. It was only the thought of her mother which made her change her mind.

On Saturday, feeling more determined, she trawled through some of the shops on the secretary's list. The displays were so dazzling, the prices so extortionate they made her gasp, and the whole experience was an exercise in obscenity at the thought of anyone spending that amount of money on clothes.

After a confrontation with a particularly snooty sales assistant in Bond Street, she gave up on the idea of new clothes and headed home. Walking past the market, she bumped into Charlie weighed down by grocery bags.

'Why the long face?'

'I've been out shopping,' said Helen, and since she wasn't carrying any bags, offered to take some of Charlie's.

'Window shopping, was it?' said Charlie.

'I was trying to buy a dress.'

'They've got decent threads at the market. Come on, let's go back and have a look.'

'Nah.'

'Why not? They're good value.'

Helen hesitated. Charlie had become a friend, and she didn't want to alienate her. 'It's not that sort of dress. I need something a bit smarter.'

'Have you been to Next?' Charlie shifted her grocery bag to the other hand.

'No.'

'Not smart enough?'

'I need something which isn't off the peg.'

'You what?'

Helen showed her Letitia's list.

'Bloody hell!' said Charlie. 'Someone's having a laugh. You could feed a whole family for the price of a handkerchief in one of those shops. What do you need a dress like that for?'

'A party in connection with work.' It was sort of true.

Charlie chewed her lip for a moment. 'We'll ask Fay.'

'Why Fay?'

'She trained as a dress-maker in prison. She's very good.'

'I don't want to ask Fay.'

'Why not?'

'I just don't, okay.'

'You want a dress or not?' Charlie caught her by the sleeve and almost dragged her back home. 'Come on, it'll be fun.'

Conflicting emotions flew through Helen's head. Excitement over going to a party – she hadn't been to one in years, and never in Knightsbridge. Irritation that she had to go through this ridiculous, girlie ritual of dolling herself up in order to find out more about her mother. Worry that she'd stick out like a sore thumb, when all she wanted to do was to blend in. *And* she had no one to go with.

But worst of all was the idea of wearing a dress made by the same hand which had probably taken her mother's life.

The thought gave her goose pimples.

Chapter Twelve

Back at the house Charlie dumped the groceries on the kitchen table and dragged Helen upstairs to Fay's room.

'Helen needs help.'

'What sort of help?'

Fay looked pale and tired, and her eyes were red-rimmed. Through the open door Helen could see into the room. It was tidy, with furniture similar to her own, as if Jason had bought in bulk at IKEA. She also had a small two-seater sofa, a bookshelf brimming with paperback novels and an unobstructed view of the unkempt back garden. The room smelt of a mixture of jasmine from the garden and something more exotic, perhaps one of her candles.

But what caught Helen's attention were the photos, which were everywhere.

Fay quickly blocked the view as if she found Helen's curiosity invasive.

'She needs a dress,' said Charlie.

'What kind of dress are we talking about?'

'It's for a posh work thing, so she needs something glam.'

Helen held up her hands against Charlie's onslaught. 'It's all right. I've got a couple of skirts, and one of them will probably do.'

'Sounds like what you need is a cocktail dress.'

'I'm fine. Honestly. You don't have to—'

'Helen,' Charlie snapped, 'stop being so bloody difficult. I told you Fay would help. That's what friends are for.'

But I don't want Fay's help, Helen wanted to shout. *She's not my friend. She can never be my friend!*

'I might have something in your size,' said Fay. 'What are you? A ten or a twelve?'

'Somewhere in between.' Helen shrugged and wished she'd left the party invitation in the bin. She didn't want to be indebted to Fay over a stupid dress, and she resented Charlie's pushiness. In fact, she resented all of them, and just wanted to climb into bed and pull the covers over her head.

'Wait here,' said Fay.

She went back into her room, closing the door behind her, then returned a few minutes later with a short-sleeved black dress wrapped in protective plastic. She pulled it out and held it up against Helen. The dress was made from thick velvet and had a daring neckline, and it reached to just above the knees. A hand-written price tag was attached to the zip at the back with a silken string.

Feeling the material in her hand, Helen remembered 'Laura's dress'. And shiny black shoes, so shiny she could see her own reflection. She saw Aggie's house, her mum in burgundy velvet, a wine glass in her hand and her blonde hair in a clip on top of her head. A much thinner Aggie carrying a tray of tiny bits of food which Helen didn't like. Ruth laughing. Letitia glittering. Men in black jackets and bow ties.

They'd both had 'Laura' dresses, she realised, not just her.

'Mummy, when can I meet your friend Laura?' she'd asked for the umpteenth time.

'One day soon.' Mimi smiled and ran her hand over Helen's hair.

But of course, they never went to see Laura or any other friend. Instead it was curtains drawn in the daytime, the phone unplugged, and shadows closing in.

Abruptly she stopped fingering the dress. The memory was so happy and so painful at the same time that tears welled up in her eyes. Impatiently she wiped them away.

'Ah, bless,' said Charlie.

'You can give it back when the party's over,' said Fay. 'It's no skin off my nose.'

Helen shook her head. She couldn't accept this, it was a step too far. 'No, I can't let you do this. What if I ruin it?'

'You won't.'

Helen fingered the material again, but to her disappointment it didn't bring back any more memories. 'If you're sure ... I'll need to try it on, though.'

'Go on,' said Charlie. 'We'll be in the kitchen.'

It was only after she'd put on the dress and twirled in front of the mirror, both satisfied and surprised at this magical transformation, that she realised she'd forgotten all about shoes. The dress was crying out for stilettos, except she'd never owned a pair in her entire life.

She tried on several pairs of sandals, but they either screamed 'hippy' or were too worn to do the dress justice.

'Bugger,' she muttered.

Which left only her Doc Martens boots. Heaving a sigh, she pulled them on, then spent half an hour touching up her make-up and hair, before going downstairs to the kitchen to get Charlie's opinion.

'Hey, snazzy,' said Charlie from her usual post in front of the telly.

'I don't have any other shoes,' Helen explained and glanced at her wrist watch. 'Any decent shoes shops around here where I can get a pair of high heels?'

Charlie got up from the sofa. 'You don't need them.'

'Are you serious? This just doesn't go together.'

'Who says?'

Helen sent her an exasperated look. 'I think I'm expected to wear something a little more, um, elegant.'

'Why elegant when you can be grungy? Trust me, you'll turn heads.'

'Yeah, won't I just?'

'No, seriously, you look good.' Charlie switched the TV off. 'Anyway, why try to be something you're not? They took you on because they thought you'd be a good little worker. If they're gonna give you the sack for having an original taste in clothes, they're not worth the bother.'

'I'm not convinced.' This wasn't the time to tell Charlie that the invitation had nothing to do with work. As for what she wore, did it really matter? She wasn't planning on impressing anyone.

Jason and Fay came into the kitchen, and Jason put the kettle on.

'It fits, then,' said Fay.

'Very nice,' said Jason. His gaze roamed over her outfit then settled on her hair, which she'd piled on top of her head. 'Going somewhere?'

Helen's stomach did a curious flip. Maybe there *was* one person she wouldn't mind impressing. Just a little bit.

'She's off to a glamorous party in Knightsbridge.' Charlie took an apple from the fruit dish and started crunching noisily.

'Shouldn't you wash it first?' said Fay.

'Why? What's gonna happen if I eat a dirty apple?'

'You'll get polio and die.'

Charlie flicked back her blonde dreadlocks. 'I'm vaccinated.'

'You're too much sometimes.'

Helen and Jason left them bickering, and Helen burst out laughing when she'd closed the kitchen door.

'Fay's right, Charlie is a bit full on sometimes.'

'You haven't seen half of it yet,' said Jason. 'So, Knightsbridge, eh? What's the occasion?'

'Oh, one of the clients of the company I work for has invited some members of staff to a dinner party.' Helen tried to be vague to avoid discussing the family connection.

'Who's the client?'

'A collector. A Russian business man. He imports vodka, I think.'

He sent her a long look, and a sharp tone crept into his voice when he asked, 'What was the name of your company again?'

'Ransome & Daughters. Why? Do you know it?'

'I've heard of them.'

'Really?' Ransome's wasn't exactly Sotheby's, despite the family's pretensions in that direction. 'I didn't think they were that well-known.'

Jason shrugged but didn't explain how he'd heard of them, and she couldn't very well ask if she hoped to side-step his questions.

'Well, I'd better get a move on, then,' she said instead. 'See you.'

'Have fun.' He smiled and saw her to the door.

A moment later when she turned around to wave, she noticed him frowning furiously.

For the second time in a fortnight Jason watched Helen turn her back on him and disappear at the end of the road.

A Russian business man. A 'connection', as Trevor called it. Russians certainly had a way of popping up all over the place around this woman. Damn. He banged his fist against the door jamb. What was it about him that he couldn't find an ordinary English girlfriend?

And what was Helen involved in?

He needed to get himself invited to the same party, and he knew exactly how to go about it.

Heading back downstairs to his rooms, he picked up his mobile and dialled the dreaded number.

Derek Moody answered on the fifth ring, a sign which told

Jason that his beloved dad found him a pain in the arse. The thought produced a grim smile.

'I'm on my way to a business dinner. Is this important?' Derek's clipped tones hinted at a man in a hurry.

'Yes, I'm after some info,' said Jason. 'You're usually up to speed with the London social whirl. Heard of any art-collecting Russian business men throwing parties this evening, by any chance? In Knightsbridge.'

'As a matter of fact, I'm heading to a party at a Russian's right now. Why?' His father sounded suspicious.

'I have my reasons, and I want an invite. Can you wangle it?'

'That depends.'

'On?'

'You hate these functions. What was it you said once? Something along the lines of "a gathering where scum could forget that they'd just crawled out of the sewer"? I seem to remember your statement included me.'

Jason sighed. This was going to be more difficult than he'd thought. His father was toying with him and obviously enjoying it. 'Not really. You're more ... evolved.'

Derek laughed. 'A rare compliment from my ungrateful son.'

'I'm not ungrateful.' Why did his father have this infuriating ability to bring out the worst in him? 'I appreciate everything you've done for me. I just don't want you meddling in my life.'

'Nuff said.' Derek cut him short. 'Tell me the reason you need an invitation.'

'I thought it might be interesting. Maybe I could establish some business contacts.'

'Pull the other one. This lot close some of the biggest art deals in the country. They don't have time for market traders. No, I want to know what it is if I'm to get you entry.'

Jason hesitated. Perhaps he should abandon the idea altogether and let Helen go to this dinner on her own. He was about to tell his father to forget it and hang up when he thought of her in a home-made dress and Doc Martens boots in a room full of people who'd be decked out like Christmas trees. He was familiar with this, but she wasn't and would be completely out of place, a lamb thrown to the wolves, or something like that. He couldn't let her go without back-up.

'A friend of mine is going,' he said, 'and is bound to, er … stick out a little. I thought I'd come along and offer moral support.'

'A female friend?'

Crunch time. No matter what he said, his father would find out anyway, through his network of spies. Why delay the inevitable?

Recalling that Derek never went to any function without having a copy of the complete guest list beforehand, he said, 'Her name is Helen Stephens.'

Derek went quiet for a while, and Jason heard the rustling of paper. 'Yes, there's a Helen Stephens on my list. No company name though,' he added as if this counted against her.

'That'll be her.'

'I see, and how do you know this girl?'

His father had abandoned his usual hectoring tone, which puzzled Jason until he realised that Derek must be thinking that if his son was 'in' with a girl who was invited to dine with a prominent collector, there was a chance he was finally moving in the right circles. He nearly laughed, knowing that he'd have to disappoint him.

'She's renting a room in my house.'

'Another charity case?'

Jason said nothing.

'And how, exactly, does one of your strays get herself invited to a black-tie dinner?' Derek asked, no longer jovial.

'It's to do with her job.'

'What does she do?'

The change in his father's mood warned him to backtrack, but with Derek a bargain was a bargain. Besides, now that his curiosity was vetted, he'd dig and dig until he knew everything there was to know about Helen. And he wouldn't be wearing kid gloves either.

'She works for an auction house,' he explained. 'As some sort of assistant.'

'Which auction house?'

'Is that important?'

'Why don't you let me be the judge of that? Which auction house?' Derek pressed.

'Ransome & Daughters. Perhaps you've heard of them.'

There was a long pause, and all he could hear was the sound of his father's breathing and the purring of the chauffeur-driven saloon.

'Yes, I have,' his father said at length. He gave a muffled order to his driver, then said to Jason, 'I'll send the car back for you. Give my name when you arrive. An invitation will be waiting for you.'

Hanging up, Jason became aware that his palms were sweating, and he wiped them on his jeans. What was the matter with him? He and his father didn't see eye to eye, but Derek had never had that effect on him before. Ice prickled between his shoulder blades, and his mouth was dry.

Was this how it felt when you made a deal with the Devil?

Chapter Thirteen

On the bus Helen attracted a few typical London stares: look up, assess, look away, pretend not to see nor care. Because it was Saturday night the bus was full of young people going out on the town as well as a few downcast individuals, mainly immigrants, who looked like they'd just finished a long shift in the sort of job no one else wanted.

Her uncle's house was a four-storey London town house of yellow brick with tall windows and black-painted railings. Steps flanked by columns led up to the ground floor where two topiary bay trees stood guard on either side of the front door.

A maid with a thick Eastern European accent let her in. She cast a suspicious glance at Helen's outfit, then her invitation, as if she couldn't quite believe the two went together, and eventually showed Helen into a drawing room already brimming with other guests. Through the crowd Helen could just about make out the leather furniture, Oriental rugs, and glittering chandeliers. At the end of the room facing a window stood a baby grand piano with a vase of orange lilies on top. The din of people socialising while sipping champagne and eating canapés was almost deafening.

The women sparkled in their sequinned dresses on toned bodies, with jewels as big as robins' eggs around slender necks and waxed legs ending in silver-heeled stilettos. The men wore dinner jackets and exuded power, and the air in the room was redolent with expensive perfume, fake tan, and the subtler scent of dirty money.

Helen gulped.

This was the world she was supposed to belong to, and

a part of her had to admit she was ready to, ready to belong somewhere, while another part knew she never would.

She accepted a canapé from a passing waitress and a glass of champagne she wouldn't be drinking due to her epilepsy. She took it mainly because it seemed like the required accessory, then sidled along the wall until she found a large Yucca plant to hide behind. When she was sure no one was looking, she emptied the glass into the flowerpot.

She wasn't allowed to hide for long, though.

'There you are.' Her uncle emerged from the crowd to greet her with kisses on both cheeks, which again left her numb. Noticing her empty glass, he muttered something in Russian, snapped his fingers and a waiter magically appeared to refill it. 'And how are you today?'

'I'm very well, thank you.' The requisite answer.

'Good. I'm so happy. And you look – how do you say? – a pretty picture.' Arseni assessed her, glancing briefly at her boots, then smiled. It was a pleasant enough smile, all white teeth in a distinguished face, yet too well-practised to be genuine.

He turned away to greet another guest who had come in just after her, and it gave her a moment to reflect. It struck her that her uncle's overly effusive Eastern European mannerisms, which could easily be seen as both comical and dim-witted, were the perfect disguise for a sophisticated ability to manipulate others. She suspected he was using Letitia's infatuation with him to further his business interests, and it made her wonder what he could possibly want with her. She had to be on her guard against his charm, and not fall for his ploy about the long-lost niece.

Across the room she spotted Letitia, talking to a man. There was something frosty about him, and he appeared to be speaking in a low voice because Letitia had cocked her head to one side, apparently straining to hear what he was saying. A frown creased her forehead as if she didn't like what she was hearing, and she pulled back abruptly.

Helen watched her walk off and wondered whether she ought to go and speak to her, but her aunt's testy expression warned her not to right now.

She pretended to sip her champagne and met the gaze of the cold-looking man over the rim of her glass. Cocking an eyebrow, he lifted his own glass in a mock salute, giving her the impression that he knew exactly who she was. Something curdled inside her, and she put her glass down on the tray of a passing waiter.

Perhaps Letitia had a good reason to be pissed off.

A hand on her shoulder made her swing around. It was her uncle again.

'I want to talk with you a little,' he said, making the *L* at the beginning of the last word sound as if it had a *J* attached to it. Helen almost laughed; his accent was phonier than ever.

'Sure,' she said.

'In private.' He indicated a door at the back, and she followed him with a mixture of curiosity and trepidation. When the door closed behind them, the hubbub of voices was reduced to a faint echo, and they crossed the marbled hall, the rubber soles of Helen's boots squeaking loudly.

Just as well I'm not drunk, she thought. Whatever he wanted to talk to her about, something told her she needed to have her wits about her.

'I want to apologise,' her uncle Arseni said when they were ensconced in what must be his home office.

'Oh?'

Helen sat down on a squashy brown leather armchair in front of his large desk while her uncle went to the bar cabinet and reached for a decanter. Like the drawing room, his office was richly furnished but also spoke of a person who liked his comforts.

'Whisky?'

'Have you got a Coke or something?'

'Of course.'

He opened a small fridge disguised as a wood-panelled cabinet, found a can and poured the contents into a crystal tumbler.

'Thanks.'

Facing her, uncle Arseni leaned against his desk and regarded her with what looked like regret, but she couldn't be sure. 'I have been a bad uncle. I should have taken you under my wing when your mother was killed.'

'Why didn't you?' Did he realise this was like waving a red rag at a bull?

'I was back in Moscow, although I stay in touch with family in London. Taking an English child out of England would mean red tape. Your mother made Mrs Ransome guardian of you in her will. I could do nothing.' He sighed. 'Then you disappear.'

Helen nearly choked on her Coke. 'I *disappeared*? I don't remember disappearing.'

'Your grandmother would not tell me where you were. No one else knew. She said you were being looked after by good people.' He looked at her with a thoughtful expression. 'Were they good people?'

Humiliation. Disgust. Isolation. That's all she consciously remembered of her childhood, even though she knew some of the foster families had been kind and welcoming. She shrugged. 'Sometimes.'

He smiled suddenly, and his seriousness, which she wasn't sure had been earnest or not, was replaced by the teasing expression she'd come to associate with him.

'How would you have liked living in Russia? You might have liked it, *nyet*?'

'I don't know. Isn't it supposed to be very cold in the winter? I don't like being cold.'

'Pah! Not if you are properly dressed. You would have been my daughter. I would have dressed you like a princess.' He paused and glanced at her Doc Martens again. 'I can still help you.'

'Yes, well, I'm sorry you didn't get a chance to be my daddy, but it's a bit late now to tell me what I can and can't wear, don't you think?'

He gave a Slavic shrug which was almost comical. 'I didn't mean your clothes. I was referring to the woman who killed your mother.'

Helen felt it as if a bucket of ice had been emptied into her dress. 'What about her?'

'She is out of prison, I think?'

'What if she is?'

'I could – what you say? – arrange an accident? Make her an offer she can't refuse?' This was the second film joke he'd cracked in her presence.

'No.' Helen rose abruptly, sloshing Coke onto his Persian rug. 'And could you cut the KGB crap, please. It's like being in a bad movie, and it's getting on my nerves.'

'Yes, yes, I know,' he said holding up his hands. 'Bad uncle. But I have contacts.'

'I wouldn't want you to. Besides, two wrongs don't make a right.' It wasn't so long ago she'd thought the same herself, but he didn't know that.

'But it makes us feel better.'

Helen was just about to protest again when Arseni's mobile phone rang. Mouthing an apology, he answered it.

'*Da.*'

He launched into a lengthy conversation in Russian, too

fast for her to follow, although she did catch the odd word. Her Russian was rusty and limited to the language of the fairy tales and nursery rhymes which she'd picked up in the Russian-speaking nursery she went to before her mother died.

While he spoke she decided to explore his office. Apart from the rich furnishings, he'd collected an interesting and rather odd assortment of antiques and trinkets displayed in locked glass cabinets.

In one of the display cases lay old sailing implements: nautical prints, compasses, a brass barometer as well as a sextant. The same cabinet also held an old leather-bound volume covered with writing in a spidery hand and black ink. Looking more closely, Helen read the words 'Captain's log, November 1868, Straits of Magellan'. A seaman's journal and probably quite valuable in historical terms.

'Let me speak to Johnson,' she heard her uncle say in Russian.

Johnson must have come to the phone because Arseni switched to English. 'Listen, I picked up an Art Deco lampshade for three thousand the other day. Tell Vitali he can have it for five grand.' Pause. 'I'm sure he will, but he's a millionaire. Press him, okay.'

Grinning because now her uncle sounded more like East London than Moscow, she moved to the other display cabinet, which contained a collection of curiously shaped Lalique vases, and next to those a smaller hoard of gold and silver snuff boxes.

'Don't forget whatever costs him five, he sells for nine,' Arseni continued. 'If it costs ten, he will flog it for twenty.'

Turning her attention on the display, Helen's eyes fell on a pair of paper knives on a red velvet cushion, and her uncle's wheeling and dealing faded into the background. Completely identical, the knives were about twenty centimetres long with lapis lazuli stone handles and gold mounts. Just like what she'd described to Detective Wilcox as a child.

Realisation slammed into her, and she quelled the profanity on her lips with her hand. She'd poured over the folder with the clippings Sweetman had given her, in the crazy hope that the articles could offer a new insight into what happened that day, but the list of possessions from her mother's house had represented everything she lost, and she'd been unable to do more than just glance at it. If Wilcox was right though, her mother's knife wouldn't be on that list.

Two missing knives, one murder weapon …

Where had her uncle got them from?

'They are beautiful, aren't they?' Her uncle had finished his phone call and was standing beside her as she bent over the display cabinet.

'Yes.' Her heart raced, and her scalp prickled with unease at how close he stood.

'They were set of four paper knives made for the tsar's daughters by Fabergé. You've heard of Fabergé?'

Four knives? Letting out the breath she'd been holding in, she nodded.

'My great-grandfather acquired them after Revolution,' he said, pointing to a silver-framed sepia photo of an Edwardian family, husband and wife with four daughters and a son. It took Helen a moment to realise she was looking at the last of the Romanovs. 'They've always been in my family.'

She ignored the fact that 'acquired' likely meant that her great-great-grandfather stole the knives in the chaos after the tsar's abdication. Her mind was reeling from this new information. 'You said there were four. What happened to the other two?'

'They were your father's. When he died, they became your mother's.' He eyed her curiously. 'I'm surprised you don't know this.'

'I'm not.'

'Eh?'

'Who was around to tell me?'

'Poor princess,' he said and put his arm around her shoulder.

She freed herself as tactfully as she could without being rude. His touch still left her emotionless. 'That's the thing, you see. I'm not poor at all.'

The look on his face told her differently, and while the irony struck her that an opportunistic wheeler-dealer like Arseni could see that money wasn't everything, it also made her uncomfortable that he could read her mind so well even though he hardly knew her. 'Perhaps we'd better get back to the party,' she said.

'Yes,' he muttered. 'But remember, my door is always open to family.'

Family.

'Thank you.'

Back in the crowded drawing room the head waiter announced that dinner was served, and the guests milled into the dining room, a large rectangular room with French windows overlooking the garden. The windows were curtain-less but indoor bamboos served as natural screening. Another set of dazzling chandeliers lit a long table covered in crisp white linen and decked with flowers, crystal wine glasses, fine bone china and enough silver to make a dent in the national reserves.

Helen found her seat and was just about to pull in her chair when a familiar voice – a *very* familiar voice – said, 'Here, let me do that for you.'

Chapter Fourteen

'Jason?' Helen swung around in surprise. 'What are you doing here?'

He shrugged and sat down beside her. 'Well, it would seem I'm your dinner partner.'

'That's just crap!'

'That I'm your dinner partner? I'm so sorry. Here I was, hoping that we might—' He spread his hands wide with a mock hang-dog expression.

Helen elbowed him in the side. 'Pack it in. You know what I mean. When I left, you looked like you were settling in for the evening. And now here you are, dressed—'

She took in his dinner jacket, crisp white shirt and slicked-back hair. She'd noticed several times how good he looked in jeans, but in a suit he was the embodiment of success and power, and she experienced an odd constriction in her chest. She'd always had a suspicion he was completely out of her league. Now she knew for sure.

'—well, all smartened up. How did you get here so quickly? And who invited you?'

'I have a fairy godmother.'

'Oh, please!'

A waiter interrupted them with a basket of bread rolls. Helen shook her head. Bread was one of those food stuffs her medication transformed into the taste equivalent of wood chippings. Jason accepted one and broke it into smaller bits, making a frightful mess on his side plate and the white table cloth.

Helen watched him out of the corner of her eye. Only a person used to going to this sort of party wouldn't worry about his table manners. The thought put her on her guard.

'My father sent a car for me,' he said finally.

'Why?'

'So I could join him. He likes me to accompany him to business dinners because Mum can't leave the dogs, or so she says. I usually say no thanks.'

'Your *father* is here? Which one is he?'

Jason bent his head towards someone further up the table and continued to munch on his bread roll. Helen knew who he meant before she turned to look – she'd felt his gaze on her ever since she came in the dining room.

'That's him over there. Salt 'n pepper hair, sharp suit.' As if acknowledging the description, Jason's father held up his glass in a silent salute. Again Helen met the cold stare and gave a little involuntary shudder.

'Yes, he has that effect on people,' said Jason.

'You said he was just a self-made business man.'

'Let's not beat about the bush. He's a crook.'

'I don't think he likes me,' she said.

'He doesn't like anyone. I wouldn't take it personally.'

The starter arrived, a fancy concoction of seafood in a fragile basket of pastry encircled by a white sauce which had been artistically swirled into a pattern on the over-large plate. Pretty, but her appetite had vanished. She picked at the food, managing only a few bites, and then rearranged it artfully on her plate so it looked as if she'd at least tried to eat it.

'So if you don't normally accept his open-invitation to these things, why are you here tonight?'

Jason put his fork down, touched his napkin to his lips, and turned to face her. 'Well, that's obvious, isn't it?'

'Not really.'

He smiled. 'You.'

'What's that supposed to mean?'

'I knew you'd be here, and I thought it might be nice to spend some time together.'

A diversionary tactic. She wasn't going to fall for it. At the same time she couldn't help feeling just a little bit tempted to believe him. 'But how did you know I was going to be *here* and not at some other dinner party?' she insisted.

'I called my dad. He confirmed your name was on the guest list.'

That sounded plausible enough, but it didn't explain why, the moment she'd met the eyes of the man who'd then turned out be Jason's father, she'd had a nasty feeling he knew exactly who she was.

'Did he say anything else about me?' she asked.

'No, why would he?'

'No reason.'

Jason took a sip of his wine. 'There's something you're not telling me.'

Plenty, she thought. 'And what would that be?'

'Why *you* are here? The kind of people my father rubs shoulders with don't usually bother to socialise with lowly assistants.'

The waiter cleared their plates away, and the interruption gave Helen a chance to think about her answer. Could she trust him? As soon as the thought entered her mind, she realised that this wasn't a case of whether she could trust him or not. She'd done nothing wrong – not yet anyway – and her connection to Arseni was just that, a connection. It was more a case of whether she dared to open up about herself to him, to anyone.

She had to learn to do that. To expose herself a bit more, and to hell with the risks. Take a chance.

'I only met him recently,' she began, 'but as it happens, the host is my uncle. Arseni Stephanov.'

Jason stared at her as he mentally connected the dots. *Stephanov, Stephens.* Here was the link between Helen and the woman called Mimi in the newspaper clippings, whom both Helen and the host were somehow related to. It wasn't a quantum leap, and it made total sense. If you wanted to start a new life while keeping a part of your identity, choosing a name close to your own was a reasonable compromise.

What he didn't quite get was why she was here at all, if the point of changing her name had been to distance herself from her family in the first place. With the kind of money on display, this guy could obviously pull strings all over town, could probably get her any high-flying job she wanted, yet she chose to work in a really lowly one.

It was almost as if she'd deliberately disassociated herself. Like Jason did from his own father. Maybe they had more in common than he'd thought.

'That might explain why my father doesn't like you,' he joked.

'Why? Like I said, I've only just met him and—'

'And you've only just moved into my house,' Jason pointed out. 'I have a confession to make. When I asked about the guest list, my father wanted to know why I was interested in you, and I had to explain that you lived in the house. He wasn't too happy about that.' Derek must have worked it out. Or spied on him and the others in the house. Or both. Always one step ahead of his wayward son.

'What do my family connections and living in your house have to do with each other?'

'He probably sees you as a bad influence on me. Turning away from moneyed family is a sore point for him.'

She turned her head and looked down the length of the table at Derek, who was deep in conversation with the lady on his right.

Jason knew better. He sensed his father's awareness and knew Derek's apparent concentration on his dinner partner was a cover for studying everyone around him, including his own son.

When Jason had first entered the crowded reception room earlier, he had spied his father across the room talking to someone whom he took to be a business contact. A woman, attractive, well-to-do, but too old to be one of his father's lovers. It didn't appear to be a pleasant conversation, and in the end the woman left as if she'd heard enough.

Derek Moody hadn't looked in his son's direction, but something about his body language, a slight shift in his posture perhaps, told Jason his father knew he'd arrived. Most children would have welcomed this sort of awareness in their parent; for Jason it felt as if an invisible net had been cast around him. Involuntarily, he'd taken a step back and accepted a glass of champagne from a waiter.

And then he'd seen where his father's attention had shifted to. Helen, half-hidden by a large house-plant, as much out of place in this joint as he was.

Sitting next to her now, the devil took hold of him, and as he felt his father watching without actually watching, he leaned closer to Helen and blew gently at the base of her neck.

Make what you will of that, you old goat.

Helen gasped. 'What are you doing?'

'Getting your attention.'

'What for?'

'Because I've thought of one other reason my father doesn't like you.'

'Yeah, what?'

Jason took a hearty swig of his wine glass. Dutch courage, he thought. *Boy, do I need it.* 'Because *I* like you,' he said.

She stared at him, in that inscrutable way of hers he'd come to respect.

'Why should it bother him that *you* like me?'

He couldn't back down now. She'd never trust him if he did, and it had become important to him that she should.

Not only that, but she had an uncanny ability to see right into his soul. If he fobbed her off with banalities, she'd know he was lying.

So, he decided to tell her something he'd never told anyone other than Lucy and Trevor.

'There was a girl once,' he began. 'Like you in many ways, blonde and tanned. And very different in others. I was twenty-three, got her pregnant, and wanted to marry her. Do the right thing, you know.'

Helen nodded.

'But my dad didn't think she was good enough for me, so he paid her off and she chose to have an abortion. I suppose a part of me still grieves for the loss of that baby. A life that ... could have been. Silly, really.'

She regarded him silently, and he turned away from those beautiful, all-seeing eyes. Swigging from his wine again, he suddenly felt a little woozy. She must think him a right tosser.

'I'm sorry,' she said. Gently she prized the wine glass from his fingers and put it back on the table. 'That you had to go through something like that. No one ever thinks about what it might be like for the man. But why should it be any different?'

'Thanks.'

Briefly he put his hand over hers, touched by her understanding. Then again, why shouldn't she be? Helen came across as far more mature than many girls her age and had what he could only describe as an intact core self, despite the tough times she must have been through. Her words to him showed that, simplistic though they were, and he wanted to safeguard it.

'You'd better stay out of his way, though,' he said.

She rolled her eyes. 'Like you need to tell me that.'

Helen experienced a shiver of unease. She remembered

Letitia's reaction to Jason's father earlier; she clearly wasn't the only one who wished to avoid him.

Jason had no need to worry on that score. She'd do everything she could to stay away from this man.

Their main course arrived, whole quail served with tiny new potatoes and stir fried vegetables arranged in a narrow stack, again encircled by gravy in a beautiful pattern. The combination of seeing the small bird along with the hard lump of uncertainty in her stomach made Helen lose the rest of her appetite.

'What I want to know is, if Stephanov is your uncle, and you have access to all this'—he made a gesture indicating the opulent dining room—'why do you choose to live in squalor?'

That question she could answer. 'It makes me feel at home. Why do you?'

Jason responded with a frown, then he attacked his dinner with savage stabs of his fork and didn't say anything else on the subject.

Something had changed. It was subtle, but it was there. He'd said he liked her, and she'd felt it too, it wasn't just words, but it still wasn't clear what he wanted from her, or if he wanted anything at all.

Instincts had made her hold back, and she'd been proven right: she would have to be extremely careful if she was to walk this continued tightrope between her life in the house and outside it.

When dinner was finally over, she told her uncle she was tired and left. It had started to drizzle, and she stopped at the top of the steps to breathe in the London air, that not completely unpleasant mixture of wet tarmac and traffic fumes.

Although she'd tried to push the thought aside, something about Jason's father interested her, in the same way a large spider might. Clearly he did business with her uncle, but his connection to her aunt she could only guess at. Perhaps he was a customer of the auction house. She had seen for herself how her wheeler-dealer uncle liked to invest some of his money in art and collectibles, and it seemed a safe bet that Jason's father, who was of a similar ilk, liked to do the same.

Then again, Jason had also described his father as a crook.

Helen nearly gave him the slip, but fortunately Jason managed to catch up with her on the pavement. 'It's raining. Let's get a taxi.'

'Taxis are expensive. I'm happy on the bus.'

'But I'm not, and I'm in charge.'

'Oh, yeah? Since when?'

'Since right now.' He twirled her around and planted a kiss on her lips.

Helen drew back with a slight scowl on her face. 'What was that for?'

'Oh, nothing. I'm just glad I know you. Happy to be alive, that's all. And out of there.' He tossed his head in the direction of her uncle's house, and, hiccupping loudly, he tried hailing a taxi. The driver ignored him.

'You're drunk,' she scoffed.

He grinned. 'A bit. Your uncle serves good wine, apart from that awful champagne. Yuck.' He had drunk a fair amount and was feeling pleasantly mellow, especially now he'd escaped his father's presence. He was also less drunk than Helen supposed.

'Didn't stop you knocking it back, I imagine.' She wolf-whistled for a taxi, which did a U-turn and came to a halt beside them.

'Impressive,' he muttered as they bundled into the back.

When they got back, the house was completely dark. Jason

flicked the switch in the hall, but the bulb went out with a ping.

'Bugger. I'll have to sort that out in the morning.'

An awkward silence fell, and he hoped she didn't think he'd engineered for the bulb to pop. Making light of it, he said, 'Well, thanks for seeing me home safely. It's nice to know someone's concerned for my welfare.'

He felt rather than saw her smile. 'Oh, you know, Women's Lib and all that. It was fun. I enjoyed being with you,' she added, then stopped abruptly as if she worried she'd said too much.

'Are you having a laugh? I've been grumpy all evening.'

'Only half the evening.'

Laughing, he placed his hand on the wall beside her head, and looked down into the only thing glinting in the darkness, her eyes. 'I suppose this is where we say goodnight.'

'I suppose so.'

He remembered how she'd reacted to him the last time he'd nearly lost himself in her. That should have been enough for him to keep his distance. Instead, drunk partly on alcohol and partly on her presence, he had, before he knew it, done the exact opposite of what he'd planned to do, had moved up close and was kissing her with abandon.

Forcing her against the wall, almost knocking the wind out of them both, he pushed himself between her legs, and let her feel just how much he wanted her. She responded by rubbing shamelessly against him, and the lust for her which he'd hoped to put a lid on just got ten times worse. Her lips were soft under his and quivered like he felt his own body shake with the effort of holding back.

'Oh, God!' she breathed before he shut her up with his mouth again. He had no awareness of anything other than her; her skin, her scent, the inviting movements of her hips, the way her breasts moulded themselves to the shape of his hand.

His shock was therefore palpable when she shoved him hard in the chest, and he had to step back in order to regain his balance.

'What?' he gasped.

'I like living here,' she said, and the amusement had gone from her voice. 'If we get involved, we might ruin that.'

'You're probably right.' He brushed a strand of hair away from her face, feeling like a cad. 'Do you know what, you're more beautiful than you realise?'

'That's a bit patronising. How do you know what I realise about myself?'

He smiled. 'Good point. I just wanted to say that you're very beautiful.'

'How can you tell? It's dark in here.'

'I meant on the inside.' He kissed her on the forehead and tore himself away while he still had some decency left in his bones. 'Good night.'

He left her with a sense that more needed to be said on the subject.

She had eyes in her head, she knew she had lovely hair, a good body, and a pretty face, but even Fay with her magic wand and the loan of a velvet dress couldn't change how she saw herself. Attractive on the outside, but inside she was like the elephant man, grotesque, twisted, and horrible.

Closeness to other people meant at some point she'd have to tell them about her epilepsy, but when and how was always an issue. They either overreacted or ended up defining her purely by her condition, or both. Sometimes they even saw her as abnormal, like she did herself.

A freak. The spaz kid. By pulling back she protected herself before it came to that.

At the same time it was probably the nicest thing anyone had ever said to her.

She paused on the landing to touch her lips, which were still warm from kissing Jason, and smiled when she heard a scuffling sound at the top of the stairs.

Lee, she thought. He might freak Charlie out, but it gave Helen a certain comfort knowing he was up there. It was almost as if he was watching over her.

The feeling of comfort lasted until she opened the door to her room. Cool, damp air hit her, and she switched on the light and noticed the open window. She'd forgotten to close it. Or had she? She couldn't remember, and not being able to remember whether she'd closed it or not made her flesh crawl.

It was nothing tangible, more like a sense that the walls and the furniture had witnessed a violation of her privacy while she was out.

She flicked the light switch again and, hidden by the darkness, went to peer outside. Everything seemed normal. Then, in the sparse light from the street lamps, her eyes were drawn to a car parked opposite the house. It was a dark car, nothing special about it, and inside it she could just about make out the silhouette of a person and the intermittent glow from what might be a lit cigarette. It had probably nothing to do with her, but after meeting Jason's father earlier and finding out about his tenuous connection to her family, and that he wasn't pleased she was living in his son's house, she couldn't prevent the little hairs on the nape of her neck from standing on end. Her body was telling her what her mind refused to accept.

Had Jason's father sent someone to spy on her?

A sudden paranoia hit her. Sweetman had told her where to find Fay. Sweetman worked for Aggie, the co-founder of the company headed by Letitia who might be having a fling with her uncle, who in turn did business with Jason's father. And Jason owned the halfway house where Fay, and now also Helen, had ended up. Whatever was happening here, Helen couldn't see through it.

For most of her life she'd tried to blend in and just be an anonymous face in the crowd, and succeeding pretty well except for the times when her epilepsy had brought unwanted attention. Now, everyone's eyes seemed to be focused on her, and it both alarmed and irritated the hell out of her.

She shut the window and drew the curtains roughly. Whoever was out there, for whatever reason, could just sod off. For the moment she had plenty of other things to worry about.

She kicked off her boots and shrugged out of the velvet dress, recalling Jason's hands on her as she did so. Her skin tingled where she'd felt the press of his fingers, as if he had scorched her through the fabric.

What had possessed her to push him away like that? She wanted him, and he wanted her, that was obvious. But how much did he want her? Was he prepared to take on all of her; the body afflicted by epilepsy, the soul damaged by years of bitterness and self-imposed isolation, both elements the cause and the curse of her whole being? No one in their right mind would, surely, and she wouldn't blame them.

She liked Jason. She didn't want him just physically, however gorgeous he was, and before she took that leap of faith, she had to make sure he didn't want her just physically either.

Enough. I can't think about this right now.

Sighing, she pushed the thought aside and slipped on a night T-shirt. With the bed covers tucked around her in the still-cold room, she was about to switch off the bedside light when she remembered the knives in Arseni's study. She'd believed him when he said there were four. That wasn't it.

She fetched the list Sweetman had given her and returned to bed, where she forced herself to read through it. She had so few memories of her mother, and if she could only picture some of the items in their house or even her mother holding something, anything, then maybe she could get those lost years back.

But she drew a blank. Nothing stood out, it was just things, with no memory attached to them at all. She'd expected it to be a slightly painful exercise, even when she read it for the second time. What she got instead was a gut-wrenching nothingness.

Wishing Jason was next to her, she curled up on the bed with her face buried in the pillow, and lived through the loss of her mother for the hundredth time.

Chapter Fifteen

From the top of the basement stairs Jason heard her close the door above. There was a certain finality to it, and he cursed himself for having so many scruples.

He wanted to go to bed with her, and she didn't seem repulsed by the idea, so why hadn't he pushed her harder?

Because his kind of trouble was the last thing she needed.

Everything about her screamed vulnerability, and there was too much she wasn't prepared to share. What had happened was probably for the best, because the more interested he was in her, the more his father would be too, and he had to spare her that.

Which meant controlling his urge to sleep with her. And that was bloody difficult.

Hearing movement on the top floor, he realised Lee was up there, lurking, watching, minding his own business, as usual, and everyone else's. He wondered if Lee fancied her too. It wouldn't surprise him. Helen's unique blend of independence and fragility could turn the head of any red-blooded man, but now Jason thought about it, he couldn't remember ever seeing Lee with a girl. Lee had never talked about girls, not that he talked much, and he even seemed afraid of women, Charlie in particular.

Perhaps Lee saw a kindred spirit in Helen, someone else who liked to hide in the shadows, and was trying to protect her. The thought of a mugger as her knight in shining armour made Jason smile.

He took the last few stairs down and closed the door to his own room behind him. Tossing his keys on his bedside table, he thought about his father's reaction when he'd mentioned the company Helen worked for. If he got involved with her, chances were he'd find himself slap-bang in the centre of his father's world despite all his attempts at keeping out of it.

Perhaps he ought to ask her to leave the house, under the pretext that they were getting too close for the whole flatmate scenario, but where would she go then? He could see now what Charlie had meant when she used the word 'trouble'. Helen was hot, in more ways than one, and he was bound to get his fingers burnt, but perhaps he was trouble for her as well.

Especially now that his father had become part of the equation.

Monday after work Helen decided to see Aggie. It was dark by the time she got there, and Mrs Sanders took ages answering the door.

'I'd like to see my grandmother.'

'What, now?'

'Yes, and? Do you have set visiting hours? She's not in a home yet.'

Mrs Sanders's lip curled with dislike. 'Mrs Ransome needs her rest, but now that you're here, you'd better come in, I suppose. Though I can't say if she'll be pleased to see you.'

In the back parlour Aggie was in bed with the cellular blanket across her legs, accompanied only by the light from a bedside lamp.

'She's asleep.' Mrs Sanders tried to block Helen from moving towards the bed.

'Then I'll wake her.' Side-stepping the nurse, Helen took Aggie's hand. It was heavy and swollen, yet the skin felt paper thin as if it had reached bursting point and couldn't hold the expanding flesh in place for much longer.

Aggie opened her eyes. 'Oh, it's you, girl. Thought you could fit me into your busy schedule, did you?'

'That's right.' Helen let go of her hand, then on impulse pressed a kiss to her forehead.

A vigilant gleam entered Aggie's eyes which hadn't been dulled by her diabetes. 'Are you going sentimental on me, child?'

'Is that a problem?'

'Not at all.' Aggie glanced at Mrs Sanders who was still hovering determinedly. 'Thank you. That'll be all.'

Scowling, the nurse left, closing the door behind her with enough force to make her aggravation known, yet not quite hard enough to cost her her job.

Aggie sighed. 'Such a temper.'

'Why don't you get someone nicer?'

'Oh, I haven't the energy. Anyway Mrs Sanders is very efficient. It can't be much fun for her being cooped up here with me.' Her fat face cracked into a wicked grin. 'You know, she puts me to bed early so she can watch *EastEnders* or another one of those horrid, tedious soaps.'

'Some people love them.'

'Then they haven't the sense they were born with!' Aggie waved a hand at her. 'Don't just stand there, girl. Pull up a chair. And switch on some lights. It's too dark in here.'

Helen switched on all the lamps in the room, and Aggie added another command.

'And the curtains. Mrs Sanders closes them too early. It drives me positively insane.'

'Do you want the door open as well? It's a bit stuffy in here.'

'Please.'

Immediately the air, crisp and fragrant with dewy roses and dampened earth, restored Helen's spirits. Aggie seemed to feel the same.

'Who would've thought Kensington could smell so sweet?'

'Not as sweet as Goa.'

Aggie opened her eyes. 'Do you miss it?'

'A bit. Strangely, I felt like I belonged there.'

'Nothing strange about that. We all need to feel we belong somewhere. Why not Goa?'

Then why did you reject me? Helen caught the words in time and just shrugged.

'So what's the reason for your visit today?'

'To see you.'

'You're not very adept at lying, my dear.'

Helen grimaced. When other people saw right through you, it didn't give you a chance to prepare what you wanted to say. 'I have some questions.'

'Hah!'

'You left a folder with Sweetman for me to read. Why didn't you give it to me yourself?'

Aggie sent her an unfathomable look, then made a dismissive gesture. 'I'm getting old. Thought I might forget where I'd put it if I kept it here. It was safer with Sweetman. He may not seem particularly organised, but he is.'

'Why did you give it to me?'

'I thought you might like all the facts. Didn't think you'd ever had a chance to read the whole story before.'

'Oh, come on! You collected those clippings years ago. Why would you do such a morbid thing?'

Aggie was quiet for a moment. 'I've often wondered if perhaps Fay might have been innocent.'

'How could she be? She was there. I saw her.'

'Yes, but what did you see exactly?'

Helen shuddered at the memory of that horrific scene.

'No one ever came forward, you know,' Aggie continued. 'There must've been other witnesses besides a five-year-old girl. It was early morning, yes, but this is London. There are always people about. Dog-walkers, commuters, rubbish men.'

'It was on the Common,' said Helen. 'It's like an island

among the traffic.' She shared Aggie's doubts, but Fay doing it was the only thing which made sense to her.

Who else had been there? She racked her brain, but found only disjointed images. She'd told Detective Wilcox about the dog, but someone must have been there with it. Why hadn't he or she come forward? Had they left before her mother was murdered?

She'd had a seizure in the car, but wasn't sure if she remembered it because she'd been told about it, or whether she truly remembered. How long had she been out? Seconds? Minutes?

The loss of her mother was such a personal issue that she couldn't see it strictly in logical terms, and she had to separate her emotions out if she was to think clearly. If you murdered someone, and there was a witness, what would you do with the witness?

The level-headed answer would be to get rid of the witness. The expression on Fay's face, shocked, distraught, apologetic, was etched on her mind, and no matter how many times she ran through the scenario, she couldn't picture Fay harming a child.

Who else, then, would kill only the victim and not the witness? Had they not noticed her on the back seat, or were they disturbed before they could finish?

A shiver ran down her spine, and she shuddered again. 'Who else could it have been?'

'In our line of work we make a few enemies,' said Aggie.

'What kind of enemies?' The image of Jason's father raising his glass to her jumped into her head.

'Business rivals. Disgruntled buyers or sellers, perhaps. An auction house only sells the work after it's been valued, and although we make every effort to check the provenance of what we sell, it's not always easy. Sometimes there are disputes.'

'Provenance?'

'The paperwork detailing ownership and source of a work. That sort of thing.'

'Are you saying things aren't as they should be at the company?'

'Of course they are,' Aggie snapped. 'But it's tricky. And then there was that uncle of yours. I never liked him. Couldn't bear his smarmy ways.'

'Was that why you kept me away from him, from my *only* living relative, because of his "smarmy" ways?'

'No, I ...' Aggie shook her head, slowly as if it was too much of an effort. 'It was the way he looked at Mimi, his sick brother's wife. And at you, too, as if he wanted to eat both of you. He was questioned by the police, you know. It didn't sit well with me. I ... well, I made a choice. But maybe I made a mistake.'

'Only one?' Helen made no attempt at hiding the sarcasm. Just then she noticed Aggie's ghostly pallor and that her lips were cracked. 'Are you comfortable? You look like you might be thirsty.'

'Parched, actually.'

Helen poured her a glass of water from a jug on the bedside table, and Aggie drank it down with heavy gulps. 'The blanket,' she said when she'd finished.

'You want me to pull it up a bit? I can close the back door as well, if you like. You mustn't get cold.'

'The blanket will do for now. The air is doing me good.' Aggie winked, and her face wobbled. 'But do remember to close it before you go otherwise I'll get in trouble with my jailer.'

'And we can't have that.' Helen pulled up the blanket and patted Aggie's hand. Perhaps this wasn't the time to talk about her mother's belongings. Then she looked at Aggie who lay with her eyes closed, and thought she may never get another opportunity. 'Aggie, why was everything sold?'

Her grandmother opened her eyes and sent her a puzzled look. 'What?'

'After my mother died, her things were sold at auction, by our own company, actually. Sweetman gave me a list. Who made that decision?'

Aggie frowned. 'I don't quite recall. Letitia, I think. Or it might have been Ruth. Does it matter?'

Helen let go of Aggie's hand. 'Of course it bloody matters!'

'Don't swear. It isn't attractive in a lady.'

'Whatever. I just want to know why my mother's stuff was sold. Didn't anyone think about me, about what I would like? It's as though you all wanted to wipe out every trace of her as if she'd never existed. Like I never existed.'

'Dear girl, don't carry on so. No one wanted to wipe anyone away. It was the practical, sensible thing to do. And you received the money from the sale. It's in trust, I think. Sweetman should have all the paperwork.'

'I've already spoken to him. I don't care about the money. I just want what belonged to her.' Helen's voice cracked. She knew she was acting childishly but couldn't help it.

'There wasn't anything you would've wanted anyway.'

'How do you know? There might have been some photos. I only have one of my parents.'

'It was all grown-up stuff. Mimi wasn't a great hoarder.'

'What about my toys? My rabbit?'

Aggie sent her a pitying look. 'Heavens girl, this was twenty years ago. You had some toys with you when you … when you left. As for the rabbit, I'm sure it went to a good home. Maybe the pet shop took it back. Either way it'll be long dead now.'

'How can you be so sure? Maybe the aunt just boiled it.'

Missing the point, Aggie snapped, 'Of course they didn't!

Neither of them even like rabbit, especially Letitia. Oh, she was always the fussy one. Fussy with her food, with clothes, with men. That's why she never married, you know. Because no one was ever good enough. I sometimes wonder if this striving for perfection was her way of compensating for the fact that she isn't much to look at. I think she envied your mother.'

'Why?'

'Because your mother was very beautiful. Both my girls resented that. When William and I got together, it never entered into our minds that there'd be so much dislike between our children. How they fought over the company, like toddlers squabbling over a toy. And when your mother died, Ruth, well, all the fight went out of her. She took a back seat, and Letitia was left holding it all together. I suppose one might say she got her way as far as the company was concerned, but I suspect that if she'd had the chance, she'd have wanted things to be different. She works too hard.'

'What do you mean "she got her way"?' Helen asked, a sudden suspicion niggling.

'She wanted to be in charge. To run it her way. Couldn't stand it that your mother had different ideas.'

A cold feeling stole over Helen and she clasped her hands tightly in her lap. She had to ask Aggie more about her aunts, to make sure they couldn't have been involved, unlikely as it was.

'About the company, well, it's big business, right? A lot of money involved. Do you think Ruth or Letitia could've had something to do with what happened to my mother? So they could get their hands on her shares?'

Aggie sent her a horrified look. 'Good heavens, girl! What goes on in that head of yours? These are my daughters we're talking about. They may have resented her a bit, but murder … well, you can rest assured that's not what happened,' she said firmly.

'I just need to know, that's all,' said Helen. She didn't particularly like either of her aunts, but welcomed Aggie's vehement protest and allowed it to quash her short-lived suspicions. Arseni's role in everything, *that* she wasn't quite so sure about.

Aggie suddenly remarked, 'Like I said, there wasn't anything worth keeping.'

'Excuse me?'

'Your mother's things. You were asking about them.'

'Well, yes, but …' That was way back in the conversation. Her grandmother's mind was obviously wandering.

'There was nothing of any real value.'

Why don't you let me be the judge of that, thought Helen, and resentment flared up again.

'Except she had some lovely antiques. And that Fabergé paper knife. Yes, that is a shame. I wonder what became of it.'

Helen thought of what her uncle had said, that Mimi had owned the other two. She also remembered Wilcox's explanation that Aggie had provided information on the knives. 'What can you tell me about my mother's knife?'

'It had a blue handle, sort of square if I remember correctly, and some intricate metal work.'

'It wasn't on the list Sweetman gave me. Do you think my mother might have sold it herself, before she died?'

Aggie shook her head. 'I very much doubt it. She used it all the time, always kept it on her desk in her office. You probably remember it. You know, the room just off the drawing room, with the yellow drapes and the view of the garden.'

'No, I don't,' Helen retorted. 'I don't remember any office or any paper knife. As it happens, I don't remember anything at all. Just my rabbit and one of my mother's handbags. The rest is a blank, more or less.'

Aggie put a swollen hand on Helen's arm. 'How dreadful for you not to be able to remember your mother. It's all my fault. I didn't do you a very good turn, did I?'

'No, you didn't.'

'I let you down.'

'Yes, you did,' Helen whispered, tears pressing.

'I wanted you away from that ... that man, and I didn't think you'd want to live with me.'

'Why wouldn't I have wanted to live with you?'

Aggie smiled wistfully. 'I was a cranky old woman. I couldn't have children under my feet. And you ... your epilepsy frightened me. I was terrified of the responsibility. Didn't think I could do it.'

'And now?'

'I'm sure you'll agree that I'm still a cranky old woman.'

'Uh-huh, but that's not what I meant.'

Heaving a sigh, Aggie sank back against the pillows. 'I think differently now. I could've hired a nurse. I could've rearranged my home in such a way that it would've been safe for you, for a child with your condition. You would've had access to private health care, private education. You would've gone to university—'

'Maybe not.'

'All right, maybe not,' she conceded, 'but you would've had the offer. Oh, hindsight is a wonderful thing, isn't it? Or a terrible thing, depending on how you look at it.'

Helen's anger deflated. She now understood Aggie's reasons for taking her away, and it took the sting out of what she'd always seen as her grandmother rejecting her. Suddenly that mattered more than anything else. People made mistakes, but it took an extraordinary person to admit to it. And it took an even more extraordinary person to forgive.

Can I forgive, she thought? *Is my heart big enough for that?*

She looked into Aggie's rheumy eyes and saw the uncertainty behind them, held firmly in check by a traditional upbringing and the 'stiff upper lip' morals which were probably instilled in her from birth. Another piece fell into place.

'Isn't it just?' She tucked the blanket more firmly around her grandmother's bloated figure. 'I expect you're tired. Sorry for pestering you with all my questions.'

'Don't apologise. If anyone's entitled to answers, you certainly are.' A sad, little smile creased Aggie's features. 'Do an old lady a favour and sit with me while I fall asleep.'

'Of course.'

'I'm glad you came. Thank you.'

'So am I.'

Aggie closed her eyes and settled back against her mountain of pillows. The silence between them was soothing. Things had been said, the air cleared, and inside Helen a small flutter of happiness rose as she watched the old lady's chest rise and fall.

Suddenly Aggie's eyes flew open again. 'I do think that woman, the one who went to prison … oh, what was her name again? I'm so forgetful these days.'

'Fay.'

'Yes, Fay. How could I forget?' Aggie smiled weakly. 'I do think she conveniently played into someone else's hands.'

Helen stayed for another hour, mulling over Aggie's theory about Fay. She'd never thought of that, but had to now when her own doubts were getting stronger every day. She'd have liked to discuss it with Aggie but had probably taxed her enough. She'd have to wait, but not too long. It was possible that Aggie didn't have much time left.

When her grandmother was fast asleep, she tiptoed around the room switching off the lights except the lamp by the bed, closed the garden door and drew the curtains again. Mrs Sanders saw her out and locked up behind her.

At the sound of the last bolt being driven home, the mental image of a jail door clanging shut leapt into her mind. She shivered and told herself not to be so silly.

But the image stayed with her.

Chapter Sixteen

Jason had called Trevor with what he'd learned about Helen's background and was now waiting impatiently for more information, but Trevor hated being chased, and Jason didn't want to piss him off.

He no longer believed her story that she'd accidentally caused the death of a child, so his concern about vengeful parents wasn't an issue any more. But instead of relief, he now felt even more concerned. Who was she really hiding from? Why had she only met her uncle for the first time a few weeks ago? And what was Mimi Stephanov's connection? Trevor's paranoia about dodgy Russians was rubbing off on him. Jason needed to find out as much as he could about the old murder.

He remembered the folder she'd been so reluctant for him to see and found himself outside the door to her room before realising he was about to break the most important of his own house rules.

Damn.

He retreated to the kitchen to mull this over and found Lee munching toast and poring over a large, glossy atlas.

'Got yourself a library card yet?' he asked.

Lee shook his head.

Jason put the kettle on and dropped a teabag into a mug. 'You know, what you're doing could technically be construed as stealing.'

'I always b-bring them back.'

'You borrow books without permission.'

'Yes, *borrow*.' Lee frowned.

Jason laughed. 'Oh, you're hopeless.'

'That's w-what everyone keeps telling me.'

'I didn't mean it like that.' Jason softened. Thwarted in his attempts at playing detective, by his own principles no less, he'd forgotten why he was running this house. He didn't know Lee well but noticed he'd read anything, from the backs of cereal packets to computer manuals, with the same deep concentration. Perhaps this was a way to reach him.

'I have some books in my room. You're welcome to borrow them whenever you like. I won't fine you if they're late.'

Lee's dark eyes lit up. 'What sort of books?'

'Well, what are you interested in?'

'History, geography, art. P-plants and animals. Space.'

'Ri-ight, I probably have some of that. Just knock on my door sometime.' Jason glanced at the huge atlas on the table. 'Anyway, how do you smuggle such a big book out of the library?'

Lee grinned. 'I have a b-big bag.'

Sipping his tea, Jason watched Lee turning the shiny pages slowly, almost reverently, and knew he didn't have to worry about his books being returned in poor condition.

It came to him in a flash. Borrowing, returning. *Library*.

Two librarians were on duty, one a young woman, the other an older man with a pair of reading glasses balancing on the tip of his nose. He approached the older of the two.

'Hi,' he said, 'I'm looking for some information on a local murder, but I'm not sure of the date.' He gave the librarian the few details he had.

The librarian frowned. 'Hmm, it does ring a bell. I think it might have been twenty or twenty-five years back. Let me take a look.'

Together they quickly found the microfiche dated from where the librarian suggested Jason start his search, and he began looking through old articles.

Shortly before closing time his eyes were smarting

from staring at the backlit screen. This was tedious in the extreme. Perhaps he should call it quits for now and wait until tomorrow, or until Trevor rang with whatever he had managed to dig up.

Then he remembered the way his father had looked at Helen at the dinner party. Interested. Just how much did his father know about Helen?

He returned to the screen with a burst of new energy and flicked through the newspapers again, faster this time. It had to be there.

'We're closing in five minutes.' The woman librarian hovered nearby. 'I'll have to turn off the computers now.'

'Just give me one more minute.' Jason flicked to another screen. *Come on, come on.*

And there it was. The screaming headlines, the teasers, the hue and cry, enticing a righteously angry public to buy the newspaper and read the whole sordid tale on the inside pages.

Girl, 5, Witnesses Brutal Slaying ...
'Don't Hurt My Mummy', she pleaded ...
Child Identifies Mother's Killer ...

He flicked to page two of the last article, but just then the screen went black.

Thwarted for the second time Jason went to check on the stall, which Neil was manning for him.

'Thanks for helping out,' he said.

'No problem.' Neil slipped back to his own stall. 'I managed to shift that Led Zeppelin album you didn't think anyone would go for.'

Jason's eyebrows rose. He'd priced the mint condition vinyl lower than online sellers, but it was still in the three figures, and no one seemed to have that kind of money to spend these days. If anyone could sell the unsellable, it was Neil. 'Wow. You're better at this than I am.'

Neil grinned. They both knew it was true.

'Winston around?'

'Having his tea.' Neil nodded in the direction of the refreshments stall, where a mop of greying dreads stood out in the dusk.

On his way back from the library an unpleasant thought had sneaked up on Jason. He'd asked Trevor to check if Helen was one of his father's spies, but hadn't really believed it. Now he wondered again how she had known about the room. If she wasn't a spy for Derek, could she be working for someone else? One of his father's enemies perhaps? As much as he hated the idea that his father was right to worry about his welfare, he needed to debunk that theory sooner rather than later.

'Winston, my man, I have a question for you.'

'Round here answers cost money.' Winston pronged a forkful of baked potato into his mouth.

'I'm hoping you'll answer this one for free. You know the new girl who's moved into my house?'

'I seen her a coupla times. Blonde, curvy. Pretty if you like de misrable kind.'

'That sounds like her. Did you tell her about my vacant room, by any chance?'

Winston eyed him disdainfully. 'You want an estate agent, mon, you look in dem Yellow Pages. I tell her nothing.'

Once again Jason found himself outside Helen's door, but this time he had no problem with breaking his own rules.

He'd always known she was lying to him, or rather withholding certain elements which made up the whole truth. It hadn't bothered him, and he'd merely seen it as her way of protecting herself, just as he wanted to protect her. People did it all the time, even those who had nothing particular to hide, mostly to present themselves in a better light.

When he'd started digging, he suspected that her reality was slightly different. A little white lie, involving Winston, had got her into Jason's house. Normally he wouldn't worry too much about that if it hadn't been for who his father was.

He half-expected the door to protest as he violated her personal space, and he almost felt the silent outrage when he touched the few things she had. Her desk was tidy, and in the desk drawers he found only pens, paper and a hand-written letter postmarked Goa, which he resisted reading. There was plenty of space between the clothes in her wardrobe, and the sock drawer below held nothing personal except a jewellery box made from Indian rubber wood. He didn't even glance at her underwear. Only a perv would do that.

Tempting, though.

There was only one place left to hide things, something ex-cons did a lot, which was incongruous because he was now sure she hadn't been to prison. Lifting the mattress, he found the folder he was looking for.

'Bingo.'

Riffling through it, he recognised some of the articles he'd seen on microfiche, as well as some more in-depth ones. The worst of the fat headlines had been cut off.

His anger turned to horror as he read the full story of the five-year-old girl who'd seen her mother stabbed to death. A chill ran through him as he imagined her terror and confusion, and an ache spread in his chest for the kid whose life had been destroyed.

Then he turned a page to an article where names withheld during the trial were finally released.

The child had been Helen. And she was here because of Fay.

Thankfully Helen was on her own when she came back.

What he had to say to her was between them, for the time being. He waited for her in the kitchen, and when she saw his expression, her eyes immediately took on a wary look.

Smart woman.

'Perhaps you'd like to explain the meaning of this,' he said before she could come up with another lie, and tossed the manila folder on the kitchen table.

'Have you read …?' There was panic in her voice.

'Yes,' he replied. 'The whole damn thing.'

She paled.

'I searched your room,' he said. 'And before you get your knickers in a twist over that, let's get one thing straight. I own this house. People here are vulnerable, particularly Fay, though she doesn't show it. You came here under false pretences. What were you planning to do? Hurt her?'

'To begin with.' She met his eyes defiantly.

Well, at least she was honest.

'And now?'

She shook her head.

'What changed?' he asked.

'I like her. Didn't think I would, but I can't help it.' Her shoulders sagged, and she sighed.

'What about the dead child? Another lie?'

'I guess it depends on perspective.'

The look in her eyes squeezed his heart. He realised it was a part of *her* that had died as a child.

'Are you going to throw me out?'

He had every right to, but he just couldn't do it. She was vulnerable too. 'You say your feelings for Fay have changed. How can I be sure of that?'

She picked up the folder and held it to her chest, not defensively this time, but as if the yellowed clippings inside represented something precious. 'I think that … maybe …'

'Maybe what?' he interrupted, more harshly than he intended.

'That maybe she didn't do it.'

It had never occurred to him that Fay could be innocent. It wasn't for him to judge. But if Helen believed it, he supposed that might be enough top keep the peace in the house. He so hated the idea of having to show her the door.

'Okay, I believe you, but at the first sign of trouble you're out on your ear, do you understand?'

She nodded, eagerly. Again he had the feeling of walking all over someone who couldn't defend herself. At the same time, after what she'd been through as a child, she wasn't completely broken, and the thought filled him with awe. If he could only get close to her.

'Will you tell the others?' she asked.

He'd said he believed her, but having her in the house was still a risk. For a moment he tossed the various scenarios in his head, then made his decision. This was one way of earning her trust, her respect. Maybe even her affection.

'No.'

'Jim's had an accident.' Bill caught Helen on Tuesday in the packing room where she was tagging a consignment of antique furniture.

'Jim? How?'

'Got knocked off his scooter at Hyde Park Corner. The bike's all right, but he's been carted off to Chelsea & Westminster hospital. A constable just brought the scooter back to the yard.'

'Will he be okay?' She hoped so, having begun to appreciate the youth with his glass-half-empty outlook. It made her own glass appear rather full.

'I don't know how bad it is.' Bill's face was pale, and he

was twisting his work coat between his hands. 'My sister's going to kill me. I was supposed to look out for him.'

'What's your sister got to do with it?'

'Jim's my nephew, ain't he? Got him the job and all, though she weren't too happy about him whizzing all over London on a glorified bike.'

Well, what do you know, Helen thought. *This company is just one big, happy family.*

'I'm off to see him now,' he said, shifting from one foot to another. 'The thing is, love, I'm not good with hospitals. They give me the willies.'

Helen tied a last tag on the leg of a Regency chair. 'You want me to come with you?'

'That'd be great.'

After letting Mrs Deakin know she was going with Bill, they both changed out of their work clothes and took a taxi. Bill was still pale when they pulled up in front of the hospital, possibly even paler, but whether it was the prospect of entering the place, or the uncertain fate of his nephew, or even the wrath of his sister, was anyone's guess. Perhaps a combination of all three.

A modern building, Chelsea & Westminster hospital featured a marbled atrium, white walls and an upward view of a glass-covered roof. Works of art some twenty feet tall were strung across internal garden areas, and only the wheelchairs and dressing gowns gave away that this was a hospital and not a museum of modern art.

That and a god awful cocktail of smelly bodies and disinfectant. Helen wrinkled her nose.

On the ward they found Jim in a bed with his leg plastered and in a sling, and wearing a glum expression on his face.

'Jimbo, my lad, glad to see you're okay.'

'Okay?' Jim whined. 'I've only gone and broken me bleedin' leg, and you think I'm all right?'

'It could've been worse, the way you drive.'

Jim sent Helen a funereal smile. 'So the old gaffer managed to drag you down here with him? 'Fraid of hospitals, he is. Are you gonna have a go at me too?'

'Not unless you want me to.' Helen sat down on the end of the bed.

After Bill and Jim had gone over every detail of the accident, Jim said, 'It's me job I'm worried about. I'm gonna lose it if I don't get someone to cover for me.'

'I know someone who might stand in for you while you're in hospital. I'll ask my au— er, Ms Walcott if you like.' Bill's eyebrows shot up.

'Thanks, you're a mate,' said Jim.

'I don't think she'll care who's doing the job as long as someone is.'

'Yeah, people like that don't know who does the real work.' Jim went gloomy again. 'They drive around in their fancy cars and go to fancy board meetings while the rest of us work our arses off. To them I'm just a nobody.'

Bill said nothing, but kept his eyes on Helen, and she read the mixture of horror and amusement in them as if he'd discovered the missing link.

Talk about putting your foot in it. Or rather a scuffed Doc Marten boot.

'I should've known,' said Bill when they left the hospital. 'You have your mother's chin.'

Helen sent him a sideways look as they crossed the road. 'The cat's out of the bag, then.'

'The cat most certainly is.' Bill stopped in the middle of the road and got hooted at. Ignoring the irate driver, he swept her up in a bear hug, swung her around, then put her down again as if she was made of porcelain, wiped his eyes on a handkerchief and blew his nose noisily. 'To think you came back, after all that.'

'I have a stake in the company, as it happens.'

'My, my, Mimi's daughter. You know, I knew your mother from when she was this high.' Bill put his hand out at around hip height. 'That little love was always with her father. Sitting on his desk, painting and drawing while he worked. Pretty as a picture. Never knew her mother, as far as I recall.'

That makes two of us, thought Helen. Why did people insist on creating this fiction that a relationship between a widowed father and his daughter was something enchanted when in reality not having a mother was a pretty shitty situation for a little girl to be in?

'Of course, I went with your grandfather when he and your gran merged the companies,' Bill went on. 'It was an exciting time, though not easy for your poor mum. Them other two were a right pair of witches. Didn't like their mother marrying again or some such.' He sniffed. 'But you couldn't keep Mimi down. I think they came to respect her in the end, especially your aunt Letitia. The other one hated her guts, but obviously she was too much of a nob to show it.'

Lost for words, Helen stared at him. One more link to the past. Bill had known her mother and, like Mrs Deakin, actually liked her. The permanent ache inside her grew a little weaker as she fitted another piece into the puzzle.

She had a million questions, and hardly knew where to start, but since Bill had known her mother in a work capacity, maybe this was the place to begin.

'You knew her well?'

'So-so,' he said with a little hand gesture. 'First she was the boss's daughter, then she was the boss. We didn't socialise. She was nice to work with, though.'

'What was her involvement with the company?'

'As involved as you can get in a family business. Knee-deep. Had great plans for it, although her plans didn't always go down well with the other two.'

This squared with what she'd learnt from Aggie. But there was more, so much more, and before she could stop herself, the questions spilled out of her like water from an overflowing tub. She bombarded Bill in the taxi and out of it, and he answered what he could.

'What were her work practices like? Am I anything like her? To work with, I mean?'

'As you might expect. And no, you're nothing like her.'

Bill clammed up all of a sudden, and she chewed over his guarded reply. The company had meant a lot to her mother, that much she'd understood, but where Mimi's commitment was concerned, whether driven by family pride or just making money, she was none the wiser. Just because money meant very little to herself that didn't mean her mother had been the same.

When they got back, an auction selling Dutch masters was in full swing, but Helen managed to pull Letitia aside to talk about Jim's predicament.

Her aunt listened with only half an ear, distracted by the sales for which Ransome & Daughters would earn a hefty commission. Helen glanced over Letitia's shoulder. As always the chauffeur wasn't far away, and it struck her that he seemed more like a bodyguard than a driver. It made sense for Letitia to have one, if she was associated with people like Jason's father, but his presence made her prickle with irritation.

'Yes, fine.' Letitia waved her hand dismissively. 'Do whatever is needed. Does this friend of yours have her own transport?'

'Jim's scooter hasn't been damaged. Bill checked it earlier. Charlie could use that if it's okay with you.'

'Sure. Just don't bore me with paperwork. Speak to Mrs Deakin.'

Helen left her and hunted down Mrs Deakin who promised to prepare the paperwork in case Charlie took the temporary job.

'She's been unemployed for a while, so I think she will.'

Mrs Deakin sent her a look suggesting that there was a reason unemployed people stayed unemployed, and it wasn't an approving one.

At the house she sought out Charlie and told her the good news. Charlie tossed the TV remote aside and flung her arms around Helen almost violently. For a moment Helen went rigid, then allowed herself to enjoy the contact.

'When do I start?'

'Tomorrow, if you can. And you'll need to spruce up a bit. Get some of those rings out of your nose.'

'If I *can*? Are you joking? I can start now!' She skipped to the cupboard and pulled out two shot glasses and a bottle of vodka. 'Let's celebrate.'

'Not for me, thanks.'

'Well, I'll have one.' Charlie filled a glass to the brim.

Helen moistened her lips with her tongue. She didn't particularly like vodka, but the idea of being able to have a drink, just like that, without second thoughts, filled her with envy. She may be fabulously wealthy now, certainly by her own standards, but money couldn't cure her epilepsy or remove the restrictions it imposed on her. Nothing could.

It was a pain in the butt.

Charlie knocked back the vodka, and instead of making her high as a kite, the alcohol seemed to bring her down to earth. 'What sort of job is it?'

'Courier, mainly, and general dogsbody. Can you drive a scooter?'

'I'm sure I can learn.'

'It doesn't bother you that Jim fell off it?'

'No. It'll be fun.'

'God help us!' Charlie's optimism was infectious. Grinning, Helen shook her head.

It took Charlie only two days to charm everyone she came into contact with, and she quickly settled in with the dull, daily routine, which seemed less dull now that she was there. She went with Helen and Bill on their visits to Jim, to talk about scooters, but more likely because it broke the monotony.

Jim found common ground with Charlie as words like throttle, ground clearance and carburettor flew across his hospital bed, and his mood improved dramatically. Helen experienced a pang of jealousy, not about Jim, but Jason.

She hadn't spoken to him since he'd confronted her about the file, but he'd kept his promise about not saying anything, which must mean that he didn't mistrust her completely. Which was a good thing.

Even so, she stayed out of his way in case her presence somehow provoked him to go back on his word, and that meant brooding alone in her room. Which was a bad thing.

She enjoyed travelling to and from work with Charlie. Charlie had an ability to talk about everything and nothing at the same time, not really expecting an answer, and it gave her some head space without being separate from the rest of the world.

Leaving work on Friday evening, she looked around for Charlie, checking both the staff room and other back rooms, then ducked inside the auction room in case she was there. Bill emerged from the dark with his bundle of keys.

'I'm about to lock up out back. You've finished out there, haven't you?'

Helen nodded. 'I'm looking for Charlie. Seen her anywhere?'

'Nope. Must've left.'

Bill continued out the back, muttering to himself.

Charlie wouldn't have left without telling her, so she had to be around somewhere, and the only place left to check was upstairs. Charlie was probably chatting to Letitia's secretary, although how she'd managed to charm that sour lemon defied all reason.

But the secretary's office was empty, the furniture and computer just boxy, dark shapes. A thin blue light coming from underneath the door to Letitia's office caught Helen's eye. Had Letitia forgotten to switch off her PC, or was Charlie stupid enough to make herself at home in the big boss's office? Anxiety mingled with exasperation made her glance over her shoulder before she opened the door, but Ruth's office to the other side was empty too.

Letitia's office looked much like it did during working hours. The floor length curtains were drawn, though, and the only light came from a large flat screen monitor. Charlie was tapping away with her eyes fixed on the screen, and didn't take any notice of Helen when she came in. Her irritation rose.

'What are you doing? You're not supposed to be in here.'

'What's it look like I'm doing?'

'Trespassing.'

'I'm working,' she said. 'Entering the data of the shipment we had yesterday.'

'You don't need the boss's computer for that. Use the one in the packing room. That's what it's there for. We all use that one.'

'Someone else was doing something on it, and I was bored.'

Helen sat on the desk and watched Charlie's fingers move at a furious pace across the keyboard, a fingertip version of *Riverdance*. 'How did you get in anyway? It must have been password protected.'

'Social engineering.'

'Eh?'

Charlie rolled her eyes. 'Social engineering. You know, when you find out what people's children or pets are called, or what their birthday is, where they were born, their favourite colour and so on. Lots of people use names and dates for their passwords.'

'Oh, I forgot. That's your area of expertise. So what's Le— Ms Walcott's birthday, then?'

'Haven't a clue.' Grinning wickedly, Charlie nodded towards a glossy photograph on the desk. 'But she likes her car. That creepy chauffeur of hers told me she's named it Amanda.'

'Amanda?'

'Yes. She-who-must-be-loved.'

'Who? Letitia?'

'It's Latin,' Charlie explained. 'That's what Amanda means in Latin. I did learn *something* while I was banged up. Anyway, her password is *Amanda1*. It wasn't difficult to work out. Besides, it's just for a laugh.'

'Seriously, though,' said Helen, 'you could get us both in a lot of trouble if Security finds us in here.'

'Not as much trouble as I could land our precious boss in. Have a look.' Charlie turned the monitor so Helen could see more clearly.

'What am I looking at?'

'You tell me.'

Helen leaned closer. On screen was an Excel spreadsheet, the sort they all used for their entries, with columns for date entered, item number, owner, description, auction estimate, as well as date sold and the actual sum the item fetched. Everything looked exactly like on the main computer, except here an extra column with alternative figures had been added which didn't correspond to the figures entered when the items were sold. Helen was sure about this, because she remembered marking some of these items herself.

'She's on network like the rest of the PCs in the building,' said Charlie, 'except her hard disk is partitioned. The C: drive is her own, the D: drive is shared. This file was on her C: drive.'

A peculiar heat spread in Helen's face. Why was Letitia marking items which had been sold at a set price with a higher price in her own files?

'You say you could land her in trouble. How exactly?'

'It's obvious. She's selling for more than she declares to the tax man. Trust me, I've seen some scams in my time.'

'Maybe that extra column is just wishful thinking on her part,' Helen suggested. 'You can't be sure.'

Charlie sent her a look which told Helen precisely what she thought of that theory.

'But where does the money come from and go to?' Helen asked. 'It doesn't make sense.'

'Does it have to? Isn't it enough to know that something's going on?'

A murmur of voices rose up from the hall, and Helen started. She didn't fancy getting caught in here.

'I really think we should go. If these are Letitia's personal files, she'll know when she last looked at them and notice if someone else has as well.'

'No, she won't. I know this cute little tool which changes timestamps.' Charlie pressed a few buttons faster than Helen could follow with her eyes.

'Yeah, what does that do? Delete all traces?'

Charlie shook her head. 'It means that if you're going to

cover your tracks, you make a note of the timestamps of the directories and files you're going to access, and then after you've accessed them, you can reset the time stamp.'

Helen jumped down from the desk. 'All the same, I'd rather not know about it, so if you don't mind, could we get out of here, please? I expect you'd like to keep your job even if it is only temporary.'

But when they left Letitia's office, Helen regretted that she hadn't printed out the file.

Chapter Seventeen

Head whirring, Helen trundled after Charlie. On their way out they ran into the security guy, another one of Charlie's slaves, and Charlie said something that made him laugh. Listening to their banter, Helen wished she could just get on with everyone like Charlie did. There had to be a special knack to it.

A dark car was parked across the road, on a double yellow line. Someone was inside having a cigarette, a thin grey line of smoke escaping from the open window and rising straight up in the evening air. It looked like the same sort of car as the one she'd seen outside Jason's house on the night of her uncle's party, and although it probably wasn't, she couldn't prevent a tight feeling in the pit of her stomach.

'I might go and see Jim,' said Charlie. 'He's back home now.'

'Sorry?'

'I wanna say hello to Jim.' Charlie twirled one of her matted dreadlocks around her finger. 'He gets a bit grumpy, being cooped up with only his mum fussing over him.'

'Sure.'

'Are you okay about us not going back on the train together?'

A strange noise buzzed in Helen's ears, and she found it hard to take in what Charlie was saying. 'Yeah. No problem. I'm absolutely fine.'

'You don't sound fine.'

'I am.' She forced a smile. 'Off you go. By the way, I think Jim likes you.'

Charlie grinned. 'Jim's all right, I suppose.'

'Yeah, he is.'

Charlie dashed in the opposite direction to catch a bus, and Helen headed for the tube station. When she crossed Berkeley Square, under the shade of the trees, she noticed that the dark car was following the road around the park. At the end the driver stopped as if waiting for her, revving the engine aggressively, and suddenly sped off towards Piccadilly.

Staring after it, she took it as a warning. The only problem was, she didn't know against what.

Her feet took her to Aggie's house. On the path in front of the house she stumbled across a soft bundle, picked it up and saw it was a cardigan. She checked the pockets for identity of the owner, but found only a sterile plastic wrapper with a syringe and an unopened sachet of antiseptic wipe.

'You dropped this,' she said to the loathsome Mrs Sanders when she let her in, this time without protest.

'Not mine,' said the nurse and disappeared down the hall. Helen checked the grandfather clock. *EastEnders* was about to start. So much for the around-the-clock care her grandmother needed and presumably paid a lot of money for.

'Well, what am I supposed to do with it?' she muttered. She held the cardigan up in front of her and caught the faint scent of lemon verbena. Ruth's perfume. Perhaps Ruth was helping Aggie with her insulin injections?

None of my business.

Aggie was asleep in her hospital-like bed. Helen dropped Ruth's cardigan on a chair, pulled the curtains back and opened the window to banish the familiar stuffiness in the room. Aggie stirred lightly but didn't wake, and she drew up a chair and sat down by her grandmother's bedside. Her insides were churning with more questions and uncertainties, and she resisted the temptation to shake her grandmother awake.

The minutes ticked by, and the sound of Aggie's raspy breathing and the curtains swishing slightly calmed her and enabled her to apply some logic.

Letitia was involved in something not quite right, and Aggie really ought to know, but she didn't have the heart to tell her. Or did Aggie already know? Her aunts and Mimi had squabbled over the company, in Aggie's own words. And Aggie had been equally tied up with the company at the time of Helen's mother's death, perhaps more so than her aunt Letitia …

Was it all just one big nasty conspiracy to do away with Mimi and ruin Helen's life?

Her paranoia had it making sense, then she pushed the thought aside because the idea was frankly ridiculous. Why would Aggie urge Helen to come home, suggest she find out more about Fay, if she'd been involved herself? It would be more logical for her to avoid the subject and leave Helen to rot in India. And if Letitia, Aggie's own flesh and blood, had had something to do with it, and Aggie knew about it, she'd do everything to protect her daughter instead of stirring things up.

That's what mothers did, protected their children.

Except instead of protecting her daughter, Mimi had unwittingly exposed her to a killer.

She went back to that fatal morning. She'd had a seizure in the car and woken up to find Fay covered in her mother's blood. There'd been no doubt in her mind who was to blame.

Yet now she saw everything in a different light. Mimi was meeting someone, Helen didn't know who. There had been a bag on the back, a beaded and sequinned bag, with papers in it.

She remembered what her mother had said to her when they got in the car. 'You mustn't touch it, darling. It's got important stuff in it that someone wants.'

'But I like the bag. Can we keep the bag, please, Mummy?' she'd pleaded, but Mimi had shushed her.

And she *had* touched it. She'd been a naughty girl and ignored what her mother said because she'd been looking for her medicine, and then her mother had died. Guilty tears, irrational tears, pressed in the corners of her eyes.

The bag had disappeared, and it didn't take a genius to work out that someone had taken it and maybe her mother had died because of what was in it.

Aggie had said Helen was safer away from the family. If the papers had something to do with the company this could have led to one of the others taking matters in their own hands, but then why would Aggie want the real killer exposed instead of leaving the blame with Fay as it had been for twenty years, especially if it turned out to have something to do with either of her daughters? It went against the grain, and she didn't believe that this was Aggie's perverse way of making amends for her neglect. Her grandmother was too direct for that. In fact, hadn't Aggie pointed out it was Helen's uncle that she didn't trust?

She looked at her grandmother's sleeping form, at a face she'd both hated and loved. The hatred had gone now. Aggie couldn't be involved, she just couldn't. The thought was too unbearable.

On Monday morning Letitia called Helen into her office. To her surprise Ruth was there too, standing by the window, arms crossed. She sent Helen a sour look.

Uh-oh, Helen thought, when Letitia didn't invite her to sit down. Despite Charlie's reassurances, had Letitia discovered they'd been on her computer?

But her aunt threw her with her question. 'Are you the careful sort?'

'Er, yes, I think so.'

'Good, because I want you to pick up a parcel for me. From Stephanov's house. Your loving uncle,' she added as an afterthought, any spite too well-disguised to be noticed.

From her position by the window Ruth uttered a contemptuous snort.

Helen ignored her. 'A parcel? Don't the drivers normally do that?'

'They're all out on other jobs, and I need it before eleven.' She handed Helen a business card. 'Here's the address.'

'I know where it is.'

'Oh, you do, do you?' Letitia's pencilled eyebrow rose a notch.

'I was there at his dinner party.'

'Of course, you were. I'd completely forgotten. Quite the little family reunion, I should imagine.'

This time there was definitely a hint of spite. 'Not really. I don't have a lot to say to him.'

'Mm, a shame, since he's the only family you have.'

Helen looked from one aunt to the other. Letitia was drawing the lines very clearly, but Ruth looked like she wanted to add something, then thought better of it. It shouldn't hurt because neither of them meant anything to her, but the barb found its mark. Letitia had changed from the woman who'd welcomed her back only recently and had fed the hope of some sort of normality in Helen's life. Why had she turned cold again if she didn't know about that business with the computer?

Because of Arseni? Hell, she was welcome to him.

And Ruth? She seemed the same, neither cold nor welcoming, just … watchful, maybe.

Helen's anger rose, but she kept a lid on it. She was a co-owner of this company and had just as much right to be here as either of them. 'What's in the parcel?'

'Never you mind.'

'I think I'm entitled to know what goes on around here. After all, I own a percentage of the shares. Voting shares, as far as I know.'

Ruth laughed suddenly. 'Looks like she's got you by the proverbials, Lettie.'

Lettie? Helen turned to Ruth. There was genuine mirth in her eyes, and she gave an imperceptible nod of what looked like approval. Warmth spread in her chest, and she bit her lip to stop herself from smiling.

Letitia's nostrils flared. 'I hope you don't mean that the way I think you do,' she said, ignoring her sister.

'I dunno, you tell me.'

'When you've worked yourself up to my position, ask me that question again, and I might give you a different answer. Until then, no, you're not entitled to know everything that goes on around here.'

They stared at each other across the desk, tension crackling. Despite Letitia's arrogance Helen had a grudging respect for her. It was also possible she was in trouble, and Helen had lost so many people already, it was beginning to look like carelessness. She couldn't back down over this.

Sighing, Letitia was the first to break eye contact. 'It's a valuable Russian icon which belongs to your uncle, and now he wants to sell it. On the quiet. It's not going in the catalogue. Satisfied?'

'Just about.'

'Now would you please get yourself into a taxi and go over there? I've arranged for a private buyer to be here for lunch. I need it before then.'

Helen hadn't seen Arseni since Aggie had voiced her distrust of him, and a low anger had simmered inside her afterwards knowing it was partly because of him that Aggie had sent her away. And if Aggie was right? Had he played an even bigger role in Helen's fate? Perhaps this would be an opportunity to ask some of her many questions.

However, getting to her uncle's house and back in time for the deadline turned out to be problematic. Stuck in the back of a taxi, Helen could only watch as the traffic moved along at a snail's pace. A coach, having attempted an illegal U-turn along Piccadilly, was blocking the road. She rapped on the glass screen separating her from the cab driver. 'What's happening?'

'Looks like he's broken down,' came the reply. 'You in a hurry?'

'I am, actually.'

The cab driver shook his head. 'Well, your best bet is to get out and walk it, then. We could be stuck here for a long time, I reckon.'

'All right. Thanks.' Helen paid the driver and began walking in the direction of Knightsbridge. After her battle of wills with Letitia, she wanted to show that she was able to carry out instructions to the letter. A small part of her told her that her mother would have approved.

A screech of brakes made her turn around.

'Fancy a lift?' Charlie was astride Jim's scooter with the engine sputtering and the visor of her helmet pushed up.

'On that thing?'

'Got a better idea?'

Helen looked at the traffic around her. The coach was still blocking the road accompanied by a cacophony of impatient car horns, and the coach driver, a scowling dark-haired man with a five o'clock shadow, was leaning out of the nearside window, shouting and gesticulating in a foreign language which needed no translation.

'Good point.' She climbed on the scooter behind Charlie. 'Where are we going?'

Helen rattled off Arseni's address. Charlie turned the

throttle, and with a blast accelerated down the road like an angry wasp, narrowly missing the back of the coach.

'Wait!' Helen screeched. 'I haven't got a helmet!'

'Oh, come on. Live a little.'

She closed her eyes as Charlie weaved in and out through the slow-moving traffic, mounting the pavement when gaps between cars were too narrow for the scooter, but after a while she began to enjoy the crazy ride. The wind played with her hair, and her insides did a flip every time Charlie drove off the edge of a pavement and they found themselves airborne for a second or two.

When they pulled up outside her uncle's house, her heart was hammering wildly, her cheeks flushed, and she was relieved to be alive.

Charlie took off her helmet and gawped at the house. 'Wow, fancy place. Why are we here?'

'A pick-up for Letitia. I'd better go in alone.'

'No way.' Charlie locked the scooter to a sign post with a chunky chain. 'Why should you have all the fun?'

Helen sighed. So much for the opportunity to ask questions.

The maid showed them into Arseni's office.

'Helen. My dear niece.' Arseni cocked his head to one side as if she was a stray puppy who had finally found its way home. 'How lucky I am they sent you.'

Helen felt Charlie's eyes on her and cursed herself for not insisting she waited outside. She could have spun some yarn about client confidentiality or something like that. Jason knew about the connection but had not, as far as she was aware, told anyone about it. Charlie was going to give her hell.

Her uncle spotted Charlie. 'And who is this charming young'—he looked her up and down and raised a quizzical eyebrow—'*person*?'

'Charlie,' said Charlie. 'Charlotte,' she added with a mutinous expression and dug her hands deep in the trouser pockets.

'Ah, a beautiful name for an English rose.'

Charlie snorted

'The traffic was bad,' said Helen, 'so Charlie gave me a lift on her scooter. Letitia told me to be as quick as possible, and that the parcel is small enough.' She hoped her uncle would hand it over straight away. The sooner she and Charlie were out of here the better.

'On a scooter? Is it safe?'

'As safe as any kind of courier.' Arseni's attempt at playing the concerned relative all of a sudden irked her, but she decided not to mention Charlie's inventiveness when it came to negotiating London traffic.

Mollified, he unlocked a desk drawer and took out a flat packet wrapped in brown paper. It was small, smaller than a sheet of printer paper and roughly three inches thick. He passed it to Helen as well a large envelope, which she tucked under her arm.

'This is important paperwork. Your aunt will know what to do with it.'

Helen felt Charlie stiffen behind her at the word 'aunt' and hoped she didn't make the connection. 'We need to get back,' she said.

Arseni cocked his head to one side. 'So soon? You are not staying for lunch? You can bring your friend too. We can be one big happy family.' He held out his arms. 'Have you a kiss for your old uncle?'

'*One big happy family?*' Charlie mimicked when they were back on the pavement. 'This greasy snake is your uncle? I'd rather cut my leg off than be related to him.'

Irritation prickled between Helen's shoulder blades. It's

all right for you, she wanted to say, then realised that Charlie didn't have much family either. 'I didn't choose him.'

'And who's this aunt of yours?' said Charlie. 'What's she got to do with Ransome's?'

Helen hesitated. Keeping secrets was a knee-jerk reaction from having always relied on herself, but keeping them from friends meant you risked losing them. She'd nearly lost Jason's respect when he'd found the clippings folder. She could, of course, pretend her uncle had been referring to a wife and put the ambiguity down to the well-studied accent, but what about next time? Secrets always came out, one way or another.

'Letitia.'

'*Letitia?*'

'Letitia's my aunt. Or my step-aunt if you like. My grandfather on my mother's side was married to her mother. It's a family company.' Helen opened the scooter's top box and placed the parcel and envelope inside.

'You're having me on. Really?' Charlie flicked back a greasy dreadlock. 'But she's loaded! And what about your parents? Where are they? Aren't they part of it?'

'My parents are dead.'

'Oh.' Charlie looked agog for a moment, but her surprise didn't last long. 'You, then,' she insisted. 'You must have a share in it. So what the hell are you doing, fetching and carrying and getting your hands dirty? You should be off on some Caribbean island eating lobster and sipping cocktails and doing whatever rich people do.'

'I don't have a lot of experience of rich people.'

'I don't get it. You must have. You were born with a silver spoon in your mouth, for Christ's sake!'

Suddenly all the rage Helen had kept under control for so long spewed out of her, and she swung to face Charlie, an innocent but convenient target.

'What if I don't want any of it?' she spat. 'What if they all let me down when I needed them? What if they're all trying to buy me back into their lives with their bloody money? Can you understand that? How it makes me feel?'

A wounded look crept into Charlie's eyes, but again she recovered quickly. 'Yeah, I can understand that. They pissed on you, and now you're too proud to forgive them. I wasn't blind in there, you know.'

Regretting her outburst, Helen bit her lip.

'You don't have to want it for yourself,' said Charlie. 'You could exploit those capitalist pricks the way they've probably exploited a whole bunch of people to get so filthy rich in the first place. Do some good with the money. You know, rob from the rich and give to the poor.'

'If only things were that simple,' Helen replied as hysterical laughter threatened to well up inside her. 'I'd be stealing from myself.'

'Details.' Charlie shrugged. 'Come on, let's have a look at what's in that packet.'

Never you mind.

Recalling Letitia's warning, Helen glanced up at her uncle's town house and the dark windows. He was probably watching her right now, from behind his curtains.

'Okay. But not here.'

They drove to a nearby pub tucked away from the main road and almost deserted at this hour of the day. Helen ordered two Cokes, and they chose a table in a secluded booth at the far corner of the pub away from windows and prying eyes.

Charlie undid the string securing the parcel and pushed the paper aside to reveal something that looked like a wooden book. Wrapping her hands in the sleeves from her jumper for protection, Helen opened it, folding back one page to the left then the other to the right.

'What is it?' asked Charlie.

'It's a Russian icon. A triptych because it has three panels.'

She looked at the centre image of the Virgin Mary holding Baby Jesus depicted as a miniature adult. The left was from the annunciation with the archangel Gabriel, and the right showed Mary in the cave with the shrouded Jesus. Three scenes from the life of the Virgin on a Russian icon, just as Letitia had said. Nothing strange about that.

Charlie reached out to touch it, but Helen stopped her. 'You can't touch art with greasy fingers.'

'Well, la-di-dah. Is it very valuable?'

Helen held it up to the light. The surface was slightly uneven where the original coat of varnish had cracked and then been restored. She had learned about icons at school. Apart from enjoying Art as a subject, the fact that they were Russian, and a part of her ancestry so to speak, had captured her imagination and provided her with a way of holding on to her identity at the same time. She probably knew more about them than most people, even Letitia. Pictures of saints, and often the Holy Virgin, they were painted on wooden board with *gesso*, a kind of chalk, as well as with egg tempera, which was made from mixing powdered pigment with egg yolk, and then coated with finishing oil. This one had also been overlaid with engraved silver leaf on the garments, the halos, and the backgrounds.

'Letitia said so. It depends how old it is, but the paperwork should tell us that.'

'Well, what are we waiting for?' Charlie slipped a dirty, chipped fingernail under the flap and opened the envelope without damaging the glue, glanced at the papers, then handed them to Helen. 'See what you can make of it. It's all Greek to me.'

'Close. It's Russian, you dork.'

'Well, what does it say? You're the one with the Russian uncle.'

'I'm a bit rusty, but'—Helen waved a sheet of paper under Charlie's nose—'here's a translation. Lucky me.'

'Go on, then.'

'It says,' Helen read aloud, 'that the Ministry of Culture of the Russian Federation certifies that this is an icon of one hundred years in age and that exporting it from Russia is within the law.'

'What does that mean?'

'There's some law forbidding exports of icons older than a hundred years. This one obviously comes direct from Russia where they're quite strict, but sometimes they're smuggled into the Baltic countries and won't have a certificate.'

Charlie looked at the icon. 'A hundred years old? I'm no expert but this one looks older.'

'Maybe it is.'

'But the certificate says it isn't.'

Helen smiled. 'That doesn't mean it's true. What if you paid someone in the Ministry of Culture to say it was one hundred years old just to make it easier to get it out of the country?'

'Corruption. Okay, I buy that. But why is it so urgent that it has to be back before lunch?'

'Because Letitia has a meeting with a private buyer. Which is why we need to get back.' She returned the papers to the envelope, wrapped the icon carefully and got up.

Charlie caught her arm. 'Sit down. I have an idea. I don't know much about art,' she said, 'but I know about stealing stuff.'

'We don't know if it's stolen.'

'All right, listen, imagine running off with the *Mona Lisa*.'

'I've been to the Louvre. It's pretty impossible. They don't even let you see it half the time.'

'Just go with me here.'

Helen sighed. 'Okay. We steal the *Mona Lisa*. Then what?'

'That's it. That's exactly it. What would you do with it?'

'Hang it on the wall.' Helen shrugged. 'Try to sell it.'

'And how'd you flog her? On *E-bay*?'

'No, I'd go to a private collector. Someone with money who'd buy it off me.'

'Where'd you find this collector?' Charlie persisted. 'They don't advertise in the local paper. "Stolen fine art bought and sold. Competitive rates."' She snorted. 'You need to find a middle man, someone who knows all the buyers and sellers, who's selling what, and who wants to buy what. That might explain those numbers on Letitia's spreadsheet.'

'You're saying my aunt is a fence?'

'Not really. She just facilitates the sale. And charges a commission which she doesn't declare to the tax man.'

'But some of those figures had to do with objects already sold through the auction house.'

'So the auction is rigged, then,' said Charlie.

'The bidding is open to the floor,' Helen pointed out. 'You can't rig an auction unless the auctioneer is in on it.'

'Probably gets a bit on the side.'

'There are rules and regulations, Charlie. Guidance from the Department of Trade and Industry, the Office of Fair Trading—'

'You can easily get by those.'

Helen laughed. 'You watch too much TV.'

'Maybe,' said Charlie, 'But I wouldn't be surprised if there's a hefty trade going on, and a lot of money involved. And if some of that money changes hands under the table, it's usually because it's dirty.'

Helen went still. This could be bigger than she'd imagined. If Charlie was right, and if this scam had been running a long time, some of Ransome's clients were very ruthless, ruthless enough to kill if there was someone interfering.

Or perhaps Mimi had been a dodgy dealer too, and ended up on the wrong side of one of these individuals?

It was *her* mother who'd agreed to meet her killer at some godforsaken hour, irresponsibly bringing her five-year-old daughter. *Her* mother that had brought a bag of paperwork to the meeting.

Her mother who'd choked on her own blood, while her child lay helpless on the back seat, potentially the killer's next victim.

The thought that her whole world may have been turned upside down over something as base as dirty money twisted inside her like a knife slicing through butter, but she couldn't back down now. She had to get to the bottom of it, whatever 'it' was.

Even if it meant finding out things about her mother she'd rather had remained buried.

'Please don't say anything about my *connections*,' said Helen when they got back. 'I'm not exactly proud of them.'

'Why?'

'Just … don't, okay?'

Charlie shrugged. 'Sure, have your little secrets. It's nothing to me.'

'Promise?'

'Cross my heart and hope to die.'

Don't say that, thought Helen. *Don't say that.*

She handed the parcel to Letitia, who was on the phone and only acknowledged her with a nod. She would have liked a chance to speak to Ruth, to see if she'd imagined the look that passed between them earlier, but Ruth was no longer there, and she was left alone with her thoughts. Cup of tea in hand, she sat on the steps to the loading bay, a favourite spot for the smokers, but no one chose that moment to sneak out for an unscheduled cigarette break.

It was funny how lies always begot more lies and landed you in a right old mess.

Now both Jason and Charlie knew who she really was. She could probably trust Charlie not to say anything for the moment, but soon she'd have to come out with it, and what would happened then? When she left India, she'd never expected to make friends with her colleagues and her house mates, and suddenly a lot more was at stake than finding out what happened with her mother.

She thought of her new friends in turn. Jason and Charlie. Bill and Jim. Lee, after a fashion.

Fay.

The name echoed in her head. Her mother's killer.

Or not.

Fay was guilty of harassment and stalking, but she may be innocent of murder. If Helen's mother had been a whistle-blower or involved in something bad, and got herself killed in the process, then instead of committing murder, Fay could have, by following Mimi around, actually saved Helen's life simply by being there. By going down for it despite not being able to remember anything, she had ensured no one came looking for a five-year-old witness.

Helen had harboured feelings of hatred and resentment for twenty years, feelings which had played a far greater part in making her into the person she was than the actual loss of her mother. Was it possible she should have been feeling gratitude all of these years instead?

Chapter Eighteen

Jason turned the key, revved the engine and felt the motorbike thrum to life under him. The bike was Trevor's, an old Triumph Bonneville he'd spent years restoring, and it had taken a great deal of persuasion on Jason's part to get him to hand over the keys in exchange for Trevor needing to borrow his van for the day.

'Just make sure you bring her back in one piece, or you're dead meat,' grumbled Trevor. 'Oh, and one other thing, that company name you mentioned, the one your bird works for—'

'She's not my bird.'

'Well, whatever. Anyway, I think I've seen that name before. Lucy sometimes brings work home, and I'm sure I saw it in some of her papers. Why don't you ask her?'

'Okay, will do.' Jason revved the engine again and grinned when Trevor waved him off with an impatient gesture.

He'd made Trevor feel guilty about not being able to operate his stall without his van to cart everything back and forth, but truthfully he didn't mind. He needed to work on the house anyway. But as he rode home, something Lee had told him this morning in the kitchen, about Helen standing outside the door to Fay's room at night, was playing like a loop in his mind. Jason had believed her when she said she wasn't planning to harm Fay, but what if he'd made a mistake? Why was she creeping around?

Okay, so Lee crept about too, but he didn't live under the same roof as someone convicted of murdering his mother.

Jason changed course and headed towards Helen's work. He'd see if she could take a break, maybe invite her out for coffee, then give her a chance to explain herself.

Just as he pulled up to Ransome & Daughters, he saw Helen get in a taxi. On the hope that she'd have a few minutes to spare for him when they got to wherever she was headed, he gunned the engine, pulled out into the traffic and followed. When she got out on Piccadilly and hopped on the back of a scooter, his first thought was that she'd seen him and was trying to give him the slip.

Then another thought hit him. She had a boyfriend she hadn't said anything about.

She didn't have to, of course. Tell him about her private life. But that didn't stop the feeling of jealousy creeping up on him. Flexing his fingers, he tightened his grip on the handle bars. He could hardly accuse her of playing with him, but when they were together, he'd got the sense that there wasn't anyone else.

When Helen and Scooter Man pulled up outside Stephanov's town house, and Scooter Man took off his helmet, Jason nearly laughed. What an idiot he'd been – he'd completely forgotten that Charlie was working as a courier now.

That didn't explain why Helen was introducing Charlie to her uncle though, when she'd asked Jason not to mention the connection. At least he knew it couldn't have anything to do with harming Fay, because Charlie would never be party to that. But why were Helen and Charlie covertly meeting up in the middle of traffic, sneaking off to meet with her Russian uncle?

Spying on Helen was ridiculous. He should come forward, let her know he was there. Or better yet, drive away. But if his instincts were wrong about her, and Fay or Charlie suffered for it … He drove around the corner and into a small side road, where he had a view of the house without being too obvious.

They emerged fifteen minutes later. Helen, carrying a smallish flat parcel and an envelope, stopped on the pavement and they seemed to debate something. Then Helen glanced around her, resting her eyes on him for a second, but he was safely disguised by Trevor's helmet so she didn't recognise him. The girls got back on the scooter.

Jason followed them as discreetly as he could, but Charlie's driving was erratic and in total disregard of the Highway Code, and he nearly lost them. They stopped outside a traditional pub with seating outside and hanging baskets planted with ivy and trailing petunias. He drove past and parked the bike behind a large van, then walked back and peered through the window of the pub. They were sitting in the far corner with the parcel on a table between them, and Charlie had a 'don't-argue-with-me' expression on her face.

Uh-oh, he thought, *I know that look.*

Helen opened the parcel, but he was too far away to see what it was, and he couldn't go inside because they'd recognise him. He leaned against the wall and wondered what to do.

A gate opened to the pub's back yard, and a youth came out dragging a garden hose with a long spout. Watching him watering the hanging baskets, Jason had an idea.

'Would you like to earn a quick fifty quid? Don't worry, it's nothing dirty,' he added when the kid sent him a horrified look.

'What do I 'ave to do?'

'See those girls there at the back? I want you to find out what they're looking at.'

'Thass all?'

'That's all, yes.'

'Gimme a minute.' The youth dragged the hose back into the yard, and Jason followed him just inside the fence in case Helen and Charlie came out while he was waiting. A few minutes later the youth returned holding a cloth and a Tupperware of water. 'I pretended I was, like, wiping the tables,' he said, clearly pleased with his own cleverness. 'They didn't even no'ice.'

'Did you see what it was?'

'Money first.'

Jason handed him two crumpled twenty pound notes and a tenner, which were crammed into a jeans pocket faster than lightning.

'It's some kind of wooden book, but it's like a painting as well, know what I mean?'

'Not quite. Did you see the motif?'

'Eh?'

'What was on the painting?'

'Something you might see in church. Like a saint.'

Like a saint, Jason thought. Grinning, for the first time he actually found himself thanking his father for his expensive education. It sounded like they could be looking at an icon. It was the right size for the parcel he'd glimpsed in Helen's hand, and it fitted with the Russian connection. But was it significant? He had no idea, but wondered what had made them open it. Couriers didn't normally open the parcels they were carrying, and he'd even heard of some who'd carried drugs or cash without knowing it.

He could hardly ask them. With a sigh he got back on the bike and drove in the direction of Tower Bridge. There was one other person he *could* ask.

Ms Barclay pursed her lips when he entered the inner sanctum. 'We're in a foul mood today. Be warned.'

Jason grinned. 'I'll call you if there's any trouble. He respects you.'

'I bet you say that to all the girls.'

'Wouldn't you like to know? In the meantime, could you look after this for me, please?' He passed her the motorcycle helmet. 'I can do without a cross-examination.'

223

'Very wise.'

Derek was on the phone. He held up a hand to stop him from interrupting, and Jason dropped into one of the squishy armchairs, content to wait. The office hadn't changed since the last time he was here apart from a vase of strongly scented roses in pride of place on the desk. Ms Barclay, he thought, probably from her garden, although he doubted if his father could tell the difference between home-grown and shop-bought. That woman could tame lions.

'What do you want?' Derek snapped when he'd finished on the phone.

'Nice to see you too, Dad.'

Derek smiled, of sorts. 'How are you, son?'

'Very well, but I didn't come here to discuss my health. You're a collector of rare and expensive items.' He flung out his arms to indicate his father's office in general: the paintings, the statue, the desk with its gilded ink stand and period-piece paraphernalia. 'Tell me what you know about icons.'

'Turkish? Greek? Russian?'

'Yes, Russian,' Jason replied.

'What do you want to know?'

'Market. How they get into this country. Authenticity. Anything else which might be relevant.'

Derek's eyebrows rose, and he looked amused. 'Market is good, not saturated, but they're expensive. Collectors' items only. They come from Russia, obviously, or other countries belonging to the Russian Orthodox Church. Value depends on age and condition. The older they are, the more they'll fetch. The Byzantine ones are incredibly valuable. But that's all stuff you can look up on Wikipedia. Why come to me?'

'I want to know about the darker side of the trade.'

His father laughed. 'And you think I know?'

'Well, don't you?' He held his father's eyes.

Derek rose and went to mix himself a drink from a silver tray on a wall-mounted cabinet. Like the rest of the furniture in his father's office, the cabinet was sleek and modern. One of the doors concealed a mini fridge, and his father pulled out an aircraft-sized can of tonic water.

'Drink?'

'A tonic without the gin would be very nice, thanks.' It was a delaying tactic, and Jason decided to lull his father into a false sense of security by giving him time to consider his answer. He'd get it soon enough.

His father handed him a tumbler of tonic water with ice, poured himself a drink, then sat back in his office chair with his hands behind his head. The posture signalled superiority, but Jason saw through that too. It struck him that he'd managed to rattle his father's cage, and that he was trying hard not to show it. He sipped his tonic to hide his own smirk.

Interesting.

'What if it was really old?'

'Well, there are rules and regulations about that. Russia tends to hold onto her treasures these days. Anything over a hundred years old is hard to come by.'

'And if I wanted to buy a really old one anyway? Like a Byzantine one.'

Derek heaved a sigh. 'You could buy one which has been "authenticated" to be newer than that. There's always a way.' He sent Jason a hard look. 'Thinking of starting a collection?'

'Yeah, with what?'

'Or is it another Russian you're interested in?'

'As far as I'm aware she's not for sale.'

'Everyone has their price, even Little Orphan Annie,' said Derek. 'Yes, I've done my homework,' he added in response to Jason's surprise. 'Now, if that's all ...?'

225

The realisation that her mother may have died because of dirty money was strangely other-worldly, and Helen made one mistake after another in her work. Bill didn't hide his frustration. 'Come on, come on, this is no time to hang about. We need to mark up this lot 'ere before the end of the day.' They were working on a consignment of Chinese vases which were being auctioned off the following morning.

Shutting out Bill's grumbling, Helen lifted one of the vases out of a packaging crate and turned it over in her hands. According to the accompanying notes, it originated from China, *in the style of* Ming Dynasty antiques, but if Charlie was right, it could be an original. Not being an antiques expert, she had no way of telling.

She was still studying it when Letitia walked past the door to the packing room in a swish of Shantung silk and clattering stilettos.

On a whim she let the vase drop, and it smashed on the concrete floor.

'Oops,' she said. 'God, I'm so sorry.'

The room fell silent, and Bill stared at her, mouth opening and closing like a goldfish. Letitia stopped, turned, and reappeared in the packing room, the clattering heels echoing in the silence.

Helen stuck out her chin. 'Just as well it was only a copy.'

'A copy?' A small muscle worked in Letitia's jaw.

'It says so in the paperwork. But you can take the money out of my pay anyway.'

Letitia cleared her throat. 'No, there's no need for that. We're insured against human error, among other things. Have to be in this business.' She looked at the shattered vase on the floor, drew herself up, then smiled coolly. 'I'd better call the owner. The overall responsibility is mine.'

She left the room, and the scent of her perfume lingered in the air with a sense of doom.

Bill grabbed Helen roughly and dragged her to the staff room, then slammed the door. 'What's your game, girl?' he hissed. 'What are you playing at?'

'It's no game.'

He shook her hard, then let go of her. 'If you know what's good for you, you stay well away. You hear?'

Rubbing her arm, Helen winced. The old geezer had fingers of steel.

But it wasn't steel which tinged his voice, but regret, when he added, 'Said the same to your mother a long time ago, but would she listen?'

'What do you know, Bill?'

'Nothing. Nothing at all.'

'Bullshit.'

He glared at her and stabbed her in the chest with his finger. 'And neither do you.'

'This is important to me,' she said, crossing her arms. 'I've waited all my life to find out what happened to my mother and why. I'm not going to stop now. If you don't tell me what I need to know, I'll just keep digging until I find out for myself.'

'I bleedin' well hope not. 'Cos you might just be digging your own grave.'

'Is my aunt a fence?'

Bill sent her a startled look. 'What makes you say that?'

'Well, is she?' she repeated, cross with Charlie for planting the idea in her head in the first place.

'First and foremost, your aunt's a successful business woman,' he replied with a pained expression.

'And apart from that?'

'Many things, I suppose. She has a good standing in the industry. A lot of contacts, as you'd expect, some of them from the, shall we say, shadier side of life. Sometimes she bends the rules. But a fence … that's a bit strong. You'd

227

better be careful throwing words like that around. Someone might take it amiss.'

'I've got nothing to lose.'

Bill didn't comment. Instead he said, 'I'd like you to stay in here for the rest of the day until I figure out what to do with you. Can't have you in the packing room if you're going to be Miss Butterfingers. It'd be my head on the block if you break something else.'

'In here?' Helen protested. 'But there's nothing to do, not even a magazine to read!'

'You can tidy up.'

'No way!'

'Or you can go home for the day.'

Jutting out her chin, Helen weighed up the humiliation of cleaning the staff room or having to leave and miss something important. In the end she settled for the staff room.

'Thought not,' he said smugly. 'Tidying up it is.'

Helen mouthed an expletive behind his retreating back.

By the door he turned. 'Here's what I think. Everyone's got something to lose.'

Helen began clearing up, wrinkling her nose at the overflowing bin, the dregs of tea and curdled milk left at the bottom of mugs, and a table top which surely hadn't seen a wet cloth in years.

She thought of what Bill had said, that everyone had something to lose. Of course they did, but there were degrees of loss. Losing her mother and her whole world at the age of five and never having had a real substitute, his words didn't have much impact. Unless he meant her losing her life.

Her mother was concerned about something suspicious going on twenty years ago. If she was killed because of it, that would exonerate Fay, wouldn't it? Or had Fay, as Aggie suggested, played into someone else's hands?

Grimly she began washing the dirty mugs.

Bill was just a cranky old coot. She'd met plenty like him over the years. People who liked things just so because the slightest change in their usual routine made them feel unsettled. Fair enough, he was cross with her for breaking a vase, because she didn't doubt Letitia would hold him partly responsible for that, telling him to supervise his staff better.

She picked up Charlie's jacket, which had fallen off the back of the chair where she'd flung it earlier, and hung it on a coat hanger. Something hard fell out of one of the pockets and clattered to the floor. She bent down and saw that it was a knife.

And not just any old knife.

Stunned, she stared at the blue-handled paper knife. It was one of Arseni's Fabergé knives, and how it had ended up in Charlie's pocket was an easy guess. A laugh escaped her. Charlie was too much sometimes, but her quick fingers could work to Helen's advantage. Ever since she'd spotted the knives in his display cabinet, she'd been itching to examine them.

The chunky lapis lazuli handle had a good weight to it, and the leaf detail on the end was worn thin from the many hands which must have held the knife in the last century. The blade, made from white gold she guessed, was unexpectedly sharp.

Curiously, it wasn't a particularly good stabbing weapon, something she discovered when she tested it on the sponge scourer in the washing up bowl. Her hand slid down the handle towards the sharp knife edge, and it was clear that the force one would need to drive the knife into the throat of a person might be enough for the murderer to do themselves a minor injury.

You'd have to wear gloves, another indication that her mother's murder had been premeditated, even carefully planned. Fay, her brain addled by drugs at the time, didn't strike her as a meticulous planner, more likely she was so unhinged that she simply grabbed the nearest thing she could find.

To her surprise, the act of stabbing the sponge brought home to her that even though she wanted to know the truth about her mother's death, she was now able to step back from the personal loss and regard it from a more investigative perspective. This had to be a good thing, surely?

The paper knives puzzled her. There had been four in total, two belonging to her uncle, and the other two to her mother. Mimi had given one to Fay. Aggie was adamant Mimi wouldn't have sold her own, and it wasn't on Sweetman's inventory list. One had been at the crime scene, then disappeared, and the fact that Fay's husband could confirm Fay's knife was missing from their home had, combined with Helen's testimony, been enough to convict her.

She weighed it in her hand. If Fay had been set up, it would have to have been by someone close enough to both Mimi and Fay to know that Fay had a knife like this. Arseni might have, if Mimi had told him that she was breaking up the family set, and Fay's husband certainly did. Who else? Letitia and Mimi worked together and must have seen each other socially despite their mutual dislike. Perhaps Letitia knew. Ruth might have known too. Then there was Bill and Mrs Deakin, although they'd said nothing but nice things about her mother.

And there was Aggie.

She thought back to their conversation, when her grandmother talked about Mimi's yellow curtains. Had she mentioned knowing back then about Mimi giving one of the knives away? Or was that something Aggie had learned during the court case? Helen couldn't remember now. But if Aggie had known, as an antiques dealer she'd probably have hated the idea of the set being broken up. Why *did* her mother give away something so precious? And who might Aggie have told? Even if it had only been a chance remark to the wrong person, it could account for Aggie's bad conscience. Now that Helen had come to know her better, she hated the idea, but had to accept it was possible.

It still didn't explain what happened to the last of the knives.

Another problem was what to do with Charlie. If she confronted her about stealing the knife, she'd only be defensive, and she might go back on her promise and mention Helen's connection with Letitia and Arseni.

She decided to leave it. A secret for a secret. Besides, she didn't care that her uncle had lost his revolutionary loot. He could go to Hell.

She hid the paper knife in her own rucksack. When Charlie found it missing, she might think she'd lost it on the ride back to the auction house. And if Charlie chose to confront *her*, she'd just say her uncle wasn't someone you messed with, and that it was probably best if she simply put it back next time she visited him.

That she had no intention of returning it, she'd keep to herself.

No one was in when she got home. She paced around in the kitchen for a bit, then eventually cooked some pasta which she didn't finish eating and tried unsuccessfully to follow a comedy quiz show on TV.

She had to speak to Fay. Not to say anything in particular, but just talk, get to know her. Find out if she knew more about that morning, but without giving the game away.

But before she spoke to Fay, she wanted to speak to Jason, to tell him that even if Fay was the murderer, Helen wanted to be able to forgive her. If anyone could understand just how complex those feelings were, it would be Jason. She may be one of his projects – and it hurt her vanity to think so – but she still wanted him to know how far she had come from having a massive chip on her shoulder to the person she was now. She wanted to tell him that his kindness towards her had changed something fundamental in her, even if she was far from his favourite person at the moment.

That wasn't the only reason she wanted to see him. Her face went hot when she thought of the way he'd pressed her against the wall in the hall, almost knocking the air out of her. That short display of passion had both frightened and excited her. Did he have any idea how he affected her?

'Argh!' Talking to him and explaining herself, yes, but anything beyond that … she groaned and pressed her face into her hands to block out the thought.

Early evening turned to late evening, and still no one turned up. She gave up on the telly and sat for a while in the deepening quiet, listening to the muted sounds of family life next door. Nearby a cat meowed, and through the open door to the garden she could hear something rustling in the undergrowth, a frog perhaps. She went outside to investigate. Sure enough a frog was hopping around in the flower bed.

Kneeling down, she gently prodded its moist body with her finger, then watched, amused, as it scampered away from her as fast as it could. A sudden furious barking from the dog next door made her jump, and as she scrambled to her feet again, she caught a movement at the back of the garden and went still.

Beyond the fence ran a little-used right-of-way, gated at either end to deter drug-pushers and tramps from hanging out behind the houses and to stop the alleyway from being used for fly-tipping. It was meant for people to bring their garden waste or bicycles out to the road without traipsing through the house, but Jason's gate hadn't been used in that way for a while, and ivy had grown across it, blocking the access.

At the same time the gate was only a glorified metal grate, and where the ivy didn't cover it you could see through it.

What Helen saw now was a shadowy figure, tall and bulky, probably male, and the glow of a cigarette. Remembering the dark saloon, she jumped up and ran back into the house. Her hands shook wildly as she pulled at the door handle and nearly whimpered with relief when she managed to lock it. Then she yanked the curtains shut.

Stepping back, she put her hands to her chest to still her racing heart, to stop the hot flow of adrenaline in her veins. Black spots danced before her eyes, her skin went from sweaty to cold and clammy.

Not now.

She fumbled her way backwards through the kitchen, knocking into the edge of the table and narrowly missing the ironing board which some genius had left out. Steadying herself against the wall, she tried to even her breathing, to pull her mind back from the abyss it was threatening to fall into. The prospect of having a seizure alone, at night, terrified her.

Calmer now, she listened out for unusual sounds. A squeak of metal, as if someone had climbed the rickety gate, then a scuffing noise, footsteps perhaps? She even thought she heard nails clawing on the window, until she got a hold of herself. She was safe in here, and no one was trying to get in. It was all in her silly head.

Relieved that she'd been spared a seizure this time, she switched off the lights and left the kitchen.

In the unlit hall she collided with a body – and screamed.

Chapter Nineteen

It was Lee.

'Sorry, d-didn't mean to f-frighten you.' He flicked the switch in the hall, but nothing happened, and the only light came from the window above the front door.

'What the hell are you playing at?' Helen exploded before her head did. 'I've told you not to sneak up on people like that.'

'I wasn't sn-sn-sneaking. I thought I was alone.'

'Yeah, well …' She wiped a hand across her eyes. If he'd been standing just outside the kitchen, he must have seen light from underneath the door and then noticed it being switched off, but he probably had his own peculiar reasons for creeping about. Maybe the habit went with mugging old ladies for a living.

'I'm really sorry,' he said again.

She sighed. Lee was sort of a guardian angel, and it was a relief not to be alone any more. Perhaps he could also help her with something. It was the bark from next door which had made her think of it. 'It's okay, I overreacted. What do you know about dogs?' she asked.

'D-dogs?' he repeated.

'Yes, you know, woof-woof, wagging their tails, humping your leg.'

'Ev-verything.'

'You know *everything* about dogs?' Was he for real? 'So, if I described a dog to you, would you be able to tell me what kind it is?'

'Yeah.'

'Okay,' she said, safe in the knowledge that he didn't talk to anyone much. 'I came across this dog once, and it's been bugging me that I don't know what it is.' She described the dog – size, colour, curly fur – frustrated by the way you always remembered things bigger as a child than they really were.

'S-sounds like a terrier,' he said. 'A b-big one. Maybe an Airedale.'

'An Airedale Terrier? Where can I find out for sure?'

He shrugged. 'The library? Or the Intern-net?'

So this was where her great detective skills were taking her, the library or the Internet, and probably another dead end.

'Thanks, Lee, I appreciate your help.'

Getting ready for bed, she started at a knock on her door. Charlie, she thought, and quickly covered the paper knife on the desk with a letter she'd received from Joe recently.

But it was Fay, not Charlie.

'I missed you earlier, so I brought you a cup of tea to say hello.'

'Thanks.' Helen accepted the mug.

'May I come in?'

'Sure.'

'Lee said he gave you a fright. Are you okay?'

So Lee *did* talk to the others, or maybe just Fay, but she supposed Fay had that effect on people.

'I didn't see him. The bulb in the hall's still out.'

'Jason sorted it out just now.'

Helen's heart skipped a beat. 'He's back?'

'He went out again.'

'Oh.'

Fay sat down on the bed and looked around Helen's room. 'You've made it look really nice in here. Have you changed something?'

Helen blew on her tea, a surprisingly fragrant brew, maybe from Fay's private stash. 'Just a few ornaments and knick-knacks I got from the market. I like Indian stuff.'

'So I see.' She seemed to have nothing more to say but made no move to leave, so Helen took the opportunity to learn more about her.

'How long were you in prison for?' she said as an opener.

'Twenty years.'

'That's a long time.'

Fay shrugged. 'In some ways, but you just have to get on with your life as well as you can. For me it was a wake-up call. I needed to change if I was going to have a future.'

'What was prison like for you?' An odd question for the one who possibly murdered your mother, but it just flew out of her mouth.

'You're the first person to ask me that. When you've been inside, people always think you deserve everything you get. They don't ask you what it's like.'

'I'm interested in you.'

'I adapted. I had to. I was stuck with these people, and could either make it easy or difficult for myself. Mind you, I didn't have too hard a time of it. I enjoyed a certain respect.'

'How come?'

'Because of what I'd done. I stabbed another woman over a man. Most women can relate to that. It's the child-killers they don't like.'

'What do they do to them?' Helen asked, suspecting she already knew.

'Usually they're ostracised, but sometimes it's violent. There was a woman on my ward who'd killed her baby. When the guards weren't watching, they'd hold her down, pull up her sleeve and scald her with boiling water.'

'That's horrible.' Helen glanced at the mug in her hand, then put it on the desk. 'What did you do?'

'Me? I boiled the kettle. I had a reputation to uphold, for my own survival. I'm not proud of it.'

Helen swallowed hard. For years she'd thought of prison

as the end station for Fay. It hadn't occurred to her that life carried on inside, with all its politics and social pitfalls. 'What happened to her? The woman?'

'Got let off. Miscarriage of justice, apparently. Something to do with a flawed expert witness. It was quite a relief, because there wasn't so much anger simmering under the surface all the time.'

'Do you have children?' Helen asked, remembering the photos in Fay's room.

'Two. A boy and a girl.' A shadow passed across Fay's face. 'I haven't seen them in nearly twenty years.'

'Why not?'

Fay smiled sadly. 'I was declared unfit, and my husband took them away.'

'Do you know where to?'

'Up north somewhere. I lost contact when I went inside. I tried to write, but the replies were sporadic. Then they stopped. I think they just wanted to forget about me and start a new life. I don't blame them, really.' She looked at Helen. 'My daughter would be about your age by now. In some ways you remind me of her.' Stopping abruptly, she looked down at her hands. 'That's why when my friend's little girl … It was horrible. That poor child.'

I am that poor child, Helen thought.

'I don't remember much, except I do remember the child. She had this condition and went into convulsions, from shock probably. I thought she was going to die.'

She did die, Helen wanted to say. Or at least a part of her. The rest struggled to make sense of the world. But Fay wasn't to blame for that part.

'Where's your friend's daughter now?'

'I think her family adopted her. She had some aunts and uncles on both sides.' Fay grimaced. 'Sometimes I dream she'll come looking for me. It's not a nice dream.'

'Why? What d'you think she'd do to you?'

'As far as she's concerned I killed her mother. What would *you* do if you were her?'

'Wouldn't that depend on whether you were guilty or not?'

'Spoken like a truly young person. Don't take this the wrong way, but when you get to my age, you begin to understand that guilt is often on a sliding scale.' Fay smiled one of her rare, sunny smiles. 'Now, if you've finished with the mug, I'll take it with me. I appreciate the chat.'

'Me too.'

She meant it, she realised. As a teenager she'd fantasised how it would be to have a mother you could share everything with, the sort her girlfriends would have envied. Except she didn't have any friends. This conversation with Fay was the next best thing.

As Fay rose to take the mug from the desk, a gust of wind from the half-open window tossed Joe's letter aside. Before Helen could put it back, Fay reached for the paper knife, her hand closing over the blade.

'Don't touch that!' Helen dived for the knife, yanking it out of Fay's grip.

Fay shrieked as the blade cut through the palm of her hand. 'Where did you get that?' she croaked, her face contorted with shock and pain. 'It's mine!'

Helen opened her mouth to speak, but her lips couldn't form the words. Pictures flashed before her eyes, the blood on Fay's hand, her mother slumped in her seat, the horror and knowledge that something bad, bad, bad had happened, was happening.

And over it an image of the tsar's daughters, beautiful and alive, played in her head like an old newsreel.

They're all dead, everyone's dead.

Spasms gripped her, she lost the use of her legs and

collapsed on the floor, jerking, grinding her teeth. Animal groans rose from somewhere deep inside her, areas of her brain fizzed and popped like firecrackers. Conscious thought was a whirl of images, all jumbled up.

In a blur she saw Fay stretch her hand towards her, her lips moving soundlessly, and the last thing entering her consciousness before the world dimmed and went out was Fay's question:

'Who *are* you?'

Jason was met by panicked shouting when he returned home. Charlie was yelling down the stairs for Lee to call an ambulance. His stutter aggravated by stress, Lee babbled incoherently when Jason asked him what had happened.

Following the commotion, he ran up the stairs. Helen's door was open and she was on the floor, jerking as if she'd been plugged into the mains. Fay was beside her, bleeding from a cut on her hand, her face a mask of horror.

His first thought was that Helen and Fay had been in a fight, and he was too late to prevent a tragedy. Then he realised what was going on.

'Do something, Jase!' Charlie shrieked. 'I think she's on some kind of drug!'

'It's not drugs. Look, go calm Lee down, please, he's flipping out. Fay, hand me some of those cushions over there. Now!'

His words brought Fay out of shock, and she grabbed a couple of cushions from the bed with her good hand and gave them to him. Jason placed one under Helen's head, another under one of her elbows which was banging repeatedly on the floor like a flesh-coloured piston, to prevent it getting bruised.

Helen moaned and twitched as flecks of spittle spumed from her lips and ran down her cheek. Jason sat down beside her and smoothed back a lock of her hair, then wiped her cheek with his sleeve.

'I've got you,' he said.

He looked into her eyes for signs of recognition. Her stare was vacant, empty, all connections severed from what made her who she was. His gut twisted as he watched her body's conflict with her brain and knew all he could do was reassure her. The spasmodic jerking, the dribbling, the smell of urine, sharp and pungent with fear when she lost control of her bladder, there was nothing he could do. Compassion surged through him, and he just continued to stroke her hair.

'I've got you,' he whispered again. 'You're doing fine, just fine. Hang in there. I won't let anything happen to you. Ever. I promise.'

She probably couldn't hear him, but her jerking subsided a little.

'She's epileptic …?' Fay said, sounding peculiar.

'Trust me, I had a friend once—'

Abruptly she left the room, and he heard her door slam. Her reaction took him by surprise. Epilepsy was frightening to witness if you'd never seen it before. Stupid and prejudiced people said unpleasant things about it, and didn't care whether the sufferer heard their comments or not. The most stupid of them even thought they could catch it. Jason's old school friend had heard it all a hundred times because kids were cruel, but it was unlike Fay to be so intolerant.

He pushed the thought aside. Right now he needed to concentrate on making Helen as comfortable as possible until the seizure released its grip on her.

When Helen came round, she lay with her head cradled in Jason's lap while he stroked her hair and whispered soothing words that made no sense. Her mind buzzed with angry bees, and the smells of fear and urine were drying on her clammy skin.

'I wet myself,' she whispered and turned away from him. Her tongue was swollen, and the inside of her mouth felt like cotton wool.

'I've cleaned up worse.'

'Where's Fay?' Helen groaned and tried to sit up.

Supporting her, Jason said, 'Charlie's dressing her hand. Apparently she cut herself on some fancy knife of hers. She's fine, but you gave us a right scare.'

'Sorry.' Now was not the time to mention the real ownership of the knife.

'Don't be. I knew how to deal with your condition anyway.'

'I like the way you say that.'

'What?'

'"Condition", not illness.' She managed a smile. 'You make it sound like it's no worse than, I dunno, thrush or eczema.'

'Ugh, don't talk to me about thrush. Nasty.' He pulled a face. 'Do you need me to call a doctor?'

She shook her head. 'I need to get cleaned up.'

'I'll run you a bath.'

'No.'

Jason sent her a curious look. 'Why not?'

'I can't have baths. If I have a seizure while I'm sitting in it, I might drown.'

'So you've never had a nice long soak?'

'Not since I was little. My mother would … well, I think she … Oh, never mind, I'll have a shower.'

'And if you have a seizure in the shower? You could fall and hurt yourself.'

She shrugged. 'I know, but that's what I have to live with.'

'Not if I have anything to do with it.' Jason rose. 'Stay there. I'll be right back.'

Helen drew her knees up and hugged them to her chest. Her room looked like it had before, except for the overturned chair and a line of dark droplets on the ancient mud-brown carpet, leading from the desk to the door.

Fay's blood. She looked away. It would blend in with older stains – tea, make-up, dirt from under people's shoes. The incident with Fay would fade and their shared history would be unknown to whoever moved in here after Helen. Just like her image of her mother was receding into the shadows.

Dr Boyd had warned her she may have grand mal seizures, but she hadn't suffered one in years and hadn't taken him seriously.

Was it the combination of the knife and the blood on Fay's hand, an echo of that time in the car, which had made her react so strongly? Was her memory finally returning? If so, was it reliable?

Jason returned. 'I've run you a bath, and I'll stay with you while you have it.' Seeing her querulous expression, he said, 'It makes sense. And don't worry, I won't look.'

'Am I that ugly?'

'Don't be daft.' He helped her up and into the bathroom, a comforting and warm nearness to support her wobbly legs, and turned away while she took her clothes off and got in the tub. The water was deep with a froth of scented bubbles floating on top, and so hot her skin felt almost itchy. Contentedly she scratched her thighs and her stomach, slipped under and became weightless in the water.

'Thank you,' she said, 'for not laughing.'

'Why would I laugh?'

'People do. They think it's funny.'

'I'm not "people", all right.' Jason sat with his back against the tub. 'And see, you can have baths.'

'No one has ever offered to have one with me before.'

'I'm not exactly having it with you, but I can get in, if you like.'

'Yeah, you'd like that, wouldn't you?' Helen flicked foam at him.

Grinning, he flicked the bubbles back at her. 'Mm, I must say, you've got very nice, rounded …'

Helen slid further down into the water.

'… shoulders.'

'Hah-hah, very funny.'

'Glad to see you're yourself again. I was really worried. Any idea what brought it on?'

Helen turned serious again. 'I remembered something.'

'Something bad?'

'When my mother died.'

'Do you want to tell me about it?'

Jason was leaning on the edge of the bath, and it would be so easy for her to reach out and touch his hair, to run her hand down to his strong shoulder which had supported her as if she weighed nothing. She wondered how he'd react if she did.

'You saw the folder, you know she was murdered,' she said. 'And you know Fay went to prison for it.'

Jason met her eyes. 'Go on,' he said.

'When Fay cut herself on that knife it brought it all back to me. It was … the blood. And the knife as well. I'd seen a knife like that before, with blood on it.'

'Where?'

'When my mother died. I've been piecing a few things together in my head.'

'What things?'

'There were four knives, part of a set, all identical. My uncle has two, my mother had one, and Fay had one. She was there the day my mother was murdered, so was one of the knives, Fay's presumably because the police didn't find it at her house, and her husband said it had gone missing. Fay doesn't remember anything. And my mother's things were sold, at auction, but the knife was a collectible and should have been on an inventory list. It wasn't.'

'Maybe they missed it out.'

'I work for an auction house. Trust me, you don't miss an item like a Fabergé knife. Her silver salt and pepper shakers were on the list, and they're even smaller. And besides, the police had already looked everywhere for my mother's knife, to rule it out. It was definitely missing. The thing is ...' She chewed her lip. 'It all feels so wrong, and now I'm not even sure Fay did it. Kill my mother, I mean.'

'Find the knives, narrow the list of suspects, that's what you're saying. And you've just found Fay's knife, haven't you? So doesn't that point to her guilt? Like you said, she went to prison for it.'

He listened to her explanation about Charlie and her uncle's knife.

'So who did it, d'you think?' Jason asked.

Helen breathed a deep sigh. 'I don't know, but I know one of the two knives that are missing was the one I saw that day. The one used to kill my mother. Unless it was one of my uncle's knives, in which case ...'

'I don't know, Helen. This is a bit ...' He shrugged and got up to stare out of the window. He couldn't see much through the grimy glass – another job for his long to-do list – but he wasn't really seeing the dirt. He thought of the knife lying on Helen's floor, with Fay's blood all over it, and slowly a few pieces slotted together in his own head.

Abruptly, he turned. 'Could it have been your uncle?'

'He was supposedly in Russia at the time. And I think he was in love with my mother, though I don't know if that gives him more or less motive.'

'How do you know?'

She shrugged. 'Something my grandmother said. About the way he looked at Mimi. Aggie doesn't trust him, and apparently that's one of the reasons she put me in foster care.'

'And Fay's husband? He knew about the knives, didn't he?'

'Yes, I've been wondering about him too.'

Sitting down again, with his elbow resting on the side of the tub, he smiled and said, 'So, all this malarkey aside, have you changed your mind about me yet?'

'I still don't think flatmates should get involved.'

He grinned. 'Honey, we already are. All of us.'

There was a thud on the door, and Charlie came in with a tray of mugs. 'I made us a cuppa. Strong milky tea. Best cure for shock, my nan always said.'

Jason groaned inwardly. Talk about timing. He'd hoped he could persuade Helen to let him get in the bath with her. Fat chance of that now. Well, fat chance of that before.

'Thanks, but Helen's actually trying to have a bath here.'

'So what are you doing in here, then? Scrubbing her back? She owes us an explanation, you know. I've worked some of it out, and I spoke to Fay.'

Charlie handed out the mugs. Jason took Helen's and passed it to her so she didn't have to lean out of the bath. She smiled, and the colour was coming back to her cheeks.

'What does she say?' asked Helen.

'Not a lot. I gather she knew your mum, and there was some major bust-up.'

'Actually, she spent twenty years in prison for her murder,' said Jason.

Speechless for once, Charlie sat down on the loo seat with a bump.

'Yeah, that's a tough one.'

245

'No wonder you didn't want anyone to know about your uncle.' Charlie's brain was working so furiously you could almost hear it. 'Fay would've sussed it out if she knew your mum. I'm surprised she didn't recognise you.'

'I look a lot like my father, apparently.'

Charlie put her mug aside as if she'd lost all taste for sweetness. 'I feel like an idiot. I thought you were a friend, but you were just playing us, weren't you? Now I don't know what to think.'

'I'd like to be a friend,' said Helen, cautiously.

'Fay's my friend. *Our* friend. We care about her. Whatever she's done, we don't want anyone to hurt her. She's like a frigging sister!'

Charlie slammed out of the bathroom, and Jason took Helen's mug and handed her a towel, turning away as she got out of the bath.

'You'd better speak to Fay,' he said. 'She's obviously guessed who you are, so God knows what she's making of us being closeted in here.'

Charlie came back. 'She's gone.'

'Gone where?'

'Well, I don't know. She didn't leave a bloody forwarding address, did she? She's taken the photos of her children, but none of her clothes. I'm sure she'll come back,' she said but didn't sound convinced. She slammed out of the bathroom again.

Shivering, wrapped in her towel, Helen sank down on the loo seat. 'It's my fault. I should've talked to her. I wanted to, but ...'

'We'll work it out. I promise.' Jason squeezed her shoulder.

He wanted to be optimistic, but he couldn't deny that the situation was a right royal cock-up. What if Fay didn't come back, or took her own life even? How would they all feel then, especially Helen?

246

Chapter Twenty

Helen called in sick and spent the next few days laid low by tiredness and despondency. Fay didn't return, and Charlie was giving her the cold shoulder. Jason was working on his stall during the day, and although they spent some time together when he was in, he didn't mention Fay, and Helen didn't have the energy to bring it up. Not just yet.

Fed up with being cooped up, when the sun finally decided to come out she took the rug from the battered sofa and spread it out in the garden. As she watched a robin on matchstick legs hopping along on the grass in front of her, she felt movement behind her. She swung around, but it was only Lee.

'For God's sake,' she snapped, 'can't you make a bit more noise? Your pussyfooting gives me the creeps.'

'I brought you some b-books.'

He was clutching a stack of books to his chest, and didn't seem bothered by her unfriendliness.

'Books? What for?'

Silently he folded his gorgeous, slim body down on the rug beside her. 'We t-talked about dogs, remember?'

Dogs? Oh, yes, she'd asked him that on the night of her seizure. 'You said you knew everything there was to know.'

'L-listen,' he began, then stopped as if he had problems forming the words, which he might well have given his stutter. 'I'm sorry you w-were ill. It was my fault, wasn't it? I scared you so bad that you w-went out, didn't I?'

The hangdog expression in his exquisite slanting dark eyes made her smile, and she put a hand on his arm, then wished she hadn't because he drew back as if she'd burned him.

'It just happens sometimes. No one's to blame.'

Not even me, she thought. Her epilepsy wasn't some divine punishment because she'd disobeyed her mother the night she died. It was just rotten luck.

'It wasn't you,' she repeated. The words caught in her throat when she realised she was beginning to forgive herself.

'Don't cry, Helen,' he said. 'Here, look at the books. They've got all the various dog breeds in them. Then you can f-find the one you remember. Maybe it'll help.' He dropped the stack of books in her lap, still in their greasy plastic library covers.

'Thanks. That's very kind of you.'

'It's what friends are for.' He held out his clenched fist. 'G-give me skin.'

She touched her knuckles to his, and he sent her a dazzling smile.

Afterwards she sat alone savouring the joy spreading in her chest. The robin, which had flown away when Lee arrived, returned to the grass by her feet as if they were old friends. Cocking its head sideways, it studied her with its beady, obsidian eyes.

'Friends, eh?' she said to the bird. 'How do you like that? Not everyone's pissed off with me, then.'

The robin refrained from commenting, obviously, and Helen concentrated on the books Lee had brought. Five in all, one a fact-finder guide on dogs and a Dorling Kindersley book entitled the *RSPCA Complete Dog Care Manual*, which she put aside.

It wasn't as if she was planning on buying a dog.

She reached for the fact-finder guide and went straight to the index page. Lee had mentioned an Airedale Terrier, so she checked that out first. The dog had a wiry, crinkly-looking coat, brown with black markings like a saddle, triangular ears flopped forward, a short upright tail, a square beard.

She found herself back at that early morning on the

common, and the feeling that something was going to happen. She'd wanted to cry – or maybe the crying came later. Everything, then and now, was so jumbled up, but she held on to the thought she knew belonged in the past.

She'd been so bored, and then out of nowhere a dog had appeared, bouncing around in the autumn leaves, playful and cheeky. Oh, how she had longed to play, to kick around in the leaves with that dog. Her innocence and childish delight over the dog's antics couldn't weather what happened later, when that child was crushed with her mother.

'Well, I found you,' she whispered. 'I finally found you.'

She'd need more than that if she was going to convince Wilcox, though.

As Trevor had suggested, Jason sought out Lucy.

He found her at her place of work. His aunt ran a small firm of accountants on the high street near their home, with direct access from the pavement to an open-plan front office. Three members of staff were on the phone, and the low hum from their muted conversations was a stark contrast to the noise on the street.

Lucy's receptionist, Alex, a pretty Chinese woman, smiled when she saw him and knocked on the glass separating his aunt's office from the others.

Also on the phone, Lucy waved to him through the glass.

'What've you been up to?' he asked Alex. He sat down on the edge of her desk while he waited for Lucy to finish her phone call, and started playing with her pens.

She smacked his hand away. 'Oh, the usual. Working, clubbing, hanging out with me mates. And you?'

'The usual. Doing my house up, hanging out with criminals. Nothing much.'

Alex laughed and snatched a pen from his hand. 'Stop fiddling with my pens.'

Just then Lucy stuck her head out of her door, interrupting their banter. 'Stop harassing my staff and get in here.'

He jumped down from the desk. 'Duty calls.'

'What can I do for you?' asked Lucy as she closed the door. His aunt wore her usual gold jewellery and an olive-green dress with a square neckline and had piled her hair high in a tidy bouffant. She looked both business-like and stunning, and he could see why Trevor had fallen for her.

Normally Lucy would cross-examine him about his love life, what he was doing, if he was eating properly, in a way which was both endearing and depressing because he'd often wished his own mother would show the same interest. She'd never spoken to him like this before, and she must have guessed this wasn't a social visit. A new respect for her grew. In some ways she was very like his father, just nicer.

He decided to come straight to the point. 'Trevor says you may have some information about a public limited company called Ransome & Daughters.'

'Might do.' Lucy arched her eyebrows, warning him to tread carefully. 'What's it to you? More to the point, what's it to Trevor?'

'He's just trying to help me out with something, that's all.' He'd hate to be the cause of ructions between his aunt and uncle, but this was important.

'Does this by any chance have something to do with Derek?'

In response to his nod, she sighed and turned to a filing cabinet behind her desk.

'Okay,' she said when she returned to her desk, 'I have the information you're asking about, but before I share it with you, I need to know what you want it for. I know you and Derek don't always see eye to eye, and I can understand why because he's a bloody pain in the arse half the time, but he's my brother. Don't expect me to be party to anything that'll harm him, or his business. Are we clear on that?'

'I'm not going to harm him or the business. Why would I do that?'

Lucy raised her eyebrows, but said nothing.

A flicker of anger stirred in him. 'If you're referring to that episode with Cathy, I was over that a long time ago.'

'Yeah, right,' she said, but not unkindly. She hesitated for a moment then pushed a ring binder across the desk. 'This is Derek's investment portfolio. As you can see, he likes to play it safe. It's mostly fixed interest products, government bonds, although he does occasionally trade in options or invest in derivatives and hedge funds. The trick to reduce risks is diversification, spreading your investments across a range of products, but I expect you know that.'

Jason opened the folder and skimmed through the information Lucy had summarised. 'Does he buy stocks and shares?'

'Next page.'

He turned the page and ran his eyes down the list of companies in which his father owned shares. There, as he'd suspected, was the evidence of his connection to the company Helen worked for, in the form of shares, but whether this represented a small or large share would depend on the total number of shares issued, and Lucy hadn't provided him with that information.

'What's the size of his share in Ransome's?' He turned the folder around and pointed to the listing for the auction house.

Lucy gave it a cursory glance, then regarded him thoughtfully. 'Well, he's on the board of directors, so I'd say that his interest is more than just an investment.'

'How long has he been on the board for?'

'Oh, about twenty years, I'd say. What's *your* interest?'

'I know a girl who works there.'

'A nice girl?'

'Very nice. Her mother worked there too.'

'*Worked*?' Lucy pounced on his use of the past tense.

'She was murdered. Twenty years ago.'

Lucy paled. 'You're not suggesting …?'

'No, I'm not, but Dad's taking a very keen interest in this girl, and I want to know why.'

'Well, he would be if you are,' Lucy observed. 'You know that.'

Jason shook his head. 'It's more than that. I think he knows why this woman was murdered.'

'Oh, come off it. If he knew, he'd have gone to the police.'

'Not if money was at stake. *You* know that.'

Back at work on Friday, Bill fussed over Helen and practically forced her to drink a cup of tea before starting.

'I heard you were ill. Better now?'

'Yeah, thanks.'

The tea was strong and milky and with three sugars, which Bill, like Charlie, insisted was the perfect pick-me-up. Helen hated sugar in her tea but didn't have the heart to tell him.

Besides, it was nice having someone who cared.

'It wasn't anything I said, was it, love?' he asked. 'You know, all that stuff about your mother?'

'Of course not. The thing is, I …'

How would Bill react if he knew about her condition? *When* to confide was always a problem. But she suspected that Bill knew more about what Mimi had been involved in than he was admitting. If she opened up a little, he might do the same.

'I suffer from epilepsy.' There, she'd said it. 'Sometimes I have seizures. No one knows why but in me there's a connection between that and over-excitement. I have to eat properly too and get enough sleep. Pace myself, if you like.' She smiled. 'And I mustn't forget my medication.'

'I know, I was around when you were little, remember?'

'You knew? But you didn't say anything.'

'It never made no difference to me, love. We are what we are.' Bill took her hand. 'Look, I'm sorry for yelling at you. Life's been pretty crap for you, hasn't it, what with you losing your parents, and them lot shunting you from one home to another like you were worthless. And don't bother defending them. I know all about it. There's precious few secrets you can keep around here. Especially your gran, that heartless old witch. Fancy treating a child like that.'

'She had her reasons.'

'Wanted to get 'er hands on your shares, I wager.'

'I think she was trying to protect me.'

'Hah!'

'No, seriously, think about it. Where was I when my mother died?' She stared hard at him.

'You were a witness,' he said when the penny dropped.

'Except whoever did it might not have known about my epilepsy. He or she didn't know that I hadn't actually seen anything. Because I was out.'

Bill frowned. '"He or she" you say, but wasn't it that woman … sorry, can't remember her name, but wasn't it some personal thing? A jealousy drama?'

'I used to think so.'

'You think it has to do with something your mother knew?'

'Yes.'

'About what went on here back then?' he continued.

She nodded.

'Jesus Christ, love!' He got up abruptly and started pacing the cracked lino floor, running his hand back and forth across his bald pate. 'If you know what's good for you, you stop right there.'

'Names, Bill. Dates, places, overheard conversations. Anything you can think of.'

'No.' He scowled at her.

'Please.'

'It'll end in tears,' he warned.

'But it won't be mine.'

'You don't know what you're messing with, love.' He reached for his mug, then grimaced after a slug of cold tea. 'Promise you'll be careful? Not go barging in and getting a name for yourself in the wrong places?'

'I promise,' she lied.

'Well,' he sighed, 'I don't remember much, but it was around the time the company was going to float that rumours started flying that some of the clients weren't what you'd call completely kosher.' He crooked his fingers in the air. 'Anyway, your mum was furious and looked into it. Then there was that nasty business about that woman who was following her around, and the next thing we hear is that she's been murdered. It was a shock.'

Helen nodded with a sense of relief. She'd suspected that her mother may have been involved in something illegal, something worse than what Letitia was doing. Hearing that she was a whistle-blower was a relief. 'Any names?'

'A few.' Bill didn't meet her eyes.

'Which ones?'

'You won't know most of them. Some aren't around any more.' Bill rattled off a handful of names, quickly as if he hoped she wasn't paying attention. He'd been right, she didn't know any of them. Except one.

Derek Moody. Jason's father.

Chapter Twenty-One

Convinced that Wilcox would want to know about the dog she'd mentioned last time she saw him, she managed to get another appointment with him. She told Mrs Deakin she wasn't well enough to be back at work after all and left early. Lost in her own thoughts, she crossed the paved square in front of Scotland Yard and didn't see the cyclist until she heard the screech of brakes.

'Why don't you watch where you're going?' he yelled after her, and she made a rude gesture at his retreating back.

Some people.

Wilcox was less pleased to see her this time, but he asked her to sit down, offered her coffee. She said no thanks and watched him slouch in his chair with his hands behind his head.

He was either arrogant or overconfident. Or maybe both. At least she knew where she stood with him.

There was a younger officer in the room with them, a blonde-haired woman with piercing blue eyes. Wilcox introduced them. 'Detective Inspector Karen Whitehouse. Helen Stephens, a former witness in a murder case.'

The DI just nodded, but her indifference had the same effect on her as Wilcox's arrogance. Neither of them were going to make this easy for her.

'What can I help you with this time?' asked Wilcox.

Helen decided to come straight to the point. 'Fay Cooper.'

'Was released from prison earlier this year.' He opened a file, glanced at it perfunctorily as if he already knew the contents front to back. 'For good behaviour, no less, but then again she never struck me as a troublemaker. It's funny how you can tell. What about her?'

'I've met her, and I don't think she did it.'

His eyebrows rose. 'I see. And you base her innocence on, what, exactly?'

Oh, no, he wasn't going to make this easy at all.

'The knife,' she replied. 'Her husband knew she had one like that. I wonder if he might have set her up.'

Wilcox nodded. 'It occurred to us at the time, yes. But it turned out he had a rock solid alibi. He'd taken their children to visit his sister in the south of France. Besides, if he was trying to set her up, why would he remove the knife from the car?'

'Maybe he paid someone else to do it.' Something flitted at the back of her mind, a thought annoyingly just out of reach.

'That occurred to us as well, but it would have made more sense for him to try to get rid of a troublesome wife rather than kill his lover, wouldn't it?'

At the word *lover*, Helen flinched. She still had trouble picturing her mother as a home-wrecker. But she wasn't giving up. 'You told me to come back to you if I remembered something. It's about the dog I mentioned last time. I now know what sort it was. An Airedale Terrier.'

As she said it, the image of it came back to her, stronger than ever before. Brown fur, lolling tongue, long legs dancing with boundless energy.

'You're sure?'

'Positive. I've looked into it, and that's the dog I remember.'

'Was it there on its own?' DI Whitehouse spoke for the first time, in a voice soft and husky like a 1940s Hollywood starlet. A hand gesture accompanied her question, and Helen noticed her long pale fingers, nails shiny with a clear varnish, sheer perfection.

'No, it wasn't a stray, the owner was there too. He wore a big overcoat with a hood or something, I'm not sure. I wonder if he saw something.'

'No one came forward, Helen,' said Wilcox.

'Maybe we could track them down.'

'If they didn't come forward back then, they're not likely to now, are they? No, I think—'

There was that thought again, and this time she managed to pin it down. 'Something else has actually just occurred to me. A cyclist nearly ran me over outside this building, that's what made me think of it. There was a cyclist there that morning. I remember him quite clearly now. He was dressed all in black, with gloves and a hat, and something across the lower half of his face, a scarf perhaps, I don't know. And his bicycle was one of those racing bikes with curved handle bars, quite low down so you're sort of crouching over the bike, if you know what I mean.'

Wilcox sighed. 'If those men were there, why didn't Fay Cooper mention them? She was facing a murder charge.'

'She was high, she could've forgotten. It's worth a try, isn't it?'

He regarded her thoughtfully. She stared back without saying anything, gave him time to process what she'd just said in the hope he would agree it was worth following up on. The only sound in the room was her own breathing which came in short bursts from her excitement at being this close.

Then he frowned and crossed his arms. 'Are *you* under the influence of any kind of substance?'

'No!' The sudden rage at having her hopes dashed made her clench her fists, and she saw from his smug smile that he'd noticed. Immediately she put a lid on it. Blowing her top at one of Scotland Yard's finest would get her nowhere. 'I don't drink. It interferes with epilepsy medication. That's a well-known fact. Weed can help, but I'm not doing that either.' Not any more, but he didn't have to know.

'I wasn't aware of that, but I'm learning all the time.'

He flashed her the smile she remembered from that day at the police station twenty years ago. It was a smile that said 'I know something you don't'. Her five-year-old gut instinct didn't trust it back then, and she didn't trust it now either. What did he know this time that she didn't? Had he and the DI discussed her before she came?

She could almost hear them. 'An interesting case … a child witness, unreliable … making up stories in her head … can't come to terms with what happened … an epileptic, you know … blah blah blah'. She imagined them laughing at her, and bit down hard on the inside of her mouth.

'There's something else. My mother …' Helen stopped. What could she say? She had no proof that something was going on with the company back then, only what Bill had said which wasn't much. No proof of Moody's involvement either. 'I think my mother might've been involved in something which got her killed,' she said instead. 'She had a bag with her when she died. With papers and computer discs in it. I've mentioned that before as well.'

Wilcox sent her an exasperated smile. 'You've mentioned the bag, yes. You never said anything about any papers or computer discs. And I've tried to tell you, there was no bag.'

'What sort of papers?' asked Whitehouse.

'Just papers. I remember finding them boring.'

'"Just papers",' the detective repeated. 'Can you be more specific? Business documents, leaflets? Closely typed or with lots of pictures?'

'The company's logo was on them, but that's all I know. I was only five.'

'What company?'

'The family company that my mother worked for. Ransome & Daughters.'

Assessing her, Whitehouse said, 'Why would papers from your mother's own company make you draw the conclusion that she was involved in anything? It seems, well, tenuous.'

Helen hesitated. 'In the world of auctioneering …' she began, then stopped. She felt a certain loyalty to the company, which was unexpected. 'Well, let me put it this way, not everyone who trades through an auction house has a clear conscience. Sometimes art and antiques are sold without a provenance. There's usually a good reason for that, like if it's been in your Auntie Edna's attic for fifty years, or else it …' she shrugged.

'Could be stolen.' Whitehouse finished the sentence for her.

Helen nodded and realised, stupidly, this was like preaching to the converted. Wilcox and Whitehouse were police officers and knew more about the shady side of business than she did. 'I think my mother was a whistle-blower.'

'I see.' Whitehouse nodded slowly.

Wilcox shook his head. 'Impressive.'

'What?'

'Impressive what the human mind can conjure up when it's desperate.'

Helen's rage returned, white-hot and corrosive. 'I want you to reopen the case of my mother's murder.'

'Look,' said Wilcox, 'I've got terrorists roaming the streets of London. Now, I appreciate this is very real for you, but I can't justify reopening a case on the grounds of practically nothing. It requires manpower and resources, and most of all, proof that Fay Cooper didn't kill your mother. If you can provide me with that, I'll reconsider.' The latter he added in an undertone which told her he didn't believe she'd be able to provide any.

And he'd be right. What did she have? Some vague memory of a cyclist and a man with a dog? There were the files on

Letitia's computer, but they proved only a current sideline. What she did have was the uncertainty of a recovered drug addict, a couple of missing knives plus a missing bag and, above all, her own overwhelming sense of loss.

She rose. Wilcox was a busy man with a career to pursue and other people like herself to fob off. He could do nothing more for her. She understood that, but she still hated him for forcing her to face the fact that her mother was long gone. Mimi was dead, and the gap left behind was closing up like a scab over a cut. Scratching it would only make things worse.

To her surprise Whitehouse caught up with her in Back Hall reception.

'Here, take my card,' she said, and held out a pristine-looking business card as perfect as her manicured fingernails. 'If you do find anything, no matter how insignificant you think it is, give me a call, and we'll chat about it. I can't promise anything, but it'll help me get a clearer picture of what happened. In the meantime, I'll read up on the case.'

'Why are you being so nice to me?'

'You sound like that doesn't happen very often.'

'It doesn't.' Except Jason, who'd been unfailingly nice, even when she'd lied to him.

Cool blue eyes sought Helen's for a moment. 'Maybe I understand how you feel.'

'How can you?'

'I lost my own mother when I was young. A hit-and-run. They never got the guy. Believe me, I know how it eats away at you.'

'Do *you* think I'm making it all up? That "my mind is conjuring up images because it's desperate"?'

Whitehouse pressed the card in her hand. 'Here's what I think. I think you're confused, you've never really dealt with

260

your mother's death, and you were an unreliable witness. But, no, I don't think you're making it up.'

Helen left with a feeling that it hadn't been a complete waste. DI Whitehouse was going to read up on the case. She may well come to the same conclusion, that she hadn't enough to go on for the case to be reopened, but it gave her an element of hope.

Also, without meaning to, Wilcox had given her an idea. If he wasn't prepared to try and find the old witnesses, she would find them herself.

Jason was having a quiet day at the market when his mobile rang.

It was Trevor. 'Any chance you could come by the house this afternoon? There's something I need to talk to you about.'

'I can come now. I'll close up for the day. Unless you want to tell me over the phone.'

'Face to face is best,' said his uncle, and hung up.

Trevor opened the door before Jason had a chance to knock. 'I'm off to the park with Jessie. Walk with me.'

The Rottweiler was sitting by his feet, lead in mouth, wagging her tail. Trevor clipped it on and locked the door behind him.

'Someone's excited,' said Jason as Jessie pulled them along the pavement, muscles rippling.

'Best thing she knows. Some dogs love food, others just want to laze on the sofa all day. For Jessie it's walkies. Here, girl, look what I've got.'

Trevor pulled a rubber ball out of his pocket, and Jessie whined and bounced up to grab it off him with what Jason could only describe as a big grin on her face. One day he'd like to have a dog like Jessie. That, and a houseful of kids. Then he remembered why he was here.

'What did you want to—'

'Not here,' said Trevor.

At the park Trevor unclipped the lead and gave Jason the rubber ball to toss. Jessie ran after it, brought it down like it was prey, then trotted back, but ran off again as soon as Jason reached for it.

'So that's how you wanna play.'

Jessie growled in reply and moved out of his reach when he tried to take the ball again.

'Oh, she'll have hours of fun doing that. Never tires of it. Let's indulge her.' Trevor took a step towards the dog who kept running off and coming back, always keeping the ball just out of reach as they moved along the path. Finally she placed it at Jason's feet and allowed him to toss it again.

'I wanted to talk to you about my time with your dad,' said Trevor. 'Something I've never told a living soul, not even Lucy. You know I started out as his chauffeur. A few years after, I moved on to personal security, although I still did a bit of driving. There wasn't a job description as such.'

'Like Jones?'

'Yeah, a bit like Jones.' Trevor's lip curled, either from humour or distaste. 'You'd be surprised how much of a commitment it is to keep a man like your father safe. You've gotta have an eye on every finger 24/7 and be ready to act if you see any threats. No good hesitating. Like being on presidential detail, I suppose.'

'Did you ever have to, er, get rid of any threats?'

'Might've hospitalised one or two. Never had an official complaint, though.' He grinned. 'Of course, Lucy put a stop to that when we met. Wanted me on the straight and narrow, or I'd be out on me ear, thank you very much. Her exact words.'

'Sounds like her,' said Jason. It shook him a little, hearing Trevor refer to the job of guarding his father as nothing more than an ordinary day at the office. Despite his efforts he'd never quite succeeded in making himself immune to what his father did for a living. 'Did it involve guns? Knives?'

'Sonny, this is your father we're talking about. He's as legit as they come in his line of business. Just don't make the mistake of taking legit for softness. There are many ways a person can be persuaded, know wha' I mean.'

'I can guess,' said Jason drily.

'So twenty years ago, give or take, I was driving your old man around. This was a job with very anti-social hours. Late into the night, early morning sometimes. Including one morning, at Ealing Common.'

Jason swung around, and blood rushed to his head with a *whoosh*. 'What?'

'Sorry, I didn't click, not until you asked me to look into the Mimi Stephanov thing. Then I remembered more than I wanted to. Never told a living soul, and I wasn't planning on telling you either. Not until Lucy ... well it was something she said last night. Something to do with the length of Derek's involvement in that company. I knew he met with someone that day.'

'Who?'

'I didn't see.' Trevor shook his head. 'I was told to stay in the car. I didn't like it and said so. He told me he didn't pay me to have an opinion. So I stayed put. Later I heard a woman was stabbed, but your dad assured me he had nothing to do with that.'

'You believe him?'

Trevor shrugged. Just because he didn't work for Derek Moody any more that didn't release him from the obligation to keep his mouth shut. Jason knew that.

'Do you think he met with Mimi Stephanov?' he asked.

'I couldn't say.'

'What can you say?'

His uncle sent him a dark look. 'Lucy will have my guts for garters,' he muttered.

'Lucy is the least of your problems right now.'

'You're not married to her. Okay, what I *can* say is he wasn't gone long. Came back looking …' Trevor whistled for Jessie who was straying too close to a group of mums with toddlers. A little girl was crying, and her mother lifted her up and held her on her hip.

'Could you keep your dog on a leash, please?' she said.

She was pint-sized, and Trevor, a six-foot-four ex-bodyguard with the advantage of probably a hundred and fifty pounds, towered over her. He slipped his finger under Jessie's collar.

'She'd never harm a kid no matter how excited she gets,' he said.

'Maybe not, but my daughter doesn't know that.'

'You're absolutely right, madam. I suppose when you're that age, big dogs can be scary.' Trevor smiled at the little girl who'd stopped crying and was now staring at this mountain of a man with huge eyes. She'd stuck her thumb in her mouth, and her dark lashes were still dewy with tears.

Jason experienced a curious kick inside. She reminded him of Helen, of what she must have looked like as a child. He could almost hear her crying, like a twenty-year-old echo.

'Thank you,' the woman said when Trevor had clipped the lead back on.

'He came back looking like … what?' Jason asked when they turned down a less crowded path in the park.

'Sort of sick, worried maybe, not sure. He got back in the car and told me his contact didn't turn up. He'd taken his suit jacket off and draped it over his hands inside out. When we found out later what had happened, he reassured me he had nothing to do with it, like I told you, and I never pressed him, not even after we became related. No point with your old man.'

'And that's all?' Jason couldn't help the mixture of disappointment and relief warring inside him.

'Pretty much, except he told me to stop at an all-night petrol station. Wanted to use the gents. When he came out, he'd scrunched his jacket into a bundle. I didn't think it the proper way to treat a bespoke tailored jacket, but I thought it best not to say anything.'

'Could he have wrapped something in his jacket?'

Away from the toddlers and their concerned parents, Trevor released Jessie and tossed the ball again.

'Possibly. You tell me.'

Chapter Twenty-Two

On Saturday while Jason was out, Helen had found the contact numbers for three local papers and placed an advertisement under 'Classified', appealing for the owner of an Airedale Terrier who'd been walking his dog on that particular morning to come forward if he had he seen something relevant to a murder which took place.

She hadn't said anything to Jason about the way his father's name cropped up in connection with R & D. She sensed that he really liked her, and didn't want to spoil it by blackening his father's name before she knew if she had any real reason to. She also had mixed feelings about placing the ad. If the dog owner had anything to do with her mother's death, she was potentially exposing herself. Even though contact would only be through the editor, it wouldn't protect her against someone determined enough to find her, but it seemed like she had no other options left.

It was like trying to find the proverbial needle in a haystack.

There'd been no calls on Sunday and so far Monday was proving to be uneventful, other than the fact that Ruth had come to the office, which had only happened once in the three weeks Helen had worked there. She thought back to last Monday, when Ruth had seemed almost approving of Helen standing up to Letitia. Where did Ruth's loyalties really lie? It was time to find out.

The front office was empty, the secretary out to lunch maybe. Steeling herself for a possible confrontation, Helen put her hand on the door to Ruth's office, but stopped at the sound of a high-pitched voice, bordering on the hysterical.

Ruth.

'You just can't wait to get rid of her, can you? So you can get your hands on her shares.'

'Don't be ridiculous,' retorted Letitia, in her characteristic low voice. 'Those shares would be divided between you, me and Helen. It won't make any difference to Mother other than giving her the rest she needs, and the three of us will have more power on the board.'

'Yes. Helen,' Ruth spat. 'What made *you* take her under your wing?'

'That's what Mother wanted. You see, I *do* listen to her. Besides, she works hard.'

Helen half-snorted at that. The aunts could say what they liked about her; she had Aggie's affection, and that was enough. She thought of barging right in, if only for the satisfaction of seeing their red-faced shame, but something held her back.

Listen and learn.

'That's all you ever think about,' Ruth complained. 'Money, shares, the company. It's like a stuck record.'

'If you'd shouldered your part of the burden when we needed an extra pair of hands, things might've turned out differently. But oh no, you had to go off and try and have babies, spending a fortune only for them to tell you that your ovaries are shrivelled up like dried prunes.'

There was a shocked gasp from Ruth, and she was silent for a moment. Despite her resentment, Helen couldn't help feeling sympathetic.

'You can be so cruel sometimes. You always know exactly where to stick the knife, don't you?'

'I'm just being realistic, Ruthie. And to think, there was a ready-made child you could've had,' Letitia added. 'Too bad that didn't work out.'

Didn't work out? Helen stiffened. What did that mean? Had Ruth wanted her and not been allowed? But who hadn't allowed it, the law or Aggie? It tallied with what her grandmother had said about wanting to keep her away from Arseni. As a blood relation he would have had a claim, but Ruth wouldn't.

Letitia sighed exasperatedly. 'But why don't we put it behind us for now? I do think it's best for Mother to go into a nursing home. I worry about her mental capabilities, and the daily care is really too much for Mrs Sanders. She's told me so on a couple of occasions.'

Hah, thought Helen, still just outside the door. From what she'd witnessed of the nurse's engagement, it had seemed like a pretty cushy job to her.

'There's nothing wrong with her mind,' Ruth snapped. 'Her disability is physical. Mrs Sanders stays, and we engage a male nurse to do the heavy lifting.'

'You're not thinking straight. If she stays for now, six months later we'll be faced with the same problem. By then she may have donated her shares to a cat society or something equally eccentric.'

'Maybe thinking straight isn't my strongest point, but I know for a fact that Mother would prefer to stay in her own home for as long as possible. And even if she's in a nursing home, she'll still have her solicitor to look after her financial affairs, so you may whistle for those shares all you like!'

'Despite your low opinion of me I just want to make sure she isn't being exploited. This Sweetman character ...' Letitia paused, 'well, he's hardly our kind, is he? Who knows what sort of hold he has over her? Their association never made sense to me.'

'Maybe I'll ask Helen what she thinks,' said Ruth.

'Helen? She has nothing to do with this.'

'She should do. Mother is very fond of her, you know. I could probably persuade her to be on my side in this.'

Letitia scoffed. 'I doubt it. Not after the way you let her

down. You could've been her new mummy but you didn't want a child that wasn't perfect. You didn't even try to make her love you.'

'I never said—'

'Not only that, but she was the child of the woman who slept with your husband. Admit it, you couldn't even bear to look at her. You'd have made a terrible parent!'

Helen stifled her horror with her hand. She'd heard enough. Trembling and battling with a sudden headache, she tiptoed backwards and left as quietly as she had come.

On the stairs she met the secretary clutching a greasy sandwich bag. 'Can I help you?'

'No.'

Screw them both, she thought.

Screw them *all*.

She collected her rucksack and jacket from the staff room, then stormed out the front, baffling the security guard. She had to get away. Away from the aunts and their poisonous, complex relationship. Aggie who manipulated them all like a giant toad in her nest, Arseni and his cloying attention.

Away from Fay and the feelings of wanting revenge, which hung over her like a dark cloud. From the doubts which sucked all the energy out of her.

Everything which stopped her having a normal, proper life.

In her bag she had what she needed: money, phone, medication, the picture of her parents. The rest could come. She would jump on a train out of London, to Scotland maybe, and leave it all behind. Start again.

She was halfway to Kings Cross station when she realised this meant leaving Jason too.

This is no good, she thought, as she stood outside the imposing entrance to R & D again. She'd overheard enough to cause her immense pain, but she owed it to Ruth, and to herself, to get the whole story. The danger of eavesdropping was that it gave you only half the picture.

Thoughts of Jason had cooled her anger, like a glass of milk on an ulcerated stomach. He wouldn't just walk off. He would stay and get to the bottom of things, do what was right, not for himself but for others. He could have thrown her out of the house when he discovered the truth about her, but he didn't. She admired him for that.

More than anything, it was the idea of never seeing him again which had stopped her from beginning a new life in the Outer Hebrides. She'd run away once before, and it hadn't solved anything. This time she wouldn't.

'Thought you'd got the sack the way you took off earlier,' said the security guard.

'No, not the sack,' she replied, and clomped up the stairs to the offices again.

Neither of the aunts were there, the secretary informed her. 'But Mrs Partridge will be back soon. You can wait in her office.'

Helen sent her a questioning look.

'I know about the family connection,' she added. Was it Helen's imagination, or was she just a bit less sniffy?

'Thanks.'

Ruth's office was as richly furnished as Letitia's. Gleaming desk, Persian rug, grandfather clock, a hideous but expensive onyx globe in the corner. It was also completely devoid of anything personal, not even a magazine to read, probably because Ruth was rarely here. Helen dropped down into a shiny leather sofa to wait for her. After half an hour Ruth still hadn't returned, and when she stuck her head out of the door, the secretary's station was empty and her computer switched off.

Helen debated with herself whether to continue waiting or maybe catch Ruth another day, except she had no idea when Ruth would be in the office again. Then she spotted her aunt's handbag on the floor beside the desk, and decided to snoop. She had no reason to, other than feeling bloody-minded. And, she had to admit, a hope that Ruth would come back and say ... well, something. Anything to take away the feeling that nobody could be bothered with her. That she was nothing but a nuisance.

But there was nothing interesting in Ruth's handbag, so she tried the desk drawers instead. There had to be something personal somewhere. Even though it was an office, it wasn't right that there was so little life in it.

But the desk drawers contained only stationary. She was thinking about turning on her aunt's computer when her eyes fell on the grandfather clock. It was one of those longcase clocks with a pendulum and weights, the kind that would tick so loudly the sound would fill the office. Except this one was either broken or hadn't been wound in a while, because it wasn't ticking.

On impulse she opened the door to the pendulum casing. Nothing looked broken, but then again, she wasn't an expert on clocks. Then she noticed something at the bottom, reached down, and pulled out a bundle wrapped in chamois leather.

The parcel was long and thin, heavier at one end than the other, and she unwrapped it carefully.

Inside was one of the missing paper knives.

Her head spun. Which knife was it? Her mother would never have given it to Ruth, certainly not after the vitriol Ruth had spouted about Mimi earlier, which meant either way she'd stolen it. But from Mimi or Fay?

Her headache grew, became a steady thumping in her

skull. She needed to lie down, but was damned if she was going to do that here – she might wake up with a paper knife in her own throat.

The sound of the phone ringing in the secretary's office reminded her that the door might be opened at any moment, so she closed the clock again and put the knife in her rucksack. She was back in the secretary's front office just as Ruth appeared at the top of the stairs.

'Did you want something?'

'I was just leaving.'

Ruth made a face which might have been a smile, and her features softened. 'You don't have to, you know. Leave, I mean.'

'Perhaps it was better if I did.'

'Why don't you come in?' Ruth went back into her office. Helen shrugged and followed her, watching as her aunt opened the onyx globe which housed a small bar and poured herself a gin. 'Would you like a drink?'

Despite there being nothing personal in Ruth's office, the bar was well-stocked, Helen noted. Funny how drinks were a requirement for some people in their working environment.

'I'm all right. But thanks.'

Her aunt closed the globe again and turned, tumbler in hand. 'I'd like to try and make things better between us. I think we got off on the wrong foot when I saw you at Mother's.'

'There's an understatement,' Helen muttered.

'I'm just not sure where to start. Perhaps we should get some questions out of the way first. I imagine you must have plenty.'

'I'd like to know more about my mother. What she was like and all that. Your relationship.' *And* why you're in possession of her paper knife, she nearly said, but decided to keep that to herself for the time being. There had to be a way of using it to her advantage.

'My sister often tells me I need to clear my conscience,' said Ruth. 'So I'll be frank. You may not want to hear this, but I'm going to say it anyway. Please don't judge me too harshly. I was so jealous of your mum. She was beautiful and successful, knew what she wanted. And she was a mother. She had Aggie's ear, and not many people can lay claim to that. Cantankerous old bat.' This time her grimace definitely was a smile, a rueful one. 'Whatever she touched, it turned to gold. I really resented her.'

'But it didn't,' Helen protested. 'It wasn't all gold and jewels and half the kingdom. Her husband died very young, and her child – me – has epilepsy. I can drop dead at any time, did you know that? "Sudden death in epilepsy", they call it. How's that for happy ever after?'

'I see all that now, but back then, I had a *thing* about your mother. An obsession I suppose. And then there was that nonsense with Jeremy.'

'Aggie called your ex-husband a "disaster".'

'Mother says the strangest things sometimes.'

'Was he unfaithful to you? With my mother?'

Ruth sighed, then nodded.

'When your father died, she needed a shoulder to cry on. She could've taken her pick of men, but for some reason she chose my husband.'

'Well, she wasn't very likely to cry on yours,' said Helen, 'if you resented her so much.'

'I suppose not,' Ruth replied mildly. 'Turned out it had been going on for a while. Since around the time she got pregnant with you.'

Helen's head jerked up as the possible implications hit her.

'Your father was being treated for leukaemia before you were born,' Ruth continued. 'Cancer drugs are known for causing infertility. I thought you might be Jeremy's child, because you were so blonde. It completely knocked me sideways. We'd been trying for so long, you see.'

'Is that why you murdered her?'

Ruth gasped, and the gin went down the wrong way. Coughing violently, she turned puce as she heaved for breath, and tears sprang into her eyes from the discomfort. Helen crossed her arms and did nothing to help her.

Go on, choke on it, she thought. Just like my mother choked on her own blood.

'I didn't kill your mother!' Ruth wheezed when she got her breath back. 'What a preposterous idea. I might be an old soak, but ... Good heavens! I was about to say that for a *while* I thought you were his child, but later I knew I was wrong. Your features are very much like Dmitri's. Although—' She stopped abruptly.

'Although what?'

Ruth lifted her glass to take another sip, thought better of it, and put the crystal tumbler down on the desk where it made a ring on the polished wood. 'Your father was seriously ill and receiving treatment. At that time, twenty-six years ago, IVF wasn't readily available, if it even existed. Your parents could've arranged for his sperm to be frozen and kept, but whether they did that or not, I don't know, your mother didn't tell me. If they didn't, he's unlikely to be your biological parent.'

'Then who is?'

Ruth sent her a tired look. 'Do you really need to ask? Your uncle, of course. And that didn't sit well with Letitia because *she* had her eyes on him.'

Because her headache was getting worse, Helen took a taxi home rather than the tube. The journey passed in a daze. Either Ruth had killed her mother in a crime of passion, or the murder weapon was still missing.

So Letitia had had her eyes on Arseni. Did they have a relationship back then? Did they still? she wondered, just as she had wondered when she first met her uncle. He never married, but that meant nothing today. If Mimi had come between them, could Letitia have lost her rag and had her bumped off? It wasn't impossible, except Letitia was far too aloof to squabble over any man.

Then what about Arseni himself? Mimi may have used the next best thing to her husband's sperm, his brother's, in order to have a child. Enough to incense a proud man when he realised he'd been exploited, and it could explain why he was all over Helen now, with his peculiar mix of guilt and attentiveness.

Neither scenario painted her mother in a particularly positive light, and it left a bad taste in her mouth. She'd loved her mother, hadn't she? Or had she merely loved the memory of having a mother, since she couldn't remember their time together?

She rubbed her temples while trying to make sense of it all. Instead of having her questions answered, she'd been presented with a whole heap of new ones.

The taxi pulled up outside the house, and she climbed out to find her path blocked by a broad-shouldered and black-suited individual. A hard lump formed in her gut, and she took a step back to collide with a similar obstacle. Her legs began to shake.

The first man put a heavy hand on her shoulder, and before she could even squeak, his other hand clamped over her mouth. She found herself being lifted across the road, too shocked to struggle, and deposited by a dark car she hadn't noticed when the taxi pulled up. Wordlessly the other man opened the door, and a light came on, revealing luxurious cream leather seats and a bar. Crystal decanters threw prisms of rainbow colours across the interior, dazzling her before she saw the guy inside.

He looked familiar, his voice was not. It was as smooth as a marbled egg and as alluring as the prospect of a viper's kiss.

'Miss Stephens, perhaps you'd be kind enough to step inside.'

Chapter Twenty-Three

It was an order, not an invitation. Jason's father wasn't used to being disobeyed.

She thought of making a run for it, but one goon had a firm grip on her arm, the other looked like he could give chase without breaking into a sweat. They would probably hurt her if she resisted them.

She allowed the first muscleman to push her inside the car while she clutched her rucksack to her chest. If Jason's father was planning to do away with her, he probably wouldn't do it in his nice, clean, posh car.

'Who the hell do you think you are? You can't just go bundling people into the back of bloody cars!'

'Language, Miss Stephens, language,' Derek Moody signalled to the man to shut the door.

Having done so, both goons slid into the front of the car, which was separated from the back by a glass screen, and the car pulled away from the kerb.

'Where are we going?' Helen demanded.

'For a little drive.'

'Where to? The river? Are you going to throw me in with something heavy around my legs?'

'Such originality. Tut-tut.'

Helen sat back against the leather seat and crossed her arms. 'Nice car,' she sneered. 'You'd better be careful you don't get blood on the seats. I've heard it's difficult to get out, and what a shame that would be.'

'Thank you. It's my favourite.' A small smile tugged at the corners of his mouth. 'For your information, I tend to do my bloodletting elsewhere. Forensics, and all that.'

'That's reassuring.'

He laughed suddenly, a hearty guffaw, which under different circumstances would have been contagious, but Helen had lost her sense of humour at the mention of bloodletting.

'I have to hand it to you,' he said, 'you're one in a million.'

'You got that right.'

'The thing is, my dear, I only want to talk to you.'

'Oh, that's what they call it,' she retorted, emboldened by his laughter. 'Attacking people in the street and bundling them into the back of a car? That's a real conversation opener.'

He shrugged. 'Sometimes people think they don't want to talk to *me* so I need a little extra persuasion. I don't like the word "no".'

His expression returned to the glacial stare she remembered from her uncle's dinner party. Not many people would dare say no to this man and live to tell the tale. Except perhaps his son.

Jason had rejected his father's lifestyle and did what he believed in, helping others less fortunate than himself, despite the threat that his father could throw a spanner in the works at any time.

And Jason was her friend. At least she thought he was.

She stuck her chin out, the chin everyone said she'd inherited from her mother. 'You wanted to talk to me, so talk.'

He was silent for a heartbeat or two, and she regretted her cockiness. 'What are you up to?' he asked.

'What am I *up* to?'

'I didn't take you for an idiot. Please answer my question.'

'I don't know what you mean.'

Derek Moody leaned closer, his nearness in itself threat enough. 'Don't insult me. I've been in business a long time. So has your uncle. Our paths occasionally cross, but mostly we respect each other's territory. And then suddenly you pop up, in my son's well-meaning but misguided little get-up of all places. Flaunting your assets, as it were, and what red-blooded young male could possibly resist?'

He looked her up and down, implying he'd have no trouble resisting any kind of temptation, least of all anything she had to offer, and Helen, who'd never flaunted anything in her entire life, felt her blood boil.

'What does Stephanov want from me?' he asked.

'Nothing! It has nothing to do with him. I've only just met him.'

'Well, of course you have, otherwise he'd have mentioned you before. He talks of nothing else now.'

'Who? My uncle?'

'My son,' Moody replied.

'Jason?' Helen shook her head. 'I've only just met both of them. A few weeks back. I knew I had an uncle, but I'd never met him before, and Jason … well, that was a complete coincidence.'

'I don't believe in coincidences. Try again.'

'But it's true!'

The goon in the front passenger seat cranked his fat neck around and sent her a malevolent stare, but Moody shook his head, and the man turned back.

'And this?' Jason's father produced a manila folder, which he laid across his knees. 'Care to explain?'

An ordinary brown folder like a thousand others, but she knew without looking what was inside. The newspaper clippings covering her mother's murder.

'How did you get that?' She'd moved it from under her mattress when everyone found out who she was. There seemed to be no point in hiding it any more.

'Let's just say, I borrowed it from your room.'

'You stole it.'

'Taking the moral high ground, are we? Like I said, I don't believe in coincidences. That woman, Fay Cooper, lives under Jason's roof, and you'—he jabbed a finger at her—'are using my son as leverage to get closer to her. I want a full explanation, and it'd better be good.'

Helen racked her brain for a suitable excuse, but couldn't come up with anything. She had no idea whether he might have had something to do with her mother's death, but whatever she said would probably be wrong, so she decided on the truth.

'I'm investigating my mother's murder,' she said, aware how idiotic it must sound.

'Your mother's murder?' He raised one eyebrow. 'This happened twenty years ago. Have they reopened the case?'

Helen shook her head.

'I see. You're conducting your own little investigation.'

'Yes.'

'Why?'

'I think they missed something,' she said.

The other eyebrow came up. 'Let me just get this straight. Little Orphan Annie comes back after twenty years, dismisses evidence, her own witness statement, identification parade, the lot ...'

'That's right, and I'll tell you why. Because there were other witnesses, but they didn't come forward. Because the evidence was flawed. Because the person doing the identifying was me, a five-year-old epileptic kid, who'd just lost her mother, and couldn't remember much.'

Moody stared at her as if he thought she was from outer space. 'Blimey,' he said when he'd recovered. 'So you believe the Cooper woman is innocent?'

'Yes, and I intend to find out who really did it.'

'Any suspects?'

'Too many.'

'Am *I* a suspect?'

Yes, she thought, but modified her comment before it flew out of her mouth. 'Should you be?'

'Well, I knew your mother. We had some dealings together, although I didn't take to her. I could've had her bumped off and thought nothing of it. That's what people expect of me.' He flicked at an imaginary speck of dust on the sleeve of his jacket.

Helen bit her lip. There was such a thing as walking into the lion's den – where she was right this minute – but antagonising the lion further would be downright stupid.

'And did you?' she said, her mouth dry.

'I'm not likely to admit to that, am I?'

No, he wouldn't, would he? He was enjoying keeping her in the dark, she could tell, and even if he did admit to anything, what would she possibly do? An ominous silence followed, broken only by the clinking crystal decanters as they swerved around a corner.

'Well, that about wraps it up,' he said. 'You've told me what I need to know. You're free to go.'

As if on cue the car stopped, back where they started, across the road from the house. Helen hoisted her rucksack back on her shoulder. 'I'd like my folder back, please.'

'What for?'

'Because it's mine.'

'I call the shots here, young lady.' Moody held it out of her reach. 'You're not in a position to make demands.'

Red mist descended. The rancorous discussion between Ruth and Letitia, Ruth trying to make amends years too late, her splitting headache, the manhandling. And the rage, always the rage. She lunged across the seat and tried to grab the folder out of his hand.

'You effing bastard! Just give it back!'

The sliding screen was pushed aside, and she found herself

yanked against the bulkhead by the hair. A beefy hand closed over her windpipe and squeezed hard. Gasping, she clawed at the hand, but the grip was relentless. Adrenaline pumped through her veins, dark spots appeared before her eyes. A seizure threatened.

Studying his fingernails, Moody ignored her struggle for what seemed like an eternity, then made an imperceptible gesture. 'That'll do, Jones.'

The goon released her, and Helen fell back against the seat, fighting for breath, her head spinning.

'I must apologise for Jones. He's very protective.'

'Really?' Helen croaked and rubbed her throat. 'You don't say.'

Moody chuckled. 'I admire your spirit. Your mother had that in spades too. Tell me, what's so important about these papers that you'll risk life and limb to get them back? They're just newspaper clippings.'

'I don't have much of my mother,' Helen whispered, and clutched her rucksack to her chest to stop herself from shaking.

He considered that, carefully, then handed her the folder. 'Take it. I don't need it any more.'

The door opened, and Helen was plucked from the car. Moody leaned forward to catch her eyes. 'One final request. Stay away from my son.'

'And if I don't?'

'Miss Stephens.' He smiled pleasantly, just making conversation. 'There are two hundred and six bones in the human body. Twenty-six of them are in the foot. Think about that next time you cross the road.'

Clutching her things, Helen watched Moody drive off, slowly, because she was no danger to him. He didn't expect her to go against him.

281

'Arsehole,' she muttered.

Still shaking, she crossed the road and let herself in. Leaning against the front door, she drew comfort from the dry rot-infested wood.

She let out a breath, realising only then she'd been holding it in. Moody had presented her with an ultimatum, but she supposed she had a couple of choices. She could either isolate herself as she'd always done, or she could drum up the support of her friends.

Friends. She savoured the word on her tongue. She would do that, and if Charlie had a hissy fit and continued to avoid her, she would apologise. If Moody thought she was a forlorn and shrinking violet, he could think again.

Easier said than done. The house was deserted. No lights from Jason's basement flat, none in the kitchen, and the door to Fay's room was gaping wide, her empty walls a reminder of what Helen had done, of the damage lies could do.

No milk in the kitchen for a decent cup of tea was the last straw, and she slammed the fridge shut again.

'Damn!'

A scuffing noise from the garden doors sent her heart leaping into her throat, and her pulse throbbed loudly in her ears. The blood left her face. She went cold, then hot again. Quickly she switched off the light and tiptoed over to peer out by the side of the threadbare curtains which someone must have closed earlier.

There was nothing to see except one of Fay's cats on the shed roof, but she wasn't sure what she'd expected anyway. Jason's father had said what he came to say, and the man Helen had spotted in the alleyway could have been a neighbour if it hadn't been one of Moody's goons. Sneaking around the back of people's houses didn't seem quite his style anyway.

She let the curtain drop and poured a glass of water in place of tea. Her throat was dry and on fire, and her head still ached. Reaching for the kitchen door handle, she noticed her hand was still shaking, and a sick feeling curled inside her.

'To hell with you,' she muttered. Jason's bastard dad might have won the first round, but she was damned if he was going to intimidate her forever.

Her courage left her at the sound of a key in the door. Without rationalising it, she looked around for a place to hide, found it in the shape of an old coat on a peg by the basement stairs, and slid in behind it. She heard footsteps approaching and the rustling of a plastic bag but stayed where she was.

The coat had a musty odour with a hint of old man's sweat, and she tried to block her nose against the smells. Something tickled her on the side of her face, and she flicked at it with her hand. When she discovered the source of the tickling, a large house spider, she shrieked, burst out from behind the coat, and ran headlong into Jason.

'Jesus Christ!' he groaned. 'What are you doing? You nearly gave me a heart attack.'

'Sorry. It was a spider.'

She picked up her rucksack and the folder she'd dropped when she knocked into him. Some of the pages had come free of the binding and were spread all over the floor. Jason handed them to her.

'A spider?' he grinned. 'What are you, man or mouse?'

'Neither. Where've you been anyway? I was looking for you.'

'We were out of milk.' He held up a blue plastic bag from the corner shop. 'Why were you looking for me?'

No more secrets, she thought. 'Because your father's just told me this town isn't big enough for both of us.'

'What?'

'He told me to stay away from you.'

'He doesn't own me.'

'Maybe not, but he's pretty scary.'

Jason laughed. 'He's a crook, he's supposed to be. Don't listen to that old goat. He's just blustering. He wouldn't harm you.'

Involuntarily her hand went to her windpipe. She remembered Jones's grip, and Moody's indifference to her terror. 'How can you be sure?'

With a frown, Jason moved her hand. 'What's this? You have a massive bruise on your neck.'

'That was the "old goat". Well, his man Jones, actually.'

'Jones did this?'

She nodded.

'The bastard!' He whipped his phone out of his pocket and began to dial, but Helen stopped him.

'Please, just leave it be. I don't want any more trouble.'

He scowled furiously for a moment, then he sighed. 'Oh, man. I'm so sorry.'

'Don't be. It's not your fault.'

'He's only doing this because he knows I like you.' He touched a finger to her cheek. 'Look, I know how upsetting it must be for you, with Fay running off just when you had the chance to really talk to her. And now this with my dad as well, but I promise you Fay will come back. And I'll tell my dad to back off. He'll listen to me.'

She wanted to say she didn't share his confidence but was distracted by the feel of his finger on her skin. Instead, the contact between them was suddenly much more important, all heat and anticipation, and she stared into his eyes and saw that he wasn't pulling her leg. He really did like her. Perhaps a lot.

Impulsively she planted a kiss on his lips. She'd meant it

to be soft, a kiss of gratitude, but her mouth and body had other ideas. She gambled everything on this kiss.

Her mouth on his sent shock waves through his body, immobilising him. When he recovered, she'd pulled away again and was trying hard not to show how rejected she must have felt by his unresponsiveness.

'Sorry,' she said. 'It won't happen again.'

'It bloody well will.' Dropping the shopping bag with the milk, he cradled her head in his hands and kissed her back.

A muffled protest at first. Then her lips became soft and warm beneath his, and she stopped pushing her hands against his chest, letting them wander around his waist instead.

He thought he understood why. She was so damned independent and so afraid of being hurt that it was easier to deny how she felt – how they both felt – rather than risking rejection.

Or maybe she just liked it a bit rough. The masterful male and all that. He smiled at his own stupid fantasy.

'What's so funny?' she said. Her breath fanning against his cheek smelled just like she tasted, cool and fresh.

He brushed a strand of honey-coloured hair away from her face. 'Nothing. I'm just glad this is happening.'

For a moment her eyes clouded over with suspicion, then she smiled. 'Me too.'

They made love in Jason's basement flat, kissing, stroking, and giggling in the muted light from his retro lava lamp. Fumbling with protection, delighting in each other's bodies, kissing away tears of relief. Her eyes, not quite green, not brown either, and flecked with gold, held his as he moved over her, drinking him in and wrapping him in their warmth. Pupils widening as she came, cat-like smugness when, satiated and mellow, they finally lay still.

He thought, I'll never get tired of looking into those eyes.

'You're so mine,' he said. He'd never understood before, this need some people had to own another person, but now he did. He rolled off her and propped himself up on his elbow so he could continue looking at her.

'Oh, yeah? How do you work that out?' She raked a finger down his chest to his abdomen, sending ripples of renewed desire through him.

'You just are.'

Her smug smile was replaced by a guarded look. 'Your father—'

'Has nothing to do with this.'

'He won't give up. He'll push and push, and you'll give in because he's family. Family is important. I don't want to get hurt.'

'No one does.' He sighed. 'Listen, Helen, I can't promise you that I'll never upset you because it'll probably happen once in a while even if I don't mean to. But I can promise you this, it won't be because of anything my dad says or does. Family is not everything, and when it comes to being dysfunctional, mine's no better or worse than yours. We aren't Romeo and Juliet.'

She smiled. 'God forbid.'

He put his hand on her hip, savouring its female roundness. Helen was slim but not emaciated like some girls who thought they had to starve themselves to be beautiful, and his respect for her grew. She'd grown up without the support of a mother, or a father for that matter, but her sense of self seemed remarkably intact.

And despite her lack of formal education, she was very smart. If he told her what he'd found out about his father, she'd draw the same conclusions he had, that his father was somehow involved in her mother's death, or at least knew more than he was letting on, not even to his own bodyguard.

Helen would confront him, and then what? He needed to keep his father's name out of it for as long as possible if he was ever to gain her complete trust.

He'd meant what he said that family wasn't everything. But you still looked out for them.

They lay for a while, whispering, and when she fell asleep, he stayed awake for a while watching the steady rise and fall of her chest, her eyelashes casting impossibly long shadows over her cheeks in the low light. All that attitude of hers had melted away, and he felt a rush of affection, but resisted kissing her in case she woke up.

His father's attack on her had worried him more than he'd let on. Derek had threatened Cathy but as far as Jason knew had never laid hands on her. This was different. Helen was more exposed, unless he stepped in and looked out for her. Except it was very unlikely she'd let him, so he had to do it in such a way that she didn't realise it.

Following her on Trevor's motorbike was impractical, and she would notice eventually. Besides, he doubted very much Trevor would let him borrow his pride and joy indefinitely. So he had to think of something else.

He was racking his brain when the idea came to him. Slipping out of bed, he found her rucksack which she'd left on the floor, and fished out her smartphone. Quickly he installed an application which allowed the owner to track the phone via GPS coordinates, a function which was useful for stolen or lost phones and which could be activated by a text message.

Pleased with his own ingenuity, he returned it to her rucksack and climbed back into bed, then pulled her closer, never wanting to let go.

They were woken by a loud hammering on the door. A shaft of bright sunlight had found its way through the railings at street level and cut through the half-closed curtains, almost blinding them. Groggily Jason felt for his clothes which were all over the floor.

'Jason, are you in there?' It was Charlie.

'Coming.' He grinned at Helen, and she smiled back. The heat rose in his stomach at the memory of what they had done last night.

'Is Helen in there with you?' Charlie shouted.

Mouthing 'what?', she sent him a wide-eyed look. He shrugged, and she threw on her T-shirt. 'Yes, I'm here.'

When they were both dressed, Jason opened the door.

'You didn't have to get dressed on my account,' said Charlie. 'Like I don't know what you've been up too. Sound really travels in this old house.' She frowned at Helen. 'There's a call for you. It's from the newspaper.'

Chapter Twenty-Four

Helen took the call in the kitchen where Lee was having breakfast.

A clerk at the newspaper gave her the details of the respondent, and she dialled the number. A man with a strong Liverpool accent answered the phone.

'You responded to my ad in *The Gazette*,' she said.

'Yes, I did. Well, I don't know what you need to know but I was there. That morning when that woman was knifed in her car. I had the sort of dog you're asking about.'

Helen swallowed. Lee sent her a curious look while spooning Cornflakes into his mouth. Jason and Charlie stood silently by the sink.

'What can you tell me?' Helen asked. 'What you saw and heard?'

'Why do you want to know?' The voice was cautious now.

She hadn't thought much about it before placing the ad, imagining that she'd probably just ask whatever came into her head, but now she had to consider two things. He might have done it himself, and if he hadn't, why didn't he come forward when the original appeal was made? If he'd been in some sort of trouble at the time, he might clam up, and she'd be back to square one.

'Can I just explain that I've nothing do with the police,' she said. 'It's personal for me. The woman who died was my mother.'

A pause. 'You're the child in the back seat?'

'Yes.'

He whistled. A dog barked in the background, and he shushed it. So, still a dog owner, then.

'Okay, I get you,' he said. 'Perhaps we ought to meet,

though I don't know what I can do to help. There's a pub in Ealing, just down the road from the tube station. You know it?'

'I'll find it. Can you make it this evening, say six o'clock?'

'Yeah, that'd be fine. At six, then.'

'How will I recognise you?'

He chortled. 'I'll be the one with the dog. At the back of the pub.'

'You can't go alone!' said Charlie when she'd explained about placing the ad. 'I'm going with you, and so is Jase. He can close the stall early, can't you, Jase?'

'M-me too,' said Lee with a mouthful of cereal.

'It's a public place. Nothing will happen.'

As if on cue all three of them crossed their arms, and Charlie's jaw was set in that pigheaded way of hers. A warm feeling spread inside Helen. They really wanted to help.

'Okay, fine. Whatever. But stay in the background. Don't let him know you're with me. There's a reason he never came forward, and I don't want to scare him off.'

Just before six, Charlie and Jason went inside the pub, hand in hand like a couple, and Helen felt a short pang of jealousy.

She waited another few minutes, then went inside and looked around. The pub was welcoming, trendy, with a slightly threadbare look about it. Scuffed floorboards, a panelled bar, wooden furniture and gaming machines. With no curtains to soften the echo from all the hard surfaces it was a thrumming, pleasantly noisy place, and ideal for having a conversation you wouldn't want anyone else listening in on. If this was what the dog owner had in mind, he'd chosen well.

The bar staff were young and hip, and over the bar hung several clocks showing the time in London, Beijing and Riyadh, among others. Helen went to the back of the pub through a doorway decorated with acid-blue fairy lights, so bright against the red-painted walls they hurt her eyes. The room was cosy with dark wood tables and squashy armchairs.

The caller sat in an armchair by a tall window overlooking an outdoor smokers' area. He was clad in grey trousers, a shapeless anorak, and dirty white trainers, and was nursing a pint of bitter which made him stand out in the wine-bar type surroundings. A packet of crisps had been ripped open on the table in front of him, and by his feet, eyeing the packet intensely, was a large brown dog.

An Airedale Terrier.

Charlie and Jason were ensconced at a table in the darkest corner, heads close together. Lee waited outside as they'd agreed, to distract the man with questions about dogs if he tried to follow Helen.

Approaching him, she said, 'Are you the dog owner from the Common?'

'That I am, luv.' He stuck his hand out for her to shake.

His touch was warm and strong. A chunky gold bracelet hung from a wiry wrist, and the words 'love' and 'hate' were tattooed on his knuckles. Prison tattoos?

She could be shaking hands with her mother's killer, but it didn't seem likely.

'Make yourself comfortable,' he said.

Tongue-tied, she sat down on the edge of the chair. She'd started to think she'd imagined him and the dog, and now here he was, a flesh and blood person, with ill-fitting clothes, crows' feet, and a lilting accent. The questions which had been queuing up in her head were now falling over themselves to be asked, but nothing came out of her mouth.

'The name's Declan. And yours?'

Her tongue untied itself. 'Helen.'

'Well, Helen,' he said, smiling, 'I often wondered what

became of you, what sort of life you had and that, and here you are, all grown up, asking *me* what happened. Don't you know?'

She frowned. Was he testing her, trying to figure out how much she saw, and then decide whether he ought to finish the job or not? Or was he just the careful type?

She weighed the possibilities, grateful for Charlie and Jason in the corner, and Lee outside on the pavement. Her own personal backup team.

'I didn't see anything,' she said. 'I'm an epileptic and had a seizure at the time, so I wasn't aware of my surroundings. When I came to, my mother was dead.'

It surprised her how easy she found it, using the dreaded *E* word. She'd started feeling differently about her condition, but the change was so gradual she couldn't tell when.

'Right.' He sent her a look as if he thought she was having him on. Then he shrugged and took a crisp from the packet, left it on the edge of the table in front of the dog, and said, 'It's a southern bas'tud.'

The dog drooled but didn't eat the crisp. Helen was about to say something, but Declan stopped her with his hand.

'Wait.'

Another moment passed by with the dog staring down the crisp. Then Declan relented. 'Go on, boy, it's a northerner.'

The dog hoovered up the snack, then turned his large, doleful eyes at his owner who repeated the action. Southerner, yuk, northerner, yum. It was absurd.

'They're clever dogs,' he said when he'd proved his point. 'A lot of people don't know that. They just see these big, brown eyes and the floppy ears, and think Airedales are a bit divvy. I've always had Airedales, but Chuck, who I had back then, was something else. I should've listened to him.'

'Could he talk?'

Declan grinned. 'Sort of. That morning he was dashing

here and there, sniffing around in his usual zigzag pattern. You know dogs walk in zigzags, don't you?'

'Sure.' Helen hadn't a clue.

'After we'd done one round of the Common, I saw you in that car, and yer ma,' he continued. 'And there was another car with a woman in it. I walked by a couple of times, and it was obvious she was spying on you, so I knocked on her window asking her what she was up to. She got arsy, and I told her to hop it.

'Then she asked if I knew where there was a public loo. Not one open at this hour, I said. Then she got out, started shouting at yer ma who hadn't actually seen her until then. This led to a right old slanging match, and I had a real job of holding onto Chuck who was snarling and barking like mad. He was a good dog, was Chuck, but he had a temper on him.' He sighed and patted the placid dog beside him.

'Do you remember if anyone else was there?'

He shrugged. 'Not really. It's not particularly clear after all these years.'

'What happened then?'

'Yer ma gets back in her car, and that crazy women starts shrieking in some of the foulest language I've heard in my time, and that's saying some. Then she staggers across the Common towards the Hanger Lane end, all bevvied up and groggy. I don't like the look of that so I follow her, just to see she's all right. The whole time Chuck's whining and running up and down, getting in my way, pulling at me trouser leg. I got quite harsh with him.'

Declan drank from his beer and scratched the ear of his current dog as if apologising for mistreating a fellow canine.

'When I catch up with her, she's squatting with her back to a tree and relieving herself in full view of anyone driving past on Hanger Lane. Chuck suddenly starts getting interested, and I think, Jesus, I'm outta here, the woman's fuckin' nuts.'

He paused and stared at his beer, twirling the glass round and round on the beer mat.

'And that's it?' Disappointment settled in Helen's stomach

'Not quite.'

'What do you mean?'

'I didn't listen to Chuck, did I? He wanted to go back the way we'd come, but I took another route. I didn't go back to your ma's car. She could've been dead already for all I know, because I don't think that crazy woman was in a fit state to harm anyone.'

'Why didn't you tell the police this?'

He sighed. 'I read in the paper they'd caught the woman who did it, and then I thought, maybe I was wrong. When they ask for witnesses, I think, like, well, they've got her, haven't they, and they don't need me. And anyway, I was trying to keep a low profile, for reasons of me own. It's just that when I think of that child, her big eyes – your big eyes – I know there's something more, like, but I can't say what.' He looked up at her. 'That's why you placed the ad, isn't it? Because you think there's more.'

Jason fingered the stem of his wine glass, wine he didn't want to drink but Charlie had insisted.

'We're supposed to be a couple,' she'd said. 'Blokes always get white wine when they take their girlfriends to the pub.'

'Depends on the bloke,' he grumbled, hankering after a pint, but bought two glasses of white and carried them to the table Charlie had secured, in a corner. Here they had a clear view of a man sitting by the window, the only person in the pub with a dog.

When Helen came in and went straight to the dog owner, Jason found it hard not to look at her. Something inside him screamed 'she's mine', a deep-rooted instinct of possessiveness making his gut clench. A sour taste welled up in his throat, or maybe it was the wine, when the bloke rose and shook hands with her.

He noticed Charlie scribbling something on a scrap of paper. 'What are you doing?'

'Composing a love letter to my boyfriend, what do you think? I'm taking notes, what else? What this chap looks like, what he's wearing, stuff like that.'

'You're really enjoying this detective lark, aren't you?'

She looked up. 'Well, aren't you?'

'It's not a game, Charlie.'

'It is to me.'

'But not to Helen. Her mother was murdered in front of her. Imagine how that feels.'

'You're right. Sorry, I got carried away.' Charlie put the pen down and took a large swig of wine. 'You really care about her, don't you?'

He glanced at Helen. The dog owner was showing her a trick the dog could do, and Jason saw the mixture of amusement and confusion on her face. Right now he just wanted to go over there, put his arm around her, and reassure her she didn't have to go through with this, raking up old memories which must be painful to her. He wanted to tell her that life was still worth living without having all the answers.

But he didn't. He stayed where he was and watched her digging deeper and deeper.

'Yeah, I do.'

Charlie touched his hand briefly. 'Don't let her hurt you, will ya?'

'I'll try not to,' he said, thinking she was more likely to get hurt than he was.

'Look, I don't mean this in a bad way but she's a magnet for trouble. She can't help it, but she is.'

Jason grinned. 'Since when did you turn philosopher?'

'Just stay cool, know what I'm saying.'

He nodded. Charlie was more right than he suspected she realised. After Cathy he'd withdrawn into himself, shut the door on any deeper feelings he might have had and deliberately only got involved with 'safe' girls – girls who didn't have the power to break down those barriers.

That is, when he'd sought out relationships at all. He could certainly count them on one hand.

Then Helen had come along and crept under his defences with her dichotomy of guarded independence and raw loneliness. His feelings for her had grown from a desire to help her, not from the selfish needs which had characterised any other relationship he'd had. Once he'd thought Cathy was The One, and when it was over between them, he spent years resenting his father, unfairly perhaps, and pandering to his own hurt, treating it as a demanding and capricious mistress.

Except he'd mistaken a bruised ego for genuine pain. He was looking at the real deal right now, and she was about to open a festering can of worms.

If he asked her to stop, she'd become suspicious and leave him out of it, and if he let her carry on without at least trying to hinder her, she may discover something about his father which was best left alone.

Things were going from bad to worse.

Chapter Twenty-Five

Declan's account left Helen even more confused than before. She'd wanted to believe Fay was innocent, but Declan had described her as mad enough to kill. He'd also said she'd looked incapable of it, and as Fay said she couldn't remember, this left Helen exactly nowhere.

'So,' said Charlie as they sat on the 207 bus home, 'what did he see?'

'Nothing useful, except Fay, but we knew she was there anyway.'

'Oh.' Charlie went quiet for a moment, then she leaned forward in her seat, making Lee who sat next to Helen jump. 'What you going to do, then?'

'Uhm, hope someone else comes forward?'

'Is that all?'

'That's all I can do.' Helen glanced at Jason who sat across the aisle. He sent her a questioning look, sharp even, and she could tell he knew she was holding something back.

But fortunately he didn't interrogate her when they were alone in her room later, just held her tight and stroked her hair after they had made love. She rested her head on his chest, groggy with conflicting emotions. Happy to be with Jason, concerned for Fay, frustrated she was getting nowhere.

Letitia was waiting for her in the staff room, a rare occurrence because the green velvet curtain which hung between the back rooms and auction hall also doubled as a personification of the socio-economic divide.

'Bad news, I'm afraid,' she said. 'Aggie is dead.'

Dead? Aggie?

On jelly legs Helen fumbled towards one of the benches

which stood against the wall. Letitia noticed. It didn't matter. For all her pride, Helen didn't care if Letitia thought of her as weak. What mattered was that Aggie was gone.

Forever.

A large imaginary hand gripped her insides and squeezed hard, making her feel queasy.

'Oh,' she said.

Shivering, she drew her knees up and put her arms around them, wishing she'd never come back because it was easier to hate Aggie than to love her. Letitia watched her struggle with an ironic smile. 'You may take the day off if you like. Although you might prefer to continue working. Keeping the mind occupied keeps the grief at bay.'

Helen stared at her, at a small pink mole beside her mouth which she'd never noticed before. What did Letitia know about grief? Surely it was too mundane for her and reserved for lesser mortals.

Yet everyone had an Achilles heel. As the pressure grew in her chest, Helen realised she knew very little about either of her aunts, least of all Letitia.

'I'll leave you to make up your mind,' said Letitia. 'I'll keep you posted about the arrangements.'

Helen squeezed her eyes shut. Aggie was barely cold, and *arrangements* were being made?

She stayed on the bench for God knew how long, alone, leaning against the cold wall with its peeling plaster, and waiting for the tears to come, just so the pressure inside her could ease up. Nothing happened.

She wanted to scream, shout, stamp her feet like a child. That didn't happen either. Instead she tasted the bitter-sweet sadness of losing someone she had mixed feelings about. Did her grandmother know she'd forgiven her? She hoped so. Last time she saw Aggie, they'd held hands. Perhaps Aggie understood this was Helen's way of showing her feelings.

No words, just touching and seeing.

Charlie found her later and pulled her close. Helen dropped her head on Charlie's shoulder, whose hair gave off the usual oily tang. The familiar smell was comforting.

'I've just heard,' said Charlie. 'Do you want to talk about it?'

Helen shook her head.

'Bill told me,' Charlie said. 'I haven't said anything to anyone. Neither has he. We thought you'd still want to keep the family connection quiet.'

They sat like this for a while, then Charlie, ever restless, began pacing the room. 'So, what happens now? What does this mean for the company? And you? Your gran was a major shareholder, wasn't she? Where do her shares go?'

Helen shrugged. 'I don't know. To her daughters, I suppose. Or all three of us. It doesn't really matter now, does it?'

'Of course it matters. You're just as much part of this as they are. You're the founder's granddaughter. Are you just going to stand by and let Letitia do whatever she pleases? I bloody well wouldn't.'

Even Charlie had been bitten by the company bug. Like a parasite, it got into your blood. It wasn't healthy.

'Letitia works in the company's interests. Always has done. My grandmother only ever interfered on the board, never in the day-to-day.' Helen sent her a sour look. 'How come you know so much about it, anyway?'

'I keep my eyes and ears open. And use Google. You need to check your legal position. Did your gran die very suddenly?'

'Not really. I mean, she was overweight and had diabetes. I expect her heart gave out.'

'Just like that?'

'She was old.'

'How old?'

Helen rubbed her face with her hands. 'Somewhere in her eighties. Why? What are you saying?' Charlie had stopped pacing, and the sudden stillness brought a chill to the room.

'It's very convenient, isn't it? The lost granddaughter returns. Granny makes a big fuss. The aunties' noses are out of joint. Then she pops her clogs.'

'It wasn't like that,' protested Helen, but suspicion had started gnawing. When she'd overheard that distasteful confrontation in Ruth's office, she'd learned that Letitia was itching to get full control of the company. But to do away with her own mother? It was the stuff of soap operas.

Still, it could do no harm to ask Sweetman about the legal implications, and there seemed to be no one else Helen could turn to who'd genuinely liked her grandmother.

She accepted the offer of taking the rest of the day off and sought out Sweetman. She found him bent over a bullet-proof filing cabinet, rummaging through a row of green hanging folders that had been squeezed in tight in the drawer. He held another file between his teeth.

'Take a seat. I'll be with you in a tick. Aha,' he added triumphantly a moment later. 'Thought I got the date right.'

'The date?'

'I file things chronologically, not alphabetically.'

'Doesn't that get rather confusing?'

'Not for me. I've got it all up here.'

'And what if you secretary – your wife – has to find something?'

'Oh, we're two of a kind.'

That explained Mrs Sweetman's permanently harassed air. 'Obviously.'

Small raisin-coloured eyes bored into hers. 'It worked for your grandmother too. By the way, my sincere condolences. I shall miss her.'

'Me too.' Helen cleared her throat.

'One day,' Sweetman said, 'you and I will sit down over a cup of my wife's most excellent coffee and have a good old chat about Mrs Ransome. Right now, we must get down to business.'

She nodded.

'It worked for your grandmother that I do things differently,' he repeated. 'For instance that I use a filing system which isn't immediately transparent. If anyone, say, without the proper authority decides to look for a file in my office, it's pot luck whether he actually manages to find it or not.'

Helen glanced at the filing cabinets. Built to withstand fire and more, they probably wouldn't keep out a determined intruder with a lock pick. However, the eccentric filing system would defy anyone.

'Was someone interested in my grandmother's papers?'

'That's why she moved from her old firm of solicitors. She didn't feel that her interests were being safe-guarded. Literally.'

'Against who?'

'Your aunts, of course. Or one of them. In the name of client confidentiality – *their* client confidentiality – I never found out which one, but my money is on your aunt Letitia.'

'Isn't that unethical?'

'Very. But what do you expect from a city company?' He sniffed. 'Personally I wouldn't trust them further than I could spit.'

'And you helped her draw up a new will?'

'Yes, but she changed it again, you know. Only a week ago.'

'Oh.'

'It's in your favour,' he continued. 'You now own thirty-three per cent of the shares in the company, which is more than your aunts combined. It makes you the most influential shareholder.'

'Me? Really?' Helen stared at him. 'That's just crazy! What am *I* supposed to do with them?'

'Take control of the company.'

'That's a good one. Like I know what I'm doing. Who has the other shares, apart from my aunts?'

'Various investors. A couple of names spring to mind. The bigger share positions are owned by a small handful. Arseni Stephanov, your uncle. A city bank.' He sniffed again. 'And one Derek Moody. You know him,' he added when he caught her startled expression. 'He sits on the board. A nasty piece of work, in my humble opinion.'

A thick silence descended on the room as Sweetman waited for her to say something.

'Why me?' she asked. 'I don't know anything about business. I haven't even been to a board meeting yet. Aggie's expecting me to be something I'm not. Like she always did.'

'Did she really?'

Helen shrugged. Maybe she wasn't being entirely fair. 'She certainly expected me to fill some pretty big boots. All her talk about college and that. I just couldn't get my head around it. I needed to find *me* first.'

'And have you?'

'I'm coming to terms with who I am, yes. I just can't walk in my mother's footsteps.' The thought of how it had all ended for her mother made her shudder. 'I need to do something a bit more … worthwhile with my life. Some good.'

'It wasn't your mother Mrs Ransome had in mind. It was your grandfather.'

Helen spluttered. 'As if!'

'Your grandfather was a decent human being. As are you. I expect Mrs Ransome only wanted you to do the right thing.'

Her lip quivered with emotion. This faith they had in her, her grandmother and the solicitor, how could she live up to it?

Sweetman, as always, read her mind. 'I'll be with you every step of the way. I'll advise, guide, clear your path through the legal jungle, as it were. Be your right-hand man. That is, if you want me to represent you as I represented your grandmother. All you've got to do is say the word.'

She looked at him, at his white hair, his chubby face, and the striped shirt with armpit stains. Aggie had placed a lot of trust in this man, and if she could trust him, so could Helen. 'Yes, I'd like that. Thank you.'

'Good, good.' He slapped some papers down in front of her. One sheet still bore the marks from his teeth. 'Let's get to the paperwork, then. This is a contract for my ongoing services. You just need to sign here.' He flicked to the end of the document and put a pen in her hand. 'This is a leaflet detailing our services, and here's a breakdown of our fees.'

She was too stunned by this mixture of efficiency and blatant manipulation to do anything other than sign. The sheet with teeth marks was a will form.

'Why do I need to make a will?'

'Makes sense under the circumstances, don't you think?'

She met his eyes and felt a shiver run down her spine. He wasn't joking. Without quibbling, she filled in the missing parts of the will form, and passed the papers back to him.

'Talking about wills, you say I'm the sole beneficiary in Aggie's will. Won't my aunts dispute that?'

'When I said it was in your favour, I meant in the broadest sense. You get the shares, but there's the house and some valuable possessions which'll go to them. Sure, they can try, but they won't look good in court. Two greedy, wealthy women questioning the kindness bestowed on a motherless child? Only a judge with a heart of stone would allow it. I think you're safe on that score.' He smiled suddenly. 'And you'll have me as a back-up. Now, doesn't that fill you with confidence?'

As usual she couldn't tell whether he was being ironic or not. There was something else she needed to ask him, something which had plagued her since she'd found that syringe in Ruth's cardigan.

'Is it possible for me to ask for a post-mortem to be performed on my grandmother?'

It was Sweetman's turn to look surprised. He raised his bushy white eyebrows. 'A post-mortem? What's on your mind?'

'Foul play.'

'I see.' He leaned back in his chair, which creaked under his weight. 'Usually only a relative can request a post-mortem – and you're not a relative in that sense – unless the death is considered traumatic, unusual or unexpected. Then the doctor signing the death certificate will instigate it. Your grandmother was old, and she was ill. Hardly unexpected.'

'But it was so sudden.'

'Death always is for those who have trouble accepting facts.'

Helen glared at him. For a family solicitor he was taking a lot of liberties. Maybe she ought to just sack him. Instead she decided to tell him about the syringe and the confrontation in Ruth's office.

'Letitia wanted to get rid of her. She thought Aggie was losing it, and Ruth, well, for some reason she's always had a bitter relationship with her mother.'

And somehow everything comes back to me, she thought.

'Mrs Ransome always knew you'd come right in the end.' Sweetman smiled grimly. 'Try to persuade one of your aunts, although if they're involved, as you suggest, they could just refuse, and that'd be that. Unless you have some sort of leverage.'

'I understand.'

She had just the thing which might help persuade one of them.

Helen hadn't been to Ruth's house since she was five. She didn't remember the actual house nor her reasons for being there, but what stood out in her mind was stumbling upon Ruth weeping into a tea towel in the kitchen.

Alarmed, she'd run back into the drawing room. 'Mummy, Auntie Ruth has hurt herself. She's crying.'

Her mother ran a hand over Helen's hair. 'Is she? Oh, dear.' Mimi looked at Aggie and Auntie Letitia, then Uncle Jeremy, who turned away.

'Someone needs to cuddle her.'

No one said anything, and Helen had a nasty feeling she often had when the grown-ups were around, that they knew something she didn't. Frowning, she went back into the kitchen and patted Auntie Ruth on the back awkwardly.

'Where does it hurt?' she asked. 'Would you like me to blow on it?'

Auntie Ruth simply stared at her in a way which told her she'd done the wrong thing, then sobbed into the tea towel again while Helen's chest hurt as if someone had punched her in it.

Years later she'd learned the source of Ruth's unhappiness: her inability to have children. Her husband having an affair with Mimi must have made things so much worse. A small part of her hated Ruth for rejecting her when her mother died, another part understood it. Reluctantly.

Ruth opened the door in her dressing gown, an old blue towelling robe remarkably tattered for someone so wealthy. Her face was blotchy and her eyes red as if she'd been crying or hadn't slept.

'Oh, it's you,' she said. 'What do you want?'

305

'I want to talk to you.'

'What about? I thought we'd done talking.'

'Aggie,' said Helen.

Ruth sighed. 'You'd better come in, then.' She led the way to the kitchen at the back of the house and flicked the switch on the kettle. 'Coffee?'

'I'm fine, thanks.'

Her aunt switched the kettle off again with another sigh. 'But you have some. Don't mind me.'

Ruth shook her head and pulled out a kitchen chair. 'Talking about her won't bring her back.'

Helen sat down opposite her. 'I'd like a post-mortem done on Aggie.'

'A post-mortem? What on earth for?'

'I don't think she died of natural causes.'

Ruth covered her eyes with her hand and rubbed her brow as if to massage away a headache. 'Helen, please ...'

'You and Letitia wanted to get rid of her.'

'Not in that sense.'

'And I found your cardigan with a syringe in it. What do you think will happen if I tell the police that?'

Ruth looked up. Her face, with yesterday's make-up still embedded in her wrinkles, seemed suddenly ancient. 'I may have wanted my mother dead a million times, but it was just something I said. People do, you know. They don't mean it. I never quite forgave her for ... well, her lack of understanding. I just wanted to be a wife and mother, not some high-flying company executive. And when that dream fell by the wayside, she just brushed my feelings aside as if they were unimportant.

'Go ahead, tell the police,' she went on, 'but Mrs Sanders can back me up that I helped Mother with her insulin sometimes. She told me the nurse was being too rough with her, but I think she just wanted my company and didn't want to ask because it'd make her look weak. So I went along with it and accepted this was her roundabout way of apologising.'

What could she say to that? Ruth had a point. Aggie had possessed an uncanny ability to be both direct and subtle at the same time.

'Are you all right?' Ruth asked suddenly. 'When was the last time you ate? Would you like me to make you a sandwich? Or I can heat up some soup. You look like you could do with it.'

'I don't want a sandwich.'

Ruth touched her hand. 'I know it's hard for you to accept she's gone, but a post-mortem isn't going to help you.'

'I get all her shares,' said Helen pointedly. 'Sweetman told me.'

'I don't care.'

'Letitia will.'

'Oh, yes, she'll be bloody furious.' Ruth laughed. 'She might agree to a post-mortem but it'll be because she thinks *you* had something to do with it.'

'Me?'

'Yes, crazy, isn't it? We're all crazy.'

'I'm not.'

'That's because you grew up away from all of it. Small mercies, I suppose.'

'There's something else I need to talk to you about.' Digging into her rucksack, Helen pulled out the roll of chamois leather and unwrapped it. Ruth blanched.

'This knife is the twin of the one they say Fay used to kill my mother. It disappeared around the time my mother was murdered. So did the murder weapon. I don't think Fay did it, so perhaps you'd like to explain what this was doing in your grandfather clock, and where you took it from?'

Ruth sat still as a statue with her hands in her lap. Helen

could have told her there were two more knives like this one, but she wanted to see her sweat.

Finally Ruth said, 'You really don't like me very much, do you? Think me capable of the most terrible things.'

'Isn't everyone? Capable, I mean.'

'I suppose so, but why you think I did it when everyone knows there are three more knives like this one, I don't understand.'

'Who's "everyone"?'

'Me, Letitia, Aggie. Your mum's friends. Loads of people. The story goes that those paper knives belonged to a Russian tsar. It's not something you forget. Everyone also knows your uncle doesn't keep the best company, and since he has two of the knives, well …'

'Where did you get it? Did you take it from my mother's house after she died?'

Ruth sent her a speculative look. 'If I tell you, will you promise me not to jump to conclusions? I didn't take it from your mother's house. I found it at Ransome's, tucked away in the corner of the packaging hall behind some old ledgers.'

Chapter Twenty-Six

'I told you not to jump to conclusions,' Ruth said when she saw Helen's expression. 'It could be that your mother dropped her own knife there by mistake, although why she should bring it to work with her I've no idea. Then there was Mother. She and Mimi got on well, but they'd recently had a set-to, over what I don't know. She could easily have taken it for spite. As for Letitia, she was close to your uncle, and when I suspected your mother had used him as a free sperm donor, I thought my sister may have taken revenge for that. That's why I took the knife. They are my family after all.' She made a noise halfway between a sneer and a snort. 'I needn't have worried about Letitia, though, because she quickly found another man to amuse herself with.'

'Who?'

'Oh, just one of our shareholders. Some chap named Moody. He was married, and the affair didn't last long.'

Ruth didn't notice Helen jump at the name. Moody. Again.

'What will you do now?'

'I don't know.'

'Will you tell the police?'

Helen still had DI Whitehouse's card in her wallet. *Call me if you find anything, no matter how insignificant.* Except she didn't have enough pieces of the puzzle. No way was she making a fool of herself in front of the Cream of the Met again. She'd keep digging.

But she didn't want Ruth to know that. 'What's the point? The knife belonged to my mother, and now it's been returned to me. The rest is in the past.'

Ruth breathed a sigh of relief. When Helen left, they embraced awkwardly. 'Come and see me some time.'

'I will.'

She left Ruth in her big empty house, to her aimless life. Her obsession with her childlessness seemed to have pushed everything else to one side, but surely there was more to life than having babies? Things like friendships, travel. A dog maybe. It saddened her that Ruth couldn't see it.

Back home she dumped her rucksack on her bed and flung herself down on the sofa in the kitchen. The big house was quiet, almost watchful, without even Lee creeping about. It gave her the emotional space to brood over Aggie's death and her complex, bitter family, which should have pleased her. Instead it was as if the walls moved in on her, squeezing her chest so she couldn't breathe.

Shaking off the feeling, she fetched her wallet and headed for the market. As soon as she stepped under the metal arch, she was bombarded with noise, colours and materialistic gaiety, and the numbness, which had started to spread inside her, slowly bled away.

She bought some fruit and a piece of fish for a pie. By the refreshment stall the yummy mummies were out in force, but this time she didn't begrudge them their cooing, well-fed babies. Ruth's unhealthy focus had cured her of that.

An older guy was manning Jason's stall. Disappointed, she turned away. It would have been nice to lean into him and feel his strong arms around her, for him to take away some of the pain by just being there, but she was so used to dealing with things on her own that she figured it would keep.

Instead she wandered aimlessly for a bit, then stopped to chat with Winston. He gave her the low-down on the local gossip. New stalls opening up, the coolest place to hang, who'd been arrested. She let it wash over her and just enjoyed the sound of his sing-song Caribbean lilt.

'What you done with old Fay?' he asked.

This startled her. 'Nothing.'

'Then how come she sleeping rough now?'

'Fay's sleeping rough? Where?'

'In da park,' he said. 'Where else would a body sleep rough?'

Helen could think of a thousand other places: shop doorways, bus stops, dark alleys. 'Which park?'

'The one 'bout half an hour from here, on the two feet that God gave you.'

'Is she all right?'

Winston rolled his eyes. 'What planet you come from? She's unhappy.'

Helen wanted to ask more, but Winston had turned his full attention to a customer and was joking and chatting. Absent-mindedly she felt the fabrics hanging from the roof of his stall – the cottons, the woollens, the silks (hah!) – a kaleidoscope of colours and a wealth of textures.

Finally he turned his attention back to her. 'Well? You fingering or buying?'

She found the park easily enough, a typical suburban park big enough to have its own modest lake, and tracking down Fay could be tricky. She might not be here at all. Helen traversed the park from the north end towards the tube, which ran across the park at the other end, looking to both sides to see if she could spot her.

At the end was a playground behind a low metal fence, kitted out with swings, brightly-coloured climbing frames and a rubbery surface to cushion any falls. Under the watchful eye of their mothers a hoard of children were playing, their young voices shrill over the din from the train passing overhead. Outside the fence was a row of benches, and Helen spotted a familiar figure.

It made sense. Playing children would be a natural magnet for Fay.

She slid down beside her. 'Hi.'

'Hi.'

'You okay?'

Fay didn't answer. Instead she clutched a handful of faded photographs in her lap. Stupid question, really.

'You know who I am, I suppose.'

'Mimi's daughter. I always wondered what became of you. Have you come to take your revenge?'

'Not any more.'

'Why not?'

'Because I think I understand now what happened back then.'

Fay gave a dry laugh. 'Then you understand a lot more than I do.'

'I've spoken to the dog owner.'

'What dog owner?'

'There was a man with a dog that morning on the Common. I remembered him, and I managed to find him. Through a personal ad in the local paper.'

'How clever of you.' Fay smiled suddenly. 'Now you mention it, I do remember a dog that morning when I ... when your mother ...' She trailed off. They both knew what came next.

'Do you remember anything else?' asked Helen.

'Not really. It's so long ago, and my brain was pretty addled.'

'Not even going for a pee behind a tree?'

'The dog man told you that? Oh, god, how embarrassing!' Her attention returned to the photos in her lap, straightening out one which had become crumpled. Then her gaze settled on the children in the playground, and her expression pierced Helen to the bone.

'You shouldn't be here. You're just torturing yourself.'

'I can't help it. I lost so much. My life. My kids.'

'We'll find them. Okay?'

Fay shook her head. 'It's too late. They're grown up now, they wouldn't want to have anything to do with me.'

'You don't know that until you've tried.' She paused. 'You know, maybe we can get some of it back.'

'How?'

'By trying to piece it all together. If you don't remember what happened on the Common, can you remember what happened before you got there?'

Fay was silent for a while. 'Well, I was following her around a lot. Despite the restraining order I'd be parked outside your house, or near it, sometimes all night sleeping in the car. That morning I'd been there since the night before, and I woke up when your mother came out. She strapped you in your car seat.' She sent Helen a sideways glance. 'You looked sort of ill, and I thought she was taking you to hospital, but then she drove to the park instead. I got it into my head she was meeting my husband, and that she'd tried to give me the slip by getting up so early. I'm afraid I just lost it.'

'Did you see anyone else following her?'

'Not really. I mean there was a cyclist on the road. One of those fanatics wearing the whole Tour de France get-up, but you can hardly chase a car while riding a bike, can you?'

'Oh, I dunno, I've seen plenty of despatch riders on bikes terrorising other road users.'

Fay laughed quietly. Another tube train rolled past on the track above them, and the children's voices rose to a crescendo to drown out the noise.

'I've asked you this before, but did you kill my mother?'

'The truth is, I don't know,' Fay replied. 'I wish I could say for sure, but I can't. I know I wanted to.'

Their eyes met, and Helen read the apology in them. She knew she should be angry, but for some reason she couldn't summon up the feeling. If Fay was guilty, she'd paid for it ten times over. Perhaps it was time to let it go.

Reaching out, she took Fay's hand, which trembled slightly in her own, and surprised even herself by saying, 'I'm beginning to feel that it doesn't matter any more. Whatever you did do, I think I understand your reasons. I can't keep hating you, it's too exhausting. Let's concentrate on the future. I'm sorry I didn't tell you who I was from the beginning.' She squeezed Fay's hand. 'Won't you come back home with me? Charlie absolutely hates me for chasing you away.'

'Charlie can be a bit like that.' Fay rose and gathered up her photos and a few other belongings. 'But it's my fault too. I should've demanded to know what it was all about. I'm just not very strong.'

No, Fay wasn't strong at all, Helen noted as they made their way back. She'd used up all her strength in prison in order to survive, but now she'd been set free, she was just like so many other people daily trudging the streets of London, isolated, overlooked, living on the poverty line with no real future ahead of them.

She was going to change that. Together with Jason and the others they would make sure Fay had a good life, and the first thing they'd do was to track down her family, come what may.

'I'm making fish pie for supper,' she said as they crossed the road. 'Fancy giving me a ha—'

She never finished the sentence. Everything happened so fast. An engine revving, Fay shouting and shoving her in the back, making her stumble and fall towards the kerb, dropping her bags. Her knee took the brunt of the impact, her elbow the rest. Red dots swam before her eyes, and she heard a sickening thud. A woman screamed.

And then it was all over. The dark car which had ploughed into Fay turned the corner with a screech of brakes. The shock on the faces of passers-by imprinted itself onto Helen's mind. She ignored her throbbing knee and the searing pain in her elbow. Ears thrumming and eyes stinging with tears, she crawled to where Fay lay all twisted and bent, and hugged her close.

Chapter Twenty-Seven

Gentle hands lifted her away, and kind words brought her back to reality.

'You mustn't move someone who's been in an accident,' said one.

'That bag lady saved your life,' said another. 'The car was coming right at you.'

'I got some of the registration number,' said a third, a young man already on his mobile. Detached, Helen thought he looked like an estate agent, with his sleek suit and gelled hair.

They helped her to the pavement and made her sit down. A woman with a pram knelt beside her and pressed a stack of baby wipes in her hand. 'It'll help with the bleeding.'

Bleeding? Helen looked at her hands, and the horror of what she saw made bile rise in her throat.

'It's not my blood, it's Fay's. Oh, god! Is she ...?'

'Fay? Is that her name?' The woman put her arm around Helen. 'It was a bad accident, I'm afraid. The ambulance is on its way.'

Helen looked to where Fay was lying. Someone had draped a jacket over her, and her face was ashen, as if she was already dead. Blood seemed to be everywhere – on her clothes, hair, face, on the road. Helen's vision blurred, and someone helpfully pushed her head between her legs as the world swam and blackened, her heart beating like a drum. The last thing she remembered before a simple partial seizure took hold of her was the gentle hand on her neck ...

Jason pushed open the double doors to the waiting room and found Helen with her head resting against the wall.

Relief flooded through him, followed by guilt that he hadn't been there when she needed him.

He wanted to put his arm around her to make sure she was all right, but Charlie beat him to it, throwing herself down in the only available chair next to Helen.

'Lee told us,' he said.

'How is she?' asked Charlie.

'In surgery. She ... That's all I know.'

Despite her ability to hold herself together, Jason read the strain in her eyes. On the way here Charlie had filled him in on the loss of her grandmother. He knelt down in front of Helen and took her hand. How could life throw so much shit at one person? Both Helen and Fay were getting more than their fair share. 'Could you tell us what happened?'

'I'm not quite sure.'

'Try, please.' Jason squeezed her hand.

Sighing, she drew herself up. 'Winston told me Fay was sleeping rough in the park.' She glanced sideways at Charlie who sent her a fearsome scowl. 'I just wanted her to come back, didn't care about what she might have done. We were crossing the road, talking about ... food, I think. I heard a car. Fay pushed me, then she got hit. The driver didn't stop.'

Just the facts, Jason noted. No grizzly reporting of the gory details, the thud, the screams, the blood, but his mind filled in the blanks for him. He let go of her hand and stood up again, his jaw tight with anger that some people could be so cold-blooded and just drive off after an accident. Helen retreated into herself, and he realised she must think him angry with her. Relaxing his shoulders, he smiled back at her.

'And what about you? Are you hurt?'

'A couple of bruises. It's nothing.'

She looked pale and drawn, with dark shadows under her eyes and her hands clasped so tightly in her lap the knuckles had gone white.

'When was the last time you ate?' he asked.

'Ate? I ... I don't know. This morning maybe. I can't remember.'

Charlie shook her head. 'That's not good. You have to pace yourself, with your epilepsy and that. Low blood sugar can lead to seizures.'

'Says who?'

'I read up on it.'

'Well, if I have a worse seizure than the minor one I had earlier, I'll be in the right place, then, won't I?' Helen snapped.

'All right, you two, leave it out.' Jason dug inside his pocket and pulled out a crumpled tenner. 'Charlie, why don't you go down to the cafeteria and see what you can find? A sandwich and maybe some biscuits or chocolate.'

Charlie sent him a mutinous look. 'Why me?'

'Because if Helen does have a seizure, I know how to deal with it. And because I'm asking nicely.'

'Who's Nicely?' she retorted but snatched the tenner out of his hand and stalked off.

'Thank you,' said Helen when she'd gone.

'Charlie can be a bit blunt but she means well.' Jason sat down, still wanting to put his arm around her, but her body language didn't invite it so he had to be content with just sitting next to her.

'You see the good in everybody, don't you?'

'I try to.'

'There's not much good in me,' she said.

'What a load of rubbish.'

She turned. 'It was my fault.'

'How so?'

'I chased her away, then she got run over. That's what happens to people around me, they get hurt. Sometimes they die.'

'Like you're some bad-luck penny?' He risked putting his hand on her shoulder, felt her stiffen, and moved it again.

'Yeah.'

'You're not, you know. Please don't blame yourself.'

'It happened to my mother, and my grandmother.'

He nodded. 'Yes, I heard about that. I'm truly sorry. Not your day today, is it?' he added, hoping that the joke would cheer her up a little. She didn't seem to notice.

'Now Fay's been hurt as well,' she said. 'Who's next? Charlie or Lee? Maybe you? You better stay away from me if you value your skin.'

'Fat chance of that. I'm in for the long haul.'

'Are you?' She met his eyes, and he read the same warning he'd felt coming off her in spades since he got here. What was *up* with her?

'If it came to choosing between me and your father, where would your loyalties lie?'

Her question perplexed him. His relationship with his father was complex, and needed careful handling. Helen was always treading so carefully that this sudden heavy-handed approach was like shooting sparrows with cannons.

He opened his mouth to protest against being put in this situation when a doctor approached them, pulling off his surgical mask. 'Your friend is going to be all right,' he informed them. 'It was touch and go for a moment. She was bleeding internally, but we've managed to control it. Her hip is fractured, she's broken several ribs, and has a severe concussion. We're keeping her in intensive care overnight.'

'So what happens now?' asked Jason.

'I understand it was a hit-and-run, so the police will need to speak to you when they get here. Other than that, there's nothing more you can do. You might as well go home. We'll call you if there's any change in her condition, but I'm cautiously optimistic.'

He left them with a member of the administrative staff to deal with formalities and paperwork, and to wait for the police.

Helen went back to her seat, and Jason followed her. If anything she seemed more uneasy now, even after the relatively good news about Fay. It made no sense.

'I'm not sure what to tell the police when they get here,' she said.

He took her hand. 'You just tell them what you saw. No need to sweat it.'

'If I do that, then you ...' She pulled her hand away and got up.

Concern that her feelings for him had changed turned to horror as it dawned on him what she was trying hard not to say. It churned in his stomach like a raging beast waking from its slumber.

It couldn't be.

'What did you mean by your question "where would my loyalties lie"?' He heard his own voice coming from far away, disembodied from the rest of him. 'It's obvious, isn't it?'

She took a deep breath. 'Because one of the witnesses said the car was aiming for me, and that Fay saved my life by pushing me out of the way. And I saw it myself as it drove off. It was like the one your father has.'

Jason jumped up from his seat. 'What?'

'I'm sorry,' she whispered. 'I didn't want to be the one to tell you, but the witness ...'

He stared back at her, noticed how she almost cringed against the wall, then lowered his hands which he'd balled into fists without noticing. A low table stacked with leaflets stood in the centre of the room. He kicked it hard, sending it skidding across the floor, then stormed out of the waiting area, ignoring her pleas for him not to go.

In the cobbled lane outside the old warehouse which had been converted into offices, Derek Moody's black, luxurious but nevertheless nondescript car was parked. Jason knelt and inspected the front. The left bumper had a recent-looking dent in it.

Closing his eyes for a moment, he held back the anger which rolled over him in waves, but found it impossible. Instead he tore into the building, past a startled-looking security officer and up the stairs to the top floor.

'You can't just barge in,' said Ms Barclay when she saw him.

He said nothing, only held up his hand, and the woman who could have silenced a lion stepped back and let him pass.

His father was just leaving, buttoning up his suit jacket while the bodyguard held a briefcase for him. He raised his eyebrows when he saw Jason.

'Jason, what a —'

He never finished the sentence. Jason reached him in three strides and lashed out. When Derek ducked, an uncontrollable rage exploded inside him, and he struck again, this time connecting with his father's nose. There was a satisfying crunch and a yelp of pain, and Derek crumbled to his knees on the floor.

'You bastard!' Jason shouted. 'You fucking bastard!'

Moving swiftly, Jones was on him, one arm pinning him to his massive chest, the other behind his neck, poised to snap it. Jason almost didn't care.

'Jones ...' Derek groaned and shook his head. Jones released Jason as quickly as he'd seized him, and Jason stumbled forward but managed to steady himself. Jones stared at him impassively.

'What the devil's got into you?' Although his father's voice was muffled and nasal as he tried to stem the blood from his bleeding nose, it still held the usual icy authority.

'You fucking ran her over!'

'I've no idea who or what you're talking about.' Helped by Jones, Derek sat up on one of the leather sofas, and the muscle-man handed him a handful of tissues from a box on the coffee table.

'Head back, Mr Moody. That'll stop the blood.'

Ms Barclay appeared in the doorway, her hands to her cheeks in horror. 'Oh, my word! Jason, what have you done?'

'Go help Ms Barclay with the first aid box, would you, Jones.' Dismayed, Jason's father stared at the bright red stains on his white shirt and the lapels of his jacket. 'Oh, and Ms Barclay, I'll need a clean shirt and suit as well. I believe you keep a couple of spares for me.'

'Certainly, Mr Moody.' Recovered now, she sent Jason a stern look and tutted on her way out as if he was merely a very naughty boy.

Well, you ain't seen nothing yet, he thought with grim satisfaction.

'With all due respect, Mr Moody,' said Jones, 'I think I better stay here.'

'For God's sake, man, this is my son! He's hardly likely to bump me off, is he?'

Jones sent Jason a look which suggested he wouldn't put it past him, but retreated, reluctantly. Jason shuddered, not from fear of the goon, but because he realised that he'd acted just like his father, using violence to get what he wanted.

'What's all this about?' Derek asked again.

'I love her, and you tried to kill her.'

'Like I said, I don't know what you're talking about.'

'Yes, you bloody well do. Helen. You tried to run her over.'

'So she isn't dead, then?'

It might have been his imagination, but did his father

sound relieved? Jason doubted it. He was a swine through and through. 'Someone else got hit instead. Fay.'

'The Cooper woman? Pity.'

'Yes, the "Cooper woman",' Jason aped and clenched his fists to stop himself from hitting his father again.

'Is *she* dead?'

'Nobody's dead. Stop trying to hide behind this ... obtuseness of yours. No one bloody buys it. Why did you do it? Why do you have to destroy everything that matters to me?'

'How can I possibly answer that question? You're convinced of my guilt. Nothing I say will change your opinion.' Derek touched his nose carefully, then winced in pain. 'Dammit! I think it's broken.'

'Good,' said Jason. 'It's nothing less than you deserve. Your car was seen. Black saloon.'

'Black saloons are thirteen to the dozen. No reason to assume it was mine.'

'A witness gave a pretty good description. Got a partial number plate.'

'Some people will say anything for a moment in the limelight. And there are plenty of people who'd like to see me in the hot seat.'

'Your car has a dent in it.'

Derek shrugged. 'Jones and I had a run-in with a lamp post.'

'And if I go to the police? They'll impound your car.'

'Then they'll find it squeaky-clean. Just like I've always been.' He coughed suddenly and, leaning forward, hawked up blood, then he sat back again with a clean wad of tissue papers pressed against his nostrils. 'But I know you won't.'

'What do you know about me, what I will and won't do?' The rage returned, but this time there was method to Jason's madness. The thought came back to him, the one he'd had when he and Helen had talked in the bathroom after her grand mal seizure, the one he had pushed aside because he didn't want to think it through to its conclusion. He went to the desk, picked up his father's paper knife and plunged it into the sofa beside his father's head. The white gold blade punctured the softly cured leather like human skin.

His father gave a strangled squeak, and more blood came out of his nose.

'Didn't see that coming, did you?'

Narrowing his eyes, Derek regained his composure. 'What's your point?'

'My point is,' Jason sneered and leaned over his father with his hands on the backrest, 'that you were there that morning Helen's mother was murdered. I don't know exactly what your involvement with R & D is, or was, other than being a shareholder on the board, but I'm betting you arranged to meet Mimi Stephanov. Did you kill her with her own knife? Or was it Fay Cooper's?'

His father simply stared at him, a muscle working furiously in his jaw.

'Not going to answer that? Of course not. You couldn't possibly reassure your only child that you're not a murderer. Well, never mind.' Jason withdrew the knife and noted with satisfaction how a bit of stuffing spilled out of the expensive leather sofa. 'Whatever your involvement, if I present this knife to the police, you'll go down for perverting the course of justice. Or worse.'

'How did you find out?'

'Trevor.'

'I'll have his head,' Derek muttered.

'No, you won't. You'll lay off him just like you'll lay off everyone else. A woman spent twenty years in prison going through all kinds of hell because she thought she'd killed her best friend. That's not to mention the kind of life Helen has had, not knowing what really happened. And for what? So you could add another shiny trinket to your collection? Enough is enough!'

His father looked at him, with a mixture of scorn and regret. 'Whose side are you on?'

'My side,' Jason replied. 'And Helen's and everyone else's. One thing is for damn sure, it was never yours.'

He slipped the knife in his jacket pocket and brushed past a startled Ms Barclay on his way out. Behind her was Jones with the first aid box. He glowered at Jason but made no attempt to stop him.

Chewing her lip, Helen watched Jason go, convinced she'd lost him before they'd even had a chance to be together for real. He'd tried his best, and she'd pushed him away, as she always did with people.

He'd gone completely still when she'd told him what she saw, then shocked her with his savage outburst. She wasn't sure what he planned to do, have it out with his father, she supposed. What happened after that was up to him. A witness had taken down part of the number plate, but Helen couldn't bring herself to direct the attention towards Moody by mentioning her suspicions to the police. He was Jason's father, and she wasn't sure anyway. Just like she wasn't sure of anything in relation to her mother.

Charlie returned from the cafeteria with a sandwich and a couple of Kit Kats.

'Has Jase gone?'

Helen nodded.

'Why? What happened?' Charlie's face twisted with concern.

'I ...' she began, then stopped. She couldn't tell Charlie about her suspicions either. She'd go mental and probably do something stupid. 'Eh, nothing. He had to be somewhere. Didn't tell me.'

Charlie seemed to accept that and handed her the sandwich and the chocolates. 'You'd better eat before it goes cold.'

'Sandwiches are cold,' Helen pointed out.

'Whatever. Just eat.'

'And the chocolate will probably taste like sugar-coated dust bunnies.'

'Why?'

'Because of my medication.'

'Really?' Charlie sent her a curious look. 'That must be pretty shitty sometimes.'

'I'm used to it.'

While Helen ate as much as she could, grateful for the rush of energy it gave her, Charlie asked the duty nurse when they could see Fay. The nurse promised to let them know as soon as Fay woke up, and she sat down again.

A woman came through the double doors. It took a moment for Helen to register that it was Ruth. She abandoned the remains of her sandwich and got up to meet her.

'What are you doing here?'

'Is your friend okay? I went to your house, and a very nice young man with a stutter told me what had happened.'

'There's a good chance she will be,' said Helen.

'Oh, good, I'm so glad to hear that.' Ruth glanced at Charlie, who stared back, then said, 'Is there somewhere we can talk?'

'Charlie?'

'I'll find you if they call us.'

They made their way through the labyrinthine hospital to the front. Outside was a small landscaped area with a fountain and some benches, and they chose a bench at the far end, away from people talking on their mobiles.

'What did you want to see me about?' Helen asked.

'The funeral arrangements. For Mother.'

'God, my friend nearly died, and you want to talk about funeral arrangements. Ever heard the phrase "bad timing"?'

'I'm … I'm sorry. Perhaps you're right. We'll do it another time.' She clasped her handbag and got up to leave.

Helen pulled her down again. 'It's fine. We might as well talk now that you're here.'

'You're sure?'

'It'll take my mind off things.' And not just Fay lying injured upstairs.

Ruth smiled, a timid, quick smile which made her look younger, pretty even. 'Good, because I'd really appreciate your input.'

'Has Aggie specified anything? Was she religious? I think we should go by her wishes if she had any.'

'Yes, of course. You're quite right.' Ruth fell silent and stared straight ahead, at the trickling fountain, her fingers worrying the clasp of her handbag. Helen had a sudden insight.

'You didn't come to talk about the funeral, did you?'

Ruth shook her head.

'Then what is it?'

'I've spoken to Mother's solicitor. That chap, Sweetman. He … well, suspects something is going on with the company, something not … right.'

'Oh, he's right about that.'

'You *know*?'

'A little,' Helen replied. She wondered whether Ruth knew just how bad things were. Or potentially how dangerous. If Moody had no compunctions about running people over, what would he do to her aunt if she started digging? Ruth and Letitia were more or less the only family Helen had left.

'I've taken a back seat for years,' Ruth went on. 'I'm regretting that now. I wish to be part of it again, and I think it's time I reined in my sister a bit, stop her from ruining our reputation. You get Mother's shares, and if you're anything like your own mother, that'd be all that matters. She was very passionate about the company.'

'I care about it too. But I've learned something my mother didn't, that some things are far more important. Things like trust and friendship. A home.'

'That's true. I wish ...' Ruth's lips trembled briefly. 'Well, never mind that now. I need you on my side if I'm going to take a more active role in the company. With our shares between us we can make it happen.'

'I *am* on your side. At least I was until Fay was run over. It was deliberate, and it's possible they were after me.'

Ruth paled. 'You don't think I had anything to do with that?'

'Of course not. I had another candidate in mind.'

'Who?'

'One of the shareholders. Moody. You mentioned him yesterday.'

'Moody?' Ruth raised her eyebrows. 'If you die, and have no named beneficiaries in your will, then according to the Ransome's memorandum of association Letitia and I will get first invitation to buy your stake in the company. Neither of us are poor by any means, but we can't afford to buy the lot. Moody can.'

If you die ...

'What are you saying?' Helen's throat felt dry.

Ruth produced a set of keys from her handbag, unclipped one from the keyring and handed it to Helen. 'It's for Letitia's flat. She says she's no longer involved with Moody, but I think she's in trouble. If you can find anything we can use against him, perhaps we can help her. She may have to go to prison, but at least she won't be hurt. Just don't let her catch you snooping. She hates that.'

'Won't she be in?'

'No, she left for Amsterdam this afternoon. It seems our mother's death isn't worth taking a day off for.' Ruth stroked Helen's cheek, then retracted her hand as if she'd burned herself, and left.

Helen slipped the key in her pocket. She wasn't so naïve she couldn't see Ruth was using her and that the rivalry between the sisters was still going strong.

That wasn't what bothered her.

Ruth had mentioned beneficiaries. Helen *had* made a will. When she'd filled in the will form in Sweetman's office, she had, on a whim and as an up-yours against her half-family, named Jason as her main beneficiary, then brought home a signed copy for her own files.

She'd left her rucksack on her bed and the door wide open, then forgotten about it when Fay was run over. Jason had no compunction about looking through her things. What would he make of it if he saw it?

More to the point, what would his father make of it if he broke in again?

Chapter Twenty-Eight

When she returned to the ward, Charlie wasn't there. As she looked up and down the corridor, the duty nurse caught up with her.

'Oh, there you are. Your friend has woken up, so you can go in.'

'Thank you.'

'But only a few minutes,' the nurse warned. 'She's very weak and needs rest.'

The ICU room was directly across from a nurses' monitoring station. Helen stopped in the doorway at the sight of Fay with tubes and wires coming out of absolutely everywhere. Her face, hands and arms were riddled with cuts and bruises like an extra in a horror movie, and through a blanket covering her to her waist, Helen could see the outline of a cast.

Charlie was by the bed, holding Fay's hand and stroking her white hair which lay spread like a halo across her pillow, while Fay rested with her eyes closed.

It's all my fault, Helen thought, her throat constricting. If only she'd taken Moody seriously.

Instead she'd done exactly as she pleased, as always. Her obsession with finding out the truth and with what she saw as total abandonment on Aggie's part had made her blind to the kindness around her. And now Fay was lying here, having suffered possible lasting damage, all because of her own bloody-mindedness.

She couldn't stay here. She couldn't stay at the house. She had to get away from them all before something else happened.

Turning away, she walked back towards the lift. Under

the pretext of wanting to protect her sister, Ruth had given her a job, and that was what she planned to do. Screw the consequences.

'Wait!' Charlie ran after her. 'Where are you going? Don't you want to see Fay?'

'I can't.'

'Why not?'

'She's in there because of me.'

'Don't be stupid. It was an accident.'

Helen shook her head. 'No, it wasn't. That car came for me.'

'Are you sure? Why do you say that?' A couple of chairs stood against the wall opposite the lift. Charlie dragged her down into one of them. 'For God's sake, talk to me!'

'It might've been Moody. Jason's dad.'

'Why?'

'He's involved with the company,' said Helen, 'and he has a hold over Letitia. Or maybe she has something on him.' She paused. 'And there's something else.'

'What?'

'Something to do with my mother's death. He knows I've been trying to find out what happened, and he doesn't like it. The irony is, I don't actually know anything, but I doubt if he'll believe that, so I'm going to search Letitia's flat to find out what's going on between them. Ruth gave me her spare key. Letitia's gone out of town.'

'Blimey, they don't like each other much, them two sisters.'

'Can't stand the sight of each other.'

'I'm coming with you,' said Charlie.

'No.'

'Why do you get to do all the fun stuff?'

'This isn't about having fun. I just don't want anyone else to get hurt because of me.'

'Nothing will happen if she's away.'

'Christ, you can't take no for an answer, can you?' Helen rolled her eyes. 'Okay then, but we'll go later when it's dark.'

She'd go through Letitia's private papers, and in hindsight it was a good idea Charlie came too because whatever else she was, she was a person who worked systematically and methodically. Perhaps they could find something – anything – to get Moody off her back and help Letitia in the process. They had to at least try.

They returned to Fay's bedside but found Fay drifting in and out of a drug-induced sleep, occasionally mumbling something unintelligible. Unable to make contact with her, they whispered their final plans for later to combat their anxiety, until the nurse told them they had to leave.

Charlie went to the loo, and Helen cast one final glance at Fay, making sure she was comfortable.

Suddenly her eyes flew open, and she gave a drowsy smile. 'You're safe,' she whispered.

'Yes, I'm safe.' Helen took her hand. 'Thanks to you.'

'The … car …?'

'The police are questioning witnesses. They'll find it. Please don't worry about it. Just concentrate on getting better.'

Closing her eyes again, Fay heaved a sigh. 'Don't … do anything … stupid.'

'I won't,' said Helen, but Fay was out cold again.

Still shaking with anger, Jason left his father. The knuckles on his right hand were sore from where he'd hit him, and now that he'd put some physical distance between himself and Derek, his own actions appalled him. Although he'd been angry with his father many times and even tempted to hit him, he never had. Resorting to violence just wasn't his thing.

Not even close.

This time, however, he'd almost lost all reason. When Helen told him about the car, his first reaction had been disbelief, that she was making it up because it was in her interest to widen the gap between himself and his father.

Then he'd realised that this was the last thing she'd ever do. Didn't she always talk about families and loyalties? She wouldn't want it on her conscience, creating a breach between a son and his father. Derek had threatened her, but that was the same old story, no one was good enough for his son unless the choice was Derek's own.

He'd dismissed it. Rarely did he allow himself to become involved, and on top of that it had been different with Helen from the start. His father had sensed that. It never occurred to him there was more to it, not until Trevor's revelation.

But how far did it go?

Back at his father's office he'd threatened Derek with the police, but did he really have what it took to send his own father to prison?

Jason returned to the hospital. He had to talk to Helen but hardly knew where to start. For years she'd been haunted by what happened to her mother, obsessed by it even. No matter how angry Jason was with his father, he couldn't bring himself to believe that he'd run her over deliberately. Jones perhaps, acting on his own, but surely not Derek? And if he was wrong, he was in possession of the answers to all her questions.

Helen had been right about questioning his loyalties. Whatever his feelings for her, he couldn't imagine himself as the one to bring his father down. Not unless he was left with no other choice.

In ICU the nurse told him Fay had woken up briefly. 'Her friends saw her for a short while, but I warned them not to stay too long. Mrs Cooper is very weak, and we don't want to tax her.' She looked down at a clip board, then up again. 'You wouldn't be Jason, would you?'

'I am. Why?'

'Well, Mrs Cooper asked after you when her friends had left. Said she had a message for you. She said to tell you'—the nurse squinted at her notes—'that "they're up to something". Mean anything to you?'

'Beats me. Did she say anything else?'

'No, only that. Anyway, I'm glad I caught you because I'm about to finish my shift and would probably have missed you.'

'Mind if I look in on her?' Jason asked. 'I won't be long.'

The nurse smiled. 'I don't suppose that'll do any harm.'

He thanked her and found the room where Fay lay, still as death, he thought, although the monitors told him differently. He felt a pang of conscience that his first thought had been to confront his father, not Fay's well-being, but he was calmer now. Everything would be all right. He would make sure of it.

Sighing, he smoothed back a wisp of white hair, adjusted the covers, and left, wondering what Fay had meant by that cryptic message.

Helen was alone in her room when he got back. She let him in without a word, and he drew her close. The words died in his throat when she tilted her head and met his kiss. Only now did he realise how much she meant to him.

'I love you,' he whispered into her hair. 'So much.'

She went rigid, began to pull back, and he stopped her by holding her closer. With a sigh she gave up fighting and leaned her head against his shoulder. It was a relief not to see the expression he expected to find in her eyes, the kind of regret and pity which spoke of appreciation but not reciprocation.

'I'm no good for you,' she said.

'We're not having this argument again.'

'But it's true.'

'Why don't you let me be the judge of that? Do you think you could, perhaps just once in your life, try not to take everything on your own shoulders? Show a little faith?'

'Faith?' she repeated with a hint of amusement and looked up at him, back to her inscrutable self, although he read a certain amount of contrition too. 'I'll try. But you know what they say about old habits.'

Laughing quietly, he cupped her face and planted little kisses on her nose, cheeks, lips, eyebrows.

They made love on Helen's bed without bothering to get under the covers. Jason wanted her with an urgency he didn't stop to consider. To feel her under him and believe in an ownership he didn't quite have. She responded without hesitation, opening up to him, and they shared the wonder and mystery as they came together.

Afterwards, as she lay in the crook of his arm, he put his hand on her waist and curled one leg over hers, tying her to him as they slept.

But Helen wasn't asleep. She rested her head on his chest, enjoyed the sound of his steady heartbeat. She'd heard something once, that if you placed a ticking clock in the dog basket of a young pup which had been taken away from his mother, he would calm down because it was the closest thing to the sound of his mother's heart.

The regular rhythm from Jason's chest had a similar effect on her. Just knowing that he lay next to her, warm, alive, and half-draped over her, was reassuring.

After a while he shifted his position and rolled over on his stomach, still fast asleep. Helen rested on her elbow and studied him in the moonlight, took in the thick, dark hair, a little messy now, his shoulder blades curved like angel wings, his spine ending in a dip at the waist, then rose again in two firm and perfectly sculpted mounds. The strong thighs, downy with fine hairs, long legs, and soft, slightly pinkish feet.

Did men moisturise? she wondered. Every inch of Jason looked as if he did, but maybe he was just lucky to have such good skin.

Without touching him, she traced the profile of his back, then on impulse placed a light kiss in the soft hollow at the base of his spine. He stirred slightly but didn't wake, and she breathed a sigh of relief. She'd wanted to kiss him just there, in that spot halfway along his body, but without him knowing.

He loved her, he said, and an incredible sense of pride and warmth spread in her chest as her lips pressed against his soft skin.

'I love you too,' she whispered. There, she'd said it, and it was true even if he wasn't awake to hear it. It seemed simple enough, but for her to ever appreciate him as an important part of her life she had to let go of the past, and that was easier said than done. The need for revenge – or justice perhaps – still burned inside her.

She might not be able to prove Jason's father had anything to do with her mother's death, but she and Charlie were going to find out what sort of hold he had over Letitia, and how that might link him to Mimi's death. What the next step would be after that, she didn't know, but she suspected she'd have tough choices to make.

Which meant leaving Jason to sleep and not asking him to come with them.

Quietly she rolled out of bed and got dressed. He still hadn't stirred, and she picked up her keys and her wallet from her desk.

Jason mumbled something in his sleep and turned over on

his side, reaching out as if he was searching for her. She slid a cushion under his arm, and he went quiet again.

Charlie was waiting for her in the hall. 'What took you so long?'

'I wanted to wait for Jason to fall asleep.'

'Mm, I suppose you were at it like rabbits again.'

'It does help with the falling asleep bit,' Helen replied, glad that Charlie couldn't see the colour rush to her cheeks. 'And anyway, that's none of your business.'

'Absolutely. The less details, the better. Come on, we'd better go while we still can.'

Letitia's penthouse flat overlooking Hyde Park was deserted. They entered through a hallway which led to a large sitting room with floor-to-ceiling windows and a balcony, and moonlight streamed in through the tall windows, bathing the room in a pale bluish light.

The living room was elegantly furnished with a dark leather suite and a glass coffee table, a wall-mounted wide screen TV, a mahogany dining table and chairs, and a sideboard with a silver drinks tray on top. Above the sideboard hung an Expressionist painting, which looked very much like a genuine Kandinsky.

Two rooms led off the living room, one the bedroom, the other a home office.

'Bingo,' said Charlie when she spotted Letitia's computer on the desk.

Helen wasn't so sure this was a 'bingo' moment. She and Charlie were looking for two different things. Charlie for evidence that Letitia was 'dirty', Helen for a convincing link to Moody.

Unlike the pristine living room, the office was crammed with filing cabinets, folders, box files, magazine holders, CD racks and four elegant leather boxes filled with papers.

'Where do I begin?'

'Start with anything that's locked,' said Charlie.

Helen tested the filing cabinets, but they weren't locked. She wondered if Letitia had a safe and looked under the few pictures on the walls. Nothing, but that didn't mean she didn't have one somewhere else.

The desk, modern, made of blond wood with a traditional blotter pad of tooled leather, stood with the back to the window. Charlie had already cracked whatever password Letitia had – no doubt using the same social engineering skills she'd used last time – and Helen tried the desk drawers on either side. The left-hand drawers were unlocked and contained nothing but stationary, the right-hand drawers held personal items like hand cream, lipstick, breath mints, and a phone charger.

The bottom drawer was locked. Using a trick she'd learned at the children's home she'd lived in for a while, where everything was always under lock and key, even food, she pulled out the drawer above it, then lifted it out of the catch which stopped it from sliding all the way out, and put it on the floor. Then she ran her finger inside the bottom drawer, flicked the locking mechanism at the front, and pulled it out.

The drawer was full of papers and folders. Helen began riffling through the contents. There had to be something important in here, what, she didn't know, but the fact that the drawer had been locked spoke volumes.

'Aha,' said Charlie.

Helen looked up. 'You found something?'

'Did I find something? I hit the jackpot!' She pointed to a spreadsheet on the screen, similar to the one they'd found on Letitia's office computer. 'And there's more.' She minimised the open document and clicked on the directory. File after file appeared on screen, each given a name and the year

338

which the figures covered, stretching back years. Evidence that Letitia's little scheme had been going on for a long time.

The numbered files didn't go as far back as the year Helen's mother was murdered, so whatever had led to that, it couldn't be this. Unless it was because they didn't use computerised records back then.

'She didn't even have a password on this directory,' Charlie said with a disgusted snort. 'Probably thinks she's completely safe.'

'By why would she keep the information going back that far? If she was investigated, it'd be an open and shut case.'

'To keep all these people on their toes, I imagine. See all those names in the file? And I bet this isn't the only copy.'

Helen ran her eyes down the list, looking for one particular name, but Moody wasn't on it. Now she definitely was disappointed – he'd fitted the bill of the cold-blooded killer so well.

'It looks like our lady boss likes to live on the edge,' said Charlie. 'Or maybe she just likes to open a file to see how clever she is. Personally I think she's being bloody stupid, but there you go.'

'So do we print this out?'

'I'll e-mail it to my hotmail account. And don't worry, she won't even know I was here.'

Charlie opened the e-mail, sent the file, then deleted any traces of her intervention, her fingers working so fast Helen couldn't keep up.

'Let's see who talks to your aunt,' she said, and opened the most recent e-mails, skim-read them until she stopped at a subject heading entitled Final Stage. 'This was three days ago.' Charlie read out pertinent bits. '"delivery of the statues ... Warehouse 14, off Nine Elms Lane ... time 2.00 a.m., date 27 July." That's in two hours' time. Is this warehouse one of ours?'

'Don't think so.'

'We need to go there.'

'How do we get in? I don't have any more keys.'

'We'll figure it out when we get there. I'll just forward this to myself, then we can go.' Charlie's fingers flew across the keyboard, and when she'd sent the e-mail, she took a picture of the screen with her phone, as well as of the computer with recognisable items in the background. 'There,' she said, 'now it'll be obvious where and when we read this e-mail.'

Grinning to herself, Helen went back to the papers in the drawers. She sensed Charlie was getting nervous. She was anxious to get out of here too, but still hoped to find something to point the finger at Moody. Nothing stood out, nothing that she'd understand at any rate, although an officer in the Fraud Squad might.

At the bottom two empty foolscap folders had been jammed in sideways, stopping whatever was underneath them from accidentally spilling out. Helen removed the folders as carefully as she could without ripping them, then lifted up a flat, biscuit-coloured item.

She turned it over, then sat back on her haunches in shock. Her heart beat loudly against her chest, and her head echoed with a cry she hadn't uttered. She was holding something she thought she'd never see again.

Her mother's elephant bag.

Chapter Twenty-Nine

There was no doubt, it was Mimi's old shopping bag. Hugging the rough canvas to her chest, she allowed it to invoke memories of her mother, the house they lived in, the life they had with all its ordinariness. Memories so strong she was transported back to the car, to that moment of childish anxiety where she'd fretted over the medicine and not wanting to disturb her mother about the lady in the other car.

With her adult's hindsight, those worries seemed so pointless now. How she'd give anything to have that moment back no matter how imperfect it was, knowing that if she'd only spoken out, she might have changed the course of her entire life and never been any the wiser.

Instead it had ploughed on relentlessly to this painful point where she could do nothing but hug her dead mother's bag and mourn her loss.

Unable to stop herself, a strangled sound escaped her throat.

'What is it?' said Charlie.

Helen didn't answer, couldn't answer. The words stuck in her throat as it constricted until she could hardly breathe. Waves of nausea rolled over her, smoke clouded her vision. A star exploded behind her eyes.

'Oh, shit, not here!' Charlie tried to shake her back into consciousness. 'Come on, for God's sake!'

Her panicked voice was the only fixed point in this black hole. Helen tried to hang on to that, concentrated on Charlie's voice, on Charlie's hands on her shoulders.

'I've got to get you out of here!'

Through her numbness Helen sensed Charlie lifting her

off the floor, placing her in a chair, heard crashing and banging although it didn't really register.

Slowly the sensation returned to her fingers, then her arms, torso, neck. Her joints were leaden, and she felt bone weary. The world began to make sense again. She saw that Charlie had switched off the computer, everything was what it had been like before, pristine and impersonal, except the bottom drawer which was still open. The only real difference was the jute bag in her arms.

She took a deep breath and exhaled raggedly.

'You scared the hell out of me,' said Charlie.

Helen opened her mouth to apologise but nothing came out.

'Is it always like this?'

She nodded.

'I'm sorry.' Charlie put her hand on her shoulder. 'I think we'd better get out of here. We got what we came for. What's this bag?'

'It was my mother's.'

'Are you sure?'

'As sure as I can be. I was only five when she died.'

Charlie frowned. 'You need to put it back where you found it.'

'No! I want to keep it! I want to show it to the police as proof.'

'Proof of what?'

'That my aunt killed my mother!'

'I thought you had Moody down for that.'

'I don't know, I just don't know, okay!' Helen clutched the bag.

'Don't lose it, all right,' said Charlie. 'Listen, it doesn't prove anything. Maybe Letitia has the same sort of bag. She probably bought it in Marks & Spencer's or John Lewis or somewhere like that. There are probably hundreds of them and—'

'Then why hide it?'

'Maybe she isn't hiding it. She just keeps it there for, I dunno, carrying stuff around. Anyway, why would she keep it if she killed your mother? She'd have thrown it away. I know I would.'

Charlie reached for the bag, but Helen held it out of her reach, and she sighed.

'Okay, let's say for argument's sake it *is* your mum's bag. If you take it, to show it to the police or whatever, Letitia will know you were here and wonder what else you've seen. You want to risk that?'

She shook her head, still clutching the bag. Even if Charlie was right, leaving it behind would mean cutting the ties to the only true memory of her mother. She couldn't do it. 'It may not be proof enough for the police,' she said, 'but at least I'll have something of hers.'

'You can't take it,' Charlie insisted, 'but tell you what, we'll take a picture of it.' She used her phone again and snapped a picture of the bag. 'Now, can we please get out of here?'

They checked everything was back in place and left. They'd found no link to Moody, but maybe they would have more luck at the warehouse.

What Helen *had* found was proof of how easy it was for the picture she'd built up about her own world to be smashed to pieces. Again. She'd suspected her aunts of being involved in her mother's death, then dismissed it, then suspected it again, and now she had proof of … well, exactly nothing, as Charlie had put it, because there could be hundreds of bags like this one.

Her life wasn't an Agatha Christie mystery where one clue after another was uncovered, leaving no doubt in the investigator's mind of the guilty party and how they should be punished. People were complex. They had both good and bad in them. Accepting that was the first step towards growing up, she saw now with a sudden clarity.

The moment she was the closest to finding out what happened was ironically also the moment she realised she'd been five years old inside for the past twenty years. Perhaps her mind had filled in the gaps between what happened, and what she thought happened, so it wasn't all just a big empty space, but she was pretty certain the bag wasn't a false memory. She'd sat on the back seat next to it and seen it for herself, stuffed full of papers and computer discs. The bag in the drawer was identical, if not *the* bag, whatever Charlie said, or Wilcox *would* said. It wasn't her 'desperate mind' making things up …

As they slipped out of Letitia's apartment building, an engine revved on the other side of the road, startling them both.

'What the hell was that about?' said Charlie.

A cold feeling curled down Helen's spine, and she followed the sleek, dark car with her eyes as it sped down the road where it turned a corner in a screech of brakes. The image of Fay's broken body came back to her, and she swallowed hard.

I'm seeing ghosts, she thought. The world was full of dark cars. Nothing to worry about.

'Probably nothing. Someone in a hurry.'

'Made me jump, I can tell you.'

'I don't think we should go to that warehouse,' said Helen. 'I have a really nasty feeling about this.'

'Oh, come on, we want to find out what Letitia is up to. Now's our chance. And we may get Moody too. That's what you want.'

No, Helen thought, I want my mother's killer. Whoever that may be.

Jason woke feeling cold and found himself sprawled on his stomach, clutching a cushion. The room was dark apart from the street light across the road, but he needed no light to tell him he was alone.

He sat up and felt the space on the other half of the bed where Helen's warm naked body had been, but the bed cover was quite cool. She hadn't just slipped to the bathroom, then; she'd been gone for a while.

Fumbling on the floor for his clothes, his hand bumped against something. Helen's rucksack. Some papers and a notebook had spilled out of the open top. He switched on the bedside light and gathered up the papers, putting them back in the bag without looking at them. He'd already gone through her personal things once, and didn't want to do it again.

The notebook, bound by silver-green Indian silk and tied with a ribbon, intrigued him, though. For a start, it was very girlie, unlike Helen, and also because it looked like the sort of notebook a woman might use for a diary. He'd be a right shit if he intruded on her private thoughts, but what if it contained some information about his father? He wanted to know what she knew.

He was disappointed. The notebook contained nothing more than a few notes detailing various tasks relating to her job, a couple of shopping lists, and a loose piece of paper with a list of clothes shops – no, *boutiques* – in the most expensive part of London, and not her kind of places at all.

He was closing it again, when he noticed a pocket on the inside cover with what looked like a business card sticking out of it. Pulling out the card, he whistled when he saw the logo for Scotland Yard and the name of a Detective Inspector K. M. Whitehouse. Detectives didn't just give out their business cards to the general public. Whoever this chap Whitehouse was, he must have a good reason to expect Helen to call him.

Hearing footsteps, he grabbed a pen from Helen's desk, copied down the number on his hand, then quickly put everything back as it was. But the footsteps turned out to be from the house next door, the walls not being thick enough to muffle the sound completely.

'Jumpy or what?' he muttered, thinking it might help if he stopped sneaking around.

He leaned the rucksack against the bed, dressed and left the room. Helen was probably downstairs, and she'd better have a good excuse for leaving him like that. Any decent girlfriend would at least cover up her naked man.

Not that he knew much about having a girlfriend.

She wasn't in the kitchen either. He touched the kettle; no one had boiled it for some time, so he went back into the hall and knocked on Charlie's door. He waited a few moments before knocking again, then broke his own house rule and opened the door, but the room was empty. He checked the bathrooms and Fay's room. There was no sign of either of them.

Strange, he thought.

On the top landing he knocked on Lee's door. After a moment there was a muffled reply, and he pushed it open just as Lee was sitting up in bed, rubbing his eyes.

'Whassup? Fay okay?'

'Concussion and a fractured hip. Plus some other trauma, but they reckon she'll recover.'

'G-good. I'm glad.' Lee swung his legs out of bed and reached for a pair of tracksuit bottoms from the back of a chair.

'You haven't seen Helen and Charlie anywhere, have you?' Jason asked.

'They w-were here earlier. Didn't they c-come back with you?'

'Shortly before me, but they must've gone again.'

'It's in the m-middle of the night!'

'You're telling me.' Back on the landing he recalled the nurse's message from Fay. *They're up to something.*

Probably. But what? And where were they at half past one in the morning?

A feeling of dread crept up on him. Had they discovered something and decided to look for themselves? It was exactly the sort of thing Charlie would do, just go for it and bugger the consequences. And Helen? He knew the answer to that. If she thought she was getting closer to what she needed to know, whether real or imagined, that anger he'd always sensed in her, lurking right below the surface, would propel her forward despite any dangers. He'd felt deeply uncomfortable about the meeting with the dog owner in the pub, but nothing like he was feeling now.

Or had it been the other way around? Had trouble come after *her*? Cold sweat trickled between his shoulder blades, and his heart was pounding.

He returned to the kitchen where he'd left his phone and dialled Helen's number, but it went to voicemail after a couple of rings. Either she couldn't hear it, or she'd switched her phone off. Hesitating for a moment, he weighed up his concern for her safety against the invasion of her privacy, then sent the text message beacon he'd configured her smartphone tracker to listen out for. Obviously it wouldn't work if she really had switched hers off, but he hoped she hadn't. And if she realised he was tracking her by GPS, he hoped she'd understand his reasons. He waited a few minutes, then finally her phone pinged back its location.

'Yes!' He punched the air, relieved. 'I'm a genius!'

Then he saw the location and frowned. His father used to have a warehouse almost in that spot, but how accurate the tracker was he couldn't tell.

A coincidence? He didn't think so.

The moment had come where his loyalties would be put to the test, just as Helen had predicted, but she'd been wrong in assuming he would hesitate.

Quickly he dialled the number he'd copied down on his hand. He expected to be given the run-around, but Detective Whitehouse – who turned out to be a woman, and whom he'd clearly woken – listened to his ramblings without interruption. Not pausing to draw breath he told her how Helen's mother had died, mentioned the company she worked for, as well as the hit-and-run.

'I think my father might be involved, at least with the hit-and-run.' A sick feeling churned in the pit of his stomach as he said it, knowing that he might just have condemned his own dad. 'I've been tracking her phone, and the GPS coordinates show that she's at his warehouse. I'm on my way there now,' he added.

'Whatever happens, you stay outside. Got it? We will be there.' All sleepiness had gone from her voice now, and Jason heard the jangling of keys. Then she hung up.

Warehouse 14 was on an industrial estate backing onto an elevated over-ground railway near a postal sorting office and a large fruit and veg market. Behind loomed Battersea Power Station, its four chimneys bone-yellow against the sky as if a giant animal had keeled over and died.

The warehouse was a modest storage facility at the end of a row of identical buildings, with a sectional door designed to fold to one side when open, and square windows at the top, too high to look inside.

The place bore signs of not having been used in a while. Disintegrating cardboard boxes and crates were stacked in front of the door, and the air smelt rotten. Something dark and nimble scurried among the boxes, and the shiny black button eyes of a rat stared back at them before it scuttled away.

Helen picked up a ball of shredded packaging from the ground. It was fresh and springy, so someone must have been here recently.

'Let's hide behind those bins over there,' she said to Charlie, and both of them ducked instinctively as her words echoed back from the empty buildings.

The road ended in a wire fence behind the warehouse and was sparsely lit by sodium yellow street lamps. They hid behind a row of bins. Here the smell was stronger, coming from a woollen blanket which reeked of wet dog. A tramp's hidey-hole perhaps.

Time ticked away slowly. It was uncomfortable to crouch down, but neither of them fancied sitting on the ground which was even more disgusting than the blanket. They didn't speak, and in the silence the realisation stole over Helen that coming here was a bad idea.

What if they had misunderstood the e-mail, and it wasn't happening tonight? What if delivery had been arranged for another place? What if they were caught? The thought made her shiver.

The drone of a van, like a purring tiger, was almost a relief. It swung around the corner, then headed straight for where they were hiding. For one long moment Helen feared the driver was going to ram into them, but then the van stopped and reversed towards the warehouse. As it reversed, she noticed a Bulgarian country sticker on the bumper.

Three men climbed out. One unlocked the back of the van, the other the warehouse. The door rattled back, and the whir from the automatic opening mechanism drowned out what the men were saying to each other.

They all seemed to have dark hair with an olive-skinned complexion – although it was difficult to tell in the yellow light – and wore trousers and short black leather jackets. One of them also wore a tunic over his trousers which reached to his knees. Indians, she thought, or maybe Middle Eastern.

The men unloaded a large crate about five feet high and wheeled it inside the warehouse on a sack barrow. A few minutes later they returned and unloaded another crate the same size. After another half hour of unloading a few other boxes from the van, and a lot of what sounded like swearing, the men locked the warehouse and drove off.

She and Charlie waited a while to make sure they were gone, then slipped out from behind the stinking bins. The men had put the rotting cardboard boxes back where they lay before, and the only evidence that anyone had been here was a few more scatterings of packaging material.

'How do we get in?' Helen asked.

'There's got to be another door, or a window somewhere. Let's go round the back.'

Charlie was right. Helen tried the glass-panel door, but it was securely locked. So were the two casement windows.

'Bugger,' she muttered, although she'd expected it.

'There's gotta be a way,' said Charlie, and went around the side to check for windows higher up.

Impatience got the better of Helen. She stepped back and rammed a Doc-Martens-clad foot through the glass in the door. A crunch and the glass shattered, but she was now stuck with one foot through the glass and some very dangerous-looking shards surrounding it.

Charlie came back, her mouth wide open. 'And the alarm?'

'Did you see a box on the wall?'

'No, but that doesn't mean there isn't one.'

'Hear anything?'

Charlie shook her head. 'I suppose not.'

'Look,' said Helen, 'do you think you could give me a hand here? Otherwise I'll cut myself when I pull my leg out.'

Charlie pulled her sleeve over her hand to protect it against the glass, and removed the more vicious fragments. Then she lifted Helen's leg out of the hole. 'Okay, I'm impressed,' she said, 'but next time, check it isn't double-glazed, all right? You were lucky today.'

Helen grinned. 'You're just jealous.'

'Wha'ever.' Charlie put her hand through the hole and turned the latch on the inside of the door, and it swung open. They were met by a curious smell, a mixture of oil and wood chippings, spices mingled with the mustiness of clothes kept in a cupboard for too long.

They found themselves on a small landing, with a loo on one side and an office on the other, and a narrow set of steps leading down to the main part of the warehouse.

A large torch sat in a recharger by the door. Helen grabbed it and flicked it on. The cone of light illuminated a path among the boxes stacked high, and she was reminded of one of those cramped grocery shops in India which sold just about everything.

Everywhere a jumble of vastly different items spilled from cardboard boxes and wooden crates: clothes, cushion covers, rugs, exotic spices, kitchenware, juice cartons, tinned food, a variety of statuettes and a whole box full of tacky plastic flowers. There were even several suites of wicker chairs and tables stacked high on top of each other against one wall. It was an Aladdin's cave for shoppers who liked cheap and tasteless imports.

And then there were the two crates standing upright in the centre of the warehouse.

Charlie pointed to the crates. 'There's the delivery. Wonder what it is. You can hardly smuggle something as big as that, so maybe that's not it.'

'Did the e-mail say anything about smuggling?'

'No, but I still want to see what it is.' Charlie found a screwdriver in a cardboard box full of brittle-looking tools and used it to lever the lid off the front of the crate. The sound of the nails grinding against the wood as the lid reluctantly gave way set Helen's teeth on edge.

'Could you hurry up, please? I really don't like this.'

'Keep your hair on. Didn't you say your aunt was in Amsterdam?'

'And the warehouse owner?' said Helen.

'We'll be fine.'

It was cold in the warehouse, and Helen wrapped her arms around herself. 'We won't find anything, you know. If it's another one of Letitia's "copies", we can't prove it. Not unless an army of antiques experts are let loose on it.'

'Don't be so negative.' Charlie loosened a last difficult nail, then tossed the bent screwdriver aside with a frown. Together they lifted the lid away, and Helen dug out the packaging material. The finely shredded wood almost crumpled in her hands, and her throat went dry from dust and something else, anticipation perhaps.

Inside was an Indian sandstone pillar a little under five feet high and two feet wide, shaped like the Hindu god Shiva. She ran a hand over the weathered surface and experienced a sudden longing for India, for Joe and her job at The Sundowner. Stepping back, she clutched her mother's elephant pendant and the silver medallion Mamaji had given her. Everything had seemed so much simpler back then.

'Here's a different one.' Charlie had opened the next crate with another screwdriver, revealing a second statue, this one the Hindu elephant god sitting in the lotus position on his throne. As Charlie removed the lid, the statue rocked ominously on its plinth.

'Careful,' said Helen, 'it might topple.' She found a piece of wood and wedged it underneath the crate.

'What are they?'

'Statues from a Hindu temple. Probably part of a pillar.

That one there.' Helen pointed to the first crate, 'is the god Shiva, the destroyer. This one's Ganesh, god of intellect and wisdom, and my favourite. Some also call him the Remover of Obstacles.'

'That should keep him busy. You seem to know a lot about it.'

'I lived in India for two years. It's hard not to become fascinated.'

'Really? You never told me.'

Helen shrugged. It seemed so long ago now.

'So, are they real?' asked Charlie.

'Well, they're not Scotch mist, are they?'

'No, I meant, are they genuine?'

Helen chewed her lip. 'I think they are. A while back, maybe a year ago, some ancient pillars were stolen from a temple. There was a big hoo-hah about it, but they never found them. Probably because they'd been smuggled out of the country immediately, perhaps by a company like the one that owns this warehouse. There may even have been some bribery involved. It was on TV.'

'You speak Hindi too? Is there no end to your talents?'

'I don't. Someone summarised it for me.'

'Are they valuable?'

'They're irreplaceable to the people who lost them. It's not about money, it's about belief.' Helen let go of the amulet and the pendant, which felt suddenly hot in her hand. 'They're very old, ninth century I think, so, yes, in monetary terms they'd fetch a fortune from a collector.'

Charlie snorted scornfully. 'If it's such a high-profile case in India, Letitia's running one hell of a risk. They're way too recognisable. Even she can't be that stupid.'

'Who isn't that stupid?'

Chapter Thirty

Letitia's cut-glass voice rang out across the warehouse just as the overhead lights came on, and they froze into living statues. On the steps behind Letitia were two men, her chauffeur and someone Helen hadn't seen before, a short, rotund Indian man with a moustache. Perhaps the owner of the warehouse.

Whoever he was, his bulk was blocking their only way out.

Charlie stepped closer to Helen, clutching the screwdriver in her hand, and Helen felt the cold metal against her trouser leg.

'Don't,' she whispered.

Charlie ignored her. 'We know all about your scam,' she shouted.

Letitia came towards them, all perfume, pearls and Hermes handbag. 'Do you indeed? That's really not terribly convenient.'

'We know how you've been at it for years, selling off stolen antiques as copies and pocketing the change.'

'Shut up, Charlie,' Helen hissed.

'What an imagination you have. I'm just a businesswoman.'

The Indian man came up beside Letitia and stabbed a chubby finger at them. 'You *know* these burglars? Who are they?'

'It'll be all right, Mr Singh. I'll handle it. One of them's my niece, the other ...' Letitia made a dismissive gesture.

'It's all on your computer,' Charlie continued, undaunted. 'There's nothing you can do. Right now copies are winging their way to every agency I could think of. The Met, FBI, Interpol, they all know what you're up to. Probably on their way here now.'

Letitia cocked her head sideways, pretending to listen. 'They must have the wrong address. I don't hear any sirens.'

'They'll be here.'

It was all bluff, and Charlie couldn't quite hide it. She hadn't e-mailed the files to anyone except herself. No one was coming. As for Helen, her anger was greater than her fear. Finally she may have found the person responsible for her mother's death. The sense of betrayal rose like a sour taste in her throat, and she swallowed it back to stop herself from being sick.

'Why?' she asked, a bitter note in her voice. 'You had it all. Money, respect, a company on its way to mega success. With a bit of careful politics you could've had it your way. Why jeopardise it? Why kill my mother?'

'Kill your mother? What makes you say that?'

'The shopping bag, with the elephant on.'

'So I have one of her bags. What of it?'

'It proves you had her killed. That bag was on the back seat, with me. I remember it like it was yesterday. You took it.'

Letitia's voice went from cool to icy. 'It proves nothing. You were a child, and no one mentioned a bag disappearing. Who'd believe you now?'

Helen's cheeks flamed, and she recalled her humiliation in Wilcox's office.

'You've been a thorn in my side ever since you came back,' said Letitia. 'First sticking your nose into my business, then wrapping Mother around your little finger so she'd bequeath you her shares.'

'I know why you killed her,' said Helen. 'She was passionate about the company, just like you, but you were going to ruin it, and she couldn't let that happen.'

'My father,' Letitia snapped suddenly, 'worked his fingers to the bone to build up the company. Before my parents met, he started from nothing and was nearly crushed by some of the big auction houses several times. When he died, my mother worked *her* fingers to the bone.'

'I know all that. What did that have to do with my mother?'

'She wanted control. Full control.' Letitia sent Helen a pitying look. 'She wanted to get rid of me and teamed up with one of our shareholders, passing him information about … my side business, that he could use against me.'

'Moody.'

Letitia smiled nastily. 'There was something poisonous about Mimi. Everything she touched just shrivelled up and died. I wasn't going to let her do that, to me or the business which my father – and my mother – gave their life's blood to preserve.'

It took a moment for Letitia's words to sink in. Her mother hadn't been a whistle-blower after all. There were no noble motives. Instead she had been just as greedy as the rest of them. The disillusionment settled like a stone in Helen's stomach.

'It was necessary. I'm sorry if you thought your mother was a saint, but there it is.' Letitia shrugged. 'I knew this crazy woman – this Fay Cooper – had been stalking Mimi. I wanted to make it look like she did it. When one of my *associates* told me your mother had another meeting planned with Moody, my man broke into Fay's house and stole a very recognisable knife, then used that.'

'And what about me?'

'Well, what person in her right mind brings a child to a secret meeting? You should've been at home, with a babysitter or something. When he spotted you in the back, the useless moron panicked and left the bloodied knife instead of putting it back at Fay's house as he was supposed to. It was pure luck Fay was there at the time and was convicted, that your condition made you so unreliable.'

Condition. Despite being a murdering bitch, at least Letitia didn't make Helen feel like a freak. If she could only keep her talking …

Then what? No one was going to come. Charlie was bluffing, and Helen suspected Letitia knew that.

Even so, it might give her a chance to think of what to do.

'If your hit man used Fay's knife, why did you steal my mother's?'

'Your mother's what?'

'Knife. They were identical, part of a set. Ruth said she found it in the packaging hall. Said you knew it was one of four.'

'I didn't steal Mimi's knife. When I heard it was missing, I worried the police would start looking beyond Fay Cooper, but in the end it didn't matter. I never knew what happened to the other knife. If Ruth says she found it in the packaging hall, she's probably lying to cover having stolen it herself, but then again, my sister is good at that.'

'I don't believe you.'

Letitia shrugged again. 'Up to you. I've lost count of the number of times Ruth has reinvented the past. She's probably told you some cock and bull story of why she won't agree to a post-mortem on Mother. One might wonder why.'

That was exactly what Ruth had done, but Helen wasn't going to give Letitia the satisfaction of having guessed that.

Instead she said, 'What about these statues? What's that all about?'

'You ask a lot of questions. They were a miscalculation, to be frank. Too recognisable, as your friend pointed out. I'll have to sell them behind closed doors. Should fetch about twenty-five grand each, after Mr Singh here has taken his cut.'

'To line your own pockets.' It was the first time since her empty threats that Charlie has spoken up.

Letitia looked genuinely affronted. 'Only some of it.

Although sometimes what we sell is sold as copies, in certain circles our reputation – *my* reputation – helps generate twice as much business as we'd otherwise have had. There's a lot of people out there who are happy to sell their valuables in a less conventional way. Ransome's was a cottage industry when I took over, and look at it now. Because I bend the rules, we generate millions.' For a moment pride gleamed in her eyes, then turned cold once again as she stared at Helen. 'I need your shares,' she said.

'Even if I die, Ruth says you can't afford to buy them.'

'Well, Ruth is wrong. She doesn't know I've been profiting off the books.' Letitia gave a short laugh and fished a hand mirror and a lipstick out of her handbag, then began applying lipstick. 'It's a pity you can't be part of it all. We'd have made a good team. And you'd have been useful, especially now that you've shacked up with Moody's son.'

Helen's eyes widened.

'Didn't think I knew, did you?' I know when everyone in that house of yours comes and goes. It was easy enough for Pete here to wait for the right moment. Trouble is, he hit the wrong person.'

'It was you? That ran over Fay?' Charlie's scowl was fearsome. 'You fucking bitch!'

Before Helen could stop her, she charged at Letitia with the screwdriver raised. Quick as lightening the chauffeur caught Charlie's arm, wrenched it behind her back and upwards, snapping the bones. Charlie screamed as he pulled the screwdriver from her paralysed fingers and drove it deep inside her back, then pushed her to the ground. She landed with a groan, a plea in her terrified eyes, then her head dropped to one side, and she lay still. Slowly a dark red stain fanned out from under her body.

Too shocked by this sudden show of deadly violence, Helen could only stare from Charlie to Letitia, then back again. Up till now she'd believed – foolishly – that Letitia would let them go, instead of facing up to the inevitable, that she was going to die.

Mr Singh was the first to react. 'Fuck!' he croaked. Covering his mouth with his hand, he fumbled his way up the stairs and could be heard retching outside.

Even Letitia looked a little queasy, her lips quivering beneath the fresh coat of lipstick. 'You brought this on yourself. If only you'd let it be.'

Enraged, Helen launched herself at the chauffeur, catching him in the stomach. She managed to unbalance him, then he regained his footing and tossed her aside like a rag doll. He pulled a length of nylon cord out of his jacket pocket and swung it over her head. Instinctively she brought her hands up, and they caught under the cord. Gasping and gagging for breath, she felt it digging into her palms, the pain immense.

Letitia's eyes met hers for a moment. 'For what it's worth, I'm sorry,' she said, and turned away.

The chauffeur loosened the cord, and Helen fell forward on her elbows, sending shooting pains up her arms. Red spots danced before her eyes as she gulped for air in short, sharp bursts.

The relief was short-lived.

Letitia's goon brought the cord around her throat again, this time without her hands acting as a buffer and almost lifted her bodily in the air with the force of it.

Her fingernails clawed at the cord, her feet scrambled for a foothold on the concrete floor, and her eyes squeaked and popped in their sockets. Her heart hammered wildly against her chest, beating out a last panic-stricken message.

I don't want to die.

Jason parked his minivan along a side road and whipped out his phone. The GPS tracker still showed Helen to be at his father's warehouse. Holding his phone, he headed down the small business park, conscious of how the squeak from his trainers echoed in the still night air, bouncing back from the hard surfaces. The business park was lit by a few street lamps and with enough distance between them to create shadowy pockets of darkness.

He'd helped out here one summer when he was in his teens, and his father's unit was exactly where he remembered it, at the end of a lane with a razor-wire topped fence behind. A perfect trap, he thought, and walked a little faster.

Two cars were parked at the end of the lane. One of them had a dent in the front left bumper. It wasn't one of his father's cars, he noticed immediately, although it was a similar shape and size. Easy to understand Helen's mistake. A sense of relief spread in his chest, followed by anger that the swine who ran Fay over was probably inside the building right now.

His heart raced. If Helen and Charlie were inside the lock-up unit, they would be trapped. Whitehouse had told him to stay outside, which made sense – they were trained police officers, they had armed response units at their disposal and all that – but he couldn't just wait here and do nothing.

Instead he crept around the back and tried the door. It was locked, and no light spilled out from the windows high up on the wall.

Odd, he thought. The tracker definitely stopped in this area. So where were they?

As he debated with himself whether he should wait for Whitehouse or try to break in, a blood-curdling scream ripped through the air. But the sound didn't come from inside his father's lock-up. Confused, he ran back to the lane and noticed the light coming from the unit opposite. All hesitation gone, he bolted around to the back of the other building, startling a man on his knees in the weeds.

'Don't …' the guy croaked, but Jason hardly heard him. Instead he slammed through a door with broken glass, tore past an empty back office, and in seconds took in the scene below. Charlie in a pool of blood, and Helen clawing at a ligature around her neck, a beefy guy with a manic grin on his face.

The blood rushed to his ears in a great whoosh, adrenaline surged through him, and with a roar he leapt over the banister and torpedoed the man from the side. The goon toppled sideways into a stack of boxes, and in a haze of rage Jason threw himself down of top of him, attacking him with fists, knees and teeth.

Out of the corner of his eye he saw Helen crawl out of the way, clutching her throat, then a fist connected with his cheekbone, and his whole head rang from the impact.

As he recovered, the goon made to punch him in the stomach, but he parried left and received a glancing blow in his side instead. Having put all his weight behind it, the other man lost his balance, and Jason launched himself at him again knocking him into a shelf of kitchen equipment. Crockery scattered and broke, and plastic flowers from an upended box on the top shelf rained down over them.

The bloke was stronger and larger than Jason, and no matter how hard he fought, even with fury on his side, he found himself being driven back again and again. With a bellow of frustration he head-butted him. The goon stumbled backwards into a wall of boxes stacked high, and the whole pile crashed down on him. Jason grabbed a saucepan, and when the other man emerged again, Jason brought it down on his head with a sickening thud. He did not get up again.

'Jason …'

He swung around at the sound of Helen's voice, saw her focus had shifted to the last person in the warehouse. He turned, saw the hand coming out of a bag, the matt-black gun, the flash of light accompanied by a bone-crunching crack, felt as if someone had shoved him in the chest. Puzzled he took in the spray of red droplets and the stain on his white T-shirt, before a searing pain registered.

'Jason!' Helen screamed.

He stumbled backwards as fire and ice spread through his limbs, blocking out everything but the horror on her face and the agony. He gasped, a long drawn-out sound which echoed in his own ears, and felt his legs give way under him.

The abrupt silence was Helen's undoing.

Her body went into spasms. Lights flickered in her head. Her jaw locked. A groan rose behind her swollen tongue. Helpless against the oncoming seizure, Helen watched Letitia advancing on her.

'I meant what I said earlier,' she said. 'I hate having to do this, but the company means more to me than anything. There's no other way.' She pointed the pistol at Helen, then lowered it for a moment and looked at her with amusement. 'Or maybe I should just let the seizure take you. On second thought, that would be leaving things too much to chance.'

'Ngnh.' Helen tried to move, to get to safety before blacking out, but her body wasn't cooperating, and the lucidity of her brain was narrowing down to a single point.

Letitia raised the pistol again. 'You've been nothing but trouble since you set foot in the country. Well, it's coming to an end now.'

Helen shook, and involuntarily her fingers twisted themselves into claws, useless like the rest of her body. Letitia would pull the trigger, and she would die. Like Charlie, who'd been stabbed by a cheap screwdriver, or like Jason, who lay lifeless on a pyre of plastic flowers. And Mimi, whose blood had coated the windscreen of her car in an all too real imitation of a Jackson Pollock.

Letitia had destroyed everyone she loved.

Her disabled body convulsed with rage and despair. Her eyes fell on the statue. Ganesh, the Remover of Obstacles. Within an inch's reach of her foot lay the piece of wood she'd used to prop it up. Struggling against the hardest obstacle of all, her failing brain, Helen willed herself into action. A single message from her mind to her foot bypassed the seizure, and she kicked the piece of wood away.

Ancient stone ground against modern concrete, and Ganesh wobbled on his base, teetered and toppled forward, crushing Letitia beneath him.

Horrified, she watched her aunt lifting her head in one last act of defiance. Blood bubbled from her twisted mouth. 'You ...' she breathed before her head dropped back to the floor with a final flump.

Then Helen entered the realm of oblivion.

She woke to a reception of flashing blue lights and a clamouring of noise, and found herself looking up into the friendly face of DI Karen Whitehouse.

'Welcome back,' said the detective. She smiled and stroked Helen's hair.

She was on the floor with a recovery blanket around her. The warehouse was packed with ambulance staff shouting orders and bringing equipment. A vague sense that something dreadful had happened stole over her.

'Jason!' she moaned.

Whitehouse took her hand. 'He ...'

Helen gasped for breath, and suddenly there wasn't enough air in the world. Choking and crying, she tried to get up but her spine was rubbery and detached from the rest of her. A strong arm was around her, supporting her, someone, Whitehouse maybe, was talking to her but the words made no sense.

'… is here. Jason's here.'

The arm was Jason's. She flopped against his shoulder and gave herself up to his embrace, weeping and yelling, tears streaming, letting out all her anger and fear of the past twenty years, pounding his chest.

Jason simply held her.

Finally her tears subsided, but her chest continued to heave with greedy hiccups.

'She shot you,' she whispered.

'In the shoulder.'

'I saw you die.'

'No, you didn't. I'm still here.' He kissed the top of her head. 'It bloody hurts, but I'm still here, and I'm not going to leave you.' He kissed her again.

'Your arm …'

He glanced at his arm which a paramedic had put in a make-shift sling. 'Will heal.'

'And Charlie?'

He held her close, wincing as he did so. 'Helen, my love, she's pretty bad. They're taking her off to hospital now, but you have to prepare yourself for—'

'No! I won't hear it!'

'Okay, okay. We'll make her better. No matter what happens, we'll be there. We're not giving up without a fight. Charlie wouldn't, so we're not going to either.' Cradling her in his good arm, he hugged her close. 'We'll make it better,' he repeated.

Chapter Thirty-One

'Are you sure you don't want us to knock you out?' asked the doctor. 'We'll need to dig into your arm to get the bullet out.'

Jason leaned back on the bed in the treatment room and shook his head. 'Just a local, please.'

He and Helen had ridden in the same ambulance to the nearest Accident & Emergency hospital and she'd filled him in on quite a lot, but they'd been separated on arrival. She'd been whisked away to be treated in whichever way an epileptic was treated – he had no idea what they were doing to her right now – and he was in a small treatment room worrying himself sick. For her and for Charlie.

No one had mentioned Charlie at all.

He winced as the triage nurse removed the temporary sling holding his injured arm in a position across his chest. The painkiller the paramedics had given him at the warehouse was wearing off.

'Aww, shit!' he groaned when the nurse cut open the sleeve of his jumper. She sent him an apologetic smile and gave him an injection near the wound. Immediately he felt a spreading numbness in his arm and began to relax. Turning his head away, he allowed the doctor to do her thing. She worked efficiently, barking curt orders to the nurse, and it wasn't long before he heard the clunk of metal in a dish.

'There, we'll just get you cleaned up now,' said the doctor cheerfully. 'Then I'd recommend we give you a sedative.'

'What happened to the woman I came in with? Her name's Helen.' He wanted to ask about Charlie too, but didn't for fear of getting an answer he didn't want to hear.

The doctor smiled. 'I'll find out for you, shall I. Won't be long.'

She left the room in a swish of her white coat, her stethoscope dangling like an avant-garde necklace, and Jason let the nurse bandage his arm.

'You were lucky,' she said. Her dark almond-shaped eyes regarded him thoughtfully. 'A bit further down and to your right, it would've gone into your heart.'

'I know. Lucky is my middle name.'

The doctor returned, and behind her was Helen, pale and shaky, but otherwise in one piece. Jason heaved a quiet sigh of relief.

'Here she is. I'll leave you to it. Other patients, et cetera.'

The nurse followed the doctor out, saying she'd be back in a moment, and it was then Jason noticed a raised welt across Helen's throat. He swallowed hard. He'd come so close to losing … No, he wouldn't think of that now. Instead he held out his good arm, and she slid into the one-armed embrace without a word. They'd both been very lucky.

He sent her a questioning look. 'Charlie?'

She shook her head. 'Her liver is ruptured, and the trauma … it's proving too much for her. They're not sure if she'll live.' Her voice was hoarse.

'No.' Burying his face in her hair, he clenched his good fist and screwed up his eyes to hold back the tears. 'No!'

She clung to him with no hang-ups about her own tears. He held her close, stroking her hair, her shoulders, her cheek, and tried to soothe her with reassuring words. Helen had been deprived of so much in her life, and despite the shock that they might lose Charlie too, a gaping hole in his chest, he wasn't fooling himself into believing he knew how that felt. Not by a long shot.

Instead he gave her what he knew she needed, his strength, realising only now that he'd always had plenty of it.

Eventually her sobbing subsided, and she pulled away. Her lips trembled as she met his eyes directly. 'It's my fault.'

'No, it isn't.'

'It is. I kept digging and digging, just wouldn't let it go.'

'Look, Charlie was …' He paused, pulled up short by his own use of the past tense. God, it hurt so damned much he almost lost the thread of what he wanted to say. 'She's unstoppable. Once she has the bit between her teeth, well, forget it. She thrives on risks, on doing crazy stuff. Not thinking before she acts.'

'I could've said no.'

'She'd have done it anyway. With or without you.'

'I suppose,' she said, wiping her nose and her eyes.

'That's the Charlie we love. The one we'll remember.' He gestured for her to come closer, but she stayed out of his reach.

'You haven't told me how you found us.' Something in her voice – suspicion? – made him sit up and take notice. She'd accepted his comfort, but he should have known this wasn't synonymous with complete trust.

'I've always wanted to help you,' he said. 'I felt like that from the moment you moved in, but I never got the whole picture with you. One way or the other you would sidestep me. So, I broke every single one of my own rules and started prying. I even downloaded a GPS tracker on your phone. That's how I knew where you were.'

'You *what*?'

He sighed. 'I realise this is where I'm supposed to say I'm sorry, but you know what, I'm not. If I hadn't done that, you'd be dead.' And so would Charlie, he thought, and could see Helen was thinking the same. Charlie might still die.

'What about DI Whitehouse?'

He smiled. She didn't miss a trick. 'I spilled your bag on accident, but I admit I did open the notebook that fell out. When I found her card, I made a note of the number and called her when I realised you were at my father's warehouse. Except it turned out to be the wrong warehouse. Said I thought you were in trouble. She told me to wait. Then I heard screaming …'

He rubbed his brow with his good hand as the memory of the scene at the warehouse came back to him. 'Christ! What possessed the two of you? Snooping around like that when you must've known what you were up against? Why didn't you come to me?'

'Because of your father.'

'I'm not my father. I'm *me*.'

'I thought he was involved,' she said.

This was the part Jason had been dreading. 'He was, to a degree.'

He told her what he'd learned from Trevor, that his father had been there the morning Mimi was killed, and also what he'd learned from Lucy about his father's involvement with the auction house. To his relief she moved closer and put her head on his good shoulder, but he could tell she wasn't entirely happy with the way he'd gone about things.

'You should've told me this before,' she said.

'Really? Is that what you would've done if it was *your* father?'

He felt her breath on his neck as she sighed. 'Probably not.'

'There's one other thing,' he said. 'If you could hand me my jacket from that chair over there.'

Puzzled, she reached for his jacket which the paramedics had removed when they put his arm in the sling, and handed it to him. He dug inside and pulled out the paper knife he'd taken from his father's desk.

Helen gasped when he handed it to her. 'Is this …?'

'I think so. My father had it in his office. Trevor thought

he might have been carrying something when he returned to the car after his meeting that morning. He was certainly covering something up, including his hands. Dad assured Trevor that he didn't have anything to do with the murder, and now with what we know about your aunt, he was clearly telling the truth.'

'Then why did he take the knife?'

'I don't know, but you can be damn sure I'll ask him when I see him!'

'Ask me what?' said a voice from the door.

The heat left the room as Moody stepped inside. Although he wasn't a big man – shorter than Jason – he seemed to take up all the available space, and involuntarily Helen snapped for air before it got sucked up. Jason's jaw went tight. The only one at ease was Moody.

'Came as soon as I heard. What happened, son?'

'I got shot, in the shoulder. No need for you to worry.'

Helen heard the challenge in Jason's words, as if he was almost pleased to be shocking his father. It worked. The colour left Moody's face.

'Who?'

'My aunt,' said Helen, and also derived a certain grim satisfaction when he paled even further.

Only then did Moody look at her. 'I might've known. Trouble seems to follow you wherever you go, Miss Stephens. I thought I told you to stay away from my son.'

'Dad, leave it out.'

Moody ignored him. 'Hard of hearing, are we?'

'No, I just like to make my own decisions,' Helen replied.

'It's not yours to make. You're nobody.'

'Shut up, Dad! Helen ...'

Suddenly the age-old anger welled up in her. People were always telling her what she could or couldn't do, and she didn't give a shit about Moody, or that he was Jason's father – he had no right. What had happened to Charlie was still raw, for both her and Jason, but Jason seemed to have overlooked something she hadn't, that Fay might not have gone to prison if the knife had been found, and Moody had testified.

'How dare you to tell me what to do!' Her voice shook with rage, and her hand trembled as she showed him the paper knife she was holding. 'This knife was used to kill my mother. Jason took it from your office.'

'There's no evidence of that. Forensics …'

'I'm not talking about bloody forensics! I'm talking about you, being there. You must've known that my mother's murder was so much more complex than a jealousy drama, but you were quite happy letting an innocent person go to prison for it. And now you come over all *concerned* for your son's welfare. Hah! It's nothing to do with concern and everything to do with control. As it always was.' Her breath was coming in ragged bursts, and she faced Moody across the narrow bed. 'You and my aunt were two of a kind, and you have *no* right to call me a nobody when I'm so much more than you!'

'That's quite a speech but …' Moody began, when the tiny nurse came back into the room.

'This is a hospital, not a bar room. I need to ask both of you to leave. I haven't finished treating my patient yet.'

'Leave?' Moody's eyebrows rose. 'I'm not leaving. This is *my* son.'

'Yes, and you're distressing him. Now, will you please get out? And you too,' she said to Helen.

Moody puffed himself up. 'Do you know who I am?'

'Haven't a clue.' The nurse pointed to the door. 'And I don't care if you're the Sultan of Brunei. Out!'

Moody sent the nurse a look that seemed to indicate

she might find herself in the Thames with something heavy around her legs, but complied too.

As soon as the door was closed, Helen confronted him again.

'You knew what my aunt was up to, and that she'd been doing it for years.'

'What of it?' He shrugged, his jaw set in a mulish pose, and it might have been rather comical to see the Big Bad Gangsta Man acting like a school boy, if it hadn't been for her concern over Charlie.

'I meant what I said in there. My aunt had my mother killed, and you let an innocent woman go to prison for it. So why did you take the knife?'

Being thrown out of the treatment room had had a calming effect on her. For years she'd wanted revenge on Fay, had thought of a hundred unpleasant ways for her die, but even before she knew Fay was innocent, the anger had begun to subside. In place different feelings had grown: disappointment that her mother had turned out to be less than perfect, and sadness that she'd died for nothing more than money and her own greed.

Having recovered his usual composure, Moody replied, 'Well, I like to be in control, as you said. When I found your mother dead in the car, I had a very strong inkling your aunt Letitia was behind it. A man in my position recognises the need for leverage. And it looked good in my collection. Simple as that.'

Simple as that. Twenty years of ruined lives, and that's all it boiled down to for this man. 'That's disgusting.'

'Miss Stephens, I fail to see the purpose of this conversation.'

'And stop calling me Miss Stephens. My name's Helen. Stephanov, like my uncle.'

'Hardly something to be proud of.'

'Well, I am. And I'm proud to be nothing like Letitia.'

'Difficult lady, your aunt, but we don't have to worry about her now.'

You might not have to, she thought. *But I'll live with her death on my conscience for the rest of my life.*

'I warned her, you know. Your mother. Another difficult lady. Told her that her meddling would get her in trouble, but she wouldn't listen.'

'You warned her, huh?' Helen gave a bitter laugh. 'Played her, more like, so you could get control of the company after you'd picked over the spoils. Well, you didn't, and you won't in the future either. *I* own the majority of the shares. *I* am in control.'

Suck on that.

Something flickered in his eyes – a grudging respect, perhaps – but it was quickly masked. 'That's quite the bright future you've got mapped out for yourself there, Miss Stephens. I sincerely hope it doesn't involve my son.'

'Maybe it does.'

'I'm not happy with that.'

'No, I don't suppose you are.'

'I told you once to stay away from him, quite rudely I recall.'

'Yes, I remember. Twenty-six bones in the foot, blah blah blah. Don't you think it's about time you let him live his own life? Make his own decisions about who he wants to be with and what he wants to do? If Jason decides he doesn't want to be with me, fair enough, I'll give him up, but I won't do it on your say-so.'

Calmly, Moody assessed her. Then he leaned forward, fast as a snake, and hissed into her ear.

'And what about your epilepsy? That taint is in your blood. You want my grandchildren to be freaks like you?'

Helen flinched. 'I don't think it's hereditary. Even if it is, having epilepsy is not the end of the world. I should know.'

Changing tactics, Moody straightened up and regarded her from beneath hooded eyelids. 'Your mother died horribly. So did your aunt, and your friend probably will too. It's clear people get hurt around you. If it hadn't been for you, your clever friend wouldn't be fighting for her life right now. All that promise wouldn't be joining the dodos.'

He was laying it on thick, theatrically so, yet every single word, sharp as a needle, found its way under her skin, crept up under her hairline, sent her scalp tingling. Her face stung from the truth.

Her mother had died because she'd been too young to understand what was going on and to call for help, Charlie might too, because Helen couldn't forget the past and just get on with her life. She knew the horror would stay with her, the shocking ease with which a person could be written out of the script. All it took was a cheap screwdriver and some unprotected flesh. And Letitia had died for the same reasons.

Despite all the disastrous mistakes she'd made since her return, she'd learned one thing: family was important. Could she really spend the rest of her life with a man whose father she wasn't sure she could ever forgive for his small part in her mother's death? And would Jason come to resent her for his own divided loyalties?

She looked away, didn't want to see the triumph in Moody's eyes, because he knew as she did, that she couldn't argue with what he'd just said. People *did* get hurt around her. Her shoulders slumped as a sigh escaped her.

Moody looked at her for a moment longer, then nodded sombrely and left. There was nothing more to say, and they both knew it.

The nurse finished tying Jason's arm up in a foam-padded sling, then handed him a glass of water and a couple of strong painkillers.

'Are you sure I can't give you a sedative? Your body's been through quite a trauma.'

'I prefer to go without. Want to stay focused.' Especially now my father is sticking his oar in, he thought. She followed his eyes to the door and nodded sympathetically.

'Well, if you're sure.'

Jason thanked her and stepped out into the general A&E department. A number of beds had been sectioned off by curtains, but he could hear voices and the occasional groan or muffled cry coming from behind them.

There was no sign of Helen. Disappointment tore through him, followed by a mixture of gratitude and irritation as his father came towards him with a polystyrene cup in his hand.

'It's probably muck but you look like you need a cup of tea. If I'd got here earlier, I'd have made sure you were taken to a private clinic, not left you with'—he flung out his arm in a general direction—'this rabble.'

'It doesn't matter.' Jason took the cup. 'Where's Helen?'

'She went home.'

'Just like that? I don't believe you. Look, if you as much as—'

'Don't be dramatic. We had a chat, she went home.'

'What did you say to her?'

Derek shrugged. 'The truth. That you got shot because of her. That it was her fault your friend might die.'

Threatening to crush the delicate cup, Jason's hand tightened around it to stop himself from flinging the contents in his father's face. Derek was his dad after all. Instead he put it down on an empty surgical trolley.

'I need a lift,' he said.

'Jason, listen to me—'

'Now! Or I'll never speak to you again!'

Derek's mouth tightened and he tried to stare Jason down, but Jason met his gaze full on and didn't give so much as an inch. Finally, his dad shook his head and turned to head for the exit. As they climbed into the back of the waiting car, his dad grumbled, 'I didn't spend a fortune on your education for you to throw yourself away on a girl with an incurable illness.'

'Good point. Why *did* you spend all that money on my education? It's not like I've ever made use of GCSE Latin, is it?'

'So you can have the things I didn't have. Do something with your life. Think for yourself. Make decisions.'

Jason put his hand on his father's shoulder. 'That's what I'm doing, Dad. Thinking for myself.'

'She's bewitched you.'

'No. She's made me realise what's truly important.'

'Which is?'

'We understand each other. We both grew up feeling out of place. We both want to help people who're not as lucky as we are. And,' Jason added, 'I love her.'

'Love!' Derek scoffed. 'Love can be bought. With your education, your looks, and the money you're set to inherit, you can have anyone. You just need to watch out for the gold-diggers.'

'Like Cathy, you mean?' Jason winced inwardly. Speaking her name still smarted a bit.

'Exactly.'

'Cathy wasn't a gold-digger, but you're right, the relationship wouldn't have gone the distance. My feelings for her weren't deep enough.'

'But for this girl they are?'

His father already knew the answer to that, and Jason said nothing. Derek could rant and rave, or needle or threaten, or whatever he did for a living, but Jason needed to get to Helen and let her know how important she was to him. With the recent loss she'd suffered and all her uncertainties, his father might well have got to her. He needed to stop her before she did something stupid.

But why was it taking so long? It was still in the early hours, and there wasn't much traffic. It seemed as if his father's chauffeur was deliberately driving slowly.

Finally they pulled up outside the house. Jason side-stepped Jones holding the car door open for him – purposefully in his way? – and almost leapt through the dilapidated front door.

Lee appeared from the kitchen, cradling one of Fay's cats. The cat took one look at Derek Moody and the chauffeur behind Jason, hissed and ran back into the kitchen. Jason took the stairs two steps at a time, only vaguely aware of his father following.

The door to Helen's room was wide open, the lights on, and he knew before stepping through the doorway that it would be empty. All that was left of the cosiness she'd succeeded in creating with very few belongings was a slight mark on the wall where a poster had hung and a faint trace of her perfume.

It wasn't the absence of her things which punched a hole through his chest, it was knowing that she saw isolating herself from others as a way of solving things. As if it ever did.

Plus the fact that if she chose to stay hidden, no way would he ever find her.

He rounded on his father who had the grace to look shame-faced. 'You owe me. Bloody big time.'

Chapter Thirty-Two

Goa

The computer screen shone with a luminous blue light in the darkened Internet café. Outside, pewter clouds had rolled over the beach with surprising speed, and it wouldn't be long before the heavens opened.

Helen rose and went to the window. This September the tail-end of the monsoon promised to be a particularly spectacular one, and the beach, which she could see in the distance with the grey sea lapping lazily against the sand, was deserted apart from a few intrepid bathers. They were a new breed of tourists, people who came to Goa during the rainy season specifically to witness the tropical storms and the torrential rainfall.

Watching the bobbing bathers, she shook her head and hoped the season wouldn't claim too many lives. So much had been lost already.

A couple of weeks ago she'd made her own offering to the sea and cast her mother's Fabergé paper knife into the deep, the one Jason had given her and which had once belonged to Fay. Feeling the weight in her hand, she knew it was worth more than some people could ever earn in a lifetime, then, letting it go, she'd hurled it as far out as she could. Maybe one day treasure hunters would find it, clean it and cherish it, not knowing how much pain was associated with it.

The one Charlie had 'borrowed' from Arseni's display cabinet, she'd given back to him when she last saw him, but the one she'd found at Ruth's office she'd kept. Her mother had used it for opening letters, and she would do the same. Ruth had seemed more than happy to be rid of it anyway.

She returned to the computer and clicked on an e-mail from Ruth. Her aunt reported that the police were still investigating, and that the business would take a knock, but would survive. She then confirmed that she'd sent Helen a package with three months' supply of epilepsy medication and lectured her on eating properly and pacing herself. She smiled. Ruth's e-mail came across as gruff, but you couldn't mistake her affection.

Her smiled dropped a little when Ruth mentioned how she and Sweetman were in the process of winding up Aggie's estate. There was still that other matter …

After she'd left Jason's house, she'd spent a few days just hiding inside herself, but circumstances had forced her out, Aggie's funeral for one. It was a quiet affair, with only Helen, Ruth and Sweetman there, plus Bill and Mrs Deakin who'd known Aggie well. The vicar tried to focus his words on a venerable old lady who'd achieved much in her life, but Letitia's horrible death haunted everyone there, and his efforts fell flat.

To clear her mind Helen took a walk among the headstones and statues of the Victorian cemetery. Arseni found her in front of an intricately carved stone angel with one arm stretched out and a finger pointing accusingly, more avenger than saviour.

'Poor Yelena,' he said.

'Like I've said before, poor is the one thing I'm not.'

'I meant because you lose another person. Very sad, *nyet*?'

She rolled her eyes at him, and he held up his hands in defeat.

'Okay, I get it. Drop the accent. It's not easy, you know. It's become a bit of a habit.'

'A bad habit. Nothing wrong with being who you are.'

'Well, consider it dropped.'

'Thanks.' She reached into her rucksack. 'I have something for you.'

'For me?'

She handed him the paper knife Charlie had taken. 'My friend stole this from your display cabinet. At first I wasn't gong to give it back, but ... well, by right it's yours.'

'Ah, the charming Charlotte. I suspected as much.' He examined it for a second then slipped it into his inside jacket pocket. 'What made you change your mind? About giving it back?'

'You've never been anything other than kind to me. I didn't appreciate it to begin with. Thought you were just playing me, you know, like a lot of people have done. But I was wrong.'

He nodded. 'What will you do now?' he asked.

She shrugged. 'Start living again, like a normal person. I've never done that, not really, so it'll be like learning a new skill. Maybe use my own experiences to help others. Get over myself, I suppose.' And Jason, she thought, and felt her insides clench. That part would take some time. 'And you?'

He made a face. 'Fraud Squad are taking a keen interest in some of my, uhm, connections – too keen for my liking – so I'm off to Russia for a while. Let things cool down and all that.'

Helen laughed. 'I wish you well. I truly do.'

'Will I ever see you again?'

She punched him lightly on the shoulder. 'Don't be daft, of course you will. You're my dad, aren't you?'

He stared at her, shocked. 'Yes,' he admitted. 'My brother couldn't have children after his cancer treatment. So I suggested I help them out. It wasn't altruistic, I just wanted to sleep with Mimi. She was very ... desirable. I'm not proud of how you came about, but ...' He smiled. 'I'm very proud of you. You're a chip off the old block, if I'm allowed to use a cliché.'

'Clichés are allowed.'

He held out his arms, Russian-style, and she stepped into

his embrace. 'We'll stay in touch, let's make sure of that. *Nyet*?'

Ruth waited for her on a bench by the cemetery gates. 'The hearse has left. For the crematorium.'

'Uh-huh.'

'It's what Mother wanted.'

Helen sat down beside her. 'Letitia said you were good at lying.'

'It was in her will, Helen.'

'I know what was in her will. I read it, remember? Letitia also said you had your reasons for not wanting a post-mortem.' She looked at Ruth, and the pressure she'd felt building inside since she'd entered the chapel earlier threatened to overwhelm her. 'Why'd you kill her?'

Ruth paled.

'Was it money, like your damn sister? Or to get control of the company?'

'No,' Ruth whispered and bowed her head. Her fingers, nails bitten to the quick, folded and unfolded the hem of her skirt, over and over in some obsessive-compulsive ritual.

'Why, then?'

Ruth let out a deep sigh. 'When Mimi died, I wanted to adopt you. Letitia told Mother you hated me, so Mother, to spare me I suppose, persuaded me not to. Said I couldn't deal with your epilepsy. I was weak and agreed, but I resented her so much for that. When I learned the truth, that Letitia had in fact lied about your feelings for me, I resented her even more for believing my sister in the first place. And when you came back, you were so angry with all of us, and I felt so guilty for not being there for you.'

'I thought you were angry with me.'

'Never,' said Ruth. 'I was never angry with you. You were a honey. You still are.'

Warmed by this unexpected affection, Helen smiled briefly, then she frowned. 'But why would Letitia do that? It couldn't possibly bother her.'

'Oh, yes, it could. You were Arseni's child, and you had to pay for that. That was my sister in a nutshell. Just mean.'

Two step-aunts, one mean, the other a liar. The luck of the draw, Helen thought. *But this is the hand I've been dealt.*

'But I came back, didn't I? I'm here now, so there was no need.'

'That's not the reason,' said Ruth. 'Mother asked me to. She wanted her dignity back, not be this'—she flung out her arm—'overweight half-invalid. She was only waiting until she'd seen you again and made sure you were fine, that you'd forgiven her.' She plucked at a thread which had come loose from her skirt. Soon the hem would come undone.

'She asked me several times, but I just couldn't bring myself to do it. Wanted me to inject air into her vein to cause an embolism. I suppose she was physically capable of doing it herself but maybe it's not an easy thing to do when it comes to it. In the end I did what she wanted.'

Ruth covered her face with her hands. Loud sobs racked her shoulders, and tears spilled out between her fingers as she trembled with grief and guilt. Forgetting her own sadness, Helen put her arm around her and held her close.

She waited for the familiar anger but was relieved when it didn't come. So far anger had led precisely nowhere. Instead she tried to understand her aunt's reasons. Aggie had manipulated them all in the end, not maliciously perhaps, but because she was used to getting her own way. Blaming Ruth for giving into some no-doubt forceful demands was pointless.

Still, she'd have liked to say a proper goodbye. 'How was she when you last saw her?'

Ruth brought a handkerchief from her pocket and wiped

her nose and eyes. 'Uhm, I'm not entirely sure. She seemed at peace with herself, so I suppose she must've been. Mother never left you in any doubt about her opinions.'

Helen smiled. 'True.'

'She blamed herself for your bitterness. You were so sweet as a child, so trusting and generous despite that awful condition of yours. She felt she'd stolen your innocence.'

Helen shook her head. 'She didn't. The person who did that was the one who murdered my mother, and in some ways my mother is partly to blame for that. Not intentionally, of course, it just … happened that way. It wasn't Aggie's fault or yours. Anyway, I've carried enough grudges to last me a lifetime. Now I just want to get on with life, maybe do something useful with all this money. And I'll need your help with that.'

Ruth nodded. 'Anything.'

They hugged again, and Helen thought she might finally be able to move on.

As she typed her reply now, a flash of lightning flickered in the distance followed by the inevitable boom, and the café strip light as well as the computer screens dimmed for a moment, then returned to normal wattage. She looked up to see another set of ultraviolet witches' fingers claw across the sky and knew she'd better finish writing her e-mails before the power went.

There was one from Jason too, dated a few days ago, after she'd last checked her account. Her heart leapt, and she clicked on it eagerly, but it was largely trivial. He talked about work and the house, although he did satisfy her hunger for news about their mutual friends in one short paragraph.

Fay has tossed the crutches. She's renting a stall at the market and is mega busy making dresses for her grand opening in a couple of weeks. Lee got a job at a veterinary surgery, cleaning out cages and looking after sick animals. And ... you're not going to believe this (actually you probably will ...) but he brought home some cross-breed stray, and it's pregnant(!!!) God knows what the pups are going to look like. :-)

No mention of the last time they'd seen each other and the way she'd left, and she wasn't sure whether to be disappointed or relieved that he seemed to be getting on just fine without her. Apart from the fact that he'd soon have a houseful of piddling mongrels.

His next paragraph made her throat constrict.

Charlie's getting better too. She's changed a bit, though. In fact, she's a bit more sensible, if you can believe that. :-D Oh, and she has a message for you, and I quote, "I understand why you left, but I still think you're being bloody stupid". Her words, not mine.

He rounded up in the most British of ways, by talking about the weather. For a moment she let the cursor hover over the *Reply* button. She owed him a response but it was difficult. Would he believe her if she told him that every single day she regretted her decision to leave, but it still felt like the right thing to do? That she hadn't run away to protect herself, but to make life easier for him? She suspected he would understand, but saying those actual words made it all so final.

Or she could be neutral and tell him of a project she was funding with her own money, a hostel for some of Goa's many orphaned children. He would appreciate her reasons for setting this up because it paralleled his own project.

She was saved from making a decision by a loud boom.

The lights in the café went out and the monitors blackened just as the heavens opened. The rain cascaded down the windows, tapped, hammered and gurgled with its own music. People on the street were ankle deep in water almost immediately and dashed for shelter. The door to the café swung open with a clatter, and one of her charges ran in.

'Lady, lady, you come now. Mr Joe has dinner ready.'

The boy, Ajit, barefoot and with black hair plastered to his skull, knew her name well enough, but like all the other children at the orphanage preferred to call her 'lady'. Joe, who cooked for the skinny kids, was known simply as Mr Joe.

'Dinner? Isn't that a bit early? It's only four.'

The boy tugged at her clothes. 'You come now.'

'Okay, I'm coming.' Nothing more she could do here anyway. Not until the power came back on.

She picked up her jacket and rucksack and followed Ajit out into the driving rain. The hostel was five minutes away in an old Portuguese colonial house along the beach, and by the time they arrived the rain had soaked through even her jacket.

Laughing, they shook off the worst of the rain on the verandah. A huge stuccoed balcony hung over their heads and above it, large ornate windows, which Helen had learned was an influence from Portuguese settlers so that returning sailors could identify their houses from the ships.

The house had been a hotel, but the company had gone out of business and she'd bought it with some of her inheritance. In the grand salon where the house began there were still traces of the hotel trade – tourist brochures, posters and a giant rosewood reception desk with an old-fashioned bell which she'd kept because it added a certain charm.

Joe was in the kitchen stirring something on the hob. The smells of spices and fried chicken filled the air. A stack of clean plates and a cutlery tray stood on the table behind him as well as a bottle of what Joe liked to call 'the amber fluid'.

'Where's the fire?' she asked, drying her face and neck with a towel.

'Eh?'

'You called me back early.'

'In your office. Something for yer.'

Knowing that she wasn't going to get any more out of him, Helen hung up the towel and made to leave the kitchen. Ajit followed her, but Joe called him back, waving a wooden spoon at him.

'You, young thingo. Table laying.'

'But, Mr Joe ...'

Ajit's protests faded into the background as Helen made her way down the long narrow room which would originally have been the library. Now the mahogany bookcases were devoid of books, and her naked feet slapped on the bare floorboards.

Her office had inherited the grand name of visitor's salon and was a fine example of what the house would have looked like in its colonial heyday. The walls were painted with vegetable dyes, and the floor tiles were laid in an intricate pattern of terracotta red, royal blue and white, and was in good condition because it hadn't seen as much traffic as the main lounge. In order to preserve it, she had chosen it for her office. Even so, it was sparsely furnished with only a small dining table for a desk, a couple of chairs which could be spared in other parts of the house, a bookcase with a few folders of paperwork, and no computer. Yet.

She wondered what had arrived for her. Ruth had sent a parcel, but it was unlikely to be here already.

It wasn't a parcel, it was a person. Engrossed in an old map of Goa on the wall, the visitor turned when Helen stopped in the doorway, with her mouth wide open.

'You're hard to find,' said Jason.

He'd changed since she last saw him two months ago. He was no longer battered and bruised as he had been when she'd left him in hospital, but also seemed stronger and taller, as if he'd grown now that he was away from his father's influence. Days of travelling had given him a rumpled look, but despite the five o'clock shadow on his chin, the goatee, which Helen saw as the essence of him, was still clearly defined.

She'd thought of a million things she might say to him if she ever saw him again, but every single rehearsed conversation went out of her head like it never happened. In three long strides she was halfway across the room. They met in the middle, and he scooped her up in his arms and spun her round, laughing and with no attempt at hiding the tears in his eyes.

'Are you hard to find, or what?' he said again.

Without shoes, Helen had to stand on her toes. Draping her arms around his neck, she accepted a kiss from him which brought a flood of emotions to her throat, feelings she thought she'd managed to suppress by telling herself she'd done the right thing.

How could the right thing feel so wrong? And how could the wrong thing be so right?

She gave up thinking and clung to him, feeling every muscle, every curve, every bulge of his body. She wanted him, but there would be plenty of time for that. Right now he deserved to know that he meant so much more to her than that. Laying herself bare, she whispered words she'd never dared to say to another person in her entire life, and had only ever said to Jason once before while he was asleep. Over and over she said them, unable to stop herself, and she saw that he understood, that he had always understood how difficult it was for her.

They were both breathless when he finally let her go. Her rain-sodden clothes had left a dark mark on his shirt.

'You're completely soaked,' he said.

She shrugged. 'It's still the monsoon. I'll dry.'

He curled one of her wet tresses around his finger. 'Helen, why?'

'I thought it was for the best I left. You said nothing in your e-mails so I thought you agreed.'

'I didn't, but I wanted you to tell me face to face. Except you covered your tracks pretty well. Even your aunt's as tight as a clam. And I didn't want to ask my dad.'

'That's what I pay her for.'

'You *pay* her to be your aunt? Poor Helen.'

Helen laughed and thumped him on the shoulder. 'Don't be an idiot. So how did you find me? Not that I mind,' she added and covered the hand caressing her cheek with her own.

'Jim,' he said. 'Apparently he posted a parcel to you from your aunt. He comes around a lot now that Charlie is better. Says he wants you and me to have a happy ending too.'

'You think that's even possible?'

'We won't know until we've tried, will we?'

He crouched down and opened the top of his rucksack. Typical backpackers' gear, Helen noticed, with padded waist belt, chest strap, and criss-cross elasticated string at the front, which was holding a pair of Wellington boots in place. Jason handed her a large brown envelope.

'Here, my father asked me to give you this.'

'What is it?'

'Info on the guy who was hired to kill your mother. Who he is, where he lives, right down to what he eats for breakfast if I know my father.'

Helen slipped her finger under the sealed flap and began to tear it open. Then she stopped, filled with suspicion. 'Why's he doing this?'

'That's the one thing I *did* ask of him. I told him he owed it to you. He's probably only doing it because he's hoping you'll give me up. Something for something, that's how my father operates. He doesn't understand anything else. But only you and I can make the decision about being together. Not him.'

Helen stared at the envelope in her hand, then dropped it on her desk. It wasn't the fact that Moody thought he could buy her with this information which made her put it away, it was the sudden realisation that it wasn't important any more. Whoever he was, this killer, he was just another name. He meant nothing to her.

For years she'd used her epilepsy and the tragedy of her mother's death to isolate herself from other people. She'd held onto her condition this way because she'd had a seizure the last time she saw her mother alive, made it into a shield, safeguarding all her anger and loss, but it hadn't stopped her caring about other people, nor losing them in the end.

She blamed herself for Charlie nearly dying – and as a child even her mother's death – but knew it wasn't quite that simple. People made their own choices, and sometimes those choices led to bad results. Despite warnings, her mother had arranged a meeting on a deserted park lane in the early hours. Aggie had involved Ruth in her assisted suicide, and Ruth had had the choice to refuse, but not the will. Charlie had insisted on opening those crates, delaying their escape ... although they were equally to blame for that.

And Jason had travelled halfway around the world to give Helen another chance to get it right.

'I'll open it later,' she said. Once she would have resented that comment he made, about paying her aunt to be her aunt, now she just let him put his hands on her hips and pull her close. She dropped her head to his shoulder with a sigh 'Will he ever come around, I wonder?'

'A couple of grandchildren will no doubt melt his heart. Imagine him bouncing a baby boy on his knees.'

Helen shuddered. 'Sorry, I know he's your dad and everything, but that's a pretty disturbing thought. How about a houseful of Indian orphans for the time being?'

'Hm, wouldn't go so well with his reputation for being a hard bastard.'

'And you?'

'Right up my street. For the time being,' he added softly before kissing her long and hard.

A sudden fizzle and crack of thunder made the whole house shake, and the lights dimmed for a moment. Startled, Jason pulled away.

'Blimey, that was close!'

Helen smiled. 'You know, you're going to be so glad you remembered your rain gear.'

About the Author

Henriette grew up in Northern Denmark but moved to England after she graduated from the University of Copenhagen. She wrote her first book when she was ten, a tale of two orphan sisters running away to Egypt fortunately to be adopted by a perfect family they meet on the Orient Express.

Between that first literary exploit and now, she has worked in the Danish civil service, for a travel agent, a consultancy company, in banking, hospital administration, and for a county court before setting herself up as a freelance translator and linguist.

Expecting her first child and feeling bored, she picked up the pen again, and when a writer friend encouraged her to join the Romantic Novelists' Association, she began to pursue her writing in earnest. Her debut novel, *Up Close*, won the New Talent Award in 2011 from the Festival of Romance and a Commended from the Yeovil Literary Prize.

Henriette is married and lives in London.

The Elephant Girl is Henriette's second novel. Look for her next release, *The Highwayman's Daughter*, in January 2014.

Follow Henriette:
Twitter – @henrigyland
Facebook – www.facebook.com/henriette.gyland
Website – www.henriettegyland.wordpress.com

More Choc Lit

From Henriette Gyland

Up Close

Too close for comfort …

When Dr Lia Thompson's grandmother dies unexpectedly, Lia is horrified to have to leave her life in America and return to a cold and creaky house in Norfolk. But as events unfold, she can't help feeling that there is more to her grandmother's death than meets the eye.

Aidan Morrell is surprised to see Lia, his teenage crush, back in town. But Aidan's accident when serving in the navy has scarred him in more ways than one, and he has other secrets which must stay hidden at all costs, even from Lia.

As Lia comes closer to uncovering the truth, she is forced to question everything she thought she knew. In a world of increasing danger, is Aidan someone she can trust?

Visit www.choc-lit.com for more details including the first two chapters and reviews, or simply scan barcode using your mobile phone QR reader.

More from Choc Lit

If you loved Henriette's story,
you'll enjoy the rest of our selection:

Visit www.choc-lit.com for more details
including the first two chapters and reviews

CLAIM YOUR FREE EBOOK

of

The Elephant Girl

You may wish to have a choice of how you read
The Elephant Girl. Perhaps you'd like a digital version
for when you're out and about, so that you can read
it on your ereader, iPad or even a Smartphone. For a
limited period, we're including a **FREE** ebook version
along with this paperback.

To claim, simply visit ebooks.choc-lit.com
or scan the QR Code.

You'll need to enter the following code:

Q191304

Introducing Choc Lit

We're an independent publisher creating
a delicious selection of fiction.
Where heroes are like chocolate – irresistible!
Quality stories with a romance at the heart.

Choc Lit novels are selected by genuine readers like yourself.
We only publish stories our Choc Lit Tasting Panel want to
see in print. Our reviews and awards speak for themselves.

Come and support our authors and join them in our
Author's Corner, read their interviews and see their latest
events, reviews and gossip.

Visit: www.choc-lit.com for more details.

Available in paperback and as ebooks from most stores.

We'd also love to hear how you enjoyed *The Elephant Girl*.
Just visit www.choc-lit.com and give your feedback.
Describe Jason in terms of chocolate
and you could win a Choc Lit novel in our
Flavour of the Month competition.

Follow us on twitter: www.twitter.com/ChocLituk and
facebook: www.facebook.com/pages/Choc-Lit/30680012481,
or simply scan barcode using your mobile phone QR reader:

Twitter   *Facebook*